Bliss

By Karen Trotter Elley

Corbitt Creations Press

DEDICATION

To my husband, Michael Elley, the man who
knew me long before we met.

Special thanks to Thom King for his photos and cover
design, Maryglenn McCombs for her encouragement
and
Susan Marsh for her proofreading skills.

To: Amy
Love is the magic!
And that's you.
Love,
Karen

*To cheat oneself out of love is the
most terrible deception,
it is an eternal loss for which
there is no reparation,
in either time or eternity.
—Kierkegaard*

Prologue

In one important area of her life, Gabrielle sought the emotional support of her parents and received it. Both her mother and father recognized and appreciated their daughter's unusual, natural aptitudes and abilities. On their planet Arias, chameleon and telepathic gifts were the norm, but their daughter's skills far surpassed others of her age, or of any age. So, it came as no surprise to them when Gabrielle was selected by the Elders to be a channel for Divine communication and healing, and it was also a huge relief. Now they would not have to wonder what would become of her, their youngest daughter, who seemed to lack even the most rudimentary social skills.

But Gabrielle did understand others. In fact, she saw right into the heart of the matter and fully comprehended any underlying motives and agendas. To heal, it was necessary to see the cause of an illness as well as its effects; a process that required heightened sensitivity, strong intuitive powers, and emotional empathy. Gabrielle was a natural healer and accepted the energy and "knowing" that came through her without any doubt or hesitation.

As part of Gabrielle's training, a Spiritual Guide from the fifth dimension had been appointed by the Elders as her teacher. They had chosen an entity that had never incarnated on the material plane, reasoning that Gabrielle would also provide balance for her guide and insight into life in the mundane world. Each span she spent more and more time in the Transmutation Chambers of the Elders in the presence of her Spirit Guide, Andreas.

Although she was in awe of him, Andreas immediately put her at ease. "The only difference between us," he conveyed to her, "is that I live in the embrace of Spirit and a state of awareness to which you are just awakening." Each contact with her Guide was an exciting adventure.

When their minds touched in a tentative exploration, the light of the Guide's love and understanding embraced her. Andreas never chided or reproved her. He never expressed any doubt, disapproval or disappointment even when she failed to understand or act on his guidance. Her parents continued to criticize and find fault with her, Andreas was always loving and supportive and imparted his wisdom with a gentle kindness, but Andreas, he found pleasure in communicating with an emotional, sensitive, and empathic being with such an appreciative nature and gracious spirit.

Andreas helped her perfect her gift of seeing into the bodies of the people who came to her for healing and intuitively sought and eliminated the cause and effect of their disease or ailment. In the fullness of their time together, she learned much about staying open to guidance and use her discernment to select the proper techniques and herbs for each patient. Andreas also encouraged her to live in the moment, stay in the flow of life and let it simply unfold.

As time passed, the teacher and the taught together created a new teaching. Little by little, they strayed from the Elder's curriculum, probed other realms and embarked on a new path. Before long they had entered uncharted territory and in one fateful encounter—an ancient rite of passage—they touched at a deep, soul level. The spirits of Andreas and Gabrielle merged and melded, and in the joy of the moment each acknowledged having found a missing part of themselves. They were twin flames, born into being, at the same instant, from the heart of God.

Their time together continued as before, but the relationship deepened and changed. The more Andreas expressed his will to be with her, the more masculine he became, and the more at one with Gabrielle he felt. It was a sensation of pure bliss for both of them, and it became her term of endearment for him. Gabrielle affectionately referred to Andreas as her Bliss. However, it was not possible for Bliss to achieve a complete physical manifestation Before long, he chafed at what he came to perceive as restrictions and limitations imposed on him.

Bliss could see her mundane world but he could not touch, taste or feel it. As for the emotions Gabrielle lay claim to, except for the higher forms of love and compassion, Bliss knew nothing of them. He was fast losing the objectivity and lofty detachment so vital and necessary for a Spirit Guide.

The Divine plan for him included the option of incarnating at some point. Until now, Andreas had been in no hurry to take up those challenges and opportunities, finding it more fulfilling to guide others. In his dimension, there was no time, only the *now*. But in the descent into Gabrielle's world, he experienced time and sensed its temporal, incremental power over him.

On one hand, it hemmed him in and on the other, offered an infinite vista of possibility. He knew that at any time or any when, he could choose to incarnate and cross paths with Gabrielle. But it was too late for any such considerations. Andreas was already contaminated by the contact and frustrated by his inability to fully experience all of the pleasures of the lower plane. His forays into the physical world became more frequent as his intentions focused on the material world.

Meanwhile, Gabrielle's parents had grown uneasy and increasingly suspicious concerning the inordinate amount of time she spent at her training. One evening, they checked her sleeping chamber and found it empty. Searching for some control over the situation, her parents scheduled a meeting with the Elders who immediately arranged for Gabrielle to be chaperoned whenever she entered the Transmutation Chambers. Under the new restrictions, Bliss could no longer materialize in a physical form for his sessions with Gabrielle. Denied the physical focus of her intense love, Gabrielle suffered from withdrawal symptoms and reacted in a most uncharacteristic but common fashion for one of her youth—she rebelled.

In the dream state, Gabrielle communicated a plan to Bliss. After their next scheduled session under the watchful eyes of the Elders, the two met in secret on a solitary strip of sand near the foot of the Kaperth Mountains. An abandoned private sanctuary, it was a place of great natural beauty where crystalline mountains loomed above the water and caught the fading sun's rays then beamed them back on the waves of an emerald sea. The enormous protective peaks formed a portion of the powerful energy grid encircling Arias. At the base of the formations, there was a wide beach of silky sand composed of billions of minute shattered crystal fragments that shimmered, danced, and made love to the light.

The lovers could not have chosen a more powerful place for their encounters. The huge crystal formations served as a booster for energy, magnifying and amplifying their intentions and desires.

The moment Gabrielle arrived home that evening, she knew something was wrong, very wrong indeed. Fear welled up within her and her heart thudded in her chest as she approached her parents. Although their greeting was cordial, she sensed the conscious shielding of their thoughts from her. *So be it*, Gabrielle thought as she gave in to her premonition, squared her shoulders for battle and raised her chin in defiance. She hesitated for a moment in the doorway as she attempted to still her thoughts and slow her breathing.

"Daughter, there is something we wish to speak with you about," her father said in a voice that brooked no rebuttal. "You have come of age. In your best interest, we have arranged a Zaroulis with Aryon," he informed her, as if he were speaking of the current climate conditions.

Gabrielle was stunned. Her mind reeled. "No, Father," she blurted out, "I am not ready, I must finish my training."

"Aryon has loved you for a long span, child—surely you are aware of his affections," her mother interjected.

Of course, she knew. Aryon was a childhood friend, someone she had loved all her life, but not in the way she loved Bliss, with her body, mind and spirit. Although she did not wish to hurt Aryon, the situation forced her to reveal her true feelings for Bliss. She took a deep breath, relieved that at last the truth could be told. "Father, I am in love with my

Spirit Guide Andreas, not Aryon, I wish to have the Zaroulis performed with *my* choice for a lifetime partner. My choice is Andreas, known to me as "Bliss."

"Daughter, you cannot be mated with a spirit guide. It's impossible. Be reasonable," her mother insisted.

"It is possible, Mother, Bliss can choose, he has free will. He has not yet incarnated on our plane, but he can do so, now, if he chooses."

Her mother sighed and Gabrielle plunged on before the confused woman had a chance to speak. "I know he will wish to do so." It was a decision Bliss had not yet made, a fact Gabrielle chose to ignore. "Bliss finds completion with me, we are twin flames. There is much good, much service for him in our world."

"There is more good for him where he is," her father countered. "You are fooling yourself, child, and interfering in things you don't understand. It will never be, trust me in this matter. Such a thing is simply unthinkable."

"No, you don't understand, Father," she said, a note of defiance creeping into her voice. "I know, I am certain—our paths are preordained. There is a mission, a purpose for us. Perhaps it's not here on Arias, perhaps it's somewhere I haven't even dreamed of yet, but it haunts me. It is something neither one of us can hope to accomplish without the other. Please don't ask me to explain any further because I can't. I just know."

But her father had already stopped listening. "A mating with one of your own kind will put an end to this lunacy," he said. "What you need is someone to provide stability—a male with more of a future and less of a past." He crossed his arms and closed his mind.

Gabrielle sent out a telepathic message to Bliss, but she received no answer.

Not far away in a crystal cave near their secret meeting place, Bliss had arrived at the answers he sought, and in this place of power, he forged ahead to put them to use. Although he had already made his decision, Bliss still hesitated, finding it difficult to leave the oneness and the all-encompassing love of his dimension. Yet from the worldly viewpoint, it seemed simple. *It is but a step*, he reminded himself, *along a path that always leads home. But what a step*, he acknowledged, *more like a leap off a cliff.*

He focused his spiritual energy and brought all his consciousness to bear on a spot in the center of the large, vaulted room. In a matter of seconds, out of the nothingness of the clear, cool air a fire mist formed. It glowed with the deep rose hues of sunset, and moved with the forces of creation. In a heartbeat, the swirling cloud of luminescent light began to congeal into the shape of a head, then shoulders, arms, torso, trunk and legs. It shrank inward, solidified, and started to change colors in rapid succession, moving through the spectrum—red, orange, yellow, green, blue indigo, violet — blending into a brilliant white that gleamed like frozen starlight.

Gradually, the light dimmed to reveal a male form with a tall, lean, muscular body and a handsome head crowned by a halo of pale hair the color of moon glow. Up until that instant, Bliss had functioned at a level of pure consciousness; now, he had invoked self-consciousness, created an image and immersed his spirit-self in it.

Abruptly, his focus shifted from the higher realms of spiritual, intuitive knowledge and began a dizzying descent into the physical. In spite of his unorthodox entry into the physical world and the scramble in the fifth dimension to appoint spiritual guides for Bliss, the Finger of God found him. Now it touched him at the point between his eyes known as the third eye and his memory of his former life in the fifth dimension began to fade.

Bliss quickly found that in order to maintain life in the material world, he must give his full consciousness to it. Totally open and aware, he was suddenly bombarded by a multitude of new sensations, the beat of his heart, the flow of blood pulsing through his veins, his breath rushing through his nostrils, and the weight of his arms were all new to him and strange. He turned his hands palm up and stared at them. Pressing them together, he felt the density of his own fingers, awed by the feel of skin against skin and the experience of touching himself.

A newborn in an adult's body, he experienced everything for the first time. Alone with no interpreters, no teachers, Bliss learned at his own pace. He had no parents, no childhood, and no belief systems. He just *was*. Meticulously, he examined his body and explored the cave and his surroundings. Bliss spent time as if it were sand on the beach, inexhaustible. Being in the physical demanded a means to establish and measure in order to create and maintain the illusion of reality.

Smells, sights and sounds assailed him and ultimately lured him from the cave and down to the ocean. He walked slowly, fascinated with the warmth of the sun on his face, the wind in his hair, the texture of the silky sand, and the cool water that lapped at his toes. Deeply enthralled, he touched, sniffed and tasted. He picked up shells and examined them; he ran after birds and chased fish. Each step, each new thing took him farther away from his meeting place with Gabrielle.

Time passed.

Meanwhile, the Zaroulis ceremony took place as scheduled.

Afterwards, Gabrielle lay on the marriage bed in the pavilion provided by their respective parents, her face averted from Aryon, gazing at the stars through the peephole in the ceiling. After Aryon had realized she might be forced to give him her body according to the laws, but never her heart, he had at first been angry. But they had talked through much of the night, and when he fully understood the depth of her commitment to Bliss, Aryon wept for both of them, and Gabrielle comforted him, holding him close until at last, he fell asleep. She slipped into a deep slumber as Aryon turned over and pulled her closer to him for solace.

Unfortunately, Bliss chose that moment to come to grips with his situation and back track in search of his beloved. He was eager to tell her of his great sacrifice, for now Bliss knew what he had gained and what he had given up. Although his previous existence was fast becoming a hazy dream, the memories of the time he had spent with Gabrielle in the physical world were available to him with great clarity. His telepathic, soul connection with Gabrielle remained intact and eventually the energy led him to their pavilion. Pulling back the gauzy, hanging tiers of fabric, he found Gabrielle fast asleep in Aryon's arms.

Unaccustomed to any emotion except his love for her, the sight of her familiar form locked in another male's embrace temporarily unhinged him and a tidal wave of feelings swept over Bliss. The sight of the tender curves of her body melded to another, combined with the thoughts of what had passed between them—an intimacy long denied him—drove Bliss to the brink of madness. In the region of his chest, something dark and cramped moved, grew and coiled around his heart to cut off the flow of love. Unendurable jealousy and hatred consumed him, and Bliss trembled with a fierce rage. For the first time, he experienced the desire for vengeance and simultaneously, the urge to kill.

Yet, a residual memory of his former life remained, rendering Bliss incapable of expressing his growing rage. Jealousy was a strange, unknown condition, and he feared it, and then he feared the fear. Bliss turned and stumbled out, fleeing the scene, eager to escape the tormenting visions and debilitating feelings.

Bliss closed himself off completely from any communication with Gabrielle because he blamed her for his situation. Trapped in the third dimension, his true spirit retreated even further in the face of his growing chaos. For a span of time, he went into hiding on Arias. Bliss was lost and confused. Then his basic survival instincts surfaced, and he focused on absorbing knowledge about the material world as quickly as possible.

His only plan was to get as far away from Arias and Gabrielle as soon as possible. Before the anniversary of his first birth day, Bliss had stolen a space cruiser from the universal portal and launched the vehicle into orbit around Arias. As soon as the craft fully powered up, Bliss engaged the warp drive and space jumped out of the galaxy.

As for Gabrielle, she never knew why Bliss had not returned. But each twix-light at the setting of the one sun, she waited on the beach at their appointed meeting time. She always faced the ocean and stared out at the emerald green waves, mesmerized by the undulating rhythm of the sea. It helped her to enter the trance-like state of her daily meditation where she focused on Bliss. *What is he doing now? Does he think of me? Is the connection still there?* Their love had been so strong, so clear, and so pure; she prayed it might be the homing signal for his wayward heart.

Gabrielle had a deep abiding faith—too much, perhaps— in the eternal life process by which the Elders said everyone would eventually be provided with everything they needed. She continued to wait for Bliss, believing love would eventually come to her. Even at the moment of her transition to the next life, Gabrielle never acknowledged it had not come, or expressed any regret for the wasted spans. For always in her heart and soul she knew—there was always the future and her destiny would not be denied.

Meanwhile Bliss existed solely for the future, living for the next conquest, purging the memory of one female in the arms of another. His Arian form, with its innate telepathic, chameleon abilities gave him a major edge, one he knew how to use and of which he took full advantage. Few females could resist him. He simply read their minds and became exactly who and what they desired. Bliss was addictive and addicted. He sensed that something in the sexual vibration held a link to his cosmic identity. During moments of intense passion, he felt himself lifted up and out, and for an instant, hovered on the brink of some important discovery.

Bliss lived on the edge, imprisoned by his own perceptions and his warped view of Gabrielle's alleged betrayal. The injury festered and spread until it manifested as a vengeful quest aimed at the heart of any unfortunate victim who entered his star-crossed path. Spans passed in his mindless pursuit of the elusive, perfect female. Bliss grew older, and in some aspects wiser, except for one area— his knowledge of love. For him, it was something that no longer existed except for a half-remembered dream, dimly glimpsed in a profile or in the sparkle of deep, green eyes. But in unguarded moments, a still small voice whispered, *remember . . . remember.*

Chapter 1

Bliss was running from himself, but no matter where he went or how far, there he was.

He drifted aimlessly for several spans as he spaced from one planet to another in a relentless quest for new experiences and adventures. He lived for the immediate gratification of his sensual nature and his previous spiritual identity remained unknown to him except for a few vague promptings—intuitive gut feelings that Bliss, for the most part, chose to ignore. More and more he fell into the mortal's trap of trying to reason everything out and make things happen.

Bliss was proceeding on course to the planet Scorpious in spite of an increasing sense of disquiet about his decision. The dubious place wasn't his destination of choice, but one of necessity. His Carduvarian crystals, the power source for his ship, had been damaged. Operating at less than half-power, he needed replacements in a hurry. One more emergency space warp might leave him stranded in deep space—not his idea of a good time.

Recrystaling was costly, doubly so for him, because Bliss could not obtain the crystals through normal channels. With a stolen cruiser, his options were fewer, and he had to be more creative. On Scorpious, it was rumored anything could be had—for a price. Other intriguing stories hinted at a certain female, irresistible by all accounts. Bliss smiled. *So am I*, he thought, *so am I.*

Whatever the price on Scorpious, he was prepared to pay it. His current activities bordered on the nefarious, and he was wealthy by some standards. Bliss trafficked in highly prized commodities, ferrying them from planet to planet without regard for interplanetary trading rules or regulations.

He believed the Tribunal laws had been formulated by those who wished to line their own coffers and felt no regret for his actions. Females and resources were all the same to him, his for the taking.

By the time he landed on Scorpious and slipped his cruiser into a slot in the spaceport, it was too late in the timespan to do anything about the crystals. Bliss shrugged, he believed that one should never put off until tomorrow the pleasures of today. Besides, the delay gave him the opportunity to explore the ruling city of the Planet of the Night.

But the city's architecture, composed of a maze of huge structures in dark shades of marble that loomed over narrow passageways and cast deep sinister shadows, was not to his liking. He found his surroundings morbid and depressing. The darkness came like the proverbial thief in the night; and with it, the rise of the three moons of Scorpious.

Compared to the pale light provided by the planet's one, distant sun, the glow of the three moons gave the place a whitewashing, and made it appear far more inviting. Bliss wandered the streets as they began to fill with the inhabitants of the city, who all seemed to be headed in the same direction.

Curious, Bliss joined a group of revelers and moved with the flow as they funneled into the black marble halls of a huge temple. There, they joined a large circle already formed and waiting. Across the room, a ripple of movement parted the sea of onlookers and an electric shockwave of anticipation surged through the crowd.

"Cassandra, Cassandra, Cassandra", they chanted.

The name sent a chill up his spine—it was the very woman he had hoped to meet. Although he had heard the tales alluding to her vast abilities, Bliss doubted any female could be as beautiful or powerful as the stories claimed.

Provocative, throbbing music swelled and filled the great hall. The sound entered his blood stream, and his pulse pounded in time with the rhythm. Bliss stood on his tiptoes and strained to see what was happening. Then Cassandra appeared, mere yards from him, her arms raised aloft, and her body moving in three-part harmony. She and the music were as one. Cassandra swayed seductively as she lifted her head and looked in his direction. Their eyes locked, and Bliss was smitten. Her remarkable beauty was rumored to be the result of sorcery, but Bliss cared naught about the cause, only the result—perfection.

Cassandra's naked body undulated to the music faster and faster in sensuous, riveting motions that drove the crowd to a fevered pitch. Bliss stared at her, already bewitched. She represented the ultimate challenge.

The ritual, conducted by Cassandra as High Priestess, was part of a fertility rite. The music ended at the peak of the crowd's frenzy and the enchantress wisely disappeared in a strategically placed puff of smoke, leaving the crowd to consume each other fired by her heat. All around Bliss, couples were already engaged in various stages of sexual activity. Bliss didn't think the sexual act was a spectator sport; he preferred one-on-one encounters. As he turned to leave, a buxom wench with long, tangled hair, wearing nothing but a toothless smile, grabbed him in the groin.

Bliss winced and brushed her aside, and headed for the rear of the temple. Rude hands groped at his garments. Bliss shoved one persistent masculine masher up against a stone pillar and explained the facts of life to him. By the time he reached the back of the building, he was breathing hard from his exertions. He stood in the shadows, and tried to remain unnoticed as he inhaled a few deep breaths to clear his mind and see if he could latch on to the glimmer of a plan that hovered in his brain.

A short span later, claiming to be the bearer of a gift of great value, one that must be delivered in person, Bliss gained access to Cassandra's personal chamber where a servant announced his arrival. As he entered the large room, lit solely by torches that burned brightly in each corner, the walls seemed to sway. He marveled at the misty black hangings that reached to the softly burnished onyx floors and moved by a breath of air that came from God knew where.

Cassandra appeared in the center of the room, exuding an aura of unreality as her form seemed to hover in the infinite blackness, powerful and unreachable. Was she real or an illusion?

"Welcome emissary," she said her voice husky and compelling. "What are you called?"

He stared at her, speechless, unnerved by her breathtaking beauty.

"Your name . . . you do speak, don't you?"

"Yes," he said, finding his voice. "I am called Bliss."

"My courier informs me you have a gift for me from a noble on the planet Ozarian. Tell me, who is so beneficent and what is this boon?" Cassandra was confused, for she had no connection with anyone on that distant sphere.

"It stands before you, Priestess. It is myself," he said, his head almost touching the floor in a formal bow.

"Yourself! I have no need of another servant. Who sends me such useless tribute?"

"Priestess, I must confess. I am not the gift of any Ozarian. It was merely a ruse to gain an audience with you."

"How dare you misrepresent yourself as a treasure. I could have you killed for this." Her eyes glowed at the prospect.

"Yes, you could, but you would regret it."

"How so?" Let him fence, she thought. She was prepared to play the game out.

"Cassandra, please forgive my impertinence," he said in a mocking tone. "May I have your permission to call you Cassandra?'

"Yes, you insolent fool—continue!"

Bliss smiled at her. Such impatience usually indicated the potential for unbridled passions. "I am a native of the planet Arias in the Orion galaxy," he said and paused to let the impact of his statement sink in.

"Interesting," she mused. "Precious little is known of the beings of Arias. Your home planet is cloaked in secrecy, yet I have heard rumors of rare abilities and powers."

"Our race has unique abilities few know of, and some of us are more adept at using them than others."

The knave has the audacity to wink, she thought, amused.

"You must admit you cannot fully appreciate the gift I bring, never having seen any evidence of it."

"If what you say is true," she said, "a demonstration is in order." She motioned for him to come closer.

Drawing near, he took her hand and kissed it, allowing his lips to linger a trifle longer than necessary. Then he dropped her hand and the intense gaze of his hypnotic emerald eyes; eyes seemed to penetrate the depths of her being.

Although she found the experience disconcerting, her curiosity got the better of her. and Cassandra permitted the intrusion. She had no way of knowing that he had probed her mind, rummaged through all her sexual fantasies, and now possessed an intimate knowledge of her most ardent desires, unexpressed wishes and unfulfilled expectations.

With his scan, he had discovered many emotions but found nothing to indicate a capacity for true, romantic love. By all indications, Cassandra was driven by two loves—sex and power. She exuded a strong aura, intensely magnetic to some and thoroughly repulsive to others. To Bliss' everlasting regret, he was irresistibly drawn to Cassandra and chose to ignore the intuitive warning bell that had sounded the moment he saw her.

When he released her slim, olive-skinned hand, he was schooled in the skills necessary to drive her to the heights of sexual ecstasy. And Cassandra knew that Bliss knew and was already plotting how best to use his telepathic and chameleon abilities to his advantage.

His mind examined the information gleaned from her, fascinated and repelled at the same time. She represented challenge and danger. In the darker recesses of her soul, Bliss sensed no mercy or compassion. Hers was an unusual moral consciousness, one with no outside reference, something he had never encountered before. But firsts were important to him.

Boldly looking him up and down, she tossed her head until her waist length black hair billowed around her like a storm cloud. "Come, let us put your gift to use," she said as she turned and motioned for him to follow. Bliss stood transfixed. He had not expected it to be so easy. But he recovered quickly, accepted his good fortune and relaxed enough to enjoy the mesmerizing sway of her hips as she led him to the raised platform in a dark corner of the chamber.

She drew back the voluminous floor to ceiling curtains that hung over the sleeping area and motioned for him to enter. He stepped up into the softly glowing interior. Tiny white particles of light clung to the hangings and glittered on the ceiling, adding a pale twilight hue to the already eerie atmosphere.

Cassandra's back was to him. She let her gossamer robe fall to fully reveal broad shoulders and a rich expanse of smooth, dusky skin that tapered to an incredibly small waist where the enticing flare of her hips bloomed into tantalizing fullness.

Without delay, Bliss willed his features to assume the form of her ideal male. As he shape-shifted, his face rippled and throbbed while his body bulged and shifted. He had barely completed his physical changes when Cassandra turned to face him. They both gasped simultaneously. The absolute perfection of her body took his breath while surprise and delight drew hers.

"I can't believe this. You are everything I've ever imagined, ever wanted in a male."

"So are you, Priestess. You are more beautiful than any mere words could possibly describe."

In reality, he was her masculine mirror image. When Cassandra looked at males, she saw only her own reflection in their eyes. For the first time, she would have the unique pleasure of making love to herself, which was all she'd ever wanted anyway. For her, up to this point in time, sex had been devoid of the desire for progeny or love. Deep within her was the urge to concentrate her sexual drive to a point so intense it pierced the obstruction of desire and gained release in forgetfulness. Sex always helped Cassandra to forget.

She clung to Bliss, knowing he represented the ultimate intimate experience she craved. Her fingers gripped his shoulders as she pressed her breasts against his chest. She parted her lips as they met his.

Her impetuous nature afforded Bliss no opportunity to remove his own clothing. Even so, he fumbled with his trousers in attempt to loosen them, but his motions merely excited Cassandra further. Bliss had lost control.

But she had to come up for air and when she did, Bliss made the mistake of expressing his desire to remove his garments. Cassandra pulled back and regarded him for a moment with a wicked gleam in her eye. Then, in one quick motion, she grabbed his tunic in both hands and ripped it from top to bottom. To avoid any further assistance, he dropped his trousers with lightening speed.

Then he drew her to him, and his right hand moved to the back of her neck while the left raised her chin, and his eyes caressed her face. Slowly, deliberately, he kissed her. At first, the kiss was gentle and exploratory as Bliss exhibited his mastery of his passions and regained control. When his hand slid down her satin smooth throat to her perfect breasts, his fingertips throbbed with the beat of her wild, hammering heart.

Cassandra's fevered, eager response excited him as nothing ever had—her desire was a palatable thing. Passion exploded in his veins, and the kiss became a demand as his tongue invaded her mouth. Cassandra moaned softly, moving her tongue against his. The two clung to each other, drinking in the taste, smell and feel of each other, allowing the sensations of sexual arousal to carry them away. He carried her to the mound of pillows and fell on top of her. Then starting with her mouth, he licked her trembling body, bringing her closer to the intense sexual release she craved.

Bliss knew exactly where to touch her, to what intensity, and for how long.

Consumed with desire, Cassandra grew impatient and pulled his head up, covering his mouth in a long, devouring kiss. With her other hand she guided him to enter her. Bliss took her with a primal, pounding passion. His penetration released a savage, primitive force that raged unbridled within each of them. Cassandra behaved like something wild. She scratched and clawed, and engaged him in every possible position, a few of which were new, even to Bliss.

In the dim light, sweat glistened and beaded on their bodies as they pushed themselves harder and higher. On and on the force drove them, to a moment, a place in time and space, when nothing else existed. Cassandra's passion reached a white-hot, searing intensity as Bliss neared exhaustion, but he managed to hold himself in check until they reached a simultaneous, mind-blowing culmination. It was the least he could do.

In the afterglow, Cassandra rested her cheek on his chest, quiet and thoughtful. He had drifted off to sleep but she woke him with a question. "Bliss, is it true you can assume any form I desire," she asked, "any one at all?"

He wondered where this was going. "There are no limitations, all you have to do is to touch me and concentrate—create a mental image of your desires. Whatever you can see, I can be."

"You must be a powerful wizard. Do you have other magic?"

"No, it's not magic," he said, not particularly liking the implication. "It's simply a matter of telepathy combined with a natural chameleon ability—it's as easy for me to change into another male as it is for you to charm one."

Cassandra clapped her hands like a child who had learned of a holiday. "You are aptly named, Bliss. How wonderful—such a delightful gift, mine to use as I please for as long as I please."

"Or for as long as it pleasures me," he countered.

A shadow passed over her face, and she shot him a calculating glance. "You have much to learn of the ways of Scorpious. I make the rules here, and no one leaves without my permission."

Surprise followed by irritation registered on his face, or rather on the face of the lover that he had created for her. Cassandra took notice and immediately changed her tactics. Her lips turned up sweetly, and she radiated a sunny smile that dazzled him with its brilliance, as it was meant to.

"You are a prisoner of desire, Bliss," she purred, "of desire."

Bending over him, she flicked her tongue across his lips and gazed seductively into his eyes, making him forget her implied threat with one of her patented, quicksilver mood changes.

"Pleasure me again, Bliss."

Not one to wait for an answer, she caressed his maleness and then bent her head and gave him the full benefit of her tongue and mouth.

His fatigue vanished, giving way to an immediate and substantial response. Bliss had a feeling Cassandra could raise the dead. At last, he had met his match in the sexual arena.

And to his surprise, Bliss was not at all sure he liked it.

Chapter 2

When he awoke, Bliss found himself alone in the bedchamber. He stirred and moments later as if on cue, a young female servant parted the curtains.

"My mistress told me to see to your needs," she said, softly, her head bowed. "Is there anything you require?"

Bliss sat up and wrinkled his nose. "A bath would be nice," he said.

Smiling sweetly in agreement, the girl crossed to the far end of the chamber, bent down and pressed a recessed plate. The floor slid back to reveal a long, deep bathing area, already filling with steamy fluid.

Bliss watched her, admiring her slim, young body, and the way her long, chestnut hair cascaded in polished waves down her back. But when she turned around, it was her face that captivated him. It glowed with sweetness and innocence, an almost angelic light that reminded him of his first love, Gabrielle.

"Could I have something to eat," he said curtly, reacting to the memory.

Anticipating his needs, she backed away, well on her way out of the chamber before he finished the question. Most of the mistress' visitors needed a great deal of nourishment when they awoke.

As soon as she was gone, he rose, walked to the pool and lowered himself into the welcome warmth. He lay in the soothing liquid, thinking, wondering what to do about Cassandra. She might prove to be a difficult lover. One thing he knew for sure, she had an insatiable, compulsive sex drive, but that was a problem easily handled. Already Bliss looked forward to procuring the crystals he needed and resuming his journey.

For him, the joy was in the chase. Once a female was his, he was easily bored and moved on. Some flaw turned him off, or his interest was diverted by another female; someone more interesting, more beautiful, or more accomplished. Bliss was not one to waste time on relationships where affection increased with time. His goal was to remain enticingly unknowable. Unable to bear rejection, he chose to leave before a lover found fault and tired of him.

The young female came back into the chamber, materializing in the misty vapors of the bath, to place a tray laden with delicacies on the floor beside him. Bliss scrutinized the graceful girl again. She was a tempting little morsel, if a bit young for his tastes. Yet, something about her intrigued him, something regal in her bearing that seemed out of place.

Blushing under his close examination, she turned to leave, but Bliss reached out and grabbed her hand. The contact opened up a telepathic pathway and an opportunity to learn more about her.

Her mistress chose that particular moment to return to the chamber. Cassandra swept into the room, a vision of beauty wearing a silver gown molded to her fabulous figure. Her sharp eyes appraised the scene in an instant—Bliss in his natural Arian identity, smiling up at the girl with an unaffected, boyish expression on his face, an undisguised, involuntary response to the fresh, young servant's innocence and purity.

Cassandra's face radiated her displeasure. Although she received more than her share of leering glances, no one had ever looked at her with such warm, open admiration.

Immediately, she issued an icy command. "Elena, you may go."

Bliss smiled, so that was her name, Elena.

"And what was that all about?" she demanded, the chill deepening.

"Nothing," he said, switching his charming grin to high beam in the hope of deflecting her hostility.

She crossed her arms and glared at him. Bliss was at a disadvantage, sitting naked in the rapidly cooling bath. As she stood over him, he became increasingly uncomfortable, but he remained silent and offered no further explanation.

Abruptly, Cassandra whirled and strode from the room, color high in her face, a bright hard glitter in her eyes. Although extremely possessive, Cassandra rarely considered anyone a serious rival. Jealousy was an unfamiliar emotion. Even though she did not believe Elena to be a real threat, knowing an attraction existed, however tenuous, created suspicion in her mind. Part of her irritation stemmed from the fact that she sensed Elena would retain her angelic aura no matter what befell her in life.

Her innocence had been lost long ago. Abandoned by her father, kidnapped, raped, then trained as a concubine and later sold as a slave, Cassandra felt sure a pure, unblemished character, once lost, was impossible to regain. All of Cassandra's wealth and power could not obtain such things, but she could and would destroy them if Elena got in her way.

Her thoughts were dark and dismal as she entered the anteroom where a rag-tag collection of mercenaries waited for her. Karachai, the leader of the band of ruffians, instantly took charge. Emboldened by his intense excitement, he took her by the arm and pulled her forward, toward the large computer screen in the center of the room.

"It's the mother-lode, a cargo ship," he rasped, leaning in a little too close for her comfort as he pointed at the screen. She nearly stepped back in revulsion before she brought herself under control. It would be dangerous to have him think she was afraid of him. "We've been monitoring their communications," he continued, not seeming to have noticed. "And from what I understand of their signals, the ship is having serious navigational problems." His finger touched the computer controls and a path tracked across the monitor. "It's forcing them to drift further and further into our quadrant."

Cassandra nodded in satisfaction. It was a lucky break for them. Since Scorpious wasn't in the path of galaxy traffic lanes, most of their prey consisted of just such crippled or lost ships, heading for the nearest planet for aid or drifting helplessly as this one appeared to be.

"We'll leave at first lightness," Cassandra snapped, accustomed to issuing orders. "Plot a course for interception."

"I'm doing that now," he snapped back, agitated by her automatic assumption of authority.

She ignored his attitude and sat down with the four males seated at a long table.

"You have the device?" Boon asked. He was a large reptilian type with chubby cheeks and slits for eyes. Whenever possible, Cassandra avoided looking at him.

"Yes," she said, through clenched teeth. "I have it, and I'll bring it when the time is right, I alone know how to use it—and I intend to keep it that way."

He grunted at her and averted his eyes, detesting her for the power she held over them.

The feeling was mutual, yet for Cassandra the criminal class, with its passion for secrecy and violence held an irresistible appeal. She had a tendency to gravitate to low-life humanoids—it made her feel superior. The brutal, avaricious louts gathered in the anteroom were mainly interested in the accumulation of wealth and what it would bring them. Karachai, their leader and the most experienced spacer, was a hard living, sadistic, murderous villain with a weakness for pretty females. He fascinated and repelled Cassandra at the same time.

As if he was aware of the intent of her gaze, Karachai turned and announced the results of his efforts at the computer. "Our course is completed, interception will take place at mark 17.5".

The group rose and gathered around the screen. Karachai focused intently, as he pressed buttons and consulted data. "The probes," he said, "indicate there are over 500 lifeforms on board."

"How many are females?" Boon asked, rubbing his thick, stubby hands together.

"Not many, less than one hundred."

All but Cassandra groaned in disappointment. Secretly, she was pleased. Karachai and his followers delighted in raping the females, and should one die in the process; he cut off her breasts as a trophy. Although Cassandra admired many of his ruthless qualities, she realized that his perversities vastly exceeded her own. But the alliance had been forged and there was nothing to be done about it except to try and limit the relationship.

As if reading her thoughts, Karachai's gaze fell on her ample cleavage. *I may have to resort to black magic with this one*, she thought. Cassandra shuddered, and sought a diversion. "How many crystals do you suppose a craft of that size carries?"

"Six to power her, maybe six more in reserve. There could be as many as twenty."

Cassandra's eyes glowed. "So many. This could be quite a lucrative venture, counting the cargo and the slaves."

"Slaves! What good are slaves? Scorpious is overpopulated with them as it is. There is no one to sell them to," he said, wondering why she insisted on taking more and more of them into her personal service. "Increasing their number is dangerous, there could be a revolt, an uprising."

"But, I don't think . . ."

"You know the rules," he interrupted, "I make the decisions in these matters. Any excess slaves, the old, the infirm, the undesirable will be drugged and left on board. We'll strip the ship clean and set its course straight for the sun."

She refused to think about it or to argue further. She harbored a healthy respect for the more vicious side of his nature, as he did her power. They seldom opposed each other openly. He knew she was a formidable and ruthless opponent, and to that he gave his allegiance.

The others crowded in, squinting at the screen. Cassandra stepped back, to stand apart, calculating her share of the booty and gloating over the possible crystal count, the key to intergalactic travel. Without their power to create a warp and skip in space, the transversable universe would shrink. No lifeform would live long enough to reach the distant stars. Yet, each one of the crystals, although capable of shattering the limitations of light speed, was small enough to fit into the palm of her hand. When Cassandra possessed enough of them, she would be sufficiently wealthy to change her own destiny.

But at the moment, Karachai held her future in his hands. "We'll meet here at 7 marks before lightness," he said.

Good, she thought, *before first lightness comes the darkness and Bliss.* She would make him forget all about Elena.

Chapter 3

When next darkness came, Cassandra was on her best behavior. She and Bliss dined alone. She charmed him, gazed provocatively into his eyes, flattered his ego at every opportunity and encouraged him to drink freely of the potent liquid concoction she had created especially for him. Cassandra never combined her sorcery with her lovemaking, but she wasn't above using it to mellow out a potential bedmate.

They decided to retire early. As they entered the dim interior of the chamber from the brightly lit hallway, they were momentarily blinded. Cassandra stopped to let her eyes re-adjust, but Bliss forged on, stumbled over a floor cushion, and cursed the darkness.

The chamber was lit by a single golden globe that shimmered on top of a trunk in the far corner of the room. Its soft illumination spread out like delicate fingers of light, probing the blackness, penetrating but not entirely eliminating the gloom. Cassandra quickly crossed the room, picked up the glowing orb and held it aloft in the palm of her hand. Moving her other hand in a circular motion above the globe, she spoke a command.

"Myort!"

The globe split into a thousand pieces of light, each taking flight to land on the ceiling, walls and bed hangings. Each individual speck intensified and became brighter, creating a starry night effect around the entire room.

Bliss looked around, bewildered. "How did you do that? Sorcery?"

"Yes, in part."

Plucking one of the small particles of light from the wall hanging, she held it out to him for a closer inspection. "See, they're actually small insects with iridescent bodies."

"Fascinating," he said, carefully examining one, "they glow like living sapphires." The tiny white light was intense.

"Reort," she ordered. Insects flew at her from all directions, merging into a large, glowing white ball in her hand.

"Myrot!"

Once again, the globe shattered, and the bugs lit on the ceiling, walls and hangings in exactly the same pattern as before.

Much to his amazement, Bliss recognized the star pattern; it was a replica of a distant constellation, familiar to him because he had traveled through it recently.

"Does this particular placement of the planets have a special significance to you?" he asked.

Cassandra's raised her eyebrows in surprise. "Yes, it is a reminder of a time that changed my life forever," she said, somewhat disconcerted. He didn't miss a thing. No one else had ever noticed or perhaps, understood enough to ask the question. The light pattern was her personal star map. "This," she said as she pointed, "marks the positions of the stars as seen from a deep space cruiser," she continued. "It was what I saw when I was flat on my back, being raped by my kidnappers. Later the same view looked quite different to me in the arms of my first lover. He taught me how to please a male. Those skills proved invaluable, they helped me to buy my freedom."

"He must have been one hell of a fellow. He taught you well."

"No, actually it was I who was exceptional. He turned out to be quite ordinary." Already, she had said too much. She detested pity and certainly didn't want it from Bliss. "But enough about me—I'm interested in hearing more about you. But first, let me pour you a drink."

She filled two glasses and handed him one and then raised hers in a toast. "To us and our future." Her eyes held a promise; his held alarm.

"To the future," he said, his eyes avoiding hers.

Cassandra noted his evasion, how he had sidestepped the slightest hint of a verbal commitment. She was irritated and eyed him intently as if by looking long enough and hard enough the mystery of him would be solved. Although she hated entanglements herself and hesitated to take anyone into her confidence, Cassandra enjoyed bringing to light the trusting, hidden selves of others. She often used her sorcery-sharpened senses to zero in on an opponent's psychological weak spots. And to Cassandra, everyone was an opponent.

She barely touched her drink and watched with pleasure as Bliss drained his glass.

"More?" she purred.

"Yes, it's delicious." The more he drank, the more he wanted. The mellifluous substance bubbled and swirled with a life of its own. It tasted like liquid fire and raced through his veins to burn in his brain.

She filled his glass, her satisfaction mounting as he continued to drink. By maneuvering Bliss into a vulnerable position, she hoped to learn something of value as insurance, something she could use against him later.

As they reclined on the plump bed pillows, Cassandra leaned back on one arm and posed prettily. Bliss sipped more of the brew and took a mental trip back home to Arias. From what he remembered, life there was far superior to existence anywhere else. After all his spans of roaming and searching, he was beginning to value some of the things he had thrown away in his youth; honor, commitment to others, responsibility, and the emotional security these things brought. He didn't regret the things he'd done, without them he wouldn't be who he was, but his love 'em and leave 'em lifestyle was beginning to lose its luster.

He wondered if he could go home again, perhaps find a mate and settle down. *But would one female ever be enough?* Each new conquest brought him no closer to fulfillment or any lasting satisfaction. Fear of commitment, of being hurt, drove him on. Lately, thoughts of what would happen when he aged, when he was no longer attractive to females began to creep in. As he grew older, his chameleon talents would

31

wane and eventually disappear completely and with it his ability to fulfill a woman's fantasy.

Not liking that thought at all, he attempted to drown it. Cassandra saw the play of emotions on his face and thought herself the cause of his serious contemplation. Unaware of her intense regard, he sought a diversion from the downward spiral of his revelry. With his booted feet crossed, he leaned back, sank into the comfort of the pillows and studied the ceiling. It provided a test for his mind, trying to determine the exact point in time and space of that particular grouping.

Joining him on the pillows, Cassandra lay down beside him.

Bliss pointed a wavering finger at the ceiling. "Did you ever think about what's out there—all the places you've never been?"

"No, everything I need is here," she said, as she stroked his chest.

"But Cassandra, there are a hundred billion galaxies," he continued, "each with a hundred billion stars and as many planets—ten billion trillion. All those galaxies with worlds inhabited by living things, intelligent beings, space faring civilizations, and planets brimming with life we have never seen. We could not possibly ever see them all." Bliss' face glowed as he warmed to his subject. "Don't you ever wonder what you're missing?"

"I don't think I've missed anything," she said, her voice flat. "The Cosmos is a vast, cold vacuum. Whenever I'm in deep space the stars seem achingly lonely, strange and desolate. I've created a world of my own right here; I desire no others."

"Cassandra, be serious, Scorpious is by no means a special place. It's not even a typical planet. How can you judge the Cosmos, if you never venture out to other worlds?"

Her face clouded. "I have my reasons. Other planets and their beings hold no lure for me." The subject was closed. "What is it you seek, Bliss? Is it so rare you have yet to find it in your many travels?" She knew all about his wanderings. If she could find out what it was he sought, perhaps she could provide it and keep him with her.

His mind numbed by drink, he answered truthfully. "I don't know. Maybe, it's the adventure, the excitement, the quest," he said, gesturing at the ceiling. "I'm forever chasing the beautiful in life. The perfect female I'm seeking is one who meets all of my needs, all of the time. My basic need is for variety, so no one female can ever be the perfect one. If you can accept that," he said, smiling at her, "our time together will be much more enjoyable."

He couldn't have stunned her more if he had hit her over the head with a mallet. Their lovemaking had held special meaning for her, but obviously not for him. His words pierced her heart and the first faint rustling of love she had felt for him was rendered stillborn by the sharp-edged sword of his tongue.

She forced herself to remain calm. Perhaps she had misunderstood. "Then you have no feelings for me, Bliss, other than desire?"

"Isn't that enough," he stated, venturing into even more dangerous territory. "I want you. I'm not here because I have to be, or because I'm trapped here, but because I want to be. I'd rather be here, with you, at this moment than anywhere else in the universe," he said, wondering why it was never enough and knowing it was not at all what she wished to hear.

She struggled with herself, swallowing hot words, hiding her hurt pride, wanting the joy of the moment more than the promise of the future and fearing the loss of the one by the demand for the other.

Bliss sensed her discomfort and wiped her mind clean of the pain with a series of gentle kisses. He began with her forehead, then kissed her eyes, her nose and the slopes of her high cheekbones, and stopped with his mouth mere inches from hers.

"You will find me the safest lover you have ever known," he whispered.

"The safest?" She did not feel safe.

"Yes, because I cherish my freedom, I also value yours. I'll never intrude on your privacy or infringe on your rights." He was here to play not to stay.

Cassandra closed her eyes in a vain attempt to block out his words. She sighed. "Bliss, would you do something for me?"

"What?"

"Shut up."

His answer was a brief smile before he covered her mouth with his in a long, slow kiss. As he pressed her back against the pillows, he dropped his glass on the floor, freeing his hands to remove her gown. His fingers fumbled for the fastening and found none.

"Allow me to do that," she offered.

Bliss released her and quickly removed his own garments. She slipped out of the tight-fitting gown that was held in place by methods only she understood. *Why*, she wondered, *do I spend so much time selecting clothing when I'm only going to take them off again?*

When she turned back to him, Bliss was nude, watching her with open admiration. "You have the most beautiful body I have ever seen," he said.

"And I'm sure you've seen hundreds in your quest for the perfect female," she needled.

"Make that thousands and you're a lot more on target," he retorted as he grabbed her and pulled her down on the bed as she faked a swing at him. He held her hand in his and made telepathic contact as he sought the identity she wished him to assume.

After a brief pause, he asked, "You want me as I am?"

"Is that so unusual?"

"You realize that I can become anyone else, anyone you choose," he suggested, giving her a second chance.

"I understand completely, and I still want you."

"Your wish is my command," Bliss said, taking her in his arms.

34

He was flattered and uneasy at the same time. Nagging insecurities plagued him, some having to do with Cassandra, but mostly with his fear of the time when his long spans of spacing would catch up with him. The warp and skip of galactic travel had a cumulative effect on the body. There were no middle-aged spacers, only the young and the very old. Long periods of exposure could suddenly take effect— wiping out entire spans of life in one chunk.

Bliss was nearing the point of no return in his own exposure rate and lifecycle, and it preyed on his mind, as it soon would on his body. He pushed the thought away. Bliss was in his prime and he lived for the moment.

His hands moved skillfully over Cassandra's plentiful curves as he pulled her to him and caressed her silky skin. He slid his hands upwards and his thumb caught in the gold chain that encircled her waist. Drawing back, he looked down at the small red key, turning it between his fingers.

"I meant to ask before. What is this?" She never took it off.

She couldn't help glancing at the trunk in the corner. Bliss noted it. Cassandra playfully batted her eyes and simpered. "Bliss, I thought you knew . . . it's the key to my heart."

He ran his index finger over the key. "That's why it's so small, I should have known," he said as he prepared to get up. "Let's see what's hidden in your heart."

Cassandra's black eyes spit fire, and the key between his fingers responded to her anger until it glowed and turned a deep, virulent crimson color. Pain from the extreme heat seared his fingertips and Bliss cursed and dropped the key. It instantly returned to a normal temperature.

She laughed wickedly. "No one sees inside my heart, you unclaimed son of a space whore."

"My dear, it's useless to call me names," Bliss said, rubbing his fingers. "I have no idea who my mother was, so you can't insult her." He smiled at Cassandra, eager to avoid any more unpleasantness. "Let's not fight. Forget the trunk, there are better things to do."

Bliss proceeded to show her exactly what they were. He set out to please her, using all his knowledge, worshipping at the altar of the shrine to her beauty. Appreciation was the most he could offer any female. Tenderly, he touched her, bringing Cassandra totally alive. No words were spoken. Soft moans and sighs escaped her lips as the wonder and awe Bliss felt communicated itself to her.

For that space in time, nothing else mattered, not the future, not the past. She wanted this moment to last forever, but even with all her powers of sorcery, Cassandra could not make time stand still.

A feeling of deep contentment washed over her just before she climaxed, and she wanted to hold onto it—the high lifted her up and out of herself and brought her to a point where she felt a oneness with the universe. She seemed to be knocking on heaven's door when Bliss climaxed, bringing her back to herself.

"Are you all right?" he asked as she gasped for breath.

Exhaling deeply, she said, "I'm fine."

"You're better than fine. You're extraordinary."

"I know," she said, smugly.

Bliss laughed in spite of himself. It was something he often said to females and being on the receiving end was a new experience. Bracing himself with his arms, he moved up and away from Cassandra.

The cold rush of air between them brought her back to reality. For her, basking in the afterglow ranked high as an important aspect of lovemaking. Most males turned loose and turned over. Satisfied and relaxed, ready for sleep, most of her lovers left her alone with her thoughts.

But Bliss was different, he reached out and drew her to him and held her close with her head resting on his chest while he stroked her hair and talked about his adventures, his views on life. It was confusing, the sharing. *How can he not care for me?* Her mind pulled her in two directions. Time sped up. Soon, she must leave to meet Karachal.

He sensed her mind wandering. "Am I boring you, Cassandra, with all this talk?" His hand touched hers.

"No, please, go on." She needed to go, but she wanted to stay.

"I remember," he said, as he absentmindedly caressed her fingers. His voice wove a spell that pulled her along with him, lulled by the poetry in his words.

The sound of his voice and the touch of his hand slowly opened doors she had thought closed forever, and in spite of her determination not to, she entered. She recalled the young girl she once had been, so innocent and trusting, living safely in a time of security.

Feelings of loss and regret overwhelmed her, as she relived and shared aspects of her painful memories with Bliss. She wanted him to understand that the changes that had taken place in her mind and heart had been necessary for her survival. Believing that story was the only way Cassandra could go on. If she thought otherwise, guilt and self-loathing would destroy her.

A deep sadness born of the longing for what might have been, welled up inside her, and she remembered why those doors must remain closed.

She stopped talking and realized that, for some unfathomable reason, their roles had been reversed, and she had revealed much more about herself than she had ever intended.

She pulled away from him.

"Bliss, enough. I don't want to think about the past, anymore. It's too painful. I can't bear it. Things never turn out the way they should."

"I know," he said. "it is what it is." His thoughts drifted to a distant time and place she could never enter.

Cassandra rose to her knees, her hand still firmly held in his. She tossed her head as if it would rid her of the unpleasant memories. She focused on the present, knowing it was a waste of time to remain with Bliss and weave foolish fantasies. Her mercenaries waited.

"How about a night cap?"

"I'd love one," Bliss answered, not realizing the drink was going to be more like a velvet hammer.

She fetched two drinks, a light one for herself and another one heavily laced with a sleeping potion for Bliss.

After he drank it down, Cassandra waited until the drug took effect.

At rest, his face took on a boyish, vulnerable quality. Gone was the mask of insolence, the mocking eyes shuttered, and the lips that had uttered such cruel words relaxed, soft and pliant.

Her fingers moved lightly over his face as she traced his strong jaw and felt the heartbeat pulsing in his throat. She believed his ardent response to her had to mean something. He was going to be hers. He had to be.

With a sigh of resignation, she stepped into her private dressing room and changed her clothing. A few moments later, Cassandra emerged garbed completely in black, sporting a military tunic over tight pants stuffed into knee high spacer boots. She pulled her thick mane of hair up onto the top of her head and secured it in a silver mesh cap, donned a visored helmet and the transformation was complete.

Before she left the chamber, Cassandra treated herself to one last loving glance at Bliss, secure in the belief that he would be there on her return.

Chapter 4

The span was well into mid-lightness by the time Bliss woke up from his drug-induced sleep, clear headed, and feeling no ill effects. Cassandra was nowhere in sight, but as soon as his feet hit the floor a pre-recorded holographic message automatically activated.

Marveling at the ingenuity of the device, he stepped on and off the floor, starting and stopping the message, watching Cassandra's three-dimensional image fade in and out before he let it continue uninterrupted.

"Bliss, I've been called away on business. Please, make yourself at home. I will return soon, probably by mid-darkness."

Bliss felt no disappointment at her absence, instead he was pleased to have some time alone. He planned to check on the condition of his ship, thinking it might be necessary to make a quick getaway.

As he dressed, his thoughts dwelled on Cassandra, but not in the way she would have hoped. Handling her many moods left him feeling drained, and he wasn't sure the conquest was worth the effort. Beneath her cool exterior, he sensed an explosive nature, and his hand rested on the detonator. Of even more concern, during their most recent sexual encounter, he thought he had detected tenderness and perhaps something more. But, no—it couldn't be, he rationalized not wanting to face any conflict—he must have misinterpreted her mood.

Never one to over analyze, he turned his attention to more important matters. Bliss arrived at the spaceport, only to discover that none of the preliminary work had been performed on his ship to prepare for the installation of new crystals on his ship. After a few well-placed bribes, he secured a promise of total crystal realignment by next lightness, and also learned that the repairs would go much faster and be less expensive if he procured the crystals. Bliss roamed the markets until he located a source, a supplier who guaranteed delivery as soon as possible—whatever that meant.

Bliss returned to the palace and Cassandra's chamber earlier than expected and walked in on Elena, startling the serving girl absorbed in the task of polishing the top of Cassandra's trunk. At his greeting, she jumped and her fingers grazed the globe of insects sitting near the trunk's edge. The ball rolled off and hit the marble floor with a thud. Insects flew in every direction.

"By the Gods!" Elena swore. "Cassandra will kill me." She sank to the floor to access the damage. "What am I to do?"

Bliss smiled wryly, failing to see the desperation in the situation. "Don't worry, there's no need to be upset."

Elena burst into tears. Bliss knelt down and placed his arm around her shoulders, gently turned her to face him and without thinking took Elena in his arms in a comforting embrace. Her slender frame pressed against him, and Bliss realized how defenseless she was. Elena's vulnerability brought out his latent protective instincts.

She pulled back and stared up into his face, seeing the tenderness there and taking heart from it. "Please, help me. I know this must seem like so much feminine foolishness to you, but I know my mistress. She will punish me severely for my carelessness."

"It was an accident. It's my fault. I startled you. I'll take the blame. No need to be afraid. "

Her chin jerked up. "I am not a coward. I accept the responsibility for my actions. Cassandra is not someone you can reason with, especially if there is a male involved."

"Then we will just have to set it right, before she returns," he said.

Elena began to examine the spot where the globe had landed and to her chagrin, she found several tiny, crushed bodies. "Oh, no, some of them are dead. What can we do?"

"Well," Bliss suggested, "we might hold a small private ceremony."

Elena shot him a daggered look; she saw no humor in the situation. She stood and walked the chamber in a circular path, gathering the scattered particles, one by one from the floor, the walls, and the bed hangings. The more she searched, the more insects she discovered until the sheer numbers overwhelmed her. There were thousands of them.

"This will take forever," she said as she sighed heavily and stared at the palm of her hand."

"Elena, don't worry, I think I know how to solve our problem," he said, "just stand still for a moment, don't move." Bliss didn't want her stepping on any of the survivors.

She nodded her understanding. An instant later, she stared in wide-eyed disbelief as Bliss initiated a transformation. She watched, her mouth slack and agape as his flesh flowed, rippled and changed shape. Even his clothing seemed to take on a life of its own. Elena gasped and pressed her hand to her mouth.

In the space occupied a moment before by the masculine form of Bliss, stood a perfect replica of her mistress Cassandra.

Holding out his hand palm up as he had seen Cassandra do, Bliss spoke the command. "Reort!"

Sparkling pinpoints of light flew at him from every direction and converged on his palm to form one solid, glowing unit. Bliss turned the orb in his hand, inspecting the surface for gaps or blemishes. It appeared to be flawless.

"It's whole once more, and Cassandra need never know," he said, offering the reconstructed light to Elena.

Stunned by the entire procedure, she waved it away. "No, please, you put it back. I might drop it." As he carefully placed the globe on the top of the trunk his mind flashed on Cassandra's earlier unease at his interest in the receptacle.

"Elena, do you know what Cassandra keeps in this trunk?"

"No . . . nor do I wish to."

"Any ideas?"

"Just that it must be something of great importance or value. She is the only one with a key and to my knowledge, which is limited, no one else can open it." *Or would dare*, she surmised.

"I see," he said, letting the matter drop, sensing Elena's discomfort, knowing the experience of speaking to him in Cassandra's body was disconcerting enough.

Elena was relieved. She had no desire to delve into her mistresses' secrets. For now, due to Bliss and his wondrous abilities, she had been spared Cassandra's wrath. Elena suddenly felt guilty, realizing she had not expressed her gratitude.

"I cannot possibly thank you enough for your help, for your kindness," she said. "If there is anything I can do to repay you, please tell me. . . ." she said, her voice trailing off.

Unable to resist the impulse, Bliss allowed a knowing, slightly sinister smile to creep over Cassandra's features. "As a matter of fact," he purred, "there is something I desire."

Elena's emotions took a wild, dizzying dip into a dark pit of fear, and she took an unsteady step backward.

"What is it that you wish?" she asked, with obvious reluctance and regret for having made the offer.

Cassandra's husky laughter filled the chamber. "I'd give my next scheduled orbit around Venuia for a good meal. I'm starved."

Elena blushed, having heard scandalous rumors about the sexual appetites of the females on that infamous planet. But the frank statement eased her tension, now she knew it was Bliss—the male—who dominated the body. *How typical*, she thought, *the first thing males think of is their stomach*. In Bliss' case, it was the second.

She smiled at him to mask the pity she felt, for she sensed his uncontrolled appetites and weaknesses. "Shall I serve your meal here or would you prefer the gardens? They're lovely at this time of lightness."

"The gardens? I haven't seen them. That will be perfect."

Elena gave him directions and left to prepare the meal. As soon as she made her exit Bliss, still in Cassandra's form, crouched down in front of the trunk and fingered the small red key fastened around Cassandra's waist. He hesitated, but his curiosity won out. He inserted the key, the lock clicked open and he raised the lid of the trunk.

Bliss rummaged through the contents of Cassandra's personal belongings. Among them, he recognized some valuable jewelry and rare pieces of artwork that he knew to be stolen. *So, she steals more than hearts*, he thought. Next, he examined a large book, a priceless ancient tome of sorcery secrets, the long-lost writings of a legendary master, quite possibly the only such volume still in existence. But these things were not what he was searching for. *There must be more.* While he was still in Cassandra's form Bliss intended to find out, and he was not above calling upon a form of genetic deja vu to access her memories.

With a familiar motion, he ran his fingers over the trunk's bottom and tripped a hidden trigger mechanism. The covering slid back to reveal a treasure trove secreted in a vault underneath the marble floor. His eyes widened in amazement, and Bliss let out a long, low whistle. *Crystals! Hundreds of them!* He picked up one of the translucent objects and held it between his fingers in front of the globe light, and slowly turned the jagged jewel in his hand. Bliss watched the reflected patterns of light play over the wall hangings magnified through the crystal's prism. His breath quickened and his heart raced at the sight. These were genuine article—Carduvian crystals—the most tradable, valuable commodity in the known universe.

Cassandra was more dangerously wealthy than Bliss had imagined. With these she could go anywhere and live well. Why then did she stay on Scorpious? *No one in their right mind would want to live out their lifespan here. Maybe that is the answer—perhaps she is insane.* It was not a very consoling thought. Bliss quickly placed everything back exactly as he had found it, relocked the box, and left her chamber.

As he crossed the threshold, one booted masculine foot hit the floor even as another feminine foot hovered in the air. With one more step, Bliss was himself once again. In a few minutes he entered the garden. The atrium was a pleasant surprise, a lush, tropical oasis in stark contrast to the rest of Scorpious.

Above his head a clear dome formed a protective canopy for the carefully controlled atmosphere. Rich hued green, yellow and bright blue foliage caught his eye, waving gently in a light breeze. To his right, water cascaded over rocky falls of pure jade and artificial sunlight glinted on the surface of the emerald pool the falls formed; an authentic simulation of the bright rays streaming down on other worlds more fortunate than Scorpious.

Bliss took a deep breath of the fragrant air and allowed his nostrils to fill with the scents of a hundred flowers. As he passed a large bower, Bliss plucked one dainty yellow bud from a bush. Farther down the path, he spied Elena. She sat on a small, low bench with her back to him as she placed several dishes on a half-moon-shaped table in front of her.

His practiced eye approved of the thick braid of chestnut hair and the long, slender neck that begged for a whisper-soft kiss. In many ways, she appeared fragile, but he recognized an underlying strength. He suspected she possessed a noble character, and like the tender bud in his hand, she would soon blossom. But unless fate intervened, Bliss feared Elena might bloom unseen, wasting her sweetness on the arid air and the sense-dulled males of Scorpious.

He spoke her name softly, and she turned to face him. Her unguarded, trusting look conjured up a fleeting memory of Gabrielle, and Bliss suddenly felt as if it his heart had been squeezed by a giant hand. He brushed the memory away.

Then Bliss held out the flower, offering it to Elena. "A tribute to your beauty, sweet lady."

"But it is so small," she teased. Elena was in a much better mood.

"The bud will unfurl and fulfill its promise, even as you will someday." His voice was light but his eyes were serious.

"I accept your tribute, thank you."

"You're as welcome as this sunlit garden," he said, spreading his arms wide in delight.

Elena remembered her duties and busied herself serving his meal. Bliss sat down at the table and watched her intently with undisguised pleasure until she finished her work and prepared to leave.

"Elena, won't you join me?"

"I can't, my mistress ..."

"I insist," he said, "sit down," more in the manner of a command than an invitation.

Reluctantly, Elena perched on the edge of the bench as far away from him as possible, feeling a stab of joy and at the same time, confused by her reaction. She was eager to be near him, yet nervous about being near him.

"There's nothing to be frightened of," he said, "all I want from you is your companionship. I detest dining alone. Please, have some wine." *Why do females always think I want their bodies*, he wondered. He flinched, realizing it was because he always did.

Indulging him, Elena sipped from the glass he handed her, impatient to end this insane encounter before Cassandra came back and found them together. To her surprise the drink produced an almost magical effect, infusing her with a warm glow of well being, unlike anything she had experienced since her arrival on Scorpious. Elena allowed herself the luxury of basking in the beauty of her surroundings in a rare moment of peace.

"Tell me about yourself," he said. "I'm curious. How did you come to be here? It's evident you weren't born into slavery." That much was obvious, submission was not her normal state.

"My father was a Councilhead on my home planet, Althea." Her words took on a tone of formality. "At the time of my capture, I was on an interplanetary journey to Kryon where I was to be united with another family of equal status, the mate for their only son, Betonia. The joining was to serve as a bond between our people. Our worlds had warred many times in the past, and our pairing would have been a symbol of our mutual peaceful intentions."

She knew all too well that one of the stipulations of their mating had demanded that the female be pure of heart, mind, and body. Although her body remained untouched, Elena secretly feared for the state of her heart and mind, feeling degraded and tainted by the depths of her desire for revenge.

"Were you alone on the journey?" he prodded.

She lowered her eyes and sighed heavily. "No, my father was with me and others of our party."

"Where is your father now?"

She did not reply, and the silence lengthened. Elena struggled to control her emotions. For so long, she had tried not to think of her father.

"He was killed," she confessed, "trying to protect me during the takeover of our space cruiser." Her eyes clouded, stung by the smoke of a distant fire, the memory of her father's lifeless body stretched out in the cargo bay, left on board their ship with the course set for the nearest sun.

"I'm sorry, Elena," Bliss said, moving closer.

"What's done is done," she said, wiping stray tears from her cheek. "My tears will not bring him back. They are useless. My father would not be pleased at my having shed them. On Althea, we celebrate the passing of our loved ones ... we show joy when their spirit is released to a higher plane."

He nodded. "The beings of my home planet, Arias, do much the same."

"Father always said, 'You come into the world with nothing and you leave with nothing—except character and the lessons you've learned in life.' He left much wealth in wisdom," she said, pride shining in her eyes.

"You honor him with your respect for his memory. I'm sure he would be pleased."

"Yes," she said, distracted, her mind caught up in the past, working her way through the familiar paths of pain.

Bliss felt a rush of compassion for her, but knew in spite of her present circumstances, there were far worse fates than being a servant. Many males despised virgins; they considered them to be frozen assets.

"It's a good thing Cassandra purchased you at the slave mart, instead of some unscrupulous male. You are fortunate," he said.

"Fortunate!" Elena's face flushed hot with anger. "Are you completely mad," she spat, "has she taken your reason from you with one of her spells? Cassandra didn't buy me. I was captured, and she's the one who staged the raid. It's what she does."

Bliss sat unmoving, shocked into silence.

His lack of response added to Elena's fury. "By the Gods, do you think it is *fortunate* to be the servant of the female who caused the death of my father—to spend the rest of my life in this dismal place, with her as my mistress? Of course, you are free to leave," she spat, her voice dripping with scorn, "while I am a prisoner. Do not speak so casually to me of my good fortune."

Bliss was lost in a mental orgy of guilt. What a fool he'd been—nothing else but piracy could account for the huge number of crystals in Cassandra's chamber. "Elena, believe me, I didn't know. I don't approve of slavery, much less piracy and murder. But Cassandra seemed harmless enough, merely another female gone mad with a little taste of power. What you've told me merely confirms the uneasy feelings I've been having."

She shook her head in disbelief, thinking it beyond her understanding. Why were males so attracted to females like Cassandra, couldn't they see beneath the surface? Or didn't they care? Even the best of them fell under her spell. She breathed a deep sigh, and glanced around, once more aware of her beautiful surroundings. "This garden reminds me of my world, of Althea—sunlit and happy—and so very far away."

"We're never so far away, we can't get back." Bliss said, softly.

"Get back?"

"I plan to leave here soon. You can go with me, Elena, I'll take you home."

'Home!' The word made her heart ache; the longing swelled and rose into her throat. She swallowed hard, afraid his words might be a trick of some sort, a cruel joke. Elena knew so little about him, could she trust him? *Why would he do such a thing*, she wondered, doubt evident on her face.

"Please believe me, I'd never hurt you, Elena. Trust me," he pleaded. "I can't explain it, but there's something about you that brings out the rescuer in me." Something Bliss had long thought dead.

"Why would you do this, Bliss, you don't really know me—or I you."

"Help me finish this wine, and I'll tell you my story. Then decide for yourself what my true motives are." Bliss left nothing out. He began with his first memories and poured out his life story, sharing his feelings in a way not possible with a female he wished to dominate physically. Elena listened intently as he told his tale.

"In my former existence, I was a spiritual guide for the beings on planet Arias," he began. "I was chosen to serve as a teacher for Gabrielle, a young female healer, mainly because I had never incarnated on the material plane, and the Elders reasoned that Gabrielle might give me insight into life in the mundane world."

"You mean were once an angel?" Elena said, her voice dropping to a whisper.

"Something like that, I don't remember much of what took place before I met Gabrielle. To make a long story short, I fell in love with my pupil and her world."

"Oh, my!"

"Indeed." Bliss stared off into space, lost in his thoughts.

"What happened?" Elena prodded.

Gabrielle persuaded me to take on a physical form, something I was able to do for short periods of time. Of course, it didn't take much persuading."

"The more time I spent in the physical world the more frustrated I became by my inability to fully experience all the pleasures of Gabrielle's world—taste, touch, sounds, smells. I could see her, but I couldn't hear her voice, or smell the scent of her, or kiss her, and hold her in my arms. She wasn't real to me."

"So, what did you do? You seem fully realized now. Although Elena was eager to hear the rest of the story, she was also concerned that Cassandra might return at any moment.

"I met with the Elders in the Transmutation Chambers and announced the renouncement of my spiritual birthright and my intention to incarnate as a fully grown male on the planet Arias. They were not amused, but there wasn't much they could do about it—free will and all. During the time of my transformation, I was forbidden to communicate with Gabrielle until the change was complete."

"How long did it take?"

"I don't know. At that point, I had no concept of time or space. It could have been a month, a year or a hundred years. I've never thought about it before. I thought she hadn't waited for me. Maybe she did, but for how long, I'll never know."

"It must have been difficult, like a newborn waking up in an adult's body," Elena said.

"It was strange," Bliss said. "I had no parents, no childhood, no teachers and no belief systems. I just *was*. Although my previous existence was fast becoming a hazy dream, the memories of the time I had spent with Gabrielle in the physical world were available to me with great clarity. My telepathic, soul connection with her remained intact and eventually her energy led me to her, and I found her in a bridal bed—in the arms of her husband."

"Oh, my God, Bliss. You must have been devastated."

"It drove me to the brink of madness. Unendurable jealousy and anger consumed me. I experienced most of the lower emotions—hatred, rage, the desire for vengeance and the urge to kill—for the first time."

"Oh, I'm so sorry, Bliss. Did you ever see her again?"

"No, I stumbled out of their pavilion and fled. All I wanted to do was escape, I was trapped in the third dimension and as far as I was concerned, it was Gabrielle's fault. I never wanted to see her again. I went into hiding, lost and confused until my basic survival instincts kicked in. Before the anniversary of my first 'birth day,' I *borrowed* a space cruiser, launched into orbit around Arias and space jumped out of the galaxy."

And you've been running ever since, she thought.

Time raced by as he quickly brought her up to date with the events of the last darkness and his recent decision to return to Arias. As he talked to Elena, Bliss began to see his own life from a different perspective.

By hearing his story, Elena had gained a better understanding of his insecurity and hidden vulnerabilities, and viewed his vindictive actions with compassion. At the same time, she felt sorry for all the females who had crossed his star-crossed path.

Her own heart was already lost to him, but with wisdom beyond her life experience, she knew nothing would come of it. Bliss saw her as a cause and cared for her only as a wrong he might right. She knew that until he learned to love himself, to forgive himself, Gabrielle and others, it would be impossible for him to truly love anyone else.

Dismissing his faults, she chose to see only the good in him. Her heart went out to him and with it, her trust. She would place her hopes, her dreams—her life in his hands. Perhaps by rescuing her, Bliss might save himself.

But their time together was growing short. Soon, all too soon, Cassandra would return.

"Bliss, I accept your kind offer," she said, taking his arm. "But you must go now, it would be dangerous to be found here together. For your own safety, return now to Cassandra's chamber. She may return at any moment." No one ever knew where Cassandra disappeared to or how long she would be gone.

Reluctantly, he stood and pulled her to her feet, smiling confidently at her to indicate there was nothing to worry about. Elena clasped his hand in hers, and pressed his fingers to her cheek. For a moment, they stood transfixed.

Then, outside in the hall, they heard a flurry of activity. Bliss herded Elena toward the doorway to the atrium where they flattened themselves against the wall. Peering into the hallway, he saw the heels of booted feet disappear around the corner.

"We must hurry," he whispered, "someone is coming from the other direction." Hand-in-hand, they slipped into the corridor, and then separated. Elena went to the right, Bliss to the left.

Bliss rounded the corner and found himself face-to-face with Cassandra.

Chapter 5

Bliss did not recognize Cassandra. Her masculine garments disguised her figure, and the space helmet further hid her identity. He passed her in the corridor without notice, his mind on his conversation with Elena and the plan they had hatched.

Relieved, Cassandra hurried past him, her eyes averted. She was in no mood for small talk, even with Bliss. She sought the solace of her gardens, a place where she hoped to bring her emotions under control.

Her heart still pounded in terror, beating out a matching rhythm in her temples. Cassandra snatched off her helmet and freed her hair from the restraint of the silver cap. As she collapsed onto the nearest bench, she placed the battle gear on the ground beside her, buried her head in her hands and massaged her aching forehead.

Over and over, the details of the raid played on the movie screen in her mind. It had been their misfortune to come upon their quarry shortly after the intended victim, transport ship the Dorian, had passed through the barrage of an uncharted asteroid field. As a result, the crew was on full alert—ship sensors on full scan.

Cassandra immediately activated the concealing device she had taken on board Karachai's star voyager, and rendered it invisible to mask their approach. But an alert navigator on the Dorian became suspicious of the void that suddenly appeared in a section of space seconds ago occupied by a distinct star pattern. The Dorian's defense shields instantly locked into place; the ship's weapons armed and ready. The crew assumed battle stations, and the merchant ship prepared to repel any attackers.

Then it happened. Karachai opened fire, but the Dorian's shields deflected his blasts, and shattered harmlessly in space several hundred spacemarks from their target.

Unfortunately, the firing trails led directly back to the invisible star voyager. Instantly, the Dorian locked onto the coordinates of the telltale trail and fired. The time lapse allowed Karachai to avoid a direct hit, but a glancing blow severely diminished both his ship's maneuverability and firepower. Karachai beat a hasty retreat, leaving the Dorian unharmed to sound an intergalactic alarm.

Inside the star voyager, Cassandra and Karachai were locked in a heated battle of their own. She demanded their immediate return to Scorpious. He, with a cooler head, insisted they take a longer, more circuitous route back to the planet in order to avoid being followed and apprehended by the Tribunal starcruisers sure to have been alerted to their presence.

Cassandra's overpowering deep space terrors stripped away the veneer covering her raw emotions. She lashed out at Karachai and his crew with bitter words of recrimination that ricocheted off the men in the close confines of the ship.

"How in the name of all that's powerful," she swore, "did you make such a witless blunder—firing on a ship with its deflector shields up? Any novice, any half-blind spacer," she continued, "would have seen them go up. You idiot, you led those blasts straight to us!"

Karachai hovered over the console control panel, laying in an evasive course, and doing his best to ignore her tirade. He seethed inside as her stinging barbs found their mark and clung. He knew the error was his and his alone.

Cassandra grabbed Karachai by the arm and screeched in his ear. "You listen to me. I command you—take this ship back to Scorpious—now!"

It was far too much for his wounded male ego to endure. In one swift move, he pinioned her arms to her sides. "No, you listen," he growled in her ear. The cold steel in his voice silenced her more effectively than any words could have. "You may be the Princess of Darkness on Scorpious, but out here in space, you're just another female. Sorcery can't fly this ship. I can. Right or wrong, I make the decisions."

With his arm around her neck, he forced her across the bridge to her seat, pushed her down into it, and strapped her in. Every snapping motion dared her to utter one more word. "Cassandra, if you want to live to see that gray pile of rocks you call home—sit there and shut up!"

Luckily, Cassandra's anger rendered her momentarily speechless. Karachai was on the hair's edge of violent anger. "One of these times, my pretty one," he taunted, "that sharp tongue of yours is going to cut off your life force. I'd leave it in the scabbard, if I were you." Then, he turned his back on her in dismissal and concentrated on the vast blackness spread out before them.

Cassandra glared at him defiantly with a cutting retort ready on her tongue. Scathing words burned to leave her mouth, but were swallowed up as her anger turned to ice, and she stared wild-eyed at the cold, limitless vacuum of deep space.

The black void was the only thing she feared. Cassandra had been space marked. It happened sometimes when the first spacing experience left an indelible, traumatic impression. At the age of 16, the terrorist group, "Fasciba," had kidnapped Cassandra. Captured with hundreds of others, she was taken on board their ship and savagely, repeatedly raped by the storm troopers. Deep space always triggered her memories and her terrors.

She could view the stars and distant planets calmly as long as the firm surface of a world was solid beneath her feet, but the star voyager with its floating, drifting feeling, stripped bare the full range of her fears.

Cassandra blamed it all on her father, Colin, the great sorcerer who had abandoned her, left her defenseless as a young child in the hands of her mother, a woman who should have remained childless. Cassandra had been home alone when the terrorists invaded.

After Cassandra had been sold as a slave and eventually won her freedom by becoming a consummate concubine, she tracked down her father. It had not been an easy task.

Early in life, Colin had felt a calling and left his family to study at the feet of the masters of sorcery. In time he became one himself and was in much demand. He traveled extensively and was seldom at home, but he did come back to see his daughter on rare occasions. After many years of service to those in high places and those who wanted to be, Colin became disillusioned and repelled by the political maneuvering and manipulations of those he helped bring to power.

The famous sorcerer had withdrawn from society, seeking peace and solitude in which to search for the true meaning of life.

Cassandra finally located him through the intergalactic Merchandising Company that delivered supplies to his isolated asteroid home every six spans. When Cassandra had shown up, unannounced, Colin was startled. In truth, he had all but forgotten she existed, never expecting to see his daughter again. He felt his estrangement from her was for the best. Even at the times when he longed to hold his child in his arms, he refrained from contacting her because he feared others might seek to hurt him through her.

But after he recovered from the shock, Colin was flattered that his daughter had sought him out and was pleased to find her interested in the one legacy he could offer her—his mastery of the mysteries. Indeed, his knowledge of magic was all Cassandra wanted from her father.

As he came to know her and learned her past history, Colin sometimes despaired for her and the uses to which she might put his teachings while at the same time feeling they might one day be necessary for her survival.

Money and sex proved to be her primary motivations. From experience, Colin knew these two root drives were the forces that every being, sooner or later, must learn to control—either control or be controlled. These drives could be converted into constructive action by the application of courageous self-discipline. By facing up to, living with, and overcoming these compulsions, Cassandra might gain power over her lower self.

For a while, she stayed with him and studied his craft, learning the basic spells and rudimentary alchemy. Soon, Cassandra had grown restless. She chaffed at the slow pace of his tutoring, resented the sparse surroundings and isolation, and longed for fleshly and material comforts. When she felt she had learned all she needed, she left him and went on to build an empire on the near planet of Scorpious, an intergalactic hideout, and a home to the dregs of the universe.

Her father was not pleased at her departure, but he knew the lessons she must learn were her own. Although Colin read the signs and foresaw the seeds of self-destruction Cassandra had sown; he was powerless to prevent the harvest to come.

Cassandra stayed on her "gray pile of rocks" as Karachai called it because she was afraid to venture any further than their raids. On Scorpious, she had status and power, knew the rules, and understood them. She knew it would be different anywhere else, and she wasn't an adaptable person, uncertainty was her enemy. Fluid situations with no predetermined references confused her. A clear aim, such as the acquisition of wealth, kept her on an even keel. Or so she thought.

Now, to make matters worse, the insecurity of her relationship with Bliss was taking a toll. Cassandra intended to have him, yet inwardly harbored serious misgivings about her ability to achieve that goal. He was the one male who fulfilled her, but his attitude and her doubts were driving her crazy.

An aching head and tense muscles drew her back into the present, away from the terrors of space and the fears of the future. Outside, light faded into darkness, and Bliss must be wondering what had happened. At least, she hoped so, prayed that he cared. She was in unfamiliar territory, and in her heart she knew his feelings weren't something she could control. She couldn't even control her own. Her thoughts sped forward to the pleasures awaiting her in their chamber, and Cassandra bit her lip in anticipation.

Later, in her chamber, much to her dismay, she found Bliss attentive, yet distracted. He engaged in sex with Cassandra, but it seemed to be more out of a sense of duty than anything else, a courteous gesture like thanking your hostess. She failed to appreciate his good manners.

She badly needed the release and relaxation of sexual satisfaction, and so she strove frantically for their earlier rapport. But somehow the natural warmth and spontaneity of their encounters had vanished as quickly as one of her sorcery-induced illusions.

She desired an act beyond the joining of their bodies; Cassandra wanted access to his heart and soul. Last darkness, the door had been ajar, and now it was locked tight. Bliss gave her his body, but his mind and spirit were already light years away. Knowing something was amiss, each of them went through the motions, feigning a deeper joy and greater passion than they actually felt; each thinking the other fooled.

A vague anger gnawed at Cassandra, driving her on, compelling her. She used her tongue, her lips, her hips, every trick she knew to revive the fervor of their former passion, but it only made Bliss more aware that his ardor had waned. Good sex was effortless, and Cassandra was working much too hard.

Just as she had decided to give up and end her efforts in unfulfilled exhaustion, Bliss responded. At last, she had struck a spark, igniting the flame of desire flickering beneath his logical, surface emotions. Caught up in her moment, he was snared in an erotic web of wanton lust.

Under the canopy of midnight blue, in the dim hued twilight—the two beings joined—united in mating movements as old as time itself. For that one moment, Cassandra felt Bliss to be completely and totally hers. No other shared in the experience, for she had wiped them all from his mind. She didn't want it to end, but it did, all too quickly with both of them achieving satisfaction.

In that instant, a die was cast, and fate and destiny converged as Bliss convulsed into her warm, waiting womb.

Cassandra smiled up into his eyes with knowing contentment.

Bliss rolled over, taking her with him, and flopping back on the bed pillows, holding her in the crook of his arm. His free hand gently smoothed back the damp tendrils of hair from her face. The salty scent of sex clung to their bodies and seeped from the tousled bedding. She snuggled against him, savoring their closeness, the feeling of oneness.

Lying in the safe haven of his arms, Cassandra felt secure. Once again breaking one of her own rules, she opened up to him, telling him of her past, her insecurities. Examining her fears, she spoke of the terrors that kept her on Scorpious.

Bliss listened raptly, armed with the information Elena had already provided, finding the female psyche fascinating and knowing no matter what she said—he would soon be gone.

It was part of his pattern. With each new conquest, he made an effort to learn as much as possible, delving into the inner workings of the female heart and mind. Each one provided him with new insights that often proved to be helpful in his next seduction. His lovers were flattered by his interest, misinterpreting his motives, even as Cassandra did now.

Perceptive and probing, his questions hit deep marks, striking a rich vein of memories, exposing her vulnerability. While Bliss interspersed her narrative with sweet kisses, Cassandra shared some of her deepest feelings and told him about the torments of her childhood and the existence of her famous father.

As their bodies intertwined, so did the convoluted pathways of their future. Cassandra's past was indelibly imprinted in his brain, and Bliss would be forced to reexamine it many times in the future.

Chapter 6

Upon leaving Bliss, in the early span of first lightness, Cassandra hurried to the central control room of the palace to review the events monitored during her absence. In that way, she kept track of all that transpired in her empire.

Seated at the master computer, her fingers flew over the multi-colored tiles, activating her electronic wizard. "Compulog 2073," she commanded. The computer acknowledged voice identification and gave her immediate access to all the events of the previous lightness.

She scanned them with a cursory interest. Finding nothing out of the ordinary, she entered the ID code that responded to Bliss' body aura.

"Requesting any available data on Bliss," she said.

A clipped, feminine voice answered instantly. "Data available on Epilog 2073, code 450, area 2, timeframe 4 kromers."

"Lock in and visualize."

"Visualizing."

The large viewing screen went from black to static, and then flared into full color in sharp focus. She immediately recognized her servant Elena and Bliss.

Cassandra watched with avid interest. Her body straightened and grew rigid as she witnessed the exchange of confidences between them. Much to her chagrin, she heard every word that Bliss had exchanged with the young girl. The conversation was more revealing and intimate than any he had shared with her during their time together.

Her face flushed and her breathing intensified. *I bared my soul to him last darkness, and he has betrayed me*, she thought. *Not only is he anxious to leave me, he plans to take Elena with him. To warm his bed, no doubt, the little whore.* Cassandra saw no incongruity in herself, a wanton adventuress, calling the innocent girl by such a name. Nor did she remember that it was she who had saved Elena from losing her highly prized virginity.

In her mind, she had been dealt a mortal blow. For the first time, Cassandra had allowed herself to feel something more than desire. The knowledge that Bliss did not, would not, could never return her love, cut through her, severing any connection between emotion and reason. Logic might have told her that she did much the same with the males in her life—she used them and moved on—but reason had no voice loud enough to be heard above the internal chaos created by the pain of Bliss' rejection.

The sickness of jealousy is a monstrous thing and it grew in Cassandra's chest until it seemed too large for her body to contain. The ache spread to her brain and blotted out every thought except one. She raised her fist and called on her powers of sorcery, "I will have my revenge," she shouted.

Her anger continued to rise, and then it erupted.

Cassandra stood up abruptly and knocked over the stool she had been sitting on and then kicked it out of her way. She stalked the computer complex, running both her hands through her long black hair, as she rubbed her forehead and muttered, "I'll kill him, I swear, I'll kill them both."

Suddenly, she shrieked and ran at the four tall columns that stood in a row at the end of the room. Her rush of adrenaline gave her super strength, and she shoved the first column until it toppled and then created a domino effect. The columns served as the settings for the display of her collection of priceless antiquities. Now, these heirlooms from vanished civilizations, all irreplaceable treasures, lay shattered on the floor. Cassandra cursed and crushed the fragments under her feet.

With some of her fury finally spent, she stood trembling amid the debris. Hatred glittered in her eyes, and there was more than a hint of madness about Cassandra as she shook her fist at the ceiling.

"By *all* the powers of sorcery," she swore, "Bliss *will* have what he wants and *more*, for longer than he ever dreamed possible. I shall see to it." She stood in the pose, motionless, her eyes closed. When at last she moved, her shoulders were back, her head high and any vestige of a potential for kindness and compassion was gone from her face.

In a short span, Cassandra was dressed for travel. Although she despised spacing alone, she dared not divulge her destination to anyone. No one on Scorpious knew where she went during her unannounced absences. No one even suspected that she traveled to see her father, Colin, in his self-imposed exile. As an antidote to her fears, she placed herself in a hypnotic trance for the trip and awoke as her cruiser went into orbit around the asteroid.

She disembarked and approached the entrance to his cave; a yawning mouth slashed across the face of a towering slab of rock. She called out a greeting. "Father, it's Cassandra. Are you there?" She waited outside for his reply.

From deep within the cavernous depths, she heard the echo of footsteps striking stone before a male figure broke through the dimness at the entrance to the cave. He was tall and lean, with a feral grace and strength evident in his stride. His long black robes decorated with silver symbols denoting his superior powers of sorcery, fluttered around him.

"Daughter, it is good to see you," he said, taking her outstretched hands in his and placing a welcoming kiss on her hot cheek. "You're as bewitchingly beautiful as ever."

Cassandra stared into onyx eyes the exact replica of her own. The light of a distant sun bounced off his full head of hair, white as moon's glow glistening on still water. Something in his stature, and the way he carried himself, reminded her fleetingly of Bliss.

"What brings you here again, so soon," he asked. "I'm pleased to see you, Daughter, but surprised."

"I need your help, Father."

Her tone was icy, and it sent a chill of premonition through the old one's heart. *It must be a serious matter*, he thought, *she rarely calls me Father*. Motioning her inside, he said, "Come inside and tell me what brings you here in such a state."

Together, they entered his subterranean asylum. On the way, she told him of Bliss' betrayal and briefly outlined the form her plan for vengeance would take as they emerged from the tunnel into a large, roomy area with a high ceiling.

Colin made no comment; he remained thoughtful and silent. The devious, vindictive act Cassandra plotted would strike to wound, not to kill. Her intent was to ruin rather than destroy. To him, the punishment seemed greatly in excess of the crime, if indeed there was one.

When Colin expressed his feelings, the ensuing argument echoed through his grotto home until it threatened to shake the very rocks from the walls. Cassandra paced, and gestured wildly. Her face contorted with rage as her father tried to reason with her.

"But Cassandra," he pointed out, "surely this male suffers enough merely by being what he is. There is no need to curse him any further. Let him go on searching for something that doesn't exist—the perfect woman—there's no such thing. Let him leave if he wishes to. Forget about him, he's not the only male in the galaxy. I won't help you in this foolishness."

"All right then, I'll kill him. I'll have the skin stripped from his body, piece by piece, and feed him to the worm mites! The sorry son-of-a-space whore! He will pay for his plotting."

"What plotting?" he demanded in exasperation.

"To take Elena away with him, to steal my property. To return her to her home planet, he says. But I know what he's up to, I know what he really wants!" The thought of them together sent her emotions on a fresh rampage.

"How do you know all this? Surely, neither Bliss nor your slave girl has confessed these things to you."

"Don't be stupid, of course not! I have surveillance devices in every chamber of the palace. Visual and sound recordings are automatically activated by the magnetic energy field surrounding any being who enters—with the exception of my chamber,' she added, "there are no monitors in my private quarters." Some things Cassandra didn't want recorded, among them were her antics on the raised platform. "While I was away, Bliss conspired with Elena without realizing he was being overheard."

The playback of that scene haunted Cassandra. Bliss spoke candidly to Elena about Gabrielle—his early rejection and hurt—the cause of his fear of commitment. Not only did he confess his own vendetta against females, and his craving for new lovers and experiences, he also revealed his anxieties about aging. To Elena, a mere servant girl, he had confided his homesickness, his wish to return to his home planet Arias, and the desire to change the path of his life.

But his complete and total undoing was his eagerness to leave Cassandra. His obvious relief at escaping what he described as a feeling of being smothered and trapped. Those words had sealed his fate.

She related all of it to Colin, becoming more worked up each time she rehashed the events. Her olive skin flushed deep red with the heat of her agitation and her hands shook, so uncontrollably that Colin became genuinely concerned for her well being.

"Come now, it's not as serious as you claim, Daughter, calm down. We'll work this out rationally," Colin said, making a solicitous move toward her.

"Don't you try to placate me," she snapped, wagging her finger in his face. "If you don't help me with this, I'll kill both of them. I swear it."

And he knew she meant it. In fact, Cassandra almost preferred it. Prolonged revenge would be sweet, but immediate retribution would serve her just as well. Colin saw the thrust of her thoughts and knew he was defeated. The only way to stop her would be to destroy her, and he could not bring himself to do that. Even as confused and crazy as Cassandra appeared to be, she was his daughter, and in his way, Colin loved her. He would help her, but it would be on his own terms. Knowing the misery she heaped on another's head would one day come back to her, he hoped to diminish those returns.

He threw up his hands in surrender. "All right, Daughter, you win. I'll have no blood on my hands. Tell me again the conditions of the evil you wish called down upon this Bliss fellow."

Cassandra once more explained the elements of the curse, and on hearing it, Colin feared he was assisting in the creation of an even more magnificent scoundrel. Patiently, he explained that countless females would suffer as a result of this folly, hoping to mitigate the terms by arousing some sympathetic reaction in her.

His words only served to further incite her. "Don't speak to me of innocent suffering. I want them to suffer. Your concern for the innocent is rather belated, isn't it, Father. Where were you when I was kidnapped and raped?"

Colin had no answer. He had made his choices and now he faced the consequences. There was nothing left to do except to concede to her terms. But his empathic, compassionate nature compelled him to add one stipulation that might afford Bliss the opportunity to redeem himself. However, Colin feared Cassandra might refuse the condition he intended to place within the spell if she fully realized the possibility of ultimate escape that it provided for Bliss.

Instead, she amazed him by dissolving in a fit of laughter. "Father, he'll never do that in a million light years. No, not even in a billion." She continued to laugh wildly and seeing his dismay, she struggled to control herself before he thought her completely mad. "By all means," she said, "let it be a condition of the curse. How very fitting. I wish I'd thought of it myself."

Colin was relieved. Perhaps Cassandra was right and Bliss wouldn't find the form of his release, but it eased his conscience to give him one, slim chance. His deeply lined face wrinkled further as he pondered what he was about to unleash upon an unsuspecting universe.

In a flash of insight, he knew there was something else he might do to mitigate the circumstances. "I add one more caveat, the females must give themselves freely to Bliss," he said, firmly, "no physical force can be used—I'll not condone rape." No matter what she thought, Colin cared.

Cassandra had neglected to tell her father of Bliss' extraordinary telepathic and chameleon abilities that made a female's cooperation practically a foregone conclusion.

With an air of resignation, Colin instructed Cassandra in the rituals, potions and incantations necessary to place the required curse on Bliss. "Cassandra, you must invoke the curse exactly as I have instructed you. If you do not, I *will* know."

"Yes, Father. Thank you."

Silently, Colin prayed that her intended victim no longer be on Scorpious when Cassandra returned.

Chapter 7

Bliss spent the time during Cassandra's absence charting his new course for Arias by way of Althea. By his closest reckoning, the trip would take one complete revolution of his home planet around its binary suns. It was a long span by some standards since Arias was located on the edge of a distant constellation, but for Bliss the lengthy journey was a welcome one. He had strayed far from his spiritual home, and the time would be well spent in introspection. His memories of his early life went as far back as his awakening in the crystal cave on Arias and no further. He had known his name was Bliss and that he loved Gabrielle, and had a vague concept of another life he had given up to be with her. *Perhaps if I return to Arias, I will find out who I really am,* he thought.

He took a break from his computations to check on his ship at the spaceport and found everything in order. The power cones had been cleaned and were ready and waiting for the new crystals to be inserted, but the supplier had not yet shown up with the crystals. Several other leads to suppliers had proved to be false, leaving him feeling powerless and frustrated.

Disgusted, he returned to the palace. Although it wasn't his first choice, Cassandra's cache of crystals might prove to be his best source. *But how can I approach such a touchy subject? She will know I want to leave.* His mind was so focused on his dilemma that Bliss ignored a vague sense of unease as he entered Cassandra's chamber.

The moment he stepped inside, someone seized him and pinned his arms behind him in a powerful, painful grip. In front of him loomed a large, ugly brute with reptilian skin, his chubby face set in a comic, yet menacing grimace as he drew back his huge, clenched fist and aimed it at Bliss' slack jaw.

Bliss lashed out with a sharp kick to his captor's shins while he ducked and dived at the same time. The fist intended for Bliss landed with a crack on the forehead of the hulk holding him. The three crashed to the floor in a pile of thrashing arms and legs. Bliss recovered first and rolled to the side in a crouch, poised for action.

His attackers, strong but not overly bright, telegraphed their moves, and Bliss evaded their blows and then picked his shots. Several of Bliss' blows landed in rapid succession and both of them fell, unconscious before they hit the floor.

Bliss staggered back and wiped a trickle of blood from the corner of his mouth. Another shadow fell across the doorway, and he tensed, crouched and prepared to do battle. Relieved to see it was Cassandra, he said, "Thank God, it's you."

"I don't think God is the one you want to thank," she said as she slowly raised her right arm into the air. From the tip of her finger, a blue flame streaked out and hit him in the center of his forehead. Stunned amazement registered briefly in his emerald eyes before they rolled back in his head and he slumped to the floor. Waves of blue-white force popped and crackled over the outline of his body and then slowly dissipated.

The next time Bliss opened his eyes, his hot cheek rested on a bare marble floor. He soaked up its soothing coolness as his confused mind wandered, unable to focus. He had no idea of how long he had been out. His head buzzed and his muscles twitched in multiple spasms. His nerve endings swelled into tidal waves of pain transmitted on so many levels it overloaded his already fuzzy brain.

Bliss tried to rise, to fight the crazy sensations that overwhelmed him, but his slightest movement magnified the torment as the room swam and danced in front of his eyes. He was pulled back from the brink of oblivion by the sound of a familiar voice.

"Don't try to move. You will have no control over your body for some time, not until the change is complete."

Change? What change? Had she turned him into a goat or a toad? His fingers fumbled in an effort to touch his face, to feel for any alteration, but it was useless, Bliss was helpless and his struggles merely resulted in uncontrollable spasms in his hand that sent Cassandra into gales of laughter.

Kneeling down beside him, Cassandra hooked a finger under his chin, lifting his glazed eyes to meet her bitter ones. "I want to tell you what has happened to you," she cooed. "I want you to know—I have given you a gift, the thing you most desire—the power of rejuvenation. You will no longer need worry about growing old and losing your attractiveness," she said with a counterfeit smile. Her eyes glittered brightly, and appeared to be pure piercing agate, black as a hole in space and as cold as a barren moon.

"Immunity from disease, great physical strength, and tremendous recuperative powers," she whispered in his ear, "all will be yours. Then she stood up and spoke in a commanding voice. "But you will remain mortal and can be killed. Guard yourself well, Bliss, or some irate male will do you in. Take good care of yourself, for you see, I want you to live for a long, long time."

She relished the puzzled look in his eyes and needled him further, pointing a taloned finger at him. "You don't understand, do you, Bliss, what I have done to you while you slept? Before the next fullness of the three moons has waned, you will know exactly what form my vengeance has taken."

From somewhere nearby he heard muffled sobs, but couldn't identify the source. *If only my mind was clear*, Bliss thought, *I might be able to reason with her*. Frustration twisted his features.

Fascinated, his captor watched him closely, enjoying his discomfort. "As soon as these changes take effect, you will leave Scorpious, taking that piece of space garbage in the corner with you," she said, shooting a stabbing look of hatred at Elena. "If you ever show your face here again, in any form, I'll have you executed, on the spot, in the most unpleasant, painful way possible."

Without any further explanation, she turned and stalked from the room. Gloating over her victory, Cassandra planned an evening with a group of fawning friends, celebrating her brilliant coup. Her crazed laughter rang in the corridors, reverberating in his bruised brain until he thought he would go mad from the sound of it, if not from the eerie churning that infested his body. It felt as if thousands of tiny insects crawled in his bloodstream, ran rampant in his veins, and gnawed at his nerves.

Although Bliss didn't believe in curses, he felt cursed. *Could such a thing be true?* With a growing feeling of dread, he replayed Cassandra's confidences of last darkness in his mind; the story of her youth, the tale of her father, the great mystic, living in exile on an asteroid. *Is it possible; the legendary Colin, is Cassandra's father?*

I'm in deep space waste, he thought as he slipped into unconsciousness. When he woke up again, more time had passed. How much he didn't know, but all was quiet, the guards and Cassandra were gone. Bliss knew he must act, now or never.

He managed to rise to a sitting position. His bleary eyes raked the room and came to rest on Elena's slim form a short distance away. At least, he knew where she was, and she appeared unharmed. At least, she still had her head.

He tried to stand, but his body refused to obey the commands of his mind. Bringing all his consciousness to bear, Bliss concentrated on separating himself from the pain and regaining control of his movements. His efforts brought success. He found his feet, staggered to the control panel, and leaned on the wall as he stabbed at the buttons. Nothing happened, they were locked in.

Resting, he looked around, examining the chamber. His eyes slid past the trunk in the corner and returned to it. In his mind, he conjured up the image of Cassandra, willing himself to transform into her image, but it was no use. Bliss was unable to complete such a complicated transformation in his weakened state. Only his hands had changed, they were now foreign feminine appendages attached to his muscular, masculine arms.

Bliss stared down at them, mesmerized, as a germ of an idea took root and sprouted into a full-grown plan. Desperate times called for reckless measures. He stumbled across the room to the trunk, knelt down in front of it and held out his index finger. Bliss concentrated all his powerful intellect on the single digit of his hand and visualized one detailed image. With all the sheer force of his thought, he focused on his finger and watched as the digit stretched, cracked and then the skin split open to reveal a shiny, red key where seconds before a bone had been.

Wincing with pain, he inserted the key in the lock, and smiled as it clicked open. Glancing over his shoulder to make sure the guards had not returned, Bliss pulled off his tunic and spread it on the floor. Then he opened the trunk, and pressed the hidden release. When the bottom slid back, he reached down and began to scoop up the crystals with both hands. When the garment was full, he tied the sleeves together to secure his package.

As he closed the lid of the trunk, his life force trickled down his maimed finger. In the dimness, Bliss failed to notice the strange color of his blood.

In the corner, Elena stirred and sat up, dazed and bewildered. With his back to her, Bliss was busy, focusing all his attention on his finger, bringing the bone back to its original shape. The split skin would eventually heal, but he would forever bear a scarred fingertip as a reminder of Scorpious, as if he needed one. Wrapping the wound in a piece of cloth torn from the bed hangings, he turned.

Elena released a sharp intake of breath followed by an anguished cry. "Oh, my God, Bliss—what has she done to you?" Horror registered briefly on her face before she veiled the expression. His features ebbed and flowed with the motion of undulating ripples beneath his skin, then abruptly, the movement ceased, and Bliss seemed more normal.

She called out to him again and asked what was wrong, but he put his finger to his lips. There was no time for talk or lengthy explanations. When she started to open her mouth again, he silenced her questions with a curt, "Not now."

Remembering her earlier promise to follow his instructions without hesitation, she watched uneasily as he removed a small implement from his boot.

"What is that?" she couldn't resist asking.

"It's a compukey, equipped with universal readouts and relays. I'll use it to trip the threshold door locking device." He whispered as he passed it over the control panel and the door slid open.

Bliss led her from the room and guided her down the corridor toward freedom. To his dismay a lone sentry barred the exit. With a hard motion of his hands, he signaled Elena forward to divert the guard's attention while he approached him from behind. She approached the guard, all smiles and dimples, making not so subtle promises. While his attention was engaged, Bliss whacked the guard over the head with his crystal filled tunic.

"Take two and call me in the morning," he said as they sprinted from the doorway. His hand at Elena's back, Bliss dashed down the narrow street as they hugged the buildings in an effort to stay hidden in the shadows. Bliss glanced back over his shoulder several times expecting to see hordes of thundering guards emerge from the palace at any moment, but only a handful of amazed onlookers stared after them.

Panting and out of breath, they reached the spaceport. Bliss entered the ship first, leaving Elena outside on guard while he checked for booby traps. When his sensors told him the vessel was safe and secure, he brought her inside and began initiating pre-spacing procedures, running through the computer system, alert for any malfunctions.

All appeared to be well. The final step remained, replacing the Carduvian crystals. As he removed them from his tunic pouch, his hands started to shake, and he fumbled, wasting valuable time, unable to lock them into the proper place where the power points intersected. Bliss willed himself into a calmer state and snapped the crystals into position.

He executed a perfect take-off, his relaxed manner belying his concern. Elena watched solemnly, praying. His steady, competent hands moved carefully, expertly over the controls. Bliss gave his full attention to the viewing screens, thinking any instant they might be blasted into oblivion, but the ship catapulted off the planet's surface without incident.

Bliss was relieved at the ease of their escape, yet troubled by it. If Cassandra was so obsessed with revenge why would she be willing to let them get away before she was finished doing whatever it was she had plotted? Then, he remembered, she planned to release them anyway before the next fullness of the three moons. It puzzled him—and he knew it had something to do with a curse. A part of him refused to even accept the possibility. *But what if it's true*, he rationalized, *how bad could it be, making love to an endless variety of females forever*. He grinned at the idea; it seemed more like a blessing to him.

Meanwhile, Elena stared out the viewport at the stars streaming past, enjoying her good fortune. In front of her was a vast array of luminous bodies, some frail and flimsy, others so large they could contain ten thousand suns; super novas emitting brilliant, fluctuating light. To her, they served as guides showing them the pathway home.

Beginning deep space maneuvers, Bliss space jumped out of the galaxy and locked in the coordinates for Althea.

"Princess, you're going home."

"Bliss, you will not go unrewarded for my rescue. My mother and my people will be very grateful, as I am."

"Well, let's not go counting my wealth just yet. It's bad luck. The game's not over."

She glanced over at him, uncertain as how to frame her question. "Do you know what Cassandra has done to you? Do you understand what she was talking about?" Elena had overhead her tirade.

"I give no credence to the ravings of a mad female."

"Cassandra may very well be crazy, but she's not stupid. Far from it, she's exceedingly clever, capable of almost anything. Don't forget she's highly schooled in the art of sorcery. I, for one, stand in dread of the things she could do, if she chooses."

"Thanks, Elena, that certainly eases my mind. At the moment, my main concern is getting you home safely. I'll worry about Cassandra's curse later."

The subject was closed; he refused to talk about it. They spoke of other things, but Elena kept turning the question over in her mind. *What are the changes Cassandra spoke of?* Although they had departed earlier than expected, it was still impossible to reach Althea until after the waning of the three moons. She'd be with him when those changes completed, whatever they were. Already doubts grew in her mind like weeds in a freshly plowed field. She caught herself casting furtive glances at Bliss as she searched for any outward signs of alteration.

Upon entering Elena's home galaxy, Bliss relaxed. He felt sure that Cassandra, so space-marked and plagued with mental terrors, wouldn't follow them this far into deep space—even to claim her stolen crystals. He pressed a lever to activate his console seat. In one fluid motion, it extended, and Bliss sank back into a comfortable reclining position. Watching him, Elena did the same in her seat next to his.

"Let's try to get some rest," he said, closing his eyes. "We'll reach Althea in another two spans." Exhausted, he felt like a stranger in his own body, everything seemed to moving in slow motion, his arms and legs felt like lead.

"It will be so good to be home. I'm eager to show you my planet, and have you meet my people," she said, as she turned her head to face him. His eyes were closed and Bliss had already fallen into a deep slumber. Elena closed her eyes and attempted to sleep, but it was useless, her mind so busy that no amount of meditation could still it.

She stared at Bliss, memorizing every line of his face and form to hold in her heart for the time when he would leave her. *What is going to become of him*, she wondered, feeling partially responsible. Elena should have felt elated at the prospect of going home, yet a heavy cloud of despair hung over her. She began to weep, not knowing exactly why, simply giving in to an inescapable sense of sadness. The tears cleansed her, eroding the helplessness she felt, but the process left her emotionally exhausted.

Somehow, it will work out, she promised herself. Satisfied, she slept.

The sound of Bliss moving about on the bridge woke her. An entire span had passed. She was rested and hungry. Bliss made a great show of producing the food and serving her, the former slave. His mood was infectious; she savored every bite, the flavor enhanced by her sense of freedom.

Bliss ate ravenously. Elena watched him with amusement. "You're consuming enough food to feed an army of storm troopers. Are you sure we'll have enough for the rest of the trip?" she teased.

"What business is it of yours," he snapped. "Are you with universal famine relief?

"I meant no offense," she said, a hurt expression on her face. "It was merely a jest."

"I know. I'm sorry. I'm not myself. There must have been something wrong with the food." *Had Cassandra poisoned him?*

"You're right, I must have eaten too much."

"I'm sure that's all it is," she said, unconvinced.

The meal hadn't appeased his hunger, as a matter of fact other than taste sensations; the food had given him absolutely no satisfaction. Bliss was still ravenous. Elena was beginning to look good to him, way too good.

"Would you mind if I retired to my quarters? Perhaps I'll rest better there," Bliss said, wanting to be alone as soon as possible.

"No, not at all, I'll be fine. Should I stay here?" The gleam in his eyes whenever he glanced her way made Elena feel uncomfortable.

"It might be best . . . just in case we encounter some space traffic. Before I go to my quarters, I'll show you the rest of the ship, what to do and how to reach me in an emergency."

He took her on a whirlwind tour, showing her the facility, the quarters, the process for obtaining food and other necessities.

As they walked together, Bliss began to fantasize, seeing visions of Elena in the nude. *The hunger is affecting my mind*, he thought. As they approached his quarters an intense longing swept over him, the need to touch her, hold her, to join with her. He could actually sense her heightened emotional state, the wave of fear and the undercurrents of love swirled around him.

He felt like an alcoholic with his hand on the bottle. He craved her. He needed her. He wanted to consume her, to take in the essence of what Elena was, physically and emotionally. Somehow, he knew the act would ease his hunger, but something stronger inside him fought for control and momentarily won back his one last, precious piece of dignity.

Abruptly, he took his leave of Elena and practically slammed the door in her face. She stood outside, wondering what to do.

"Bliss, are you all right?"

"Yes," he said, with his back flat against the door, suppressing an urge to open it. "Please go back to the bridge and contact me when you get there."

Elena did as she was told, for now she had an inkling of what might be happening to Bliss and wondered if there was any place on board where she would be safe. During the tour, she had seen everything except the storage bay, which was locked.

But when she contacted Bliss he had solved the problem for her. "Listen to me carefully," he said, "and do exactly as I say. We don't have much time." His willpower was waning.

"What do I do about the ship—our course? I can't handle interstellar navigation," she said as she stared wide-eyed and confused at all the unfamiliar controls on the bridge.

"Don't worry, the course is already plotted in. You don't have to do anything; the ship will take care of itself until touchdown. I can't come up to the bridge, not while you're there. I want you to use the computer to set up a new locking sequence in quarters number two. You can do that, can't you?" *And hurry,* he thought, *please hurry.*

"Yes, yes, I can do that."

"Good. Use a code word, one I don't know, have never heard of and can't possibly come up with. Then go immediately, don't waste any time—do you understand—and lock yourself in."

"I understand. I'll do it now." Elena didn't need to ask any more questions.

In his quarters, Bliss could actually feel Elena's love and concern; it was a beacon, luring him. Cassandra had known all along, he realized, *she counted on this.* That's why she wanted the girl to leave with him, but Cassandra hadn't counted on Bliss' early departure or the strength and courage of his pledge to return Elena safely to Althea.

The intercom buzzed. "The locking sequence is in." Elena said.

"Good, now go lock yourself in, and no matter what I say, or what I do, don't let me in. Don't unlock that compartment until we've landed, and I'm off the ship. Not for any reason. Promise?"

"Yes, yes, I promise. Bliss, I'm so sorry . . . thank you for everything you've done. Please forgive me . . . I love you, and I always will."

"There's nothing to forgive. Forget about me, Elena, what's done is done. I'm not for you, and we both know it." In physical agony, he leaned against the wall for support. "Just think about yourself, Princess, take care of yourself. You know I don't want to hurt you, but I feel so strange, so . . . never mind! Just get out of there—get going!"

"I'm going, Bliss," she said before she ran for the door.

A few minutes later, she entered compartment number two, punched in the new locking code and the door slid shut, sealing her into solitary confinement. When she examined her quarters, she found it to be a pretty prison, roomy and comfortable, designed to meet a guest's every need.

Meanwhile, Bliss was confined in a body tormented by his cravings, a hunger that grew more insistent with each passing moment. Seeking an escape, some relief of any kind, he drank a strong tranquilizing elixir normally used to ease the pain of laser injuries.

Marshaling the forces of his will, Bliss freed his mind from the tortures of his body, using mental control to rise above his physical condition. Mercifully, the combination rendered him unconscious for an entire span. But weird dreams and even stranger sensations marred his slumber.

When he came to his senses, the ship had already started the approach path to Althea, and Bliss neared the brink of insanity. His drugged sleep hadn't refreshed him. Weary and sick, he struggled to perform even the simplest task. In an effort to keep his mind occupied, he tackled numerous chores, and forced himself to think about something else, anything else, other than the female in compartment number two.

As the ship entered Althea's orbit, something inside Bliss broke, and the veil descended between his old self and the new one Cassandra had created. With trembling hands, he contacted compartment number two on the intership frequency. On the edge of hysteria, he inhaled and exhaled several long deep breaths before he spoke. In a soft, enticing voice, he called her name over and over until she answered.

"What is it Bliss?" she said, not liking the tone of his voice.

"You're almost home, Princess," he replied, making every word a caress. "It's time for us to say our farewells, properly. There's no need to be afraid, I've recovered, I'm fine, I found an antidote."

Elena did not respond. The voice was not the Bliss she knew.

"Your quarters or mine?"

"Neither," she said.

"Don't be afraid, Elena. I'm OK, really. Forget what I said before. I was sick, confused. The food made me ill," he insisted, forgetting she had eaten the same meal.

"I know what you told me, Bliss. You said not to let you in no matter what you said."

"But it's all right, now. Trust me. I got you safely this far, didn't I? Took chances, risked my life," he said, hoping to play on her guilt.

"Bliss, don't do this," she pleaded. Her voice shook with emotion. It was a strong enticement.

"If you love me, Elena, you'll let me in. I won't hurt you, I promise."

"I wish I could believe you," she said sadly, "but I don't. You no longer care what happens to me."

"Care? I care deeply. I can't survive without you. I need your help. You owe me! Help me!" Bliss knew he was losing control and any chance of convincing Elena to allow him to touch her. He knew he had to touch her. He had to have her.

"Think about it, I can be everything you've ever wanted in a male," he said, his voice heavy with desire." But Elena had already switched off the intercom.

Enraged, Bliss demanded she respond. His shouts were met by a deepening silence. He stormed from his quarters, invigorated by his anger. Banging on her compartment door, he screamed, "Let me in, now! Do you hear me!"

There was no answer. He continued his assault. "This is my ship. I order you to open this door!" Elena waited, hoping he would give up, but he didn't. Bliss tried his compukey, even his laser gun to no avail. One last time, he pleaded with her. "Please, please, Elena, let me in, I'm so hungry."

Hungry? "Go away, Bliss. Leave me alone," she shouted through the door.

Bliss cursed the door, its origins, Elena and her ancestors as well as his own stupidity. Then he raced to the bridge and engaged the master computer in an effort to break the sequence locking code even as the ship began its landing descent to Althea.

Feeling the shift, he abandoned the computer and headed for the storage bay where he kept his land scooter, thinking there was more than one way to solve the problem of uncooperative females.

Elena sat on the floor in her compartment, hugging her knees, praying they reach Althea before Bliss found a way to get to her. She watched the viewing screen and felt an immense relief when she saw the land scooter leave the ship's dock headed for the planet's surface. *Bliss had left the ship!*

Cautiously, Elena opened her compartment door, checked the hallway and then raced down the corridor to the bridge. In a few moments, she had opened a hailing frequency and contacted authorities at the spaceport center, apprising them of her identity. It took precious minutes to convince them. Then they walked her through the landing procedures, and she followed the step-by-step instructions.

As she punched in the last number on the computer, the ship slowed and prepared for landing, and a moment too late, she sensed a movement behind her.

She whirled around into Bliss' arms.

"What are you doing here?" she demanded. "I saw you leave."

He pulled her tightly against him, reaching behind her to cut off communication with Althea. One hand moved up to grasp the back of her head, and his fingers entwined in her hair. He yanked her head back, and forced her to look up into his face.

Elena gasped. His face had aged. The change was shocking. His starved state was taking a heavy toll. Something ugly flickered at the back of his eyes, dark and threatening.

"What you saw, "he said, grimly, "was exactly what I wanted you to see—Bodkins, my humanoid facsimile, taking off in the land scooter."

So, she realized with a sinking heart, *there had been an android in the storage bay.* A stab of fear shot through her and with a sudden blinding insight, she understood exactly what Bliss wanted.

He saw the terror in her face, sensed the energy of it and took it into his body. His hunger flared. Elena's emotional state went off the scale, and he tasted the tangible, galvanizing waves of emotion within her, as irresistible to him as the scent of hot, fresh blood to a carnivore. *Oh, this is better than sex*, he thought.

Elena felt the slight, almost imperceptible thud of landing. Bliss was otherwise engaged, his focus a laser of lust, intent on getting inside her and drinking in all that she was. But instinctively he knew—Elena must choose to give herself to him of her own free will. *I cannot simply take her.* He paused and his body began to ripple and change.

Bliss was transforming into the form of her fiancé Betonia—shorter, more muscular with a shock of thick black hair and a neat mustache, perfect in every detail. Elena stared into the face of the man she was destined to marry. He gazed into her eyes intently.

"Betonia?"

"Elena," he said before he locked his mouth on hers in a demanding, devouring kiss. Determined to overcome her resistance, Bliss relied on the fact that, somewhere deep inside, she desired at least one of them.

Bent backward by his force, Elena fought to free herself, knowing he had sensed desire in her, and maybe it didn't matter how long ago it had been. She tore her lips from his long enough for one impassioned plea.

"Please, Bliss—no! Let me go!"

But he was too far gone.

With her right hand, she searched the panel behind her, knowing her people couldn't come on board until she opened the loading bay doors, and by then it might be too late. Relying on memory and feel, she fumbled for the right button. It was her only chance. She asked for guidance and pressed.

He grabbed her chin and captured her mouth in a compelling kiss. Then, his mind invaded hers, stripping from it all of her fantasies and innermost desires, bringing them to life in her mind. His voice whispered seductively, creating word pictures as his hands moved expertly over her body as Begonia's never had, arousing suppressed reflexes. In spite of her intention to resist, Elena's body began to respond.

Bliss pressed closer as he raised the skirt of her garment and his knowing fingers traced her inner thigh and probed for the wetness of her feminine center. Everything within Elena opened to him. Her heartbeat accelerated rapidly, the blood drained from her veins, replaced by a gush of adrenaline. The sudden rush of hormones put her entire system on overload and dimmed her awareness to the point of escape.

Then Elena fainted.

She hung limply, uselessly in his arms.

Shocked, Bliss resumed his own form and eased her to the floor.

Panic stricken, Bliss tried to revive her by taking hold of her shoulders and shaking her, but Elena only moaned softly. Desperate, he slapped her hard on both cheeks.

At that moment, Althea's spaceport troops stormed the bridge, weapons drawn. Seeing Bliss assaulting Elena, they fired and stunned him into oblivion.

Elena came to as Bliss hit the deck. She sat up and shook her head to clear it. Two of the troopers helped her to stand. When she was safely on her feet, their leader said, respectfully, "We followed your hailing frequency, Princess. What in the name of All That Is has been going on here? Who is this other worlder?"

Thinking quickly, Elena took command. "He is my rescuer. I owe him my life. I became ill on landing and lost consciousness. He was trying to revive me."

"Your pardon is requested. We thought he was attacking you," the trooper said.

"I appreciate your loyalty," she said, relieved the ruse had worked. "Contact my mother, Althor at Beta, and the Biers of Theoreaus. Have them meet me here as soon as possible." Looking at Bliss sharply, she continued, "Tell them to hurry, there is much to be done—and quickly."

As he moved toward the console, she said. "Ask them to bring the best talents from the 'Hall of Healers' with them." The trooper's eyebrows arched up, but Elena added nothing to explain.

A short span later, several air cars swooped toward them from the floating city hovering on the horizon. When the large group entered the ship, their reunion was a joyous one. Her mother was elated, for she had thought her daughter lost to them forever. The two spent time alone together, and Elena spoke of all that had transpired, telling her mother what the perceptive female already knew—her husband of many years had been killed.

With her father's death, Elena as his only offspring inherited a goodly portion of his prestige and power which she called upon to assemble a group of Biers and healers in Bliss' quarters. There, they launched into a lengthy discussion to decide his fate. Elena guided the discussion feeling she owed Bliss a debt and intended to repay his kindness and courage.

Bliss was being held under sedation until a plan of action could be formulated. She sent a group of healers to examine him. They marveled at the strange composition of his physical and spiritual body, one impacting on the other.

Shaking their heads in dismay, they informed Elena that nothing could be done to alter his state, and he must be fed, soon, or cease to be. From their examination, they knew exactly what form the feeding must take and with Elena's assistance, the healers hit upon a way to solve the problem.

"It's a temporary solution," she advised the Biers, "but it will allow Bliss to continue."

The elders reluctantly agreed to do as she wished not out of any compassion for Bliss or his condition, but in order to adhere to the New Rule of Althea enacted after the recent wars. The New Rule forbade the killing of any being. To their way of thinking, starving Bliss to death was the same thing as killing him outright. Elena silently offered up a prayer of thanks for the New Rule.

With their ancient visages set in masks of stern disapproval, the Biers selected three females from the Hall of Healers. The chosen ones were victims of a mining accident on a colony planet. During the ensuing dust bath from a cave-in, the three received several small cuts and abrasions that allowed a rare, voracious space spore access to their bodies. The spores could not be killed or removed and the women were dying.

When the three females arrived, Elena herself informed them of the situation. The decision was theirs and each one volunteered to go with Bliss of her own free will. All were young with no family and each of them had hoped to find a mate on the colony planet.

At this point, the loss of their emotions seemed a minor consideration. Feelings had become a handicap. Being made love to by someone, who knew exactly how, seemed to be an answer to their prayers, and their emotions were an answer to his hunger.

Bodkins, Bliss' robotic facsimile had automatically returned to Bliss' ship in the land scooter and was immediately reprogrammed with information intended for Bliss when the sedation wore off.

Everyone left the ship with the exception of Bodkins, the three females and a trooper who would remain on board to initiate take-off and ferry the ship into orbit. After locking in a navigational course and activating Bodkins, an Althean space cruiser would pick up the trooper.

In a short span, Bliss would awaken in deep space with the three females ready to provide for the renewal of his life even as theirs ended. Elena viewed the ship's departure with mixed emotions, trying to reconcile what she had done.

Have I aided and abetted the creation of a monster?

Elena knew Bliss did not yet fully know what he had become, and she sensed that the slow realization of the extent of the curse was an integral part of Cassandra's vendetta.

I have no choice, Elena thought, chasing from her mind the terror of what he had become. Instead, she concentrated on the remote possibility of Bliss overcoming his affliction and achieving his true destiny. She formed that vision of his future in her mind and dared him to fulfill it.

Walking toward her air car, Elena turned to see Bliss' ship disappearing into the misty skies. *I miss you already. I know I will never come in contact with anyone half so interesting again.*

Seating herself in her vehicle for her victorious return to her home planet, she looked resolutely ahead, mentally preparing herself to accept the responsibilities in the coming union, joining Althea with Kyron.

To her everlasting surprise, she found her mate to be everything she had ever wanted. From the fortunate pairing came an outpouring of love and compassion as their twin spirits merged and each grew in strength and wisdom, and governed accordingly, bringing illumination to their corner of the universe. Much would have been lost—forever—had Elena not been returned home.

For Bliss, it was the beginning of the end.

Chapter 8

His recent sojourn on planet Veta had proved to be a gross miscalculation. In all the time since the sorceress Cassandra had placed the curse on him and forever changed his existence, Bliss had never before encountered a planet where the humanoid life forms were too highly evolved for him to feed. He had grown too confident and careless.

The inhabitants of Veta lived in a heightened state of awareness, and in that rarefied atmosphere emotions were no longer a necessary part of their experience. Their lives moved forward in a serene flow of cool, clear logic with no place for passionate love or hate, greed, fear or jealousy. Love and compassion existed in its purest forms so these lofty beings no longer required sex for recreation or procreation. Offspring were the results of combined, creative thoughts.

On Veta, he had found nothing to feed on, absolutely nothing.

By the time he realized his mistake, a considerable amount of his resources had been depleted. His body demanded to be fed and he had already wasted precious time and energy. Bliss needed to find another inhabited planet immediately, one with an abundance of emotional beings.

At last, he made contact with a young female that had allowed him to accompany her to a mind enhancement meeting. During a break, Bliss steered the conversation to the subject of other nearby inhabited worlds with an emphasis on emotions. "It's an aspect I wish to explore," he said.

Calistra had little interest in the subject. "Emotions are ancient history," she said, and hesitated before she continued. "But there have been some interesting developments in a nearby galaxy. I've heard reports of a planet that is about to make a quantum leap in evolution. Prior to such an event, a tremendous amount of chaotic emotional energy is released."

"Where is this planet?" Bliss asked, unable to suppress his excitement.

"Why do you ask?" Calistra lifted her delicate eyeshades several times in rapid succession.

He had searched for words Calistra would not find offensive. "I would like to drink in their essence, to experience them fully."

She beamed at him. "Of course, now I understand. You are a scientist."

Calistra had directed Bliss to a space research facility where he found everything he needed. The small blue planet on the isolated outskirts of the universe contained a large population of warm and willing women, exactly what he craved and the only way to prevent his starvation.

If only he could reach Earth in time, his survival depended on it.

A short span later, his intergalactic vehicle hurtled through the cold, limitless reaches of space; a slender cylinder moving toward a predetermined—perhaps even predestined—location. Stars shed their cold light and winked at the ship's passing as if in a giant cosmic conspiracy.

After he entered the coordinates for his journey, Bliss placed himself in a deep hypnotic sleep to conserve his waning strength. Had he been in a conscious state, the pulsating energies emanating from the planet in his approach path would have fanned the flames of his rampaging hunger beyond endurance.

As he neared the planet, still in his self-induced trance, Bliss astral traveled. His spirit left his body, and sped ahead to his destination, seeking the places where knowledge is stored. Bliss had learned his lesson; it paid to be prepared.

He swept through the halls of learning, consuming vast amounts of information at enormous speeds, mastering languages, and memorizing details of geography, world history and current events in a blink of the eye. In his furious foraging for facts, he siphoned information, alternating between shock and fascination, and ended his quest both appalled and amazed.

These beings were teetering on the brink of annihilation, flirting with complete and total oblivion. Small wonder the atmosphere was so deliciously charged with emotion. But in spite of their headlong plunge toward destruction, these beings appeared to be enjoying the ride, while doing everything in their considerable power to destroy their planet and its atmosphere.

World leaders postured and postulated, acting for and reacting to each other. Nothing of real value was accomplished because they seemed to be more interested in the primitive concept of developing weapons than in the larger, universal method of working together in a combined effort of unity to find solutions to their mutual dilemmas, of which there were many.

It reminded him of an ancient tribe in a distant galaxy, one that now lived only in memory. The Horgaths had destroyed themselves through their own fear, threats and allegations that left no room for compromise or for cooperation and the sharing of priceless global knowledge and resources.

Yet Bliss sensed an underlying element of hope—pockets of light, an awakening in the collective unconscious, and perhaps the dawning of a new evolutionary cycle. Other forces were at work, a dark, negative energy. As for the planet itself, the masculine and feminine energies were out of whack; the left-brain influence dominated the culture. More of the intuitive, creative right brain influence was needed to restore balance and harmony.

Perhaps, the Vetans have underestimated the value of planet Earth to others in the galaxy. Bliss was intrigued. His choice of a new home might prove to be a very interesting experience.

For the moment, Bliss had learned all he needed to know. His essence followed the thread of life, the glowing, silver connector that joined his empyrean being back to his physical body. Access came suddenly, sharply with a feeling of falling—a familiar feeling. Not his first fall, merely a continuation.

He was one of the Starborne. While others in his dimension had sought to open doors to cosmic consciousness, Bliss had been plagued by a persistent desire to take part in the more worldly aspects of Arias, the very experiences his ancestors had spent vast passages of time working to transform and overcome.

Bliss had willingly given up the intangible advantages of his realm for the immediate joys of the moment—the senses of taste, touch, and sound, and most importantly, and perhaps the most dangerous of all—physical love. But he remembered little of it, knowing only what he had gleaned from the archives of the ancients on Arias.

Now, he was trapped in his physical form, on the wheel of life, imprisoned by those very needs and desires. Thoughts of death by starvation filled him with an overwhelming dread, coupled with fear of what might lie in wait for him when his soul left his body. How many other lives would it take to balance the karma he had incurred during this one long lifespan?

"*It is best not to think of such things,*" he said as he brought himself out of the meditative state and slowly sat up.

"Beating yourself up again, Master," Bodkins said.

"Bodkins, I don't want any commentary, and I've asked you not to call me master," Bliss said as he touched his cheek and rubbed his fingers over deep-set wrinkles that had appeared where none had been before. His body ached from lack of use and rapid aging.

"Let's get this show on the road," he said motioning Bodkins to the ship's console. The pressing need to find a landing spot forced him to move quickly in spite of his pain and exhaustion.

"Engage," Bodkins announced. The android had been studying the information on the planet, absorbing data as fast as Bliss had relayed it. "Resistance is futile."

"Enough, earthisms, Bodkins, I need to focus."

Bodkins returned to the controls of the ship in silence while Bliss sifted through the geographical and sociological information, fighting off a foggy, floating feeling of lethargy. The choice of a landing site was crucial. There was no room for error. One area seemed to offer the most promise, with plenty of freedom of movement along with a high standard of living.

Still in the Veta form he had last assumed, Bliss realized his appearance was unacceptable, probably even frightening to Earth's females, so he must quickly make a transition into a more desirable form. An all-important choice since what he needed from females could not be taken by force, it must be freely given.

This time it wasn't going to be easy because his chameleon abilities were waning. One or two more transformations at the most—that was it. The big question was, could he hold a form long enough to survive?

Fortunately, touchdown was near. Bliss had chosen an isolated section of the Florida Everglades where his vessel would be hidden among the ten thousand islands in a labyrinth of Mangrove waterways and sawgrass marshes. He considered the native inhabitants of the area—snakes, alligators, sea turtles and a few rare American crocodiles—to be his natural allies in discouraging any pesky intruders.

After the dry cold of planet Veta, Bliss welcomed the warmth and humidity of the Glades. From his research, he suspected there were enough unfulfilled females in Florida to feed a flotilla of his kind.

Thinking in the coordinates on the computer, Bliss settled back and attempted to relax, hoping to conserve his small energy reserves. The ship slipped out of deep space into orbit around the small blue sphere over-shadowed by far too many pockets of the brown haze of pollution.

Chapter 9

At 11:45 p.m., Maggie Danvers eased her pearl white Lincoln Continental into the driveway of her Florida home. Throwing open the car door, she turned and swung her slim, shapely legs out. Then, immediately she jerked them back, startled by a long pink tongue that licked the length of her left stocking from ankle to knee.

"Daniel, damn it! You scared the hell out of me!" She caught her breath and laughed at her own foolishness. Her response sent the Doberman into a tail wagging frenzy, but she firmly pushed him aside and got out of the car. Daniel wandered off to sniff curiously at a sand dune.

"Come on, boy," Maggie called, snapping her fingers. "I'm bushed, let's get inside."

Seeming to understand her words, the dog led the way to the back door. Maggie unlocked it and entered, switched on some lights, kicked off her shoes, and dropped her purse, the mail and her keys on the kitchen counter.

Daniel trotted on ahead, dutifully inspecting each room. Deeming them safe and secure, he returned to his mistress' side and watched her every move as she checked her mail.

Suddenly, Daniel's head jerked up, his ears pricked, and he padded to the door. The animal reared on his hind legs and peered out the glass panes. Either he had heard a noise outside or the dog hadn't finished his business. Maggie sighed in resignation, opened the door and watched him bound into the night.

It was pitch black outside with no lights from neighboring houses to break the darkness. Maggie's vacation retreat was perched on an isolated peninsula in the Florida Keys. At least, it was hers for the moment. Maggie and her husband Bill had been separated for a year, sloughing through the painful process of a complicated divorce settlement.

Turning back to the pile of mail on the kitchen counter, she approached the stack of envelopes as if it were a nest of poisonous snakes. She knew instinctively what waited for her—another venom filled letter from Bill's attorney, Gordon Turnbull.

She extracted a fat manila envelope from the pile and tore it open, hoping that somehow her husband had come to his senses. She thumbed through a thick clump of pages in a quick perusal as she walked in a daze to the sofa and collapsed into the pile of pale blue cushions.

Maggie twisted a lock of hair, her eyes widening in shock as she read their latest list of demands. She did her best to decipher Turnbull's mind-boggling masterpiece of legalese. After several minutes of paper shuffling, Maggie dropped the papers in her lap. It was unbelievable, they were asking—no demanding—that she capitulate and exchange the beach house and property for a larger cash settlement.

Like hell, I will. How can Bill do this to me? Damn him! He knows how much this house means to me. Let him keep the others. It isn't fair, and it isn't like him. Someone else must be pressuring him, someone greedy, someone who wants to take away everything I have ever loved. My God, isn't Bill enough?

It hurt, more than the separation, more than the finality of the impending divorce. How could he treat her this way? Had he completely forgotten the past? *It must be damned convenient to be able to forget*, she thought, *not to have to remember how it was in the beginning.* She crumpled the legal pages in her fist and threw them on the floor.

Even if Bill had developed a case of martial amnesia, Maggie clearly remembered the early days of their relationship. Bill had loved her then, she knew it. *She* was the most important thing in his life. Everything he did, Bill promised, was for her, to build a good life for them.

His job as a sales representative for Beaker Pharmaceuticals was just the beginning. Bill had held the number one sales position for five years in a row. He won cash and trips, and they enjoyed both together.

It seemed like yesterday, she daydreamed, as she recalled the night Bill had come home with a strange gleam in his eye. Maggie thought he was in a sexy mood and sat on his lap and kissed him playfully. But he brushed her aside—his mind was on the boardroom not the bedroom. His ruggedly handsome face flushed with an excitement fueled by the heat of ambition not ardor.

At the dinner table, Bill had explained what he wanted to do. "Babe, I've made up my mind," he said. It wasn't until much later that she learned to her chagrin that her husband called most women Babe, especially when he wanted something and other times simply because he couldn't remember their names. "I could spend my whole life working at Beaker and never make it to the top. I can't sit around waiting for one of those old men to die off. Why should I continue to make all this money for other people, when I can be doing it for us? I've decided to go into business for myself."

He wanted and expected her blessing. He received that and much more. Bill used their life savings for his working capital, coerced a banker friend into a substantial loan and opened his own pharmaceutical company.

A born salesman, Bill possessed the innate ability to charm and manipulate others with ease. But he had no head for figures and absolutely no interest in them except for the bottom line—and other bottoms she had found out, much too late.

Maggie however, did have a head for figures. So, she stayed in the office, taking care of the dull, laborious work. She was the one who agonized over the books and details Bill despised. Maggie mastered handling their cash flow and learned by trial and error the bills to pay right away and the ones that could be put off.

Both of them worked day and night and together they managed to stay one baby step away from bankruptcy during the first year. Bill made most of the sales calls himself, relying on his fine-tuned sense of timing and instinctive feel for his customer's needs. The first few years had been rough going, but Bill was finding his niche in the marketplace.

When the company began to show a profit, they plowed the money back into the firm, taking small salaries for themselves. Maggie swore they lived on love for there was little else.

She didn't mind the long hours or the times they fell into bed too exhausted to make love, knowing they had the rest of their lives ahead of them. When success came, there would be plenty of time for each other and for the family she wanted.

In October of their third year in business, Bill's years on the road paid off and Danvers Pharmaceuticals took off. They lined up the financing and opened their own lab to launch the manufacturing end of the business. Products and patents brought in the big bucks.

Maggie felt their financial future was stable enough to start a family—she wanted children, but Bill balked. He fast-talked her, using all of his selling skills to convince her that she was rushing things. His dreams advanced while hers receded. All her energy and time were consumed by her desire to help him succeed. There would be time for the fulfillment of her dreams, later or so she had thought at the time.

But Bill began to spend more and more time in conferences and meetings, less and less time with Maggie. Slowly but surely, he excluded her from the decision-making processes in the company and surrounded himself with new people and advisers. Bill placed Maggie in charge of the accounting department, the dull bean counter's end of the business.

But he failed to realize accounting was the center, the heartbeat of his company. With a clear advantage in the numbers game, Maggie's perspective encompassed the big picture of the operation. Bill had the edge in selling, but she knew and understood the business of doing business including where to find the best suppliers, the distribution system, all the facts and figures, and where to go for working capital.

With the increased success of the business and the resulting workload, Bill hired additional office help. There was less for Maggie to do. More and more, the tasks she routinely performed were taken over by others. The new employees were polite but distant. No one wanted to get chummy with the boss's wife, except those who thought they could get to Bill through her. Maggie saw through them quickly and felt increasingly alone in the crowded office.

One sunny April morning, Bill had suggested they have lunch together. Maggie was surprised and elated. In the early days, they often lunched together, spreading out a picnic on Bill's battered desk. But those days were gone in a maze of high-tech furniture and new rules designed to fit Bill's new corporate image.

A few minutes before noon, Maggie headed for the rest room to touch-up her make-up. Bill stood in the doorway, waiting for her with his arms crossed and a familiar frown on his lips.

"Where have you been," he snapped. "You're late."

"Good grief, Bill, it's only five after twelve. What's the big deal?" Her lunch date dream was starting to waiver like a mirage in the desert.

"No *big* deal. I have to get back here on time, that's all, and we can't do that unless we leave on time. You're always late," he accused. "I need to be back at 1:30 for a meeting with our new Advertising Director, Kathy Elliott."

"I wouldn't want to interfere with business," she said. "Are you sure you can spare the time for lunch?"

"Don't be sarcastic, Maggie. I'm not in the mood."

"You seldom are," she couldn't resist muttering to his retreating back. If he heard, Bill gave no indication.

They left the building together, but Bill walked faster, leaving her several paces behind as usual. It didn't matter; she knew where they were going. Ciraco's his favorite restaurant—located just a few doors down from the office. As she walked behind him, she slumped, and the bounce disappeared from her step. Bill was an emotional roller coaster. He could take her from the heights to the depths in a matter of minutes.

Seated at *his* table, Bill paid an inordinate amount of attention to the waitress. Smiling charmingly, he teased the pretty young woman with an irritating air of familiarity, glancing a little too often at the shapely legs revealed by her short dress. Maggie repeatedly smoothed the skirt of her conservative navy-blue suit, feeling old and frumpy.

After the waitress took their order, Bill revealed the real reason behind his luncheon invitation. He had decided he wanted her to stay home; her services at the office were no longer required. Of course, he didn't put it so frankly or in so few words, but she knew that she had just been fired.

She sat in stunned silence as Bill rationalized her out of the business. He mistook her lack of response for acquiescence and greedily dug into his steak. Maggie's throat ached, and her eyes burned with unshed tears as she attacked her seafood salad with vehemence, stabbing at each shrimp with unnecessary vigor. Totally insensitive to her mood or determined to ignore it, Bill rambled on.

"It's a wonderful opportunity for you Maggie, a chance to do all the things you've wanted to do but never had time for."

All I ever wanted to do was to share your life, to bear your children, she thought, mentally willing him to shut up.

Glancing at his watch, he motioned for the check. "We'd better get moving if I'm going to make my appointment," he said. Then he reached across the table, took her hand, squeezed it and flashed her his most ingratiating smile, the one that no longer touched his eyes. "Thanks for being so understanding, Babe, I knew you would be. Funny, old Peterson thought you'd be upset, but he doesn't know you like I do," he said, scraping back his chair.

Maggie didn't make a fuss although her answering smile was sick and wan. But Bill hadn't noticed. Already his mind had moved on to other things, more important things. *He doesn't even know me*, she thought. *The son-of-a-bitch has just demolished my world and doesn't have a clue as to how I feel; and what's worse,* she remembered thinking, *he doesn't care.*

Maggie would never let Bill know how deeply he had wounded her, could never let him know how important her participation in the business was, how dear to her. Danvers had become her child, the one he wouldn't allow her to have. She nurtured it, watched it grow but never suspected she was nursing a viper, one that would kill her marriage.

An eternal optimist always hoping for the best, Maggie enrolled in some classes at the local college, and found she had a flair for interior decorating. She renewed her hopes for a family and pressured Bill on the subject but found him unreceptive. He wanted to "think about it," he said.

Too honest to trap him into fatherhood, Maggie continued to take her birth control pills.

As a consolation prize, Bill purchased the beach house. Its renovation kept Maggie busy and off his back. She fell in love with the rustic wooden exterior, aged naturally by the wind and the salty sea mists. The interior was another matter; dark colors and heavy furnishings made it seem gloomy and uninviting.

Room by room, Maggie transformed it into a light, airy contemporary haven. The activity kept her distracted but not so much that it prevented her from sensing that something was wrong at home. Bill worked later, more frequently, making an increasing number of business trips in the company of the young and lovely Kathy Elliott.

The handwriting was on the divorce papers lying at her feet. At the age of 39, Maggie was childless and alone. She broke down and sobbed into her hands.

Chapter 10

Unnoticed, Bliss' ship approached the Everglades. Shortly after midnight, his terrain scanners locked in on the preselected landing spot on a point of land that jutted out into a sawgrass marsh. The swamp was dotted with hammocks and salt prairies and bordered by towering mangrove and moss-covered cypress trees that formed a dense canopy over the winding waterways. The landscape formed the perfect natural hiding place.

An eerie beauty and tranquility existed within the tide-swept maze of inlets, oyster bards and mud shallows. It was a place of deep silence except for the steady drone of insects and the occasional raucous roar of an agitated alligator.

Bliss' ship swept in, flying low and slow over the Glades, until it appeared to levitate and seemed to hang in mid-air as an oval opening appeared in its shiny belly and a brilliant white light shot out from the aperture and streamed down to touch the surface. The light seemed to draw the ship down as it sank to the ground.

The intrusion of the strange, silver cylinder shattered the evening stillness. The pine, oak and palm trees that rose high into the velvet night sky were the roosting place for hundreds of land and water birds. The startled fowls took to the air with shrill cries, flapping their wings as if to shoo it away.

Meanwhile, Bliss deftly set the ship down in the soft mud without so much as bruising a blade of grass. The landing lights cast a soft glow on the twisted tree trunks where a wily water moccasin lifted its head from a gnarled root and flicked its tongue, testing the air before it slithered off down a narrow waterway into the darkness. Two horny-backed alligators, beady eyes glistening from just above the water line, viewed the proceedings with interest. Sensing the possibility of a bedtime snack, they sank below the surface and swam toward the intruder. But as they neared the object, their inner sensory system warned them off.

Inside the ship, Bliss and Bodkins shut down systems in preparation for their departure. In his haste to execute the lock down, Bliss skipped important procedures and had to go back over them again. In too much of a hurry to log in all of the coordinates on the computer, he made a mental note of his landing site so he'd find it easily when he was ready to leave Earth.

A few minutes later, with a deactivated Bodkins stowed in the rear seat, Bliss climbed into his landscooter, opened the shuttle bay doors, switched on its anti-gravitational force field and shot out of the ship's bay. Accelerating, he whizzed through the labyrinth of waterways, skimming a few feet above the shallow marshes. His lean flying machine slipped into the narrow slots between the cypress trees like a phonograph needle in the groove. Gliding over the grassy hammocks and vast prairies of shallow water, Bliss picked up speed and headed for the Florida Keys and the inhabitants of the houses in his path.

Using Highway 1 as his guide, Bliss sped past Key Largo, scanning the interior of the dwellings as he approached. Then, at a point just before Sunset Key, he found it, a lone female emitting a strong surge of emotion. Bliss honed in on the energy, and allowed it to lead him. The vibrations grew stronger until he knew exactly where they were coming from—an isolated beach house that quickly came into view. He zeroed in on the beach cottage and cut his power.

Now, the need to feed dominated him, until it owned him body and soul. He would give all he had, all he had ever hoped for to satisfy it. Although Bliss knew his first matter of business should be to hide his landscooter, he had gone way past caring about such trivialities. Instead, he plunged the scooter into a sand dune in an attempt to partially conceal it. As soon as its forward motion ceased, Bliss leapt out, all caution and stealth forgotten. Instead, he ran in a loping, sliding, dizzy dance through the sand dunes to the beach cottage and the female had sensed inside.

He topped a small rise near the rear of the house and slammed into a metal rod, the corner post of a small, fenced area and nearly impaled himself. The sheer force of his momentum carried him on. Bliss reacted instantly, grabbed the post in his left hand, rolled his body forward and followed though with a somersault that vaulted him into the enclosure.

He landed on his posterior with a thud. When Bliss recovered, he was nose-to-nose, staring straight into the glinting, yellow eyes of a startled Doberman Pinscher. The Doberman emitted a deep-throated growl and bared his fangs. The direct eye contact was a definite challenge.

Bliss took a deep relaxing breath and held the dog's gaze. Nervously, the dog shifted its weight from front paw to front paw, unsure of what action to take, confused by the unfamiliar messages entering its brain. Then the dog stopped moving and stood still as a stone statue.

Reaching out with his pale green Vetan hand, Bliss placed his slender, spidery fingers on the top of the dog's head. Except for the occasional quivering of his flank, the Doberman remained perfectly still for five full minutes while Bliss laid hands on him and withdrew information.

He slowly released the pressure of his hand, and the Doberman slumped to the sand. The animal didn't move and no longer seemed to be breathing, but there was no time to think about it now. Bliss immediately began his transformation. In a few seconds, standing beside the motionless form was the Doberman's exact duplicate—his twin.

Sniffing the air, the clone's head turned in the direction of the beach house. He wagged his stubby tail in anticipation and drooled with delight. Then the Doberman ran with a stilted, jerky trot that soon became a graceful lope as he neared the cottage.

At the back door, he whined and scratched the wood with his long toenails until he heard an answer. He sat waiting for her, his eyes bright, his mouth open in an overeager pant. As her steps neared the door, he sniffed the air and his long tongue lashed out to lick the canine lips in agitated anticipation of the meal to come.

Chapter 11

Curled in a fetal position on the sofa, nursing her grief, Maggie heard Daniel's persistent scratching at the back door. *Damn it, I wish he wouldn't do that, it scars up the wood something awful. Better let him in. From the sound of it, he's going to tear it down.*

She dragged herself to her feet, grumbling. "First, he wants in, then he wants out. Well, this is it—Buddy. You're in for the night."

Since Bill had left, Maggie let Daniel sleep in the house. Just having him there made her feel more secure. Bill hated dogs in the house, wouldn't stand for it. Lately, she had begun to realize how many things he hated that she loved. *The dog is better company.*

She opened the door and Daniel cautiously entered. Usually, after his outing he bolted through the kitchen to the mudroom to check his food dish. But instead, Daniel stayed on Maggie's heels as if he were on an invisible leash.

She sat down, and Daniel sat in front of her at her feet, cocking his head at a rakish angle. Amused, she reached out to pet him, and he dropped his head on her knees and looked up at her expectantly. Her hand smoothed his brow, and as she did, Maggie experienced a weird sensation. The tips of her fingers buzzed and a warm tingle spread into the palm of her hand. Then, something more powerful surged up her arm, flowed through her chest area and collected in her brain.

Warmth infused her, and along with it came a deep sense of relaxation and peace as her mind emptied itself of thought. She stared into inner space as time stood still.

Daniel supported her limp hand with his head. Seconds passed and turned into minutes. He whined, licked her hand and backed away. Maggie's hand dropped to her lap. She blinked, shook her head and shuddered. *What had happened?*

She didn't remember. *I must have gone to sleep sitting up,* she thought. *How strange.* Maggie put her hand to her forehead, thinking perhaps she was coming down with something. But her head was cool to her touch. Still, she didn't feel quiet right. "It's time for bed," she muttered as she got up from the sofa.

She walked down the hall, through the master bedroom and into the bathroom, flipped on the light switch and flooded the area with light. It was her favorite room. The decor was totally Maggie, done in varying shades of beige and blue, and accented with seashell motifs to bring the shore indoors. She was particularly partial to the sunken whirlpool tub, large enough for two. Bordered by lush, green plants, the huge bathtub faced the floor to ceiling windows that provided a sweeping view of the beach and ocean beyond. It was like looking at a giant painting come to life.

It was her oasis; a place to hide from the world whenever she felt troubled or needed time to think. Armed with a glass of Chablis, she would sit in the warm, swirling water of the whirlpool, seek oblivion and find some small measure of peace. For the past few months, Maggie had used the tub so often her skin should have looked like a prune, but instead her lightly tanned flesh fairly glowed with health and vitality. In fact, catching her reflection in the mirror, Maggie thought she looked pretty good for an old broad.

As she shucked off her green silk skirt and matching blouse; she eyed herself critically in the large double vanity mirror. Standing naked in front of it, she posed, lifting her hair, she piled the chestnut strands on top of her head and turned slowly to study her body from all angles, pleased with her profile.

But her pleasure was short lived. She had the eerie sensation of being watched. The hair on her arms stood up, and out of the corner of her eye she saw something move. Her heart pounding, Maggie turned quickly.

Daniel sat there in the bathroom doorway staring at her.

"Shit, Daniel! You scared me." She waved her hand at him. "Good boy, go get your food."

The dog didn't move a muscle. Now Maggie was acutely aware of her nakedness and felt the rising heat of a blush beginning. Daniel's mouth hung open in a comical leer and his eyes gleamed in a strange way. Confused by her embarrassment, Maggie grabbed a towel from the rack and flicked it at him, striking the dog on his sensitive nose. Daniel yelped and dashed to the relative safety of the bedroom.

Now, she was wide-awake and somewhat unnerved. Seeking comfort in a few of her favorite things, she pulled on an old blue robe grown soft and comfy from numerous washings. Much too keyed up to sleep, Maggie went to the kitchen in search of a liquid tranquilizer.

She opened a kitchen cabinet, seized a bottle of Harvey's Bristol Cream and poured herself a generous drink. Her eyes fell on the French doors that led from the breakfast area to the deck. Maggie pushed them opened and stepped out, breathing in deeply, enjoying the warm salty air and the rhythmic sound of the waves breaking on shore. Throwing her head back, she gazed up at the starlit canopy of the heavens.

Maggie was bone tired of being alone. With all her heart she beseeched the heavens, asking for an end to her boredom. Even when she'd been married, she'd often felt alone. *Please, dear God, let me meet a man, someone with wit, intelligence, and of course, a great body— the perfect man, one who isn't looking for the perfect woman.*

The childhood admonition of her mother flashed in her mind, "Be careful what you wish for. "

In the breakfast room Daniel paced back and forth in front of the French doors, stopping every few minutes to gaze longingly at Maggie. The dog's movements were becoming more and more impatient.

Finally, Maggie came back in and headed down the hall to her bedroom with Daniel hot on her heels. Halfway there, she stopped in mid-stride. "Oh, shit," she muttered under her breath, "I forgot to check your water dish. As she turned, she tripped over the dog. "I'm sorry, Baby, but you've got to get out of my way." He had become her shadow.

To her surprise, she found plenty of water and a full bowl of food. "Whatsa matter, Danny, you not hungry. Aww, you must be feelin' bad," she crooned.

Kneeling down, she took his slender black head in her hands and peered into his eyes, searching for any sign of illness. Warmth immediately spread from her fingers up her arms and across her chest, and the tingling sensation once again invaded her body. Maggie jerked back, rose unsteadily and took a step backward, reaching behind her for the kitchen counter top as support. Her knees were weak.

"Whatever you've got, it must be contagious. Well, boy-o, it's back to the vet for you, first thing Monday morning. Now, let's get some rest, what d'ya say, Daniel, ole boy?" He panted happily in agreement and ran ahead of her into the bedroom.

Maggie pulled a cream-colored gown from the bureau drawer, removed her robe, and stood naked for a brief moment before she slipped the garment over her head and wiggled into it. Daniel lay a few feet away and watched her every move. Feeling his intent gaze, she thought maybe she should put him out for the night.

No, she thought, *I'm not going to give into this. It's crazy to develop paranoid feelings about the damn* dog. *Maybe, just maybe—I should see a psychiatrist, or the dog should see one.* She'd read somewhere there was such a thing. *We can share a shrink, two for the price of one. A therapist might be able to tell me why I only attract boring, self-absorbed men.* Like David Trenton, Daniel's vet, the man had invented boring. Tonight, had been their first, and as far as Maggie was concerned, last date. David had called, wanting to make a day of it. So, she had agreed, actually drove into Miami to meet him at his clinic. It was an arrangement she preferred, an opportunity to avoid a difficult scene at her door when the evening ended. Most of the time, she had decided, it's better to sleep alone.

Maggie turned back her comforter and slid between the fresh, crisp sheets of her queen size bed. Out of force of habit, she slept on the left side. The right side, she mentally referred to as the "cold side of the bed", the side most husbands slept on. But even now, some mornings on waking—without thinking—she reached out to touch the man who was no longer there.

Then automatically, she reached underneath the mattress on the left side, and checked to make sure her gun was still there. Her fingers brushed the cold metal of her air-weight .38 Smith and Wesson. If an intruder got past Daniel, all she had to do was roll out of bed, grab the gun and use the mattress as a barrier and something solid to steady her hands. So far Maggie had never used the weapon. But she felt safer, just knowing it was there.

The nightly ritual completed, Maggie settled down in her bed and drifted off to sleep. Her right hand rested near the edge of the bed. Daniel rose from the floor and approached Maggie. He gently nudged her hand with his muzzle until her fingers rested on his head.

Maggie began to dream. It was such a pleasant dream; she was going to meet someone with a feeling of great anticipation. There was a man in the shadows, but it was impossible to see his face until he stepped into the light.

It was Brian! It had been so long since Maggie had seen him. She moved to meet him, melting into his outstretched arms. Her hands caressed his strong, warm back. Brian felt so good.

Then, Maggie woke abruptly to find herself embracing Daniel.

"What in the devil are you doing in this bed," she sputtered. "What has gotten into you? Daniel, you know better."

Maggie continued to express her extreme displeasure and admonished the dog severely as she ordered him off the bed. The Doberman rose slowly, and for an instant it appeared he might openly defy her. Then with a look of pure disdain,

Daniel leapt to the floor. A few feet away, the animal lay down and looked up at her with sad, accusing eyes.

"Daniel," she warned, "don't try to make me feel guilty. I don't. I won't." Maggie flopped over on her side, trying to get comfortable.

In the dimness of the room, lit solely by the glow of a shell-shaped nightlight, Daniel's gaze was unwavering.

Chapter 12

Maggie sensed Daniel's eyes on her but chose to ignore the dog. Her mind kept going back to Brian and the dream. She missed him. Their relationship had been a full-blown case of love at first sight. For over a year, the two young people had been inseparable and had spent every free moment together. In her heart, Maggie had been sure Brian was the one. Theirs was the forever kind of love, made all the sweeter and more intense because it was also a first love.

Eighteen years old and a virgin, Maggie assumed correctly that Brian at nineteen was not. But since he had started dating Maggie, there had been no one else. They necked and petted incessantly, grappling in the back seat of his vintage '57 Chevy with Maggie moaning, "please, no", but dying to say, "yes, yes, yes!" Little by little, Brian had chipped away at her will power, and wore down her "won't" power. With a tinge of sadness, she recalled the first time they had made love. *If only ...* she thought as she drifted into sleep.

Daniel jumped back onto the bed and settled down next to Maggie, his head resting against her breast. His canine body twitched and rippled.

Maggie's dream picked up where it had left off. She was with Brian at his parent's secluded cabin at Lake Arrowhead—alone. At first, the images flickered dimly as if in an old-time newsreel, then they crystallized into sharp, colorful relief and stabilized into a reality.

Brian pulled her into his arms. It felt so good to be there, so warm, safe and right. His lips brushed her forehead, and she raised her head to kiss him. His lips took hers in a sweet, tender meeting filled with promise. His arms tightened around her and his mouth became more demanding. Maggie surrendered fully to his kiss, caught up in the delicious feel of his mouth on hers and the sweet ecstasy of his hands stroking her body.

"Oh, God, don't let me wake up," Maggie moaned. *It is so real; it feels so good.* "Maggie, you're so beautiful. I've wanted you since the first moment I saw you. Make love to me Maggie. I want you so much it hurts."

He kissed her again, and a fever raced through her veins. There was nothing she could do to stop him, nothing she wanted to do. "I want you, too," she whispered in Brian's ear. The entire center of her being seemed to converge at the point between her legs and ached with a sweet throbbing pain.

The alarm went off.

Maggie awoke abruptly from her dream. *Shit*, she thought, *I forgot to turn it off. It's fucking six o'clock in the morning on the weekend!* With her eyes clenched shut she reached for the clock radio and pressed hard on the snooze button. *Damn. Maybe if I don't open my eyes, I can go back to sleep, to that dream.* It had been so vivid, so real. She didn't want to wake and have it end. Maggie could still feel the hand between her legs. *The hand . . .*

She reached up and turned on the light before opening her eyes. When she slowly raised her eyelids, she was staring directly into Brian's eyes.

No! It can't be. She knew it couldn't be true. But, it seemed real enough. Brian Donovan lay next to her, reclining on one elbow, his head propped up on one hand, smiling down at her, his other hand between her legs.

His curly black hair fell over his forehead in exactly the way she remembered. His eyes a rare clear, light blue that made young girls swoon. *He looks wonderful*, she thought. *He's exactly the same.* Brian didn't look a day over twenty. Maggie felt as if she had been transported back in time. *But how? Why?* Brian's tanned naked body was pressed next to hers, and Maggie was not sure she cared how the materialization had happened.

It must be a hallucination, she thought, closing her eyes and holding her forehead in her hands. She willed the apparition to disappear. But a warm, real hand clasped hers and drew her fingers from her forehead. Her bedmate placed a gentle kiss on the back of her hand before he spoke. "Maggie," he said, in a familiar voice, "don't you recognize me, it's Brian."

Maggie opened one eye. He was still there.

He released her hand and smiled. Maggie reached up to caress his face, letting her fingers trace the contours she remembered so well. She touched his high forehead, moved down to his classic Roman nose, over his sensual bottom lip, and ended her investigation with the familiar cleft in his chin. "Brian," she moaned.

Tears sprang to her eyes. It couldn't be Brian, and yet, somehow it was. Seventeen years had passed since Maggie had last seen him. *No, no, the last time I saw him, he didn't look like this.* But Maggie pushed the thought from her mind; she didn't want to think about that, now. She'd go mad if she did. *He's here, that's all that matters*, she thought.

"Oh, God—Brian, I've missed you so." Tears spilled and ran down her cheeks as she held him close.

"I understand. Believe me, I know what you're feeling." Brian said. He knew exactly what Maggie was feeling.

"There's no way you can know," she said, "the hundreds of times I've thought about you, longed to touch you, to hear your voice. I saw your face everywhere, and relived over and over those few, precious moments we spent together. No one else ever made me feel the way you did," she swore. "Not any of the men I've met since then, not even my husband."

"I'm here, now, that's all that matters. The other men in your life were merely pale shadows. They were the dream; I am the reality, everything you've ever wanted—right here—right now."

With his tongue, he licked the salt of her tears from her face, and drained the tension from her body. The tightness in her temples relaxed as his lips drew the stiffness from her. Then Brian's hand reached up and turned off the lamp, and Maggie lay in early morning's first light, releasing the fear and anxiety that bound her and kept her from having what she truly wanted.

"Relax, Maggie, admit it, you want me just as much as I want you. For once in your life, let go, let your feelings tell you what to do." He spoke to her gently, and soon had her riding a rising wave of soft words. "Maggie, trust your feelings," he whispered as his mind reached out and touched hers. "Allow me and I will show you pleasure beyond your wildest dreams. I will see you as you wish to be seen, love you as you chose to be loved. All you need to do is think it, and it will be so."

And it was the truth. The words he whispered in her ears were the exact phrases she had waited her whole life to hear. Maggie removed her nightgown and flung the garment from the bed in an act of wild abandon and celebration. It no longer mattered who he was or how he had gotten there.

He touched her in places other men didn't even know existed. "Yes, yes," she screamed, as all her doubts, her fears, her sense of reason, vanished in the soul swallowing depth of their passion. His mouth covered hers in a deep, soulful kiss that re-ignited the flames that had so long been banked. She shivered with delight as Brian trailed a map of kisses from her throat to her breast, and a shard of pleasure shot through her.

"Brian, my God, it feels so wonderful, so right!"

"I know, I know," he said, as he moved over her and down, penetrating her. Maggie opened her legs wide in welcome as he kidnapped her consciousness, taking her to a place of primal instinct. His hunger drove them on to greater heights as he plunged on and on until something blossomed inside her and reached out to him with an emotion so deep, so powerful, the surge left her breathless as she climaxed. "Oh, God, yes, yes," she screamed.

Then, something strange happened. Roman candles went off in Maggie's head, and suddenly she was flying down a long, dark tunnel, fighting for breath. Deep inside, something shattered and a force flowed out from her and into him. Maggie felt the siphoning surge, and then the icy edges of a numbing cold that spread rapidly through her veins like a lethal drug. Dimly, she was aware of Brian above her, murmuring soothing words. But she could not understand them. They had no meaning; these strange melodious tones that danced enticingly just out of reach in her mind. But they calmed her, and in a matter of seconds, she fell into a deep sleep with a serene, blissful look on her face.

Brian's face glowed, lit from within and fueled by her fire. The moment Maggie closed her eyes, Bliss immediately assumed his natural form, changing completely in a matter of seconds, renewed and rejuvenated. When he finished the transformation, Bliss stood at his true height of 6 feet, 3 inches. His faintly luminous, muscular body seemed more like a statue of a Greek God than that of a man. There was not one hair on his sleek form except for his head. A thick mane of snow-white hair fell to his shoulders, shiny as cornsilk. It artfully framed his face and shone like a halo.

His high forehead was unmarred by eyebrows, and his lashless emerald green eyes were the windows of an ancient soul. His face was handsome by Earth standards, an arresting combination of features set off by a wide, sensuous mouth and a strong jaw.

His skin was luminescent, renewed and refreshed, a sign that his hunger if not sated was at least, abated. He stared down at Maggie, sleeping soundly, curled in upon herself for warmth. She was totally and completely his—his source, his supply, his immediate gratification and salvation.

Bliss sighed. Once again, he had managed to survive. Now, he must formulate plans to establish a base of operation for himself. There was much to accomplish and much to learn. He must learn to fit in by becoming familiar with Earth's customs and behaviors and eliminate anything that would draw undue attention. He intended to become the perfect Earth male. *Now, there's a concept*, he thought.

But first, more than anything else, his rapidly rejuvenating body required rest. Bliss lay down beside Maggie and entered his resting mode, knowing he would awaken long before she would.

Chapter 13

Outside the beach house the world took on all the aspects of a normal Sunday morning. The sun rose as it always did in the clear blue of the Miami skies—white and hot.

The tide rolled in and deposited its early morning offerings, and the sea gulls swooped and dove above the beach, uttering their plaintive cries. Early morning runners strode across the sands, luxuriating in the feel of the fresh ocean breeze on their faces.

On Highway 1, good Miamians drove to their respective churches. Some went there to commune with God, others to make business contacts or points with their fellow citizens, and a few went to covet their neighbor's wife in the pew in front of them; sometimes all three.

At no time was there any indication of the ominous events taking place in their midst with the exception of one sensitive soul in a large city far to the north.

In her New York City apartment, Victoria Chambers was ready to begin her morning meditation. She invoked the protection of the magic circle of Divine Love, and then stilled her mind.

"I ask to be a clear channel for inspiration and guidance, nothing inappropriate can enter here, nothing inappropriate can leave me. If there is anything I need to know, Divine Source, tell me now," she said.

Victoria entered the silence. For several minutes, she heard and saw nothing. Then the images and words came in rapid succession. Some of the messages she understood, some she did not, but she knew their meaning would become clear later.

Just as Victoria was about to come out of her meditation, she saw a symbolic image of a human heart, frozen in a block of ice. Something sinister lurked at the edge of her consciousness. Then, strobe lights of information hit her, coming in too fast for her to decipher as strange people and places filled the landscape of her inner vision—incredibly strange images, even for her.

She sensed a black hole of negativity where a repulsive, vindictive force resided. Someone else carried a great burden—darkness and light, both sides of the same coin. Victoria experienced a chill from the top of her head to the soles of her feet, a familiar indication of a spiritual truth. Then, she clearly heard the words of her inner guide who always spoke the truth with love, without any judgment or criticism. *Do not be afraid, do not be anxious or worry, no matter what happens*, the voice said. *There is nothing you can get into that God can't get you out of. You are always taken care of.*

"Thank you, Father, for hearing me, thank you for always hearing me," Victoria said before she opened her eyes. But it wasn't over; she was picking up something else, coldness unlike anything she had ever experienced and a sense of someone who wanted something *so much* that it was a dangerous compulsion. Victoria's teeth chattered uncontrollably, and she hugged herself for warmth. Although it was obviously some sort a premonition, a warning, it made no sense to her.

"Angels, guides . . . help me out here? Who is the message for? What does it mean?"

Victoria was working on several police cases at one time, so it could be anything. The vividness of the vision of the frozen heart lingered and cast a pall over the picture-perfect living room. The only thing Victoria knew for certain was that the vision had something to do with her impending trip to Miami.

For the first time in a long time, she felt afraid. It was a foolish feeling without any basis, like a child's fear of going into a dark room alone, hanging back on the threshold, imagining all the kinds of demons lurking in the darkness. Victoria knew from experience that the real enemy was the fear. Only sometimes, even she forgot that love casts out fear.

"God is Love, God is all there is, Love is all there is," she chanted.

She might be able to cast out fear, but she didn't seem to be able to shake off the pervasive chill so she got up to check the thermostat. Even before she saw the digital readout, she knew it would be exactly 76 degrees. No matter—Victoria was freezing. She needed something warm.

She headed down the long hallway and stopped in front of an elaborate gilt-framed mirror that was actually the cleverly disguised door to the linen closet. She tugged it open and pulled a large blanket from the top of a towering pile. Her actions created an avalanche of sheets and other bed linens.

"Grrreat!" Victoria moaned, knowing it was going to take time to put all of this stuff back. "Why does mother have to have so much of everything?" Every closet in the place was chocked full.

Of course, Victoria already knew the answer to her own question. Her mother, Rita, was making up for the insecurities of an impoverished childhood. In Rita's case, the hereditary psychic sensitivities had skipped a generation. Rita remained firmly rooted in the material world.

No hocus-pocus for her, as she called it, just the things she could see, touch, wear or taste. Although Rita loved food, she constantly worried about her weight. Her favorite saying was, "You can't be too rich or too thin." Rita worked hard at being both.

Another shiver brought Victoria back to the moment. She picked up a blanket and wrapped it around her body Indian fashion and headed for the kitchen. She felt drained, in the world but not of it, even though she interacted with her surroundings, she felt apart from them. The memory of the vision was a like a nugget of dry ice lodged in her brain, sending out chilly drafts to her heart. Victoria searched for a touchstone to bring her back into her comfort zone, something to give her focus and a feeling of connection. Her eyes fell on the box of instant cocoa. It immediately reminded her of her maternal grandmother, Mamie—her own personal guardian angel. Mamie thought a cup of hot chocolate would cure anything. In her mind's eye, Victoria pictured Mamie, a petite woman with a sweet, kind face, and tender, loving eyes.

To appease the spirit of her grandmother, she made a cup of steaming hot chocolate and held it between her hands to absorb the warmth. Her thoughts played hopscotch, taking her back to the summer when she was ten years old and Mamie took on a much more meaningful role in her young life.

Seated on the floor at play, Victoria had suddenly looked up and interjected herself into the adult conversation flowing around her.

"Grandpa won't be coming home tonight," she remembered saying. Those words had been the result of her first vision. She well recalled the stunned silence that followed her words, and the phone call that came 30 minutes later from Granny Mamie, saying that Grandpa Arnold had suffered a heart attack. Although he had been rushed to the hospital, he had been pronounced dead on arrival.

Later Grandpa Arnold had appeared to Victoria to say good-bye, and she had been reassured by his presence. But to her mother, it was not an auspicious event. The evidence of her child's psychic ability irritated Rita. She equated ESP with sleight of hand or other parlor tricks. To her, it was a social faux pas, one she chose to ignore, hoping to thwart any repetition by pretending that the incident had never happened.

As a child growing up, Rita had been embarrassed by her mother's abilities. She cringed every time she had to pass through their parlor filled with neighborhood women waiting for a reading from her Mamie. Rita knew her father accepted these intrusions with an air of resignation because he was secretly in awe of his wife's strange, intuitive powers.

The kids at school called her mother the "spook." But when Rita entered high school, the kid's attitudes changed, and her girlfriends badgered Rita to set up an appointment for them for a free reading. They wanted to know about their love lives or closer to reality, the lack of them.

In those days, Victoria mused; no one called Mamie a psychic. She was a "fortune teller." Her clients came expecting to meet some dark-skinned gypsy: a witchy woman in garish clothing with a gold-toothed smile. Instead of an old crone staring into a crystal ball, her clients found a plump, gray-haired matron, wearing a simple housedress, seated at a rickety card table, shuffling a tattered deck of Bicycle playing cards.

People always remembered Mamie's eyes; gentle and kind, capable of seeing into their hearts and minds, knowing their deepest, darkest secrets and somehow loving them, in spite of, or perhaps because of their shortcomings.

It was Mamie who taught Victoria that love was the most powerful force in the universe. In each person, she saw a spark of the Divine and did what she could to fan the flame. Mamie had her own code by which she lived. Without the spiritual aspect—what she called a soul consciousness— Mamie felt her psychic powers might be nothing more than a frivolous gift in a class with con artists. She had taught Victoria that abusing the power of her insight by pressing too hard for material advantages or coddling her vanity would diminish the effectiveness of her gift and, eventually, it might disappear altogether.

That was the main reason that Mamie charged no set fee for her readings. She merely accepted "love offerings." The practice made her accessible to more people and still provided an adequate income. As the years passed, Mamie's awareness and reputation increased and so did her income.

Of course, Mamie wasn't surprised or upset when Victoria experienced her first vision. Her initiation had come about in a similar manner when as a child Mamie foresaw the death of her father. An emotional crisis or impending disaster was often the trigger for psychic abilities—or in some cases, a sharp blow to the head. During their early years, children often experienced strong intuitive impulses and were less hesitant than adults to make them known.

Mamie understood the importance of encouragement. These natural inclinations needed nurturing before they were stifled by well meaning adults. Since Victoria spent summers with her grandmother, she received valuable instructions designed to prepare her for what lay ahead. After a serious talking to by Mamie, Rita finally accepted the inevitable and enjoyed the freedom of summers without a child underfoot.

Victoria owed a debt of gratitude to Granny Mamie who had taught her how to harness the power within and use it as a light to illuminate the darkness in people's lives and help them see more clearly.

Mamie claimed everyone had a mission, a purpose in life. Victoria had found hers at an early age. The more she learned, the more she understood how little she knew and much of life and death remained a mystery to her. How can I help other people, she wondered, when most of the time, my own life seems such a mess?

You always know what you need to know when you need to know it.

"Yeah, right. That's easy for you to say, Mamie. I'm here, and you're not."

She drained the last few drops of cold cocoa from her cup and wiped the unpleasant vision of the morning from her mind. She felt much better; the warning had lost its sense of urgency.

Victoria went into her bedroom to pack. She had a flight to catch to Miami.

Chapter 14

At ten o'clock on Monday morning, Maggie was still in a deep, motionless slumber. Bliss knew she probably wouldn't come out of her coma-like state until near the time of the setting of Earth's sun.

The earthly equivalent of what she had just experienced was the free-basing of high-grade cocaine, a sudden release, and a rush of adrenaline resulting in a quick, sharp rise in blood pressure that constricted the blood vessels and stimulated the heart. The aftermath, the numbing, cold sensation, like a freezing wind blowing through her heart and soul, posed the greatest danger.

With highly emotional, compassionate females like Maggie, Bliss could feed on the same victim several times before they were depleted, but he seldom fed on a female more than once due to the fact that continued feeding left his victims dispassionate and heartless and forced them to exist without the restraints of compassion, love or guilt. But with Maggie, his frequent feedings were unavoidable—it was a matter of his survival.

In the meantime, Bliss took full advantage of having the house to himself. First, he explored the living room, delighted to find one entire wall devoted to bookcases. As he flipped through the books, his photographic memory stored every word. It took him only three hours and ten minutes to memorize every book, magazine and newspaper in Maggie's house.

In her study, he found a home computer and the instruction manual Maggie had never quite mastered. The home system had been for Bill's convenience, not hers. It was tied in to the master computer at Danvers Pharmaceuticals, exactly what he needed to create an identity. A quick scan of papers in the desk and the information on the computer provided most of what he needed to know about Earth's monetary systems and necessary identification documents. With the accumulated knowledge, Bliss created an imaginary past and identity.

He picked a first name from a book citing names and definitions, choosing Jonathan because it meant "Gift of God", something he felt he was to females, a little inside joke. He used Bliss as his last name, selected a social security number and established a file with the IRS and the Social Security Administration, dating back several years. *Social security*, he mused, *exactly what I need.*

Next, he tackled the task of acquiring funds. He needed money to make money. Bliss worked miracles with the computer. The simple Earth access codes of the computer systems were child's play for him. His fingers flew over the keyboard. Bliss tapped into the accounts receivable file at Danvers Pharmaceuticals and prepared fraudulent invoices for several major accounts. Included were a number of physicians, clinics, hospitals and pharmacies with a total billing of over $250,000 dollars. He quickly set up the process to pay the invoices instantly by automatic debit card transactions. Bliss then transferred those funds to a bank account he had created for himself at the First National Bank of Miami, listing Maggie's beach house address as his own. And then he wiped out all the information on the Danvers computers pertaining to his recent transactions.

When he left Maggie, Bliss planned to close the account and take the cash. He knew it would be weeks, perhaps a month or more before the discrepancies were noticed. By then, he would be long gone.

But Bliss required much more in the way of resources. He intended to amass huge sums of money since he liked to live well in luxurious comfort and great style. Toward that end, Bliss gleaned every bit of information possible from Bill's stack of Wall Street Journals. When he arrived in New York, he wanted to hit the ground running. *Even better*, he thought, *I'll establish a female contact with an insider's knowledge.*

His telepathic abilities were invaluable in making investments and the key to amassing instantaneous riches.

Bliss' hunger for material things was as strong as his craving for emotion. Boredom was his enemy and he fought it with all the weapons of wealth.

The persistent ringing of the doorbell startled Bliss.

Ding-dong. Ding Dong. Ding Dong.

He followed the sound and found its source.

Ding Dong. Ding-dong.

When Bliss finally jerked the door open, he startled the delivery boy standing on the front porch.

"Hey, mister. I was just about to leave, didn't think anybody was at home. Delivery for Maggie Danvers," the lanky teenager said as he thrust a long white box into Bliss' hands. The delivery boy looked Bliss full in the face and did an exaggerated double take. "Say, man, what happened to your eyebrows? You been in a fire or something?"

"My what?"

"Eyebrows, dude, your eyebrows," the boy remarked, pointing to his own, thinking the man must be a little dense. "Must have gotten your eyelashes, too." He stared at the unusual emerald eyes, sensing something strange in their depths. Bliss reached out and touched his hand, and a fog shrouded the boy's mind until he forgot why he was there.

"You can go, now," Bliss suggested.

"Yeah, right," the kid said, dazed.

Bliss closed the door, thinking about the repulsive outcroppings of hair. He knew he'd need the facial hair in order to fit in. Fortunately, the rest of his natural physique would do nicely.

He carried the box into the kitchen, placed it on the counter pulled the top up. Inside were a dozen pale pink rosebuds. A small card in the bottom read, "Thanks for a wonderful evening, David Trenton." Bliss tossed the card in the trashcan with a self-satisfied grin.

A lover of beauty in all its forms, Bliss lifted the rosebuds from their bed of tissue paper to appreciate them more fully. At his touch, the buds burst into full bloom in a blaze of beauty.

He found a vase on the counter, filled it with water and arranged the flowers in an artful pose. Pleased, he returned to the computer. A few minutes later, the roses withered and died, but Bliss had seen only the blossoming. If he had witnessed their early demise, he might have considered it to be an omen.

Down the hall in the master bedroom, Maggie tossed and turned, ascending to consciousness from the deep well of her sleep. She pulled the covers more snugly around her, rolled over, and stretched her hand out to touch the empty pillow. Slowly, she opened her eyes.

In her first waking instant, she was surprised to find herself alone, then relieved.

The events of the past night came flooding back in vivid detail. Maggie raised her arm and sniffed it. Brian's faint scent still lingered. Her rumpled nightgown lay on the floor beside the bed as further evidence, and the soreness between her legs was irrefutable proof.

Is he still in the house? Except for the whoosh of the air conditioning system and the soothing murmur of the sea, the house was quiet. Blinking her sleep heavy eyelids, she surveyed the room, and found it empty. Maggie stretched, inhaled a deep cleansing breath and looked at her digital clock astonished to see it read 5:15. The pattern of strong sunlight streaming in through the patio doors left no doubt; it was late afternoon, not morning.

Where is Daniel? In the kitchen, more than likely, eating the food he'd shown no interest in last night. Maggie shivered in an uncontrollable spasm. She squirmed lower in the bed, and yanked the covers up. The sheet resting on her face held the lingering odor of salty sex. The thoughts of last night's gymnastics brought on a sudden, unexpected response. Her nipples stood erect beneath the covers and a pulse of pleasure throbbed between her thighs as an intense wave of longing swept over her. Tears stung her eyes as saliva flooded her mouth. Goosebumps brought the hairs on her arms to full attention. *What in the hell is going on?*

Uncomprehending and exhausted, she lay back on her pillow, trying to sort it all out. Someone or something had made wild, passionate love to her last night, someone who looked exactly like Brian Donovan. But Maggie knew that was impossible. She should be afraid, but she wasn't. Instead, she was cold, curious and more than a little crazy from the rampaging rush of hormones.

Round and round her thoughts chased each other, playing the events over and over like an old, worn-out tape. There must be a logical explanation. *Someone, who looks exactly like Brian, broke into the house and made love to me in the middle of the night. Highly unlikely. A supernatural experience? Wish fulfillment? No, it was too real, last night had not been some vague, spirit visitation; last night was the work of a real man.*

And, she sensed—no, she actually felt him. His presence vibrated in the air, a compelling force, drawing her to him on his own personal wavelength. Maggie *wanted* to go to him but fought the urge, knowing something was wrong, maybe even downright dangerous. There were things she had to understand and questions that must be answered.

Although he was absorbed in entering more data into the computer, Bliss knew Maggie was awake. He went into the guest bedroom and searched for some appropriate Earth attire. The best fit was a burgundy Pierre Cardin robe, a trifle short, but it would have to do. Bliss slipped into the robe and donned Brian Donovan's identity at the same time. This time, he remembered to age the human's body to compensate for the passage of time.

Brian actually improved with age; a slight graying at the temples and the added character of a few laugh lines enhanced his attractiveness. Bliss paused to check his image in the mirror.

Suddenly, Maggie sat bolt upright in the bed. Whoever he was, he might not be as eager to answer her questions, as she was to ask them. *Well, we'll see about that!* Now, she was more angry than afraid. *I'd better get some clothes on,* she thought. Maggie threw back the covers and swung her feet to the floor. She raced around the bed and slid her hand along the edge of the mattress until her fingers contacted cold steel. *Let him argue with that!* She moved the gun from the right side of the bed and placed it under the mattress on the left side. Then she ran to the closet for a robe.

As Maggie pulled the garment from the scented, satin hanger, the sound of a door opening down the hall turned her to stone. She froze, held her breath and listened intently as the footsteps came toward her, closer with each of her thudding heartbeats.

She threw on the robe and dashed back to the bed and sat down on her side, her hand gripping the mattress just above the revolver's hiding place. She waited; her jaw set in a stubborn line as the door slowly swung open.

Chapter 15

The bedroom door opened wide and Bliss, once more in Brian's form, entered the room with a confident smile on his face.

"Good afternoon, love."

"Don't good afternoon me," she snapped. "Stay right where you are, don't come one step closer." She held her left hand up like a stop sign.

He smiled and took a step.

She slid her hand underneath the mattress and closed her fingers around the weapon. In a split second, Maggie had him staring down the barrel of her 38 Smith and Wesson, and she looked like she knew how to use it.

"I said, stop!"

He did as she asked.

"Now, suppose you tell me who the hell you really are and what you're doing here."

Her reaction, the weapon, and the anger in her voice surprised him. His face didn't change, but his lips tightened into a thin, straight line. Maggie should have no question as to his identity. Brian wasn't some sexual fantasy, or a figment of her imagination. He was a real person, someone from her past, chosen from her own memories.

He thought quickly, hoping to repair the damage and regain her trust. "Why, Maggie, I'm hurt, don't you remember last night? Don't tell me you'd do those things with a stranger? I'm shocked."

"Shocked? You? Don't give me that garbage." She stood and pointed the gun at him, eye level. "I asked you a question, and I demand an answer. Who are you?"

Bliss weighed the situation, knowing she was already under his influence far more than she realized, and he could easily take the weapon from her. He was intrigued by her question and decided to play out the scene. Apparently, he had overlooked some important element. For his own sake, he needed to know what it was. Bliss seldom made mistakes, but lately, he seemed to be on a roll. *What next?*

"You're not Brian Donovan, that's for sure."

"I know it's been a long time since we've seen each other, but I've never forgotten you, or our last night together at the cabin.

"Cut the crap, whoever you are. The last time I saw Brian wasn't at his folk's cabin. It was in a cozy little place you obviously don't know anything about—the Associated Funeral Home."

Bliss blinked.

"Brian was the center of attention, you see, because he was dead—in a casket. That was the last time I saw him."

In his mind, Bliss went back over the information he had lifted from Maggie's memories. He had stopped at Brian's induction into the military and his orders for Vietnam. He had been in a hurry. Apparently, he had not delved deeply enough.

He reached out and touched her hand as if in sympathy. The images flowed out to him, her mother opening the front door, two men in military uniforms delivering a telegram and then, intense grief.

A master of the expedient lie, Bliss searched for a plausible fabrication. "It wasn't me in that casket, Maggie. Earlier in 'Nam there was a mix-up, a mistake. We were captured, taken as prisoners of war, and I traded dog tags and uniforms with a Colonel to protect him. But it didn't work; he tried to escape and stepped on a land mine in the jungle. He had on my dog tags so he was identified as Brian Donovan."

"An interesting story. Tell me more, but first, move away from me and sit down over there, you're making me nervous." She motioned toward a wingback chair near the patio doors.

He eased himself into the chair and sat facing her. He leaned forward and placed his hands on his knees and continued his story, making it up as he went along. "The

POW camp was hell, Maggie, but I survived. After seven years, I was finally rescued. When I arrived back in the states, I was in the Veteran's Hospital in D.C. for 18 months. I had battle fatigue, I lost touch with reality, didn't know who I was, didn't care. By the time, I finally came to my senses, recovered and came back home; you had married and moved away. I was devastated."

"Very touching, please do go on."

"There's not much more to tell. I heard about your separation from your husband, and I came here looking for you, hoping it wasn't too late. I planned to surprise you, looks as if I did."

"As we say in the South, that dog won't hunt. Brian was never taken prisoner of war. He was killed by a land mine, you got that part of your story right, but he wasn't trying to escape, Brian was on his way to do volunteer work at a Vietnamese orphanage. His face was destroyed beyond all recognition, but he still wore the ring I gave him. Brian said he'd never take it off. His parents and I identified the body. It was Brian we buried, not your fictitious Colonel." Maggie took a deep, mind-clearing breath and steadied her gun hand. "Now, for the last time, while I'm still thinking about faces being blown away, tell me who and what you are." *Some CIA experiment gone wrong, no doubt.*

"All right, Maggie, I will tell you the truth, but I don't think you're going to believe me." It was one thing he was sure of.

"Try me."

Bliss had learned all he could from the experience so he decided to change his tactics. It was time to get on with his sojourn on Earth.

"I am a being from another planet. My home planet is Arias located in the constellation of Orion."

"No way!" The news numbed Maggie into silence. Scenes from old horror movies replayed in her mind, but somehow, she was not totally surprised by his revelation. There was *something otherworldly* about his lovemaking. *How had he managed to look so much like Brian? Why was he here? How did he know what she knew? And what did he really look like?*

"Maggie, put the weapon down. Put it down . . . and I'll answer some of those questions running around in your head."

Her indecision, coupled with the confusing messages in her body and mind, momentarily disconnected Maggie from reality. *How strange,* she thought, *I'm no longer afraid of him.* In fact, she was *drawn* to him. No panic. No terror. No hysteria.

"Maggie, lay the weapon down," he repeated. "I won't hurt you. Remember last night? Everything you've ever wanted, remember?" His voice held an enticing promise.

At the mention of last night, her brain fell below and centered on the wetness between her thighs. His voice touched her mind intimately, controlled her and claimed her. Maggie no longer cared who he was.

The only reality was the craving, an aching, growing need for him. Their recent sexual encounter had become the focal point of her existence. She must experience that high, the mind-blowing culmination, again. She couldn't get enough of that wonderful stuff.

Bliss sensed it, and in spite of himself, felt pity for her. But he brushed it aside—his needs trumped hers.

Slowly, she put the gun down and Bliss rose to meet her. Maggie went to him, ready to give herself to him. Bliss gazed deeply into her eyes, piercing her with a sweet ecstasy. "I want you, Maggie, but not now, it's too much too soon. It might be dangerous for you; your heart and your blood vessels can only take so much strain. Give yourself time to recover, you need to regain some of your strength."

But it made no sense to Maggie. She was engulfed in a steamy fog of uncontrollable desire. "I don't care what happens to me, take me to that place, that high," she pleaded.

"Yes, I understand, but first, let's talk. I'm sure you have many more unanswered questions."

Gently, with his hand on the small of her back, he guided her out of the bedroom into the living room, putting some distance between them and the bed they had shared. Normally, when Maggie entered the main room of her home, she felt a rush of satisfaction, knowing she had created a lovely place. But so much had changed in a short time, now Bliss claimed her full attention.

They sat on the sofa, he steered her to one end and he sat at the other.

"Where did you say you were from?" she asked, trying to focus on something other than sex.

"My home is Arias. It's many light years away. Do you have any knowledge of astronomy—the stars?"

"No, not really." Except for the ones in her eyes.

"Then I won't bore you with meaningless details of star maps and locations except to say that my people are very advanced by Earth standards. In the beginning, I was more like a spirit guide to others on Arias who lived in the physical realm."

"You are a spirit?" He looked solid enough.

"We are all spirit," he said. "I existed in a different dimension as spirit without a body, but I could assume a physical form for short periods of time. In my youth, I did that often, a little too often," he admitted. Since Cassandra's curse, some memories of his early life had returned, not all but some. Part of her revenge, he supposed, to let him know just how far he had fallen.

Maggie's confusion registered on her face.

"I became enamored with the material world of tangible experiences," he continued, "and while I was in the physical world, I formed an attachment for a young healer, an Arian female, Gabrielle. There were doors of knowledge I could open for her and she for me. She was very beautiful with an inner light that fascinated me. Soon, merely touching Gabrielle's mind and sharing her soul no longer were enough. I wanted total fulfillment, carnal knowledge."

Maggie's interest heightened. She envied Gabrielle. *I wish I had been the first.*

"Gabrielle seemed as taken with me as I was with her. Our tender, passionate affection aroused needs that could only be met in the physical world. It created a conflict for both of us. In order to have Gabrielle, I had to give up my role as spiritual guide and become a permanent part of her plane of existence.

"You gave up everything for love," Maggie sighed. *How romantic!*

"Not love, lust. I could have *loved* her from afar, but I wanted it all. You see Maggie; it's all about choices. I could have waited and incarnated with her in another lifetime. But no, I was too impatient, so I turned my back on my birthright and immersed myself in the physical world. Then, I went in search of my heart's desire to tell her of my great sacrifice," he said in a self-mocking tone.

"What happened?" Maggie prompted. "Did you find her?"

"Oh, I found her all right, in the arms of another."

"What did you do?"

"What could I do? Gabrielle had obviously been playing me for a fool all along. Having her know I was there, having them know I had seen them together would have been the ultimate humiliation."

Although there was no emotion in his voice, Maggie saw the shadows of pain and torment in his eyes. *His story is strange, yet familiar, not unlike my own. We both bear the scars of betrayal.* But Maggie didn't really care anymore, not about Bill or their marriage.

"Did she know what you were going to do?"

"Not really. I wasn't allowed to see her until my transformation into the physical was complete."

"But you talked with her later, got her side of the story?" *Not likely*, she thought.

"No, I never saw or spoke with her again." He looked at Maggie without seeing her, his mind a billion miles away. "She must have known, females sense these things, do they not?" It was the first time such a thing had ever occurred to him.

"Not always. Sometimes we sense it, but don't trust the feeling. A woman needs to be told, reassured. You should have talked to her, told her that you still loved her."

"Maggie, the only thing I wanted at the time was revenge, I had been betrayed. I ran away, stole a space cruiser and plotted a course for the nearest planet with humanoid lifeforms."

Humanoid lifeforms?

She finally worked up enough nerve to ask the crucial question. "How is it that you look exactly like Brian?"

"It's easy. The beings on Arias are telepaths and chameleons. I incarnated in one of their physical forms and inherited those abilities. I can read your mind and take any form."

Then she bit the big bullet. "What is your real name, and what do you really look like?

"I am called Bliss. As for what I look like in my natural form, are you sure you want to know." There was a glint of amusement in his eyes.

"Yes, I'm sure," sounding like she had just bet her bankroll on a three-legged dog at the track.

"All right, if you say so. Close your eyes and keep them closed until I tell you to open them."

Maggie nodded, eyes clamped shut, her hands twisting nervously in her lap.

"There's a part of my transition that you really don't want to see . . . it's a little messy and disturbing." As he spoke Bliss scanned the room until his gaze lit on a large-leafed floor plant. "Just be patient for a moment while I make the transformation." Making as little noise as possible, Bliss picked up the plant, brought it over to the sofa, then sat back down and positioned the plant between his knees before he made the transition into his Arian form. The leaves were at a height even with his head.

"Don't open your eyes yet. Move over a little closer to me and give me your hand."

Maggie complied. Bliss guided her fingers to one of the leaves of the plant. *Oh, my, he felt ugly, ugly, ugly.* She gingerly touched the cold, rough surface and moved her hand over the large veins that forked in both directions, forming swollen ridges, pictures forming in her mind of a huge head, bulging veins and slanted lizard eyes. She drew back her hand in horror, stifled a scream and opened her eyes, expecting to see an alien right out of the Star Wars bar scene.

Instead, a handsome face with arresting emerald eyes peeked through the leaves. "Boo!" he said before he convulsed in laughter.

"You bastard! Maggie opened and closed her mouth, at a loss for words.

He laughed again, an infectious sound with a musical quality. "Maggie, I couldn't resist. From everything I've read and what passes for entertainment on your planet, you Earthlings persist in the belief that alien lifeforms must be hideous, malevolent creatures, a grotesque parody of life on your own planet."

"I guess you have a point," she said.

"If you really believe that the God of the Universe, the Source or whatever you choose to call All That Is, created man in his or her image, what makes you think life in other parts of the galaxy is so completely different from your own?"

"I don't know, I never really thought about it." Maggie admitted. Her pulse had returned to normal. She was relieved, glad he wasn't a monster, and pleased to know he had a sense of humor, twisted though it might be. She liked humor in anyone, even an alien, even if he had made her the victim of his joke.

Victim. The word lodged in her brain and the train of her thoughts sped toward a conclusion. Then, Bliss took her hands in his; pulled her into his arms and her thoughts were diverted by a sudden switching of the tracks.

The craving within Bliss was building, but he could wait. There was work yet to be completed. Even as his lips moved down Maggie's slender neck and she moaned, he was mentally ticking off the things he needed to accomplish. He kissed her, thinking about concealing his landscooter, activating Bodkins and disposing of the dog's body.

The dog's untimely demise concerned him. Such a thing had never happened before. Bliss had joined minds with Daniel in order to communicate with his owner. From the information he had received, he knew that when he assumed the form of her canine best friend, Bliss could then easily connect with her. But Daniel had not survived the process, and it troubled him. Bliss had a respect and reverence for all life, but for none more than his own.

Bliss came back into the moment and gave Maggie a deep, passionate kiss. When he had her full attention, he pulled back and looked into her eyes. "You are feeling totally relaxed, he said in a soft, musical, hypnotic voice. "You are very sleepy; your eyelids are heavy . . . heavy. When I count to three . . . you will be asleep . . . one . . . two . . . three."

Maggie slumped in his arms. Bliss picked her up and carried her down the hall to her bedroom where he deposited her on the bed. He rearranged the covers to make her more comfortable. Bliss gazed at her fondly. *She is a lovely woman, in more ways than she knows*, he thought as he brushed the hair back from her forehead and traced her face with his scarred finger. Then he kissed her cheek and brought his lips close to her ear. "Dream of me, Maggie, of all the things you want, of all the words you long to hear. Think of them and soon, very soon, they will be your reality." She smiled in her sleep.

Bliss returned to the study and switched on the computer aware of what he must accomplish and his own pressing biological timetable. To maintain, nourish and rejuvenate his physical form, Bliss must feed at least once every few days— more was better.

He expected Maggie to be of use to him two to four more times, depending on his restraint and her recuperative powers. Eventually, she would be totally drained of emotion, and Bliss would have to move on. He hoped to leave before it went that far. Yet, he wanted to stretch out the timeframe to give himself more time to acclimate and adjust to his new world. All the information he had accumulated so far made him acutely aware of the necessity of carefully choosing his bedmates.

The knowledge they possessed was as valuable to him as their emotions. Bliss was the all-time ultimate taker and user. But in his mind, he rationalized that he gave the females what they wanted, what they were missing in their lives—a fantasy, dream lover. Somehow, he failed to see that his gift to them was an inequitable trade-off, a few nights of pleasure for the their most valuable commodity, their emotional essence. Of course, it was something Cassandra had well understood, and in spite of Bliss' resistance to self-knowledge, at some level, he was starting to get it. But the big question was, would he do anything about it?

Chapter 16

As he acclimated himself to Earth, Bliss extended his circle of activities, leaving Maggie alone for short periods of time in his quest for other victims. Although she continued to be of use to him by providing him with new contacts, his attraction to her had waned with the depletion of her emotions.

Upon his return from one of his frequent absences, Bliss found Maggie in the kitchen with a peculiar, perplexed look on her face.

"What's wrong, Maggie?"

Maggie shrugged, "It's nothing really, I'm just disappointed by the mail." She waved him away.

"That's not unusual, many females, throughout the universe are disappointed by the males."

Maggie smiled thinly; her sense of humor had been one of the first things to go. "No, Bliss, I'm not talking about the m-a-l-e, it's the m-a-i-l, as in delivered by the United States Post Office. But you were half-right. I am disappointed with one male, my lawyer. He promised to have my revised divorce settlement papers to me today."

"Ah, the about to be ex-husband."

"Yes," she said, pouring herself a cup of coffee. "It's taken months to work out the details of the financial property settlement." She cradled the cup in her hands and sat down at the dining nook's glass-topped table.

Up until that moment, Maggie's marital situation had been of no interest to Bliss. Now, he sensed there might be something to be gained by exploring the subject. "Are you pleased about this divorce?" he asked.

"No, but I thought I could handle it until I found out there was another woman involved, someone I know—Kathy Elliott." Maggie was surprised to find none of it seemed quite so important anymore. The pain was almost gone.

"How did you find out about the other woman? Did Bill tell you?" Human behavior fascinated him.

"Heavens, no. It was a psychic at Cassadaga. You know what a psychic is?"

"Yes, someone with heightened intuitive powers, I believe."

"Yes. Anyway, I went to Cassadaga with a group of friends. It's a small town filled with psychics and mediums and such. It was the first time I'd ever done anything like that, but my friends had been many times before. They recommended Victoria Chambers; she's quite well known and has a good reputation for accuracy. Anyhow, I went in as a skeptic, but she told me things about myself, personal things that no one else knew about but me. Victoria saw the divorce coming and warned me there was someone else involved."

"She named the person?"

"No, not the name, but she described her so well, I recognized Kathy right away. Victoria advised me to hire a private detective to improve my position during the divorce proceedings. She said it would be necessary to protect myself, because Bill would behave in ways that were totally out of character."

"So, you hired the detective?"

"No, I was in denial. I didn't want to face the truth; I tried to convince myself there wasn't anyone else, and that I still had a chance with Bill. When he asked me for a divorce just as Victoria had said he would, I was shocked and hurt, but I didn't want revenge. I cared too much for Bill to hurt him or make him pay for his pleasure. In the beginning the settlement was an equitable one, or so I thought." she said, thinking of the lawyer's latest demand that she give up her beach house.

"And, now, you're not sure?"

"I'm not sure about anything, anymore. It's strange, my feelings are all mixed up."

Bliss did not want to go there. "Have you been back to this psychic, recently?"

"Not professionally. We've become friends. We do lunch, when Victoria's in Miami, go to seminars together, things like that."

Good, then maybe I haven't shown up on her radar. Bliss thought.

"Tell me more about Kathy Elliott, what's she like? Young? Pretty?" He hoped so.

"Yes, to both," she sighed. "She's in her mid-twenties, pretty in a blonde bombshell sort of way and very aggressive. Bill hired her as Advertising Director for Danvers Pharmaceuticals three years ago, and she set her cap for him right away."

"Is Bill fond of hats?"

"No, Bliss, it's another one of those language things. Bill doesn't have a hat fetish—to 'set her cap' means Kathy intended to have him."

"It's very confusing. I will need your assistance in becoming more proficient in English."

"Everything I have is yours, Bliss," she said with a seductive smile.

To him, 'everything' included information about all her women friends. Two new names had been added to his list—Kathy Elliott and Victoria Chambers.

Bliss took Maggie's hand in his and gazed deeply into her eyes as his mind swept hers clean and planted suggestions. He was setting the stage for his departure, mentally auditioning a new cast of players while Maggie sleepwalked through life, living for Blissful moments that were fewer and farther between.

On Wednesday, Bliss sent Maggie out to run errands for him. He needed a new wardrobe. Then, there was the eyebrow issue. Certain implements were required for the implants and the fewer who knew about it, the better. It was much safer to do it himself. Maggie followed his instructions without question, rushing from shop to shop. Dressed in a long sleeve blouse, pullover sweater and wool slacks, Maggie was chilled to the bone in spite of the tropical weather.

When she staggered through the door in the early evening, buckling under the load of her parcels, like any typical male, Bliss announced he was hungry. Maggie looked and felt terrible. Her head throbbed, and the numbing cold had settled into a dull ache somewhere in her mid-section near her backbone, but the moment Bliss took her in his arms, those discomforts were forgotten.

He entered her body, penetrated her mind, drew on Maggie's desires and transformed her nebulous dreams into reality. She rode high on a wave of churning sexual ecstasy until it crashed in a frantic finale and her remaining essence flowed out to Bliss.

Afterward, she lay totally spent, wrapped in his arms. Maggie pressed even closer, in a vain attempt to absorb some of his body warmth.

"Bliss, I'm so cold. Did you turn up the air conditioning?" *Men are so hot-blooded*, she thought. Bliss was roasting. He glowed with heat like a wood-burning stove.

"Relax, love, close your eyes, there's a good girl," he said as he drew another blanket over her. A few weeks ago, Maggie would have bridled at his patronizing words, but under the spell of his hypnotic charms, she obediently complied.

In a few minutes, she was sound asleep. Upon reaching the deeper layers of slumber, she dreamed that she was naked, afloat on a huge iceberg, alone.

Wide-awake, Bliss stared out into the darkness broken only by a pale sliver of moonlight that sliced through the curtain break in the patio doors. Beside him, Maggie twitched and mumbled in her sleep. In the last stages of her depletion, she alternated between comatose and insomniac. Soon, she would return to a more normal physical state, but her emotional life would never be the same.

Suddenly, Maggie thrashed about wildly and moaned, as she struggled to free herself from the clutches of yet another nightmare.

"What is it, Maggie?" Bliss asked in a soothing tone. He was growing fond of her, not a good sign. He had already been here too long.

But even before she was fully awake the fear had faded, merely a residue of her former emotions, existing only in her dreams as half forgotten memories. Living without any fear can be dangerous, as Maggie would soon find out.

"It was a dream about Brian . . . and Bill," she confessed, "all mixed up with ice and snow . . . then I was alone, adrift on an iceberg."

"Forget about the past," he said. "We all have things we'd rather not think about." As he held her in his arms, Bliss had a momentary lapse, a mini-scuffle with his conscience, but it was a battle destined to end swiftly in favor of survival. In the beginning, the feeding had both disgusted and excited him at the same time. After each feeding, he had vowed he would never do it again, but once the hunger returned Bliss' resolve vanished. For the first few decades, he tried to keep the feeding at a minimum, filled with self-loathing at what he had become. But with the passage of time, his needs triumphed over any sense of integrity or ethics.

Over the eons, Bliss had suffered though periods of reversal, raging guilt, shame and denial but such confrontations with his inner self occurred farther and farther apart. He preyed on the finer emotions and experienced most of the lesser ones. On each world he visited, Bliss surrounded himself with beautiful things to stave off the loneliness, and to compensate for the lack of any real relationships.

The curse was taking its toll.

But other forces were at work, more powerful more compelling than Cassandra, bringing him closer to an inexorable moment written in the book of fate.

Chapter 17

Victoria Chambers was the last guest to arrive at Maggie's party. Cars filled the parking area near the house and snaked up and down the shoulders of the road in both directions. After a persistent search and several skillful maneuvers, she squeezed her white sports car into a vacant space. It was a tight fit. *I'm going to need a shoehorn to get it out of here*, she thought. As she hiked back up to the house, she got sand in her shoes. All in all, it contributed to her disgruntled, out-of-sorts feelings.

Inwardly, she groaned as she approached Maggie's house. This wasn't the gathering of a few close friends, she'd envisioned, it was a major event. The crowd from the beach house overflowed the pool area and spilled down to the ocean's edge. She fervently hoped Maggie hadn't invited her as part of the entertainment. Psychics were always an interesting novelty at parties whether they wanted to be or not. Like musicians, they were often expected to perform for free.

Near the edge of the pool area, she hesitated, scanning the crowd for a familiar face. Her azure blue eyes added to her look of childlike innocence and several rapid blinks betrayed her nervousness. Her gaze flicked from the pool to the house and back again. Victoria did not like crowds. Too many people, too many impressions, she was already buzzing from the energy. Standing partially hidden in the shadows, she vacillated, *should I stay or go?*

Then, someone waved at her from across the pool and Victoria was caught like a deer in headlights. She waved back and began to move toward her friend. Out of the corner of his eye, Bliss saw her at the same time. Victoria's white jumpsuit had flagged his attention as she emerged from the darkness. His eyes followed her as she threaded her way through the crowd and stopped to greet a tall attractive brunette standing with a group of people just a few yards away from Bliss.

When Victoria turned in his direction, Bliss caught her gaze and held it. She stared into the disconcerting pair of unusual emerald eyes and felt a flush creep up her chest to her throat. Suddenly, the air seemed supercharged. Embarrassed, she broke the eye contact first.

Meanwhile, as her friend Marilyn chattered on, Victoria's eyes strayed back to the tall, interesting stranger. Something in his stance, the shape of his head drew her. In her heightened state of sensitivity, she received three quick impressions: superior intelligence, supreme confidence and a passionate hunger. *Interesting, indeed.*

Then the last half of one of Marilyn's run-on sentences grabbed her attention

"He just bought the old Haley mansion. You know, the one overlooking the ocean down off Neely's point. It has the best view in Miami. The place is huge, why it must have at least thirty-five rooms. Can you imagine how much it will cost to furnish it, let alone cool it—with all those high ceilings? I do love me lots of lovely ceilings. My God, he must be loaded or crazy, or both."

"From what I've heard, the estate is in a sad state of disrepair," Victoria said. "The previous owners couldn't afford to keep it up. Perhaps the new owner will renovate the mansion. It's such a lovely old landmark." Victoria knew the house well.

When she was eight years old, she and her mother were weekend guests at the Haley mansion. Victoria had quickly fallen under the influence of the house, enthralled by the atmosphere of southern charm and elegance in the antebellum style mansion that dated back to pre-Civil War days. She intuitively picked up the remnants of a spirited past that lingered on, impressions that appealed to her romantic nature and active imagination. Playing with her dolls on the second-floor landing, Victoria had sworn to her mother that she had heard the tinkling laughter of a southern belle engaged in a happy flirtation, followed by the rustle of long, stiff skirts and crinolines on the stairs.

Caught up in her memories, it was a few moments before Victoria came back to the present and found herself once again snared by those emerald eyes. She shifted her gaze, feigning interest in the conversation flowing around her. But it was total pretense; Victoria had no idea what they were saying. She felt giddy, light-headed, glad to be alive and not knowing exactly why. The party entered an exciting new dimension of heightened senses; colors became more vivid, smells were sweeter, even the air she breathed seemed heady and invigorating.

A few feet away from her, Bliss experienced the exact same sensations as both of them existed on two levels: On the surface they interacted with the others around them, but beneath the surface churned an undercurrent of awareness of each other's every movement.

Victoria forced herself to concentrate on what the silly woman next to her was going on and on about. Meanwhile, Bliss could stand it no longer; he had to find out who she was. Excusing himself from a throng of female admirers, he moved with panther-like grace to her side.

As she turned to sneak another covert glance, Victoria found herself eyeball to eyeball with its intended recipient and recoiled in surprise. Tactfully, Bliss stepped back a foot.

"Have I met you somewhere before . . . long ago, in a galaxy far away?" he asked, his eyes deepening with pleasure. "Aren't you a princess I once rescued from dull companions?"

"I don't think so," she said, cocking her head slightly to the left, indicating the group she had been conversing with. "Perhaps you're merely the victim of an overactive imagination and an addiction to sci fi films," she said, as she extended her hand. "I'm Victoria Chambers."

"It's a pleasure to meet you. I'm Jonathan Bliss, but everyone calls me Bliss." He took her hand and gallantly brought it to his lips. With the initial contact, a wave of feelings flowed out to engulf him—compassion, kindness, and tenderness combined with purity of heart and a genuine love for humanity. The emotions were of such depth and scope that they constituted an entirely new experience for Bliss. The wave washed over him and left him refreshed like a hot shower after a day in a quagmire. *What an aura! What a woman!*

Her mouth turned up in amusement. "May I have my hand back?"

"Oh, yes, certainly. Forgive me, but now that I've found you. I hate to let you go."

Victoria extricated her hand from his and looked away, blushing. She hated that aspect of herself and her highly emotional nature, but it was an unavoidable barometer of her feelings. Unskilled in the art of flirtation and at a loss for words, she desperately cast about for a topic, any topic. She said the first thing that came into her head. "The name Jonathan means Gift of God?"

"Yes, you're right, it does." Bliss agreed.

A flash of intuitive cognition shot through Victoria's consciousness. In her mind's eye appeared a dark, sultry woman with long black hair, billowing out around her head. Loud laughter tinged with madness rang in Victoria's ears. A dark cloud threatened to engulf Bliss. Victoria attempted to warn him.

"You're in terrible danger from a dark-haired, olive skinned woman."

But is it in past, the present or the future? Victoria wondered. Time was the most difficult aspect for a psychic to nail down.

"Do you know what I'm talking about?" she asked.

"What ... no ... I don't."

"She's a powerful woman," she repeated, growing impatient with him. "I'm a psychic. I see things, events in people's lives, their pasts and futures. I pick up impressions from them." She sensed the woman's ill intent; it was virulent, crushing. "Do you know this woman?" *Maybe he hasn't met her yet.* "Does this mean anything to you? She wants to hurt you, she's after revenge."

"No, I'm sorry to disappoint you, but I have no idea what you're talking about. Perhaps you're picking the information up from someone else. There is no one who wishes me harm." Victoria's knowing unnerved him.

She sensed his avoidance, but another vision was quickly taking shape. She was picking up Maggie Danvers and a bone chilling cold. Icy fingers clutched at Victoria's heart, and a shiver ran through her. It was a now familiar feeling, akin to the one she had felt in New York during her meditation. The hairs on her arms went on alert, tiny sentinels that rose up in warning as Victoria opened her mouth to speak.

Then suddenly, a curtain fell in her mind. For the first time in her life, Victoria drew a complete blank, and the surprise of the shutdown threw her off. Confused, she stared at Bliss, her eyes clouding with concern.

Bliss put out a hand to steady her, sensing how much he had disconcerted her. Although she made him uneasy, he was fascinated by her and wanted to know more. Fearing her intuitive powers, he had erected a barrier against them. With the block in place, he was no longer concerned about what he might inadvertently reveal.

Victoria's hand smoothed her forehead, her fingers massaging her temple. "Strange, very strange. Nothing like this has ever happened before. I was receiving an impression, then abruptly, it vanished . . . like a disconnected phone call."

She eyed him suspiciously. "Are you a psychic?" It was the only explanation Victoria could think of; a negation of her powers by a similar or stronger force.

"No, not that I know of. So, you are the famous seer Maggie told me about. Do you pick up anything from me, right now?"

"Absolutely nothing," she said. It was unsettling. Victoria never had any trouble with readings, even when a client resisted her; they were always open books. It was the first time she'd been faced with dead air and a blank-page.

His eyes were riveted on her mouth. She had the most sensuous, seductive lips he had ever seen. All his thoughts centered on how it would feel to have his mouth on hers. But Bliss sensed Victoria's discomfort and brought his focus back to reality with considerable difficulty and attempted to put her at ease.

"If this were one of the times when you could read minds," he said, "you'd know that I think you are one of the loveliest ladies I've ever met." And their numbers were legion. "Tell me everything about yourself. Please, don't leave anything out, from the day you were born right up to this minute."

"Everything?"

"Yes, don't leave out a comma," he encouraged her.

"Well, I remember a long dark tunnel, then bursting into the light. I could gloss over, say the first couple of hundred diaper changes. You're sure you want to hear this?"

Bliss held up his hands in mock surrender. "Wait, I think we need to sit down for this, it might take longer than I thought." It could take forever as far as he was concerned, but he didn't have forever, or did he?

"Are you here with someone?" he asked.

"No, I have friends here, but no date, if that's what you mean." A smile from deep within her eyes reached out to gently touch his heart.

Conversation ceased to matter. Victoria was so alluring, so beautiful—she could have recited her ABC's and enthralled him. Something deep inside, grown cramped and stiff from suppression, began a delicate unfolding. The release manifested in a tremendous surge of exhilaration, Bliss was higher than a cypress tree.

Many of the guests had drifted down toward the beach, giving them more privacy. He spied a vacant table in a secluded area and grabbed her by the hand. "Come with me, Princess. Let's sit over there and get better acquainted." Bliss said as he led her on.

Victoria went willingly. Nothing short of a crowbar could pry her from his side.

144

He deftly steered her around the remaining knots of people by the pool, heading toward a table on the far side of the patio area where a flaming torch cast wavering shadows over the white wicker table. In the center of the table, white candles and orchids floated on top of the water in a clear, shallow glass bowl.

As she walked toward the table, Victoria was acutely aware of the pressure of his hand on the small of her back. The leaves on the trees stood out in sharp relief, and the night scents of sand, sea air and tropical flowers mixed and merged and yet were easily distinguished from the smells of cooking odors, perfume and stale cigarettes. Her ears picked up layer upon layer of sound; the buzz of insects, the low drone and murmur of distant conversation and the plaintive cry of a night bird.

Bliss pulled out a chair for her and motioned to a passing waiter bearing a tray of champagne glasses. They sat and slowly sipped their drinks. After the first few nervous moments had passed, it was as if a dam had burst and words tumbled out, and they behaved like long lost friends, starved for news of each other. Bliss parceled out his past in the form of a fable he felt Victoria could relate to. Both of them loved and appreciated beauty in nature, thought and form and in touching on these subjects they reached common ground.

Bliss directed his most seductive 'gets 'em every time' looks straight to her heart, but Victoria sensed the underlying pain and sadness lurking behind the Casanova eyes, and she yearned to erase the hurt although she could not seem to fathom the cause.

Their conversation touched on many topics, factual and philosophical in a meeting of mind, heart and soul. The rest of the world retreated.

Bliss admired the way Victoria used her psychic talents in the service of others. "I charge a nominal fee, I'm a poor man's psychiatrist," she said with a laugh.

"People like you could destroy the entire capitalistic concept," he warned her.

Victoria laughed at him. "Never fear, I assure you we are in no danger of mass unselfishness."

She briefly mentioned her early marriage and subsequent divorce. From her dealings with her clients and her own personal experience, Victoria said she thought marriage might well be the first step toward divorce.

Marriage often meant offspring. Having some scruples, Bliss avoided women with young children. He preferred not to inflict emotionless mothers on them, although in some cases, he thought it might be an improvement.

So, it was with reluctance that he asked, "Do you have any children?"

"Regretfully, no. However, it's a situation I've learned to live with. If you can't change something," she said, philosophically, "there's no point in railing against the fates and making yourself and everyone around you miserable. I can't change it, so I accept it. And as time goes by, I find myself truly happy with things as they are."

"What a shame there are no little Victoria's running around."

"One," she said, "is more than enough. I don't need a tiny replica of myself to experience fulfillment." Her face changed, taking on a look he couldn't' comprehend. "Sometimes parents don't even like their children, so maybe I'm not missing anything. My work is enough. My grandmother Mamie once told me the reward of helping people extricate themselves from the tangled web of their lives is more important to the soul's progress than leading a little child."

"Your grandmother was a wise woman. It must be hereditary."

"No, not always," Victoria mused. "Sometimes it completely skips a generation. Oh, I'm sorry, that's not nice, that was a catty dig at my mother. She's a pleasure seeker by profession." Victoria inwardly winced, she rarely criticized others, especially family and to someone she'd just met.

"Pleasure seeking, is that so horrible?" Bliss experienced discomfort at the notion.

"When self-gratification is the driving force in a person's life, and they do exactly as they please without any respect or consideration for others, then yes, it is horrible."

"Is your mother like that?" Bliss asked. If so, he'd like to meet the lady.

"Not really, not totally, I'm being unfair. It's just that she irritated me recently by doing something selfish, and I haven't forgiven her, yet—emphasis on the yet. Maybe mother is just a product of the times we live in. Our society is geared toward quick money, fast food, instant sex and rapid highs on drugs. I see so much of it in my client's lives. Sometimes, it depresses me, seeing so many people desperately seeking the very things that will eventually destroy them."

"You can't save everyone, Victoria."

"That's just it, Bliss. I can't save anyone except maybe myself. But I can help them to know themselves, to find some peace, and to learn to listen to that still, small voice within."

"Maybe that's enough," he said, his deep green eyes full of unreadable emotions.

"Yes, perhaps it is."

Without warning, Maggie descended on them like a bird of prey, swooping down on them in a flurry of words.

"Well, fine-ally, I've found you. I've been looking all over the place for you two, and here you are—together. Bliss, you are my escort, and the guest of honor, you should be by my side, for heavens sake."

Bliss rose, smiling sheepishly against the onslaught. Maggie took his arm possessively and molded her body to his.

"And you, Victoria—everyone is dying to meet you, the famous psychic, hoping you'll do a reading for them. You should have let me know you were here," she chided.

Victoria felt as if she'd just been nabbed by the truant officer.

Maggie smiled up at Bliss, who deliberately avoided her gaze. "At least you've met Bliss," she said, swiveling her head to beam at Victoria. "Isn't he something?"

Before Victoria could comment, Maggie bent down and whispered in her ear. "He's absolutely adorable when he wakes up in the morning."

The hand resting on Victoria's arm was unusually cold. It sent a shudder through her. At a loss for words, Victoria managed a polite nod. Suddenly, the magic of the evening had disappeared.

Maggie led Bliss away, calling over her shoulder; "We'll see you later, sweetie. Just stay right where you are. I'll send some people over."

They walked away, and as they did, Bliss glanced back over his shoulder at Victoria and mouthed a silent, "I'll call you."

How could he? Victoria's number was unlisted. She felt sure Maggie wasn't going to give it to him. She teetered on the keen edge of disappointment, doing a delicate balancing act, not wanting to fall into a pit of depression. The relationship between Maggie and Bliss was obviously an intimate one. Of course, almost no man existed without some form of entanglement, be it lover, wife or mother. She knew Bliss would have to make his own decisions about the people he wanted in his life.

Maggie seemed so different, not at all like Victoria remembered her. *Who was that masked woman?* Victoria wondered. Her entire demeanor had changed, now there was a bright, glittering hardness in her eyes and a false, forced gaiety in her voice. Maggie was putting up some sort of front, faking it, but Victoria knew her friend was no phony. The change was radical and disturbing. Maggie had not been at all happy to find her with Bliss. In fact, Victoria felt decidedly unwelcome, especially after the whispered remark designed to warn her off.

The rapport she had established with Bliss had vanished like mist in the soft night air. But she knew the connection had been real, not something she had imagined. Victoria rose and prepared to leave the party. As far as she was concerned, the evening was over. But it was too late, a gaggle of giggling young women lurched toward her, bringing their unanswered questions, problems, hopes and dreams. Victoria rarely ever drank, so she hoped the champagne she had consumed would not affect her perceptions.

One of the young women pointed at her. "You're the psychic? Right? Maggie said you'd give us a reading."

Smiling a sincere welcome, she asked, "Who would like to be first?"

The group pushed a plump girl wearing a red sundress into the vacant chair next to Victoria. She held the young woman's hands in her own and meditated for a moment. "Someone very close to you has a lump in her breast," Victoria said, tapping her chest. "Here."

The girl's eyes widened. "Don't worry," Victoria continued, "everything will be fine. It's a benign tumor. She will need to have it removed, but it's not malignant."

"How did you know? She's going into the hospital to-to-morrow," she stammered. "It's my mother."

Victoria went on to speak of the girl's childhood, her personality, touching on all the elements of her life that influenced the woman she had become. Then, Victoria mentioned an ongoing intimate relationship. "There's a man in your life who poses a threat to you. You know the one I'm talking about. He's not good for you. If you continue to see him, he will do you physical harm. Trust me, this guy is dangerous, he abuses women, including his wife. He's a tall man with dark hair, his name is Mike or Mark."

"Yes, I understand what you're saying, but I don't think I can stop seeing Mark, I love him," the girl admitted.

"It's up to you," Victoria said. "I can only tell you what I see. If you don't end this affair, quickly, he will hurt you, physically, as well as emotionally." She knew the girl was going to ignore her warning.

Victoria never ended a reading on the down side; her next words were of encouragement and hope as she steered the girl in the right direction for an upcoming career move. She ended by telling of a man in her future, one who would be right for her and bring much happiness. When the young woman rose to leave, she felt good about herself.

The readings continued for an hour past midnight, and she longed for the comfort of her bed. But as always, once engaged in the business of helping people sort out their lives, Victoria forgot about her own, absorbed by each person's situation and opportunities.

Finally, she finished the last reading and her weariness caught up with her. She dropped her face in her hands and rubbed her throbbing forehead. When she lifted her head and looked up, she stared into familiar emerald eyes.

Bliss indicated the empty chair. "May I sit down?"

"Of course," she said, as her eyes scanned the pool area. "Where's Maggie?"

"Never mind Maggie, this doesn't concern her."

He took both of her hands in his as he had seen her do during her readings. "Now, let me tell your future. There is a tall, blond stranger in it. You're going to be seeing a lot of him. But not for a while, because I'm leaving for New York in the morning."

Victoria's emotions went on a roller coaster ride-up and down-a slow climb, then a quick descent. She tried not to let the disappointment show in her face, but she was too tired to fabricate emotions.

"It's not that I don't want to see you sooner. This is my farewell evening with Maggie. We won't be seeing each other any more. My trip to New York is necessary to raise some quick cash to cover a real estate deal. I'm closing on the Haley Mansion."

Victoria's face brightened. "So, you're the one who's buying the Haley estate. I can't believe it. What do you plan to do with it? Please tell me you're not going to sub-divide the land and put in rows and rows of luxury condos."

"Goodness, no! I'm going to restore the mansion and live there. It sounds like you know the place."

"Know it, I love it! I visited there as a child. It's a wonderful home, warm and inviting. There is nothing but good vibes in those old walls, only pleasant memories live there."

"Well, since you think so much of it, I'd value your opinion on my plans for the restoration. Shall we get together when I get back from New York?"

"When will that be?"

"Oh, maybe two or three weeks."

Victoria frowned. "I should still be here."

"You don't live here?"

"I spend a lot of time here, but my home is in New York. I'm here on a missing child case. This is the third one in as many months. I can't quite get a fix on the killer, but I will."

"I hope you find this child alive," he said, showing genuine concern.

"So, do I."

"Good luck, then. I'll call you when I get back. Since I don't have an office as yet or a home phone, I'll have to get in touch with you. I'm getting a new cell phone tomorrow." He didn't plan to give Maggie his new number.

Victoria quickly found a business card given to her by someone else and penciled in her name and private, unlisted phone number on the back. As an afterthought, she added her address in Miami.

She handed the card to him. "What sort of business are you in?"

"Investments, stocks, commodities, anything with a quick turnover."

"I wish you success in New York," she said, standing. "I really must be going."

Bliss rose with her, taking her hand, "Good night, sweet lady." He gently brushed the back of her hand with his lips. "Take care of yourself while I'm away."

Their eyes met and held for an instant before she withdrew her fingers from his. "I'll say goodnight to my hostess on the way out. Do you know where she is?"

Bliss walked with her to where Maggie stood in deep conversation with a couple, their voices raised in heated argument. Victoria stopped, not wanting to intrude on a private matter. From her vantage point, she could clearly see Maggie's face; it was a cold, hard mask of bitterness.

Victoria turned to Bliss and touched his arm tentatively. "Is Maggie all right? She seems so different, so cool and aloof."

Bliss ducked his head, not wanting to look Victoria in the eye. "She's under an enormous strain, that's all. The couple she's talking to—it's her husband Bill and his friend, Kathy Elliott."

Victoria glanced back at the couple in dismay. "Did Maggie actually invite them here tonight?" Victoria wondered why Maggie would want to inflict that kind of pain on herself.

"Yes, she insisted they come. I think the idea was to have Bill meet me and, well, you get the picture."

"Yes, and now, we're seeing what develops. I'm surprised; vendettas aren't Maggie's style. On second thought, I think I'll just slip out of here, unnoticed. It's been a pleasure meeting you, Bliss."

Looking toward the troubled threesome, she added, "Good luck, I think you're going to need it."

He ignored them. "May I walk you to the car?"

"No, that's all right, I'll be fine, but I think Maggie might need rescuing." She saw Kathy tug on Bill's arm in a vain attempt at retreat.

"Or Bill," he said, with a sardonic grin. "You're something; always thinking about someone else."

"Flattery will get you everywhere," she said, starting down the drive. "Good night."

"Sweet dreams, Victoria," he called after her. Bliss stood watching her with a strange glimmer in his eyes until she disappeared from view.

Later that night, Bliss dreamed of going home to Arias.

In her own bed, Victoria slept the deep, untroubled sleep of one with a clear conscience. In her dreams, Bliss appeared with a crown of red roses on his head—the symbol of spiritual love. It was the sign of Victoria's soulmate one Grandmother Mamie had foretold many years ago. Strange that it had come in a dream. What if anything, did that mean?

Chapter 18

The next afternoon in a luxurious beachfront villa, Bliss utilized another one of Maggie's contacts. He had lifted the address from Maggie's handsome gold-tooled address book. Beneath him, supine on a peach satin comforter rested Kathy Elliott, a smile of supreme satisfaction on her flawless face. Driving home his point, Bliss achieved rejuvenation and a convoluted form of revenge for Maggie in one bold stroke. He had delayed his departure for three days just for this moment—mission accomplished.

His original intent had been to go straight to New York City, but a major portion of his bankroll had been depleted by what he deemed to be necessary expenditures; a new limousine, and earnest money as part of the contract for the Haley estate, clothing for himself and Bodkins, and their traveling expenses. Bliss needed to replenish his cash. Las Vegas beckoned.

As soon as they had registered at the Caesar's Palace Hotel, Bliss and Bodkins went up to their room, but Bliss didn't bother to unpack. It was a shame, he thought, not to stay long enough to enjoy the wide-screen TV, computerized Jacuzzi or the enticing circular bed that rotated beneath the mirrored ceiling. But these attractive extras designed to appeal to high rolling hedonists, were not the reason Bliss had chosen Caesar's. His choice was based on the fact that the hotel's casinos boasted the highest betting limits in the world, and Bliss intended to work his way up and down the strip and save Caesar's gaming tables—the best—for last.

On their way out of the hotel, they passed the open door to one of the lounges. Bliss gazed inside and briefly assessed the charms of the predatory princesses perched at the bar, waiting to pounce on unwary players and separate them from their winnings.

Bliss and the adult Disneyland in the desert were made for each other. He roamed up and down the strip, reveling in its archaic decadence and glamorous fantasy environment. To Bliss, it was like walking through a huge bakery. He drew in several deep breaths and experienced a sensual vicarious pleasure from the emotional energies churned up in the gaming palaces.

Bodkins followed at a discreet distance, watching Bliss' back. At the Luxor, Bliss strolled through the casino gathering information. His game of choice was blackjack. With his photographic memory, it was easy for Bliss to keep track of the card count and place his bets accordingly and rake in his winnings. He knew that the tables were carefully monitored and consistent winners aroused suspicion. If he won too much and they suspected him of counting cards or cheating in some way, the casino would put the word out on the strip about him and relay a full description of him to their unseen observers who would pick him up on the spot.

There was no way the pit bosses could figure out how Bliss was winning. When the scrutiny became too intense, Bliss flashed Bodkins a pre-arranged signal, cashed in his chips and headed for the men's room nearest the Luxor's casino exit. Meanwhile Bodkins had entered the restroom, located and disabled the hidden cameras and placed an "out of order" sign on the men's room door. A few minutes later, Bliss arrived, slipped into a stall, morphed into a completely different identity and placed a tall stack of bills on the toilet paper dispenser. As he left, Bodkins came in, entered the stall and retrieved the thick wad of cash and stuffed the bills into a small duffle bag. Then he pulled a baseball cap from his pocket and tugged the brim low over his eyes. Then he turned his jacket inside out, creating an instant change from black to beige. "Elvis has left the building," Bodkins said, as he strode out of the men's room. Now, they had their seed money.

Casino by casino, they worked their way back to Caesar's, winning all the way, leaving a series of befuddled surveillance teams behind them scratching their heads. On their way into the high stakes gaming areas at Caesars, they walked through several banks of slot machines. As they passed the Million-Dollar Jackpot slot, the machine dinged, announcing a small payoff. When the player at the machine cashed out, Bodkins walked over and touched the machine.

"It feels warm. I think this baby is ready to pop."

"What makes you say that?"

"Well, it's a progressive slot and it's near the end of a down cycle, entering a pay cycle, and it's located near the casino entrance where a payoff attracts a lot of attention so they rig them to pay off more often." Bodkins found any mechanical device intriguing. "This particular machine always pays off between $48,000 and $62,000." Bodkins reached out and grasped the handle of the slot. "Right now, it's sitting at $60,000. Why don't we play it?"

"Maybe it's time somebody else got lucky." Bliss said, eyeing an older woman sitting at a nearby machine with a dejected look on her face.

Molly Hayes had just bet her last dollar and lost. She sighed and rose from her chair. Bliss approached her, "I believe you dropped this."

"Why no, young man, it's not mine," she said. Molly might be poor, but she was honest.

"Well, consider it a gift from me," he said placing a bill in her hand and closing her fingers around it. With the contact he saw flashes of her life. *Definitely a good choice*, he thought. He took her arm and steered her toward the hot machine. "Play these lucky bucks in this machine, I've got a feeling about it," Bliss said as he pulled some more money from his pocket and placed the cash in her hand.

Molly hesitated for a moment until she saw another player headed for *her* machine. She sat down quickly, inserted the bills and pulled the handle. The symbols spun and then clicked into place. JACKPOT! JACKPOT! JACKPOT! Lights went off, bells rang. Molly clutched her chest and exclaimed over and over, "Oh, my . . . Oh, my . . . Oh, my." When she caught her breath and turned to thank her benefactors, they were gone.

On Sunday afternoon, millions of dollars richer, Bliss and Bodkins boarded a 747 bound for New York City. Several hours later, the stewardess made the traditional announcement. "We are making our final approach to La Guardia and will be landing in a few moments, please stay in your seats until the airplane has reached the terminal and the seat belt signs have been turned off."

Bliss thought the words *final approach* and *terminal* gave the landing an ominous sound. Earth's antiquated modes of travel were getting on his nerves. *My cruiser would have been here hours ago*. But his impatience had not dampened his enthusiasm. Bliss was as excited as a kid coming down the stairs on Christmas morning. As the plane dipped, he peered out the window, seeing the huge city for the first time. Even Bliss, jaded though he might be, could not help but be impressed by the New York City skyline. He stared in wonder at mile after mile of asphalt and stone with its forest of steel and glass jutting into the sky. His senses were slammed and buffeted by the waves of energy and emotion rising from the congested corridors of concrete below. The vibrations were intense even from that height. *New York! New York! So many women, so little time.*

After a period of what seemed like endless circling the plane landed, and Bodkins collected the luggage. A few minutes later, they stood beside a taxi as the driver threw their bags in the trunk. The dark, swarthy man hailed from an obscure Third World country and spoke in an untranslatable dialect punctuated by English expletives. Even with all the linguistic knowledge Bliss had assimilated, he could not understand what the man was saying. Finally, Bliss gave up. Bodkins drew a detailed map and wrote down the name of their hotel.

The yellow missile launched itself from the airport curb with tires squealing. The driver darted in and out of traffic like a needle in a hyperactive sewing machine. Countless decades of interstellar travel had not prepared the cosmic jockeys for the danger of a journey of so few miles. The taxi had two speeds, 70 miles per hour and stop. Bliss and

Bodkins struggled to remain upright but ended up tumbling over each other like two dice in a tin can. The taxi driver chose the long route into the city, complete with a grand tour of Harlem. As he steered with one hand, he used the other hand to blast out a staccato beat on the horn. Pedestrians ran for cover and any second, Bliss expected bodies to come flying over the hood.

"Bodkins, do you see those white lines in the pedestrian crosswalks? I thought they were safety zones, but I must have misunderstood, I think they must use those markings to measure how far a body is thrown on impact."

Bodkins sat back and closed his eyes.

In spite of the heat, and the air conditioner turned up to full freeze, the driver kept his window rolled down so he could stick his head out and curse anything that walked, talked or moved.

By the time the cab screeched to a halt in front of the Hemsley Palace Hotel, Bliss was simply glad to be alive. Totally disoriented, Bodkins kept moving his head, first to the left then to the right in jerky uncontrollable circular motions.

The elegant interior of the Hemsley Hotel was a welcome sight. Bliss checked into their suite and sent Bodkins to buy newspapers and magazines. The rooms were exactly to his taste; two bedrooms, a sitting room and bath, all furnished with an eye for comfort and luxury. The bathroom was fully equipped with every amenity, including a telephone and a large dressing area. Bliss ran a bath, settled into the steaming water and pondered his plans for the next few days.

As he plotted his next move, an errant thought crept in, out of sync with the rest. In his mind's eye, he beheld Victoria's lovely face in the candlelight. He couldn't help himself as he recalled the force of her personality and the delightful turns of her mind. He was anxious to see her again. In fact, he wanted to be with her more than he had ever wanted to be with any female. But the longing was something more than the physical, something apart from the hunger and his renewal, and it frightened him. She frightened him.

Victoria was sensitive and perceptive; a woman who tuned into cosmic vibrations, a woman not easily deceived. Anyway, Bliss didn't have relationships with women. He fed on their emotions and lived on while they aged and then ceased to be. Not that he, every minute of the day, wanted to live forever, but his fear of dying and the unknown was greater than his death wish. Bliss didn't have emotions; they had him; anger, resentment, guilt.

What would happen if he made love to Victoria? *Will there be anything left of what I find so desirable in her*? Higher emotions gave humans access to the spiritual realm, a vital part of Victoria's life. For him, that door seemed to be locked, maybe forever.

He wondered if he could nibble at her emotions, go to Victoria for occasional snacks and prolong the contact? Bliss had never tried such a thing. In all the years of his feeding, he had focused on survival, control was not an option, or was it? Questions led to more questions, without any answers. *Why do I care? She's just another female.* In all the time since the curse had been placed on him, mercy had never moved him, nor had a conscience constricted his quest for new victims. But Victoria was different, and Bliss didn't know why or what made it so.

Perhaps he should let Victoria be the one that got away. There were plenty of others, a world full of others, but she was the one woman he could not forget.

After his bath, Bliss called Victoria. They talked for an hour and a part of him felt fulfilled in a way that none of his sexual feedings had—before or after the curse. The next morning, he sent her flowers, her favorite, yellow roses. Knowing exactly what a woman liked and wanted made courtship easier.

On another level, Bliss was grateful to Victoria. Her intuitive abilities had provided the leap of logic that would help him make a killing in the commodities market. While kissing her hand during his initial contact with her, Bliss had acquired valuable information via a series of strong psychic perceptions channeled through her to him. Telepathically he had picked up information from another psychic, someone Victoria had recently spoken with. The words reverberated in his brain . . . *Impending unusual weather conditions in South America, a vision of drenching rains, an early harvest of a poor crop of reddish berries.*

Bliss knew the events were imminent, but he required more specific information. On Monday morning, he set out for Wall Street in one of the dreaded taxis. Before climbing into the deathtrap, he shook the startled driver's hand.

He glanced at the I.D. on the visor, and said, "Good morning, Amir," as he grasped the man's hand in a firm grip.

"You will drive carefully and safely," Bliss said, "or I will remove certain important parts of your anatomy with a rusty blade."

In a trance, Amir stared at the man with the hypnotic green eyes and nodded his head in agreement. Bliss shuddered and released the driver's hand, having drained the man's excess emotions in the process. Such emotions always left an unpleasant taste in his mouth, akin to rotten grapefruit. But it made for a much more enjoyable ride because Amir drove in an exemplary fashion, docile and courteous, and Bliss arrived at Trinity Place in one piece.

He strolled the narrow streets of the financial district, fascinated by the incongruity of Dickensian style counting houses of the 19th century nestled among the high rises. The vast sheets of concrete soared skyward and allowed but a hint of blue and patches of sunlight that filtered down to the pavement below. The air was oppressive, hanging heavy like syrup between the tall buildings.

To him it seemed as if New York's entire population had taken a coffee break at one time in some sort of mass evacuation. The sidewalks were filled with flocks of Wall Street canaries flaunting their power ties. Passersby bumped and jostled him and Bliss murmured polite apologies until he realized no one was paying him the slightest bit of attention. In a few moments, Bliss was acclimated, alone in a seething sea of flesh, awash in an ocean of emotion.

When he reached his destination, the stone-columned edifice housing the stock exchange looked cool and inviting. Bliss went inside to get a feel of the place. From the moment he entered, the emotion charged air inundated him. The place was a madhouse of frenzied activity at an intolerable noise level, and the push-pull of negative and positive vibrations created an emotional vortex that threatened to pull him under. Bliss contemplated a hasty exit.

Then, a tall, blond Sophia Loren look-a-like in a short black skirt brushed against him. From the contact, Bliss gleaned her name, Nancy Burgess and the fact that she was a commodities broker dealing mainly in grains and beans— coffee beans. Bliss grabbed her by the arm. She turned, looked into his eyes, and stopped in her tracks, motionless as a department store mannequin. Bliss probed her mind as the crowd surged around them. In a few minutes, he released her. With a slightly dazed expression on her picture-perfect face, Nancy resumed her hectic activities, shouting into her phone as she watched him walk away.

Next on his agenda was a magnificent building on Fifth Avenue at 42nd Street. The New York City Library was more to his liking— room after room of vital information at his fingertips and in blessed silence. He spent most of the rest of the day there among the racks, taking in section by section. He carried stacks of books to a reading table, flipped through each one, absorbed the contents in a drop of the page and went back for more.

In the magazine section, he discovered the microfilm, scanning it faster than the machine could move the film through. After two hours of searching, he found something useful in an article in *New York Magazine* from a back issue dated January 15, 1979. The subject was "Psychics on Wall Street."

The cover story revealed, "Stockbrokers, diplomats, even psychiatrists are going to psychics." The article featured an exotic Italian woman named Chiara who did pendulum readings for Wall Street brokers, inquiring into the futures of stocks and bonds. *Not exactly what I'm looking for.* The name he'd lifted from Victoria's mind had a German sound, 'von' something. Bliss knew that particular psychic could tell him what he needed to know.

The article went into more detail, putting together what it called The New York Psychic Directory: its own registry of better-known local clairvoyants with a listing of their specialties and fees. Bliss checked the list and found the name he was looking for—Stella Von Moll.

Arriving back at the hotel, he called her office, only to learn she was booked up solid for three weeks. He didn't have three weeks to waste. Bliss called information and requested the number of an Instant Messenger Service and requested a pick-up.

When the messenger knocked at his hotel room door, Bliss shook his hand, thanked him profusely and pressed a twenty into his palm, saying he'd changed his mind about the message. After the messenger left, Bliss' elastic body made the transition into the young man's form, an exact duplicate right down to his mismatched socks.

A half-hour later he was standing in Stella Von Moll's outer office, charming the receptionist out of her mind, kissing her hand and making a brain drain.

Then he asked to see the psychic.

"I'm sorry, you can't," she said, flustered. "She's with a client."

"These are from H. J. Stone," he said, holding up two white envelopes. "He needs an answer immediately. It's of the utmost importance. He instructed me to hand deliver these to Mrs. Von Moll and bring the answers right back to him."

"Wait a moment," she said, instantly reacting to the name. "I'll see if there is anything I can do."

She left the room and returned a few minutes later. "She'll see you between clients. Please have a seat, it'll be about ten minutes," she said, motioning him toward a chair.

Twenty minutes later, Bliss walked into Von Moll's office. The woman seated behind the French provincial desk certainly didn't look like the "Witch of Wall Street." Actually, she looked like somebody's grandmother.

Without saying a word, she took the first envelope, held it in front of her and concentrated. Then she wrote something on the outside. Next, she took the second one and repeated the procedure and handed them both back to him still sealed. As his fingers brushed hers, she eyed him strangely.

"Young man, do you have an eating disorder?"

"Not exactly," he said. Bliss quickly erected a mental barrier, but Von Moll continued in spite of his block.

"I'm getting an unusual sense of . . . hunger . . . some sort of addiction
. . . a craving. . .."

Bliss closed himself off completely.

She blinked and closed her eyes. The connection was broken.

When she opened her eyes, the messenger was gone.

Chapter 19

In the large, well appointed executive office on the top floor of the Danvers Building in downtown Miami, a lone figure sat in a high-back leather chair behind an antique mahogany desk. Outside, a storm raged. Traffic crept along, headlights on, as the last of the work weary waged yet another battle to get home in the dreary, premature nightfall. Gusts of wind blew blinding sheets of rain through the streets and miniature tidal waves white-capped in the vacant parking lots.

The Danvers Building was deserted except for the man in the corner office on the 16th floor. Bill Danvers sat hunched over with his arms resting on the desktop. His large hands clutched a glass tumbler half-full of golden brown, scotch whiskey, and the nearly empty bottle of Chivas Regal was within easy reach.

He took another sip, caught a piece of ice, and held it on his tongue before he crunched the cube between his teeth. It was an old habit resurfacing in a time of stress. Maggie had told him a million times how irritating it was, and not to mention bad for his teeth—unsolicited, unheeded advice. Swallowing another slug of scotch, he eyed the nine-millimeter Browning lying to his right on the desk blotter.

He put down the glass, picked up the Browning and flipped off the safety catch. The weight felt good in his hand as Bill brought the gun to his temple. The barrel felt cool and soothing against the hot flush of his skin. Pain and sorrow masked Bill's ruggedly handsome face as his index finger tightened on the trigger.

Clearly framed in the floor to ceiling windows behind him, twin bolts of lightening split the sky. The brilliant bursts zigzagged to the earth, followed immediately by a deafening clap of thunder that rolled on and on.

For an instant, Bill thought he had accidentally pulled the trigger as the boom reverberated in his head and rattled the windowpanes. A cold sweat popped out on his forehead. He relaxed his grip on the weapon, and his hand trembled as he carefully put the gun down on the desk.

He couldn't do it. He'd tried, he had wanted to, but he didn't have the courage to blow his brains out. Tomorrow, he thought he would wish he had. Bill knew with a high degree of certainty that he was probably going to lose the business. He had already lost the woman he planned to make his wife; but apparently, Bill had not lost his will to live.

Early that morning, his fiancÉe, Kathy, had moved out of his townhouse apartment, telling him there was someone else—someone younger and richer. During the heated argument that followed, she had spewed out several other venomous statements. One of them had been a scathing criticism of his abilities, or inabilities more likely, as a lover. After ripping his male ego to shreds, she had poured salt in the wound. "It will be good to make love to a young, hard body for a change," she had hissed at him.

Those were almost the identical words he had used when he left Maggie for Kathy. Now he understood how his wife had felt—instant Karma. *How could I have said something so cruel*, he wondered?

Wearily, he leaned back in his chair and drained the tumbler of the last drops of Chivas. Maggie didn't seem to mind the roll of flesh above his belt and jokingly referred to it as 'Dunlops' chiding that his stomach had done lopped over his belt. She loved him anyway.

Kathy, on the other hand, was constantly nagging him about losing weight. Now, he had lost 120 pounds, all at once. Kathy was gone. The dull ache in his head spread to his mid-section. Unshed tears stung his eyes, tears Bill would not allow to fall even though there was no one there to see them.

The whiskey was beginning to show in his face, the strong line of his jaw obscured by an unhealthy bloat. Puffy bags sagged beneath his bloodshot eyes, the result of too many long lunches and late-night client dinners with plenty of rich food and booze. But in the past year Bill's drinking had escalated.

His guilt at hurting Maggie, combined with his efforts to keep up with the much younger Kathy drove him farther and farther into the bottle, until the drinking itself became an issue in his new relationship. He tried to put a block on the booze, to slow down for Kathy's sake, but it was no use. Bill was no longer able to drink everyone else under the table. Now after a few drinks, Bill spiraled into a state of sodden, morose drunkenness.

Although Bill had fallen wildly, passionately in love with Kathy at first sight, he was not totally blind to her faults. The knowledge that she was a money hungry social climber didn't lessen his ardor one bit; in fact, it increased it. Playing God, he toyed with the appealing idea of making all her dreams come true. Now, someone else, younger and smarter would be opening those doors for her.

In the grip of his depression, Bill swiveled his chair to look out into the rain swept darkness at the lights of the city below. Unhappiness washed over him in waves like the sheets of rain he watched slide sideways across the glass. Despair deeper than any he had ever known settled in his bones. Although there were thousands of people nearby, he was alone. *Not one soul out there gives a shit what happens to me*, he thought. It was not a good feeling.

Standing, he wavered slightly as he closed the drapes and blotted out the cruel, uncaring city. Then he headed to the wet bar for another fix of scotch. *The worst of it*, he thought, *is the missing money. God damn it! What's going on? There's over two hundred and fifty grand missing!*

He was up to his ass in alligators and somebody had just drained the swamp. The new cosmetic line had required a tremendous cash outlay, not to mention the extensive, expensive advertising campaign Kathy cooked up to launch the products. Bill was deeply in debt, hopelessly in hock—personally and professionally.

166

Time was running out. How was he going to come up with the money to cover the audit? If the bank got wind of it and called his loan, his ass was grass and they were the lawn mower. "Shit!" Bill had never been any good with figures. He hated the financial side of the business, all those details. Maggie was the math expert.

Maggie, dear God! That was the answer—why hadn't he thought of it before? *She will know exactly what to do.* His alcohol befuddled brain latched onto the idea with no consideration as to whether or not Maggie would be receptive to bailing him out after the way he had treated her.

Grabbing a fresh bottle from the bar, he twisted off the cap and drank deeply. The closet door was open, and Bill inspected his appearance in the full-length mirror fastened to the inside of the door. His fingers fumbled as he attempted to straighten his tie that remained slightly askew in spite of his efforts. He ran his comb through his hair and tried in vain to button his jacket. As the company had grown, so had his waistline.

He left the office with the lights blazing and lurched down the hall, reaching out to the wall for support until he reached the elevator. When the door opened, Bill stepped inside and stood with a blank look on his face for a few minutes before he stabbed at the "B" button and missed. Focusing his eyes required intense concentration, but fortunately at that moment the buttons converged into one. He pressed it and set the machine in motion.

His Porsche, at least it was his for now, was parked in his reserved spot. He backed the car up in a wide arch, gunned the engine, and roared out into the driving rain, leaving a trail of tire marks on the concrete floor as he shot out of the garage.

Halfway down the block, a Miami Police patrol car waited in the deepening gloom with its motor idling. The Porsche sped by, throwing up a curtain of water in its wake.

"Did you see that asshole," Officer Bledsoe asked his partner, "he must have been doing at least sixty by the time he hit the corner?"

"Yeah, I saw the son-of-a-bitch when he launched the mother from the garage. Another middle-aged crazy with his toy, let's take him."

Bledsoe was pretty sure he'd seen the glint of an upturned bottle in the dim interior. Or maybe it was just the school of experience giving his intuition a nudge.

Then the police radio crackled to life and the dispatcher announced a robbery in progress at a nearby liquor store. "An officer is down; all available cars are requested on the scene. I repeat, an officer is down."

Bledsoe responded to the call. "The jerk in the Porsche just got lucky," he said as the patrol car pulled out, made a U-turn and fishtailed off in the opposite direction.

Oblivious to his narrow escape from the law, Bill switched on the radio as his car made the turn onto Highway 1 and headed south. The weather report indicated the storm was lessening. As if in confirmation, the heavy rain dwindled to a light drizzle. But visibility was still poor for Bill who was half-stewed.

The words of a popular country song boomed out, loud and strong in the close confines of the car. Another one of those love-gone-wrong songs. He sang along for a few bars before he turned off the radio.

But the words echoed on in his brain. What if he could go back in time, would he do the same things all over again? Falling for Kathy was something akin to being struck by lightning, an event over which he had no control. But if he was being honest with himself, he had to admit he wouldn't have missed it for the world, and knew he might do the same thing again, in spite of the pain he felt now, or maybe not. He wasn't sure.

His only real regret was hurting Maggie. She deserved better treatment after working side-by-side with him, loving him through all the tough, lean years. If he ever got this mess straightened out, Bill intended to find some way to make it up to her. She was a trustworthy woman, one you could ride the river with. *Maggie will know what to do, she always does,* he reassured himself.

With that ray of hope, the lump of lead in his midsection softened. Taking another generous gulp of scotch, Bill peered through the windshield in between the slap, slap of the wiper blades. In the mist ahead, he could barely make out the taillights of another vehicle moving at a safe, sane speed on the rain slick highway.

Bill dropped the liquor bottle on the passenger seat as he accelerated and swung out sharply to pass the slower driver. The bottle rolled with the motion, up on the console and then down under his feet. "God damn!" He reached under the seat and searched for the bottle as he steered back into the right lane in front of the pickup truck. His fingers grazed the bottle and Bill looked down and took his eyes off the road for an instant.

In those few seconds, the Porsche drifted onto the shoulder of the road and hit a rain soaked soft spot. The right tires sank, and the car dipped and went into a flip before it rolled down the embankment. The Porsche landed on its roof in a grinding crash and slid several yards before coming to rest in two feet of water with all four wheels spinning in the air. The unbroken bottle of scotch floated out the smashed window on the passenger side and bobbed merrily away.

On the road above, an old black man parked his pick-up on the shoulder of the road and then scrambled down to the scene of the accident. He sloshed through the knee-deep water until he reached the car and pulled frantically at the passenger door handle, but it was locked. Easing his hand in past the broken window glass, he opened the door from the inside.

When the car door swung open, Bill's body lay headfirst in the water, his neck at an impossible angle, obviously broken. His unused safety belt fluttered in the wind, making a clanging noise Bill would never hear.

Chapter 20

At 8:45 p.m., on Monday evening, the doorbell rang in Nancy Burgess' high-rise apartment, an unexpected, unaccustomed sound. Nancy worked over 70 hours a week, pulling down $250,000 a year as a commodities broker. She earned every dime of her money; the pressures on brokers were horrendous. Her career left no time for a personal life. As a result, Nancy's social life was practically nonexistent, almost everything she did related to business in some way. No one *ever* casually dropped in on her.

Who the hell is it? Security hadn't buzzed her, so it must be someone who lived in the building; her place was harder to get into than Fort Knox. Nancy put down her wine glass and turned down the music that she constantly played as the soundtrack to her life, if she'd had a life.

She kept the safety chain on when she opened the door a crack to peer directly into a set of Paul Newmanish blue eyes. No easy feat since Nancy at 6' 3" was taller than the average woman, or the average man for that matter.

"Miss Burgess?" The stranger's deep voice held a hint of a growl.

"Yes, what can I do for you?" Several things came to mind.

"I'm your new neighbor from down the hall, Vince Everett." He waved two white envelopes in the air. "I seem to have gotten some of your mail by mistake."

At least he isn't selling anything, she thought. She opened the door and stepped back, unprepared for what she saw. Leaning against the doorframe in a casual slouch was the most gorgeous man Nancy had ever laid eyes on. *Be still my heart.*

His thick, wavy, dark brown hair framed a devastatingly handsome face with high cheekbones, a strong jaw and a wide, sensuous mouth. But the eyes had it—a definite twinkle glimmered in their clear blue depths.

His body was even better. Attired in a light blue button-down oxford shirt and tight jeans, he looked more handsome in casual clothes than most men did in a tuxedo. *He's right off the cover of GQ*, she thought, *a super hunk*. Nancy didn't realize it, but that was exactly where she'd seen him.

She recovered her wits and asked him in. Vince brushed by her, and she recognized the faint scent of English Leather, her favorite men's cologne. When Vince turned to face her, his physical perfection took her breath away. Nancy stared at the open collar of his shirt where his chest hair spilled over the edges before she looked up into his eyes.

Something flickered in their depths, something strong and compelling. Vince offered the envelopes in his hand to Nancy and used the opportunity to close the gap between them. As she reached for the mail, he took her in his arms, and the move was so natural, so right, she didn't resist. His eyes clouded, smoky with desire. Nancy had never seen such hunger in a man's eyes before.

"I want you," he whispered before his lips touched hers, engulfing her in his passion. Too startled to push him away, and not really wanting to, Nancy viewed herself as if from a distance, surrendering to a stranger. *I must be losing my mind*, she thought, before she lost all power to reason.

He drew her to the floor, unbuttoned her blouse and removed her jeans with a few, practiced motions. Then, he straddled her and peeled off his shirt. All the while he was murmuring to her in a sweet, seductive tone—words that she heard in her head and felt in her heart as if he was reading the pain and longing written there.

"Open your mind to me, just let go. Allow me to know you, fully."

He found and spoke the words Nancy had waited all her life to hear. He stroked her, appreciated her, and made her feel special and exalted. Everything Nancy had ever wished a man would do in lovemaking, Vince did, without being asked, without any prompting, he fulfilled her every fantasy. He touched her in a way no man ever had before, deeply and completely. She gave herself to him with a wild abandon, her tiredness forgotten.

He moved inside her mind and body. Nancy rode high on a sweet tide of passion, so overwhelming in its intensity that it blotted out everything else. *I pity any woman who isn't me tonight*, she thought.

Vince reached what Nancy thought was his climax, but instead of coming—she felt herself going. In one sweeping, siphoning motion, something inside her flowed out to him. The drain caused a tremendous rush of adrenaline and Nancy's blood pressure soared to a dangerous height. Weakened from chronic hypertension, her blood vessels strained at the overload.

Suddenly, a numbing cold spread from the inside out. Nancy turned a sickly ashen shade and passed out from the shock to her system. Bliss bent over her, his face radiating light. He felt for her pulse and found it to be weak and erratic. Picking her up, he carried her into the adjoining bedroom. As Bliss eased her down onto the bed, her face and body relaxed into a supernatural sleep.

In the living room, he stooped and picked up the two envelopes from the floor. He would need them in the morning. *By tomorrow night, I will be wealthy by Earth standards*, he assured himself. Few of his desires were ever disputed; everything came quickly, without resistance. Earth females were lush and lovely—ripe plums waiting to be plucked by the master harvester.

But the males made it so simple. Their women were starved for attention, craved kindness, and were in awe of any small, thoughtful act. Bliss found Earth's females incredibly easy to please. *Didn't Earthmen know what their women wanted? Or didn't they care?*

The next morning, for the first time in her five years with the firm, Nancy Burgess was late for work. She had overslept, but when she had awoken, Vince brought her breakfast in bed so she lingered like a lazy lioness in awe of her king of the jungle. As she left for work, he walked her to the door and handed her the two white envelopes and repeated his instructions. Then he kissed her good-bye, a long, slow, deep kiss that made her weak in the knees.

"I'll see you this evening," he promised.

Nancy rushed into her office with a splitting headache, realizing too late, she had forgotten to take her blood pressure medicine. Her face flushed, her eyes glittering too brightly, she launched herself into the new day, fortified with caffeine and nicotine.

Before the pressures of the day closed in, she pulled Vince's envelopes from her purse. On the outside of one was scribbled, "Berries. Immediate action. Storms bringing disaster. London price, 2900 pounds sterling." On the second was written, "unusual potential, enormous returns by late September."

The man Vince represents, this Jonathan Bliss, is a gutsy one, a real risk taker, she thought. Investing $350,000 in coffee futures in a year of bumper crop predictions was pretty nervy. On a hunch, Nancy decided to invest a few dollars of her own.

Interested and excited, she checked the second envelope. It targeted a stock that had been rising steadily for the past week. Nancy reluctantly placed the order as instructed buying a large number of shares at 41.25 per share. It defied all logic, but by noon the stock had gone up another .25. In two weeks, it would split, doubling Bliss' investment.

Nancy alternated between chills and flushes. *Maybe I'm coming down with something*, she thought. Her discomfort and irritability increased with each passing minute, but her mind refused to focus on anything but the approaching night and Vince. Her work suffered and, on two occasions, she failed to react to a client's sell order and lost them money. Knowing that to continue the day was an exercise in futility, Nancy went home early—another first.

In her apartment, she counted the moments until Vince arrived, and then stopped counting anything except lots of lovely ceilings. During the night, she got up and turned up the thermostat. *It's unusually cold for September,* she thought. She got back into bed quickly, snuggling up to Vince without even noticing that his hair had turned white. Her bottle of blood pressure pills remained untouched on the nightstand.

On Wednesday morning, Bliss made his final withdrawal from the bank of her emotions. When it was over, Nancy sank back into the pillows, looking pale and wan as he gathered his things before he came back in the bedroom to say good-bye.

Bliss reached for her hand. "Nancy, I'm leaving now."

"Please, don't go," she protested feebly, her hand clutching his.

"I have to," he said, squeezing her hand. "No hard feelings?"

"None," she whispered and turned her face from him. In fact, there were practically no feelings at all.

Nancy didn't look so good. Before he left, Bliss placed a call to 911.

The coroner's report listed the cause of death as a massive heart attack.

Bliss learned of Nancy's death the next day at the stock exchange, but he was too busy making money to give her sudden demise any serious consideration. He brushed her memory aside with a weak rationalization even he did not believe. Nancy's death had nothing to do with him. He was in no way responsible.

By the end of the week, the coffee bean crop disaster was public knowledge. A devastating storm with high winds and torrential rains had wiped out most of the year's expected crop. Combined with political unrest in other coffee bean producing countries, the crop losses were more than enough to send prices through the ceiling. Bliss' bank account shot up right along with them.

To keep busy and assuage his guilt, Bliss went on a buying spree, purchasing furnishings for his new home. Having memorized the floor plan, he accurately visualized how each acquisition would look in its new home. He purchased Italian marble, fine porcelains, several exquisite French tapestries from the looms of Beauvis, and spent a king's ransom on Aubussons from France to enhance the highly polished oak floors. Earth history, period furniture, valuable antiques held no meaning for him. He chose furnishings and art based strictly on their appeal to his eye for beauty—things he would treasure for a time before he moved on.

He bought paintings and statuary by the truckload and arranged for everything to be shipped back to his mansion. Bodkins had already returned to the estate to supervise the more than one hundred carpenters, artisans and craftsmen hired to restore his new home to its former splendor.

Meanwhile, Bliss sought the bright lights and glamour, throwing his money around, making friends as fast as the mint made money. One of them was Tiffany Blake. Bliss recognized her from old movies he had watched on Maggie's DVD player. But the small screen hadn't prepared him for Tiffany in the flesh. Considered one of the most beautiful women in the world, she possessed a rare combination of child-like vulnerability and earthy sexiness.

For each and every one of her 42 years on Earth, people had paid her lavish compliments on her incredible beauty, but Tiffany never believed a word of it. Her public couldn't possibly conceive of the dismay and disappointment Tiffany experienced each time she gazed into a mirror. Riddled with self-doubt, she was highly emotional and extremely insecure, qualities that made her a great actress. But no amount of public adoration ever overcame her deep sense of inadequacy.

Tiffany had seven marriages under her belt—where they began and where they ended. No man ever reached her heart. She repeated the same error over and over, mistaking lust for love.

At the moment, she was appearing in a highly publicized play on Broadway, her comeback try on the stage, the place where her career had its beginnings. The role was the most important one of her life, and Tiffany was blowing it.

Overemotional and volatile, she created tempestuous scenes on-stage and off, and her complete lack of self-control was ruining the one thing in her life that really mattered.

Bliss took with one hand and gave with the other as fate conspired to make his conquest of Tiffany a one-night stand. For her, it was a blessing in disguise.

After he drained off her excess emotions, Tiffany left Bliss' suite at Hemsley Palace Hotel early the next morning, feeling more emotionally balanced than at any other time in her life. That evening, she gave the most brilliant, controlled performance of her career; a performance that drew rave reviews.

The next morning, Bliss woke up feeling like a 25-year-old, but there wasn't one around. Instead, he reached for the *New York Times*.

The headline brought him bolt upright.

"MIAMI SAVED!

Hurricane Sidney rips through Everglades."

He read on. "Last night while Miami braced for the storm, Hurricane Sidney suddenly veered inland, striking at the heart of the virtually uninhabited Everglades. The powerful storm with its 175 mile-per-hour winds is one of the strongest to come ashore in Southern Florida in recent memory. The devastating winds drove tons of mud across the prairie, tearing up ancient forests of mangroves and stranding 2300-pound loggerhead sea turtles in the mud far inland. Masses of concrete, along with large chunks of boats, are lodged in the mangroves."

He read no further. Bliss immediately chartered a jet and started to pack. *What if someone stumbles across my ship?* By now, Bliss had serious doubts about his own ability to locate it. The coordinates he had logged in on landing were based on landmarks—topography and geography that probably no longer existed.

Of all the space warped luck! Am I to be marooned on Earth? Bliss didn't even want to think about such a possibility. Things were starting to close in.

Chapter 21

Maggie was home in bed alone when the phone rang. Unable to sleep, she fidgeted, thinking of the one thing that dominated her mind, day and night—Bliss. The persistent ringing of the phone was an unwelcome interruption. She switched on the light and checked the bedside clock; it was 11:45, *too late for a social call*, Maggie thought, as she reached for the phone. *I'm going to give whoever it is a piece of my mind.*

The authoritative voice on the other end informed her that Bill Danvers had been involved in a serious auto accident.

"How serious?"

"Well, Mrs. Danvers . . . ma'am, it's very serious. You might want to sit down."

"I'm lying down, it's nearly midnight."

"I'm sorry to have to tell you this, but the accident was fatal. Mr. Danvers is dead." He felt like a fool for blurting it out that way. He hated to make these this type of call. He never knew what to say, and the words always came out wrong.

"To whom am I speaking?"

"Sorry, ma'am, I forgot to identify myself. I'm Sergeant Dobins with the Florida Highway Patrol."

"You're notifying the wrong party, Sergeant Dobins. Have you called Mr. Danvers' home? He no longer lives here. I can give you the number."

"Yes, ma'am, we tried there first. There's no one home. That's why we called you. The officer at the scene found your name, address and phone number in his wallet. You were listed as next of kin. You are his wife, aren't you?"

"Yes—legally, we're still married, but we're getting a divorce. What do you want from me?"

A little concern would be nice, he thought, even divorced people seemed to have some feelings about their ex when the chips were down. Dobins shrugged, you met all kinds in this job. "We need someone to tell us where to take the deceased," he said. "You know, which funeral home. And, of course, someone will need to notify the rest of the family."

"There is no rest of the family. Bill's parents are dead. He's an only child. I guess I'm it." Suddenly, it dawned on her.

"Was Bill alone in the car? Was anyone else involved?" *Maybe that little bitch Kathy was in the car with him*

"It was a single car accident. Mr. Danvers was alone. Apparently, he lost control of his vehicle. He'd just passed an old fella in a pick-up truck when he swerved off the road and rolled down an embankment. No one else was injured."

"I see," she said, not caring to hear anymore of the details. "Take the body to the Alexander Funeral Home," she said, distracted. Her mind was already speeding ahead.

"Alexander's, yes ma'am. You'll need to get in touch with them in the morning about the arrangements." *She sure is a cool one,* he thought. She had not asked any of the usual questions: where was the accident, what time did it happen, did he die instantly, did he suffer?

"I'll do that. Good-bye, Officer Dobins." Maggie said as she hung up the phone and sank back onto her pillow. Maggie knew she should be feeling something; grief, loss or regret, yet there was nothing. Zero. Zilch. Nada.

Memories of their life together flashed through her mind, and she viewed them impersonally, seeing the snapshots of their marriage with the crystal clarity of an uninvolved third party.

Her love for Bill had left the building, and in its place was an emotional vacuum. Two emotions remained—greed for whatever worldly wealth Bill had left behind and an all-consuming hatred for Kathy Elliott. It seemed that Bliss preferred to feed on the finer emotions.

Maggie plucked idly at her bedcovers before she squeezed her eyes shut, and dared to hope sleep might come.

Lately, it had been elusive and as a result, she was tired all the time. By day, she drifted listlessly from room to room, and by night, she either suffered from insomnia or ended up on the edge of comatose.

Nothing held any interest for Maggie anymore, except Bliss. Having him was killing her and not having him made her want to die. *Where is he? Why doesn't he call me? He never writes, He never phones.* She changed positions, rolled onto her side, and then flopped over onto her back again. It was no use. Her mind was a muddle. Resigned, she reached for the bottle on her nightstand and downed two of the little yellow pills aided by a gulp of water. In a few minutes, the drug took affect and dragged her down into a dreamless sleep.

Early the next morning, Maggie called Alexander Funeral Home and made the arrangements over the phone. The service was set for the following day, Wednesday at 2 p.m. She phoned Bill's business associates and her own parents, who immediately booked a flight scheduled to arrive late that afternoon.

On her way out the door to the airport, a thought hit her and she suddenly turned on her heels and ran back into the den. She rummaged through the desk drawers and unearthed a leather-bound address book. Her manicured finger slid down the page to the name: Turnbull, Gordon, Attorney. Maggie reached for the phone with a smile of satisfaction on her face, thinking revenge was, indeed, a dish best served cold.

When his receptionist came on the line, Maggie made an appointment to be in Gordon Turnbull's office on Friday for the reading of the will. Maggie wondered if Kathy would be there. Bill might have changed his will, more than likely he had, but she would cross that bridge when she came to it.

Maggie's parents arrived with every intention of staying with her, but instead, she put them up in a hotel in Miami, telling them it would be more convenient for them. Who was she kidding? It was all about her. During the ride to their lodgings, she treated them with studied indifference, so cool and aloof that even her mother, Joan, found it impossible to get past Maggie's glacial exterior.

It was a side of their daughter they had never seen before. The moment Maggie left them alone in their room after the funeral, Joan commented on her daughter's conduct.

"I can't get over it. I don't know what we've done to deserve this kind of treatment. What's gotten into her? She hasn't shed one tear for poor Bill. It just isn't right."

"She's in shock. Not everybody reacts the same way to this sort of thing," Joel said, in an attempt to pacify his wife. "Maybe Maggie's pain is on the inside. She probably doesn't want to upset us," Joel offered, trying to justify something he really didn't understand. He preferred not to delve too deeply. *One hysterical female in the family is enough*, he thought.

"But, she's so different, like a stranger. I don't even know her, my own little girl. Did you see her face when I asked about Daniel? Maggie looked at me as if to say, 'Daniel who?' Then she said, he's dead, simple as that, no explanation, at all."

"Joel, don't look at me like that! You know how much she loved that dog; she treated him like a member of the family. I don't understand any of it, maybe she's having a nervous breakdown."

"Yep," she was pretty fond of Daniel, all right," Joel said, pleased to have found one thing they agreed on. He didn't want to think about it—any of it. Over his lifetime, Joel had stuffed more things than a sausage factory.

"And she was fond of Bill," she asserted, "even with all his carrying on. But you would never know it by the way she's acting, now—sailing through the funeral, cool as you please, brushing me off anytime I tried to comfort her. She's my baby, and I'm worried about her. She's not herself. It's like she's been invaded by an alien."

"I know," Joel agreed, "maybe there's something in what you're saying, but don't you think maybe you're getting yourself all worked up over nothing? Maggie's in shock and as soon as it wears off, she'll be her old self again. You'll see." He forced himself to adopt a positive attitude, not wanting to face any more unpleasant facts.

"I hope you're right, Joel," she said, unconvinced. "I certainly hope so."

Relief was evident on both sides when Maggie's parents boarded a plane for Atlanta on Thursday morning. During their leave-taking, Maggie could barely conceal her impatience to get them airborne, her thoughts were focused, with increasing anticipation, to the reading of the will.

Friday could not come too soon for her, and on the big day, she arrived at the lawyer's office ten minutes early, and much to her surprise, the secretary ushered her in immediately. Impeccably dressed, Maggie wore a simple, elegant dark gray sheath, its severe lines softened by the milky whiteness of a matched set of pearls.

The man behind the desk appeared to be in his late fifties, with receding gray hair that framed a pleasant, inquisitive face with youthful, boyish features. He stood up as she approached.

"Good morning, Gordon. It's good to see you again," she said, extending her hand.

"And you, Maggie, you're looking as lovely as ever," he said as he grasped her outstretched hand in his. "Please accept my condolences on the death of your husband. Bill will be greatly missed."

Especially by the people he owes money, she thought.

"Thank you, Gordon. I do appreciate your concern." She knew exactly how genuine it was.

"Please be seated, and we'll begin." He motioned her toward a burgundy, leather wing back chair that faced his massive desk.

Then his phone rang, and Gordon begged her pardon as he took the call. Maggie anxiously eyed the door, expecting any second to see the chronically late Kathy Elliott make her usual breathless entrance. Everyone had been surprised when Kathy didn't show up for Bill's funeral. In fact, no one had seen her since she left her office at Danver's last Thursday.

Gordon's phone conversation continued, and Maggie glanced impatiently around the large, impressive office. The decor reeked of imitation country manor house, *the lord's library*, she thought, with its hunter green walls, tall burnished bookcases and fine art prints of English hunt scenes interspersed with an original painting here and there to add an air of authenticity.

Gordon cleared his throat to gain her attention and plunged into the reading of the will. His voice droned on, enumerating the where as's and there to's. *It's like a sleazy romance novel*, she thought; *you have to read the whole thing to get to the good parts.* When Gordon finally finished, Maggie found herself to be the only heir to Bill's personal and business fortune.

She was speechless, unable to believe her good luck. Maggie was the uncontested owner of Danvers Pharmaceuticals. *Well, how about them apples.*

Gordon mistook her stunned expression and tight-lipped silence for grief and his normal staid, conservative manner dissolved into compassionate concern for the bereaved widow. He clucked at her like some old hen. "Now, now, I know how difficult this is for you, Maggie. We won't be much longer. There are a few papers that need your signature, transferals to your name—that sort of thing."

To his credit, he thoroughly explained each document to her, but Maggie insisted on reading each one over carefully before signing. Although Gordon was irritated, he concealed it, and waited patiently until she finished. He could afford to wait.

Then he offered his advice. "Don't bother yourself with the concerns of the company, my dear. As you know, there are some serious problems, but I understand the business is in capable hands. Take some time to think things over and decide what you want to do."

He paused, pursed his lips and looked down at her through his spectacles in the perfect pose of a wise old adviser before he continued. "I've already received what I consider a very fair offer for the business, under the circumstances—should you decide to sell. And that's precisely what I recommend you do, Maggie, sell Danvers—get out from under it all as quickly as possible."

Waving his hands over the paperwork like a wizard with a magic wand that could make it all go away, he said, "There's no reason for you to be saddled with a responsibility like this. But, we can discuss this later, when you feel more up to it." The attorney ended his summation with a condescending smile.

Maggie effectively wiped the Cheshire cat grin right off his face with her next words. "Danvers Pharmaceuticals is not for sale, under any circumstances."

"But, Maggie, surely you're not thinking . . . "

Rising brusquely, she sliced his words off in mid-sentence. "No, I am not thinking. I've already made up my mind. The matter isn't open to discussion. Now, if you'll excuse me—if we're finished with the legalities, I'll be going. I have quite a few things to attend to."

Maggie stood up, turned on her heels, and marched from the office, leaving a startled Gordon Turnbull mumbling to himself and running his hand through his hair. As the door closed behind her, he grabbed the phone.

"Mrs. Peyton, get me Greenburg, the CEO at Danvers Pharmaceuticals." In a few minutes, the phone rang, "John, Gordon here—we have a problem, a big problem."

Chapter 22

At exactly 8:00 a.m. on Monday morning, Maggie strode past Ann Nichols, Bill's astonished private secretary, entered his office and closed the door behind her. Wearing a no-nonsense navy suit, her auburn hair brushed back into a bun, Maggie was ready to get down to business. Pausing for a moment, she surveyed the room as she mulled over the changes she planned to make. *Something less cluttered, more functional in neutral colors. Better have a decorator in next week*, she decided.

Taking Bill's seat behind his desk, she buzzed his secretary. But things were already buzzing out front as word of Maggie's unexpected arrival spread throughout the Danvers empire.

"Ann, would you tell Mr. Greenburg I'd like to see him immediately, please. And ask him to bring the current P & L statement with him."

"I'm sorry, Mag - uh, Mrs. Danvers, he isn't in yet. Mr. Greenburg doesn't usually come in until, oh-nine or nine-thirty."

"When he does come in, tell him I want to see him. In the meantime, send in the manger of the accounting department with that P & L. She *is* here, isn't she?" There was more than a hint of rebuke in Maggie's tone.

"I'm sure she is. I'll call her, right away," Ann said eagerly, anxious to please.

"I don't remember her name. Matthews, is that it?"

"It's Mathis, Jody Mathis."

"Thank you, Ann."

Within five minutes, a nervous Jody Mathis fidgeted in front of Maggie's desk, clutching a computer printout in her hands. Her mind raced, rumors had run rampant through the company since Bill's unexpected death, but none of them had suggested the possibility of Maggie Danvers actually taking control of the business. Jody knew Maggie had, at one time, been actively involved in the running of the company, but that was years ago. Things had changed. Jody suddenly felt dubious about the company's future and more importantly, her own.

Maggie extended her hand for the printout. "Thank you, Mrs. Mathis, there are several other reports I will want to see. I've made a list of them. I'll need them as soon as possible."

Maggie tore off a sheet from her yellow legal pad and handed it to Jody. To her dismay, Jody saw the list of items reached to the bottom of the page. Then, in an unconscious gesture of dismissal, Maggie bent her auburn head and focused her attention on the printouts covering her desk.

As Jody turned to leave, Maggie said, "One more thing, on your way out, tell Ann to get the personnel director on the phone and make an appointment for her to meet with me at 2 p.m."

By the time Ann buzzed her at 9:45 to announce Greenburg's arrival, Maggie had scanned the personnel folders and expense sheets of every department head in the firm. She carefully noted salaries, length of service, responsibilities and number of employees under their supervision. She shook her head in frustration. Management of the company had become top heavy and overlapped in several areas.

Her eyebrows knit together, and she frowned her disapproval. Bill's complete lack of interest in figures had allowed expenses to steadily creep up until they ate away at the profit margin. Each department took a small bite and continued to nibble away at slices of the Danvers profit pie. From the contents of the reports, Maggie knew that Bill had been apprised of the problem, but she also understood how reluctant he was to rid himself of the parasites attached to the company. Bill felt a personal responsibility and regard for the people who had been with him for a long time. As a result, the skim milk rose to the top at Danvers while competitors with an eye for good people siphoned off the cream.

Maggie's appraisal of the personnel folders was quick, calm and calculating. Her first official act would be to get rid of the dead wood. Unencumbered by any emotional concerns, Maggie chopped away, and unlike her late husband, she would suffer no pangs of guilt or regret.

When Greenburg entered the office, he was smiling and oozing charm, fully prepared to win his way as he always did—by manipulation. But Maggie seemed unaffected by his effusive greeting. Self-contained and regal, the woman behind the desk was nothing at all like the Maggie Danvers he had known and placated for years.

"Maggie, it's wonderful to see you. I'm so pleased you've taken an interest in the business. But I must admit I'm surprised." His eyebrows arched to denote the incredulous nature of her actions.

He couldn't have been any more surprised if Maggie had suddenly announced she was taking up auto racing. He launched into his prepared speech, telling her all the reasons why her input was unwarranted and unnecessary. When he finally wound down, Maggie did not waste her time responding to his comments or refuting his implied indulgence of "the little woman" trying to make her way in the cold, cruel business world. *How soon they forget*, she thought. *I helped build this business.*

Like a laser beam, Maggie cut right to the heart of the matter as she laid out her master plan for Danvers. She drew the big picture for him with all the enthusiasm of a child with her first set of crayons. When she had finished, Maggie issued an ultimatum: Either Greenburg agreed to give her his full cooperation, or he turned in his resignation.

An unknown side of Maggie's personality had surfaced and the self-assured executive was stunned and horrified by the unexpected turn of events. There was no reasoning with Maggie; she was imperious to his ploys. An hour later, Greenburg left the office, ashen faced and subdued.

As he exited, Jody Mathis entered Maggie's office, staggering under the load of a stack of folders. Peering over the top of the towering pile, she asked, "Where shall I put these, Mrs. Danvers?" She knew where she would like to put them.

"Right here," Maggie said, tapping the desktop. Her only other response to Jody was a curt, "Thank you," as she dove into the pile. Precariously balanced, the mountain of paperwork was about to become an avalanche. Maggie arranged the paperwork into smaller more manageable groups, so engrossed with the task she never even noticed when Jody frustrated and confused, left the room.

Maggie absorbed the information like a dried-out sponge, soaking up the data, and facts and figures with a cool, all-consuming competence. Tireless and obsessed with the business at hand, Maggie worked straight through lunch, reading and making copious notes. Employing her innate talent for reading a balance sheet at a glance, she detected any strengths and weaknesses immediately.

As she worked, her right hand automatically smoothed back stray strands of hair that fell in her face. Other than the stacking of folders and the flipping of pages, it was the only hint of action in the room. No one dared to interrupt her. Satisfied at last, she leaned back in the chair and sighed. *It's perfect. I've worked out a formula for the complete reorganization of the company.* The drastic measures Maggie planned to put into action were designed to get the business back in the black as soon as possible.

When the personnel director entered her office at 2 p.m., Maggie was armed with her list of reassignments and terminations. She had trimmed the fat in the firm and cut dangerously close to the bone, acting swiftly with the ruthless objectivity of the uninvolved. Pure logic ruled as she eliminated people and their pet projects. Clare, the personnel director, sat numb and disbelieving, nervously smoothing the perfect folds of her pleated skirt as she listened to Maggie outline her plan. *She doesn't even respect me enough to consult me or ask my opinion,* she thought. As Clare left the office, she knew Danvers was no place for her anymore and mentally brushed up her resume.

At 6 p.m., Maggie sat alone in what had once been Bill's office, having taken possession of the space and the company. Both were in for dramatic changes. Her sharp eyes flickered over the room, coming to rest on familiar objects from their shared past, but no traces of sentiment softened the hardness in her hazel eyes.

Her nimble mind locked onto the events of the present. When she had walked into the office that morning, she knew no one had taken her seriously. "They do, now," she said aloud. Whatever the others thought of her abilities, her power was something they could not ignore. Maggie took a deep breath, and savored the feeling of a new high. She had to admit it was no substitute for Bliss, but it would do.

When she arrived home and opened the day's mail, she was astonished to find a cashier's check in the amount of $250,000. It had arrived in a plain white envelope with no return address, stamped with a New York City postmark. She examined the check closely; finding it had been drawn on Citibank of New York. The only other thing in the envelope was a cryptic handwritten note that read: "I borrowed some money from Danvers to get started. Thanks for the loan. Sorry for the inconvenience . . . Bliss."

At least the mystery of the missing money had been cleared up and Bill absolved. She ran her fingers over the signature, and found herself caught up in an intense wave of longing at the mere sight of his name. "He is out there, somewhere," she whispered to herself. But the knowledge brought her no closer to him. Although Bliss had said it was over between them when he left her, Maggie had not believed him. How could two people share such a connection and never see each other again? "Of course, he isn't human," she reminded herself. But the logic of that particular piece of information provided no comfort to her. She wanted to talk to him, to persuade him to change his mind. But it was useless, when Bliss disappeared; he did a thorough job of it.

Maggie considered hiring a detective agency to track him down and she had fully intended to do it. But each time she tried to talk to anyone about Bliss, a curtain fell in her mind and blotted out her thoughts, leaving Maggie with her mouth open and nothing to say. Just thinking about Bliss, threatened her mental existence, so Maggie reluctantly placed his letter in a drawer out of sight and forced herself to think of other things.

She spent that night at the desk in her study, her weary, reddened eyes devouring page after page of endless piles of paperwork. Maggie steeped herself in the business and embarked on a new life, one where she lived only for the challenge and the excitement of making money. Weeks passed, the company turned around, and she had plenty of money but no friends. "She knows the price of everything and the value of nothing," one of her employees sniped, quoting Oscar Wilde, and he was right.

She might have gone on that way for years, if it had not been for David Trenton's phone call. David had called to invite her to a party with some of his Palm Beach friends. Reluctantly, Maggie agreed to go, thinking she could use a change of pace, and perhaps make some important business contacts.

David Trenton had been after her to go out with him again ever since their first date, a time that seemed to her a lifetime ago, B.B. (Before Bliss). The two had met on Maggie's first visit to David's veterinary clinic with her dog, Daniel. The moment David's hand had brushed hers as he handed back the dog's leash, he had experienced an instant attraction. After that, David was extremely nervous around Maggie.

David was tall, dark, handsome and boring. It didn't take Maggie long to realize that he got along better with animals than he did with people. On their first date, he started out tongue tied, completely at a loss for words and then developed a case of diarrhea of the mouth. In his struggle to make conversation, he tried to impress her by dropping names, places and prices with unrelenting alacrity, resulting in a stupefying evening for her.

Maggie accepted his current invitation, not because she enjoyed his company, but because she intended to use him as a stepping-stone to his influential friends, the ones he claimed to have. David showed up on time for their date, but managed to look slightly seedy in spite of his good looks and expensive jacket. His hair and nails were a bit too long and no iron had ever touched his shirt. In fact, it looked as if it had been lying in the dryer for days. Worst of all, his shoes were scuffed and rundown at the heels. *Oh well*, she thought, *what the hell, it's only one night; I'm not going to marry the guy.*

At the party, in the ostentatious home of one of his nouveau riche friends, Maggie networked while David pouted. He followed her around like a puppy on a short leash. But he was a petulant pet who grew more and more irritated and frustrated by Maggie's indifference to him. She seemed to find the bartender more stimulating company than her date.

As she sighted another group of people she wanted to meet, she flashed David a calculating smile and said, "Get me another drink, sweetie," as she waved him away.

Resigned to his role as waiter, David headed toward the bar. In the corner, he spied a young woman and older man in a passionate embrace and a wave of envy enveloped him. As he waited for their drinks, he noticed a silver-serving bowl piled high with small, clear vials topped with colorful plastic stoppers. He smiled as he scooped up a handful and shoved them into his jacket pocket.

Later, David asked Maggie if she wanted to see the pool area and the beautiful English gardens. "Might as well," she shrugged. At the moment, there was no one more interesting in sight.

When they were alone, David asked for her hand and placed a vial in her open palm.

"What is it?"

"Primo stuff. Ever tried it?"

"No, I smoked some pot in my youth, but that's about it." She stared at the vial, thinking the drug looked like small, crumbled pieces of soap.

David pulled a pipe from his coat pocket, loaded it with pellets and lit up. After a few drags, he offered the pipe to Maggie. "Here, try it, you'll like it."

She had never used crack, never felt she needed anything to get high. But now, things were different and good feelings were more difficult to come by. Still, something inside told her 'no', but she chose to ignore the inner voice. *What can it hurt, just one time?* Maggie closed her eyes and took a deep drag from the pipe.

Within ten seconds, the cocaine exploded in the pleasure centers of Maggie's brain, and shot her from zero enjoyment to infinity in milliseconds. The intense rush made her feel like she was zooming through the universe, doing 200-mph standing still. In an instant, Maggie's perception of reality expanded as the drug induced an extreme sense of euphoria. She suddenly experienced a tremendous surge of confidence and knew she had found the closest thing to Bliss on Earth.

Although David knew cocaine rivaled Russian roulette as the ultimate challenge for risk takers, he was one of those rare people who could use the drug casually. But Maggie was not; she had found the fast food of drugs on her first try and came up number one with a bullet, hooked from the very first hit.

In less than two weeks, Maggie was a full-blown addict, and David evolved into her supplier and her lover. Under the influence of the drug, she would do anything to get more. But the crack wore off much too quickly, and Maggie craved stronger stuff and more frequent fixes. As her habit escalated, Maggie's weekly drug expenses mushroomed from $300 to $3,000.

Crack replaced Bliss as the dominant desire in her life, more important than anything, including her business. Cocaine became her business. When she was high, Maggie reigned supreme in her own mind. With the rush in her veins, she felt invincible. *Why should I wait around for David to bring me a supply, why not make it myself*, she reasoned?

Through David, she located a pusher to supply the cocaine powder base she needed. At night, when everyone else went home, Maggie appropriated the research lab in the empty Danvers building to cook up her batch of rocks. First, she heated the powder base. Next, she added baking soda, and then rapidly cooled the mixture. True to its street name, the drug made a crackling sound, produced by the extremes of hot and cold. As it cooked, the drug gave off a sweet, magnolia smell; a scent Maggie came to love.

She bought up a stockpile of microchip vials, chopped the dried rocks into pellets and dropped two or three into each container. The vials sold for $10 to $25 each, depending upon the size of the pellets.

Meanwhile, David made himself useful by arranging for sales and distribution. Since the purity of the local crack supply was questionable at best, Maggie decided to approach the process from another angle. She used nothing but the finest, purest ingredients and as a result, her concoctions sold faster than snow cones in Hades.

In fact, her rocks contained such purity and potency that her special vials gained widespread popularity, known on the street as "Maggies." As her work and fame spread to neighboring states, clients were willing to pay more for authentic "Miami Maggies."

But its namesake grew weaker by her association with her corruptive creation. Depressed and irritable, she suffered from severe headaches and chronic fatigue. Maggie nagged, bitched and carped continually at everyone and David in particular.

"The only difference between Maggie and a pit bull is lip gloss," David complained, but not to her face.

She didn't care. Seeking the thrill of that first-time user high, Maggie smoked more and enjoyed it less. And the more she smoked, the more she wanted. The more she used, the more she needed—an endless cycle. The crack pipe became her constant companion. Alone, in her bedroom, Maggie started to talk to the pipe, making deals with the demon inside, the one who beckoned and urged her to do more coke.

Much too late in the game, David voiced his concern for her well being and his. He demanded she slack off on the coke. "It's hurting the business. All you do is stay locked up in your room with that damn pipe!" Maggie had long ago lost any interest in sex, only the profits from the drug trade held the two together.

But Maggie was no longer listening to anyone; she was too busy—a pro in a sudden death playoff.

Chapter 23

At the airport, on his way back to Miami, Bliss called Bodkins and asked the android to access the situation in the Everglades. Much to his chagrin, the reality proved to be worse than he had imagined. The terrain was unrecognizable. Tons of mud clogged the mangrove waterways, and unrecognizable pieces of boats and homes were scattered all over the glades. Tall cypress trees in the path of the twisters spawned by the hurricane had been reduced to toothpick-sized splinters.

Professionals, along with the Red Cross and volunteers had converged on the area and were struggling with the monumental task of clean up. Motels and hotels flashed "No Vacancy" signs and a tent city had sprung up nearby to house the overflow. The roads leading into the Everglades had been commandeered by a caravan of dump trucks whose crews worked around the clock to remove the tons of debris piled up by the storm. No lives had been lost, but many of the natural inhabitants of the marshes were in danger and rescue efforts were ongoing.

Bodkins one-word report, "Awesome!" did little to ease Bliss' mind.

"There are too many people, too much activity," Bodkins added. "We'll have to wait until things settle down to try and locate the ship."

Surely, Bliss thought, *we'll be able to find the ship, landmarks or no landmarks.* Stranded on Earth—it was a possibility he didn't even want to consider.

So, it was back to the game plan for them both. Bliss and Bodkins focused on the Haley estate, and restoring the old home's past grandeur. When things were far enough along, he decided to call Victoria. All he wanted was her advice and counsel, he rationalized.

"How's the prettiest woman in Miami this evening," he said when Victoria answered the phone.

"I don't know," Victoria shot back. "Perhaps you should call and ask her."

"Don't you like compliments?"

"Yes, when they're sincere. But that sounded like a line." She had immediately recognized his voice.

"A line?"

"Yes, you know, something you throw out to a woman when you want to reel her in."

"Well, Victoria, it was a sincere line."

Victoria smiled into the phone.

Bliss chatted for a few minutes, then invited her to dinner at his home on the following Friday. Without a second thought, she accepted.

Early on Friday morning, the doorbell at Victoria's beachfront condo rang repeatedly. *Who can it be at this hour?* She thought, as she opened the door.

"Mother!"

"Sur—prise!"

"It certainly is."

"Aren't you going to invite me in, dear?"

Victoria's wide eyes took in the silver limo parked in her driveway, along with the half dozen bags the uniformed driver was already lifting from the trunk. *What timing! My ESP must be on the fritz, or I would have been warned.*

"Yes, of course, come in—my house is your house."

"Precisely, I couldn't have phrased it better, myself." Her mother's eyes twinkled with mischief.

No, Victoria thought, I just beat you to it, is all. It was her mother's house, one of the several Rita owned, but Victoria had use of it whenever she worked in Miami. There was also the penthouse in New York overlooking Central Park, the villa in the Cayman Islands, and the home in Houston. Her mother acquired husbands and houses the way other people traded cars.

Rita was in her late fifties, give or take a few years. She easily looked ten years younger, thanks to plastic surgeons and health spas. *Her lifestyle certainly has nothing to do with it,* Victoria thought. Rita lived and loved hard, fully expecting to die young. Rita often lamented if she had known she was going to live so long, she would have taken better care of herself, At the moment, she was perfectly groomed, elegantly attired, complete with a fur thrown over her arm on this hot, humid late September morning.

As the chauffeur placed the bags in the hall, Victoria asked, "What are you doing here this time of year, Mother? All the 'in' people are still out-of-town."

"Not all of them, sweetheart. You stay cooped up here too much. The Jamisons are having a gala in Palm Beach tomorrow night in honor of visiting royalty, the prince of something or other."

"The Jamisons?"

"You remember them, dear. I met them when I was married to my third husband, he was Palm Beach, you know. Or was it my fourth? I lose count. Anyway, they're lovely people. Besides, I've been wanting to spend some time with you."

"That's going to be a bit difficult, since I didn't know you were coming. I have clients scheduled all day and a dinner date tonight."

Rita perched on the arm of the sofa. "A date! Splendid! Is it anyone I know?"

"I don't think so. I met him at a client's party a few weeks ago. He's buying the Haley Mansion."

Rita's eyes sparkled with interest. "The Haley place—you can't be serious. That house brings back such wonderful memories. I met your father there, you know. I'd love to see it again." Her face softened, and the worldly mask of sophistication slipped away to reveal her sentimental, more sensitive true self.

Uh, oh, Victoria sensed a plan in mid-plotting.

"Where are you having dinner, dear?"

Victoria was tempted to lie, but she couldn't. "At his home."

"Do you mean at the Haley Mansion!" Rita paused. "Sweetheart, I have a wonderful idea. Why don't I go with you, meet this new man of yours and see that lovely old house? It's just perfect."

"But Mother . . . "

Rita harpooned her. "Otherwise, we simply won't have any time to spend together. Tomorrow is out of the question. You know how long it takes me to get ready for a party of this sort.

And my flight back is early Sunday morning." The steamroller was in high gear.

"This is my first date with the man, Mother. Surely, you don't expect me to take you along."

"If he's any kind of a gentleman, Victoria, I'm sure he won't object. Besides, I don't think it's wise to go to a man's home alone on the first date. You'll give him the wrong impression." Her lips assumed a thin, disapproving line.

"Mother, if he has the wrong impression, I certainly didn't give it to him," she said, once again on the defensive.

Yet, as much as Victoria hated to admit it, her mother had a point. She was a bit uneasy, not quite comfortable, about going to his place for dinner. Victoria had allowed her desire to see him again override her normal caution.

Victoria felt a catch in her throat, remembering the recurring bone chilling feeling of premonition she continued to have, ever since that first experience in New York. A sense of impending danger haunted her, not to mention the erotic dreams that had plagued her for several nights, prompted somehow, she knew, by the phone call from Bliss while he was in New York. Suddenly, her mother's outrageous suggestion didn't seem like such a bad idea, after all.

Rita correctly interpreted Victoria's silence as acquiescence. "Well, Dear, why don't you phone what's his name," Rita prodded, "and see what he says about bringing along your lonely old mother." Her voice was vintage whine.

Victoria had studiously avoided any mention of his name. Her mother knew how to push all the right buttons. She especially liked the big one with GUILT written all over it. Sometimes, she thought Rita possessed psychic abilities, but was simply too lazy to pursue it.

Victoria gave in and dialed his number.

Bliss answered on the fourth ring with a sleep slurred, "Hello."

Victoria thought she heard a feminine giggle in the background. "This is Victoria Chambers. I hope I'm not disturbing you."

"No of course not. I was just thinking about you," he said as he smiled at the young woman in bed beside him.

"Bliss, it's about our dinner date tonight, I have a problem." She had started to say small, but it wasn't. "You see, my mother arrived in town unexpectedly, and tonight is her only free night while she's here."

"You're canceling?"

"No, not exactly, well it's up to you . . ."

Rita grabbed the phone from her daughter's hand, covered the mouthpiece and stage whispered, "What *is* his name?"

"Bliss, Jonathan Bliss."

"Mr. Bliss, this is Victoria's mother, Rita. I'm fine, thank you, and you . . . Good." Her tone took on a pleading quality, as she entreated, "If you wouldn't mind terribly, I'd like to join you and Victoria for dinner tonight. I see her so seldom, and this is such a short visit."

Listening to her mother, Victoria rolled her eyes, helplessly.

Rita forged on. "But I must confess, I do have an ulterior motive. You see your home, the Haley Mansion, has a sentimental attachment for me. I met Victoria's father there. I'd love to see it again."

Bliss chuckled. "I don't mind at all, Mrs. Chambers, it would be a pleasure," he assured her.

"Oh, it's not Chambers, it's Michaels. Mr. Chambers was my first husband. You're sure this isn't a terrible inconvenience?" she asked, not caring at all if it was.

"No, not at all, Mrs. Michaels. I'll expect you ladies at seven. My man Bodkins will pick you up."

"Thank you, Mr. Bliss, but that won't be necessary. I have my own car and driver. And, of course, we know where it is."

"I'll see you at seven, then. May I speak with Victoria?"

Rita smiled smugly and handed the phone back to her daughter.

"Bliss, I'm sorry about the inconvenience."

"No problem," he interjected before her apology could go any further, "in fact, you can bring the whole neighborhood with you, just as long as I get to see you again. Do me a favor, will you—wear something blue to match those incredible eyes of yours. I've been dreaming about them all week," he said, his voice reaching out to touch her in a soft, intimate way.

Victoria felt a hot flush creep up her neck at his mention of dreams. "Yes . . . well, I guess I'll see you this evening. Good-bye," she stammered, feeling as if he could see her red-face through the phone.

"Good-bye, Victoria—until tonight."

As she hung up the phone, Victoria had the queerest feeling, one to which she could put no name, merely a vague sense of misgiving.

"You see, dear, it worked out splendidly, he was very gracious," Rita said, beaming in triumph.

"Mother, it's a remarkable coincidence, you're showing up here this morning. Is there something you're not telling me?"

"Don't be ridiculous," Rita snapped, "can't a mother come to see her only child without stirring up a lot of needless speculation?" She punctuated her remark with an exasperated sigh. "Really, Victoria! Sometimes you take this psychic business too far." Anywhere near her personal motivations was way too far.

Victoria let the subject drop, knowing it was an old battle neither of them could win.

Rita would never admit, even to herself, how strong and right on target her intuitions were. She had felt compelled to come to Miami, sensing Victoria was in some sort of danger. What kind of danger, she did not know, only that she felt a need to be with her child. The party was just an excuse.

The day passed quickly in a blur as client after client called at the condo, and soon, Victoria and her mother were on the way to "their" date, chatting amicably on the drive out. When she allowed herself to, Victoria found her mother was actually good company.

Rita led an active, interesting life fueled by plenty of money and influential friends—one attracted the other. She married often and well. After the death of her first husband, Victoria's father, Rita went on an extended cruise to recover from her grief. She came back home with a deep suntan and rich husband-to-be. It was years before Victoria
forgave her, not understanding that her mother simply couldn't imagine life without a man.

Eventually, Victoria matured enough to accept her mother for who and what she was. In her work, she discovered many of her clients had the same problem; the need to find validation in another person, desperately searching for happiness in the outside world, never realizing it comes from within.

Victoria had been married, once, to her college sweetheart, but Brett's love had proved to be the possessive, restrictive kind. Their interests and needs grew, but not at the same time or in the same direction. Gradually, they drifted apart. Her work was the final wedge in the widening crack of the facade of her marriage.

Brett couldn't fathom Victoria's need to use her psychic gifts to help others and found it impossible to accept the fact that the therapeutic readings she gave to the depressed and disenchanted were her mission and purpose in life. He expected her life to revolve around him, his needs, his work, and his wishes. Finally, he issued an ultimatum — give up the readings or he was gone.

Victoria didn't want to make such a choice, so Brett gave up on her and their relationship. Brett found someone else to hold onto, and Victoria was alone, but not lonely, never lonely. In fact, she liked to be alone, wished she were right now, she thought as she glanced in her mother's direction.

Just then, the limo rounded a sharp bend, and the Haley house came into view with all the drama of an opening night. Located on a high point of land with the ocean on three sides, the imposing structure rose regally into the azure blue sky to dominate the landscape. With its pleasing blend of Greek revival and Georgian design, Victoria thought the mansion was one of the finest examples of antebellum architecture still standing in the South. Even Scarlet O'Hara's Tara paled in comparison.

Victoria's lips parted and she sighed; thinking it was exactly as she remembered. When revisited, sometimes childhood haunts seemed to shrink in size, but the Haley house had escaped the telescoping effects of time and loomed in front of her, larger than life.

As the limo made the last turn leading to the entrance of the circular drive, her eyes locked on a pair of identical sculptured hounds, flanking the gate on each side. The stone animals disconcerted her with their menacing, threatening stance. They appeared to be straining to break free of their concrete perch and run some hapless quarry to ground.

Victoria turned in her seat and stared back at them as the car drove on. She shuddered. The image of the hounds flashed off and on in her head. She was getting something . . . the dog . . . Bliss . . . the hound . . .Bliss . . . Maggie . . . dead air. "No! Wait!" she cried out loud.

Her mother reached out to her in confused concern. "Victoria, what is it? Are you all right?"

Victoria sat back in the plush interior of the limo and drew several deep, calming breaths. *I surround myself in the Divine Light of Love and invoke the Magic Circle of Love, nothing inappropriate can enter, nothing inappropriate can leave me.* In her mind's eye, she envisioned giant hula-hoops of white light, surrounding her for protection.

"Mother, thank you, it's O.K. I'm fine, now. I just had one of those frightening psychic flashes." Now, if she could just convince herself. Victoria rarely saw anything frightening and had not a clue as to its meaning or the cause of the sudden shutdown.

"What was it? What's the matter?"

"Nothing, Mother, really," she insisted, embarrassed.

Rita was unconvinced, but she didn't say anything more.

Victoria stared ahead, concentrating on the tree-lined drive and the house rising from the midst of a mass of overgrown vegetation that had over taken the once well-kept lawn.

Near the front, several gardeners were busy working to bring nature back under control, but years of neglect could not be corrected in a few weeks time. Yet, it was lovely in an overripe, promiscuous way. The lush landscape was dotted with huge, old live oaks, royal palms and orange trees interspersed with hibiscus, oleander, banyans and a generous sprinkling of red and yellow tropical flowers.

The limo crawled to a stop in front of the colonnaded entrance, and the chauffeur jumped out and held the door open for the ladies. Victoria gave her mother's hand a quick, comforting squeeze as they climbed the wide steps to the double oak doors—both of them feeling as if they had stepped into a time warp, half expecting their old friends to open the door.

Bodkins answered their tentative knock and ushered the two women into the entrance hall, directing the chauffeur to the rear of the house. Bliss' servant glided across the floor as if the bottoms of his shoes had ball bearings in them. Victoria received no psychic vibes of any kind from him. *Interesting.*

The absolute perfection of his body and features made her uncomfortable. No wrinkles, no blemishes, no defects, and no marks of character marred his flawless face. Bodkins looked like a department store mannequin blessed with the gift of life.

Directly in front of them, twin staircases curved gracefully toward the ceiling. Victoria's eyes were lured to a spot directly in the center of the landing, the place where she had played as a child. She turned into the vibrations of the past, happily reliving genial days gone by. The house welcomed her with all its charm and a hushed serenity that fell over her like a benediction.

To their left, Bodkins slid back the heavily carved wooden doors to reveal an elegantly furnished sitting room, formal, yet warm and hospitable. In a perfect English butler accent, Bodkins informed them, "I'll tell Bliss you have arrived. Please be seated. He'll be down in a few moments."

Twin loveseats squared off in front of the Italian marble fireplace with a huge French gold-framed mirror hanging above it. An elaborate chandelier was reflected in its depths, creating the effect of a handful of diamonds tossed in the air. The scent of flowers permeated the room, exuded by a huge bouquet of yellow roses blooming in a vase on the mantle. Smaller arrangements of daisies and daffodils, all of Victoria's favorites, adorned the tabletops. The entire room was a picture-perfect harmonious blending of beauty and style.

Rita gave the room a quick once over, selected a magazine from a fan shaped display on the glass-topped table, reclined on the loveseat and entertained herself.

Victoria remained standing and surveyed the room with great interest.

Although it was quite warm outside, a fire blazed in the fireplace and had for some time by the evidence of the glowing embers. But the room remained comfortable, chiefly because Bliss compensated by turning the air conditioning up full blast—a technique that worked surprisingly well.

Victoria drew closer to the fire, gazing into the flames, seeing a kaleidoscope of images of days past. There had been much happiness in this house, marriages, births and sorrows, too. *But the grievous times had been endured with the calm dignity of gentlefolk—no one gets through life without tests*, she thought.

Unnoticed, Bliss entered the room, taking the opportunity to observe Victoria, unaware, reflected in the mantle mirror.

She's beautiful, he thought, as he stared at her classically drawn Dresden china-doll features. Fine bones accentuated the delicate planes of her face, and tenderness and wisdom gave an alluring luster to her blue eyes. In the firelight, her petite, slender form appeared to be surrounded by a golden aura.

Suddenly, Bliss recognized Victoria's beauty for what it was, an outward manifestation of her inner serenity. A unique quality of Grace enveloped him in an unaccustomed, yet not totally unfamiliar sense of profound peace. Coming into her presence was like stumbling in from the bitter cold of a wintry day to a warm, glowing hearth in a place that felt like home. Tears threatened to fill his eyes. *If only . . . things were different,* he thought.

Victoria glanced up into the mirror and saw Bliss reflected there, standing behind her. Her face lit up with pleasure at the sight of him, and she turned to face him with a twinkle in her eyes.

"Do you always sneak up on your guests, Jonathan Bliss?"

The warmth of her smile tugged at his heart and pulled him into the room. He grinned at her and said, "Only the pretty ones. You promised to call me Bliss, remember?"

"Yes, I did, but it was so long ago, I'm afraid I've quite forgotten my promise." It wasn't true, not one tiny, infinitesimal detail about him had escaped her, but she didn't want him to know how important he was to her.

"It's only been a few weeks, but you're right, it was far too long. I have the eerie feeling you're often right about almost everything."

Although his remark was intended as a compliment, Victoria felt a hot flush creep up her neck. She tried to ignore the rising heat; feeling embarrassed by it, but it only increased her discomfort, because she knew that he knew how nervous she was in his presence. Being near Bliss somehow turned her into a silly schoolgirl with her first crush.

At that moment, her mother unwittingly came to her rescue, clearing her throat to claim their attention.

"And who might this lovely lady be, Victoria? I thought you were bringing your mother with you."

"This is my mother, Rita Michaels . . . Jonathan Bliss."

"It can't be, you're much too young." He took her hand in his, kissed it and said, "It certainly is a pleasure to meet you, Mrs. Michaels."

Rita instantly warmed to him; he had said exactly the right thing. "I'm pleased to meet you, too. I must compliment you on this room; it's lovely, simply lovely. You have excellent taste."

"Victoria, I like this woman," he said, turning toward her, his smile on high beam. "You must see the rest of the house. I'd value your opinions."

"We'd love to!" Both women spoke at the same time, having been hoping for just such an invitation.

Bliss took them on a mini-tour, apologizing as they walked guiding them through the debris scattered about by the army of construction workers. A large portion of the house was in various stages of reconstruction. The sitting room, dining room and master bedroom suite were the only rooms that had been completed.

Searching for small talk, Victoria inquired about his trip to New York. "It went fine, just fine," he said, "I made a killing in the stock market, and then I bought up half of New York City. Most of the furnishings and art work, I purchased at Sotheby's and Christi's auction houses."

Rita's interest peaked at the mention of the familiar names, "What did you buy? Tell me all about it," she said, eager to hear the details.

"I think it might be better if I showed you."

At the end of a hallway at the rear of the house, he led them into a huge, open room with high ceilings that extended up two levels. Encircling the entire room was a wide balcony. "This is the ballroom," Bliss explained. "I'm using it as a storage area until the restoration is finished." Victoria glanced up and imagined couples strolling on the balcony above, looking down on a throng of dancers below.

Rita gasped in amazement. The huge rectangular room was filled with furniture, mirrors, statues and other objects d'art. On either side of the doorway were two large ornamental urns. Bliss put his hand on one. "These beautiful urns are of Egyptian granite . . ."

But Rita finished the sentence for him, "Made during the craze for Egyptian art following Napoleon's African campaign. They're gorgeous, I love them!"

"Mother's something of an expert," Victoria explained.

"Wonderful, then perhaps she'll enjoy looking around."

Rita dove into the treasure trove, not believing her eyes or his fortune. She drank in the beauty of fine old craftsmanship, feasted her eyes on the lost arts preserved in the mellow patina of aged wood. She picked up an impressive figurine and checked for the mark of authenticity on its base.

"This is quite a collection," she remarked, "but you're mixing so many periods and designs. What interior design firm are you using?" Rita was accustomed to decorators who followed a theme.

"Actually, I don't employ anyone to make my selections. Perhaps I may hire someone to assist in the placement. Most of what matters to a decorator is meaningless to me. I simply buy what I like, what's pleasing to my eye and my own personal sense of beauty. The history of the item or the maker doesn't really concern me. Each of my guest rooms will be furnished in a different style, with items I select, personally." And each room would be occupied by a passing parade of women, but that knowledge he kept to himself.

While Rita roamed through the room "oohing" and "ahhing" over each new find, Bliss and Victoria made small talk. The words they exchanged were meaningless pleasantries, but an underlying electric current raced back and forth between them with a delicious urgency. A feeling of warmth and instant familiarity, an overpowering impression of having known one another before consumed her; feelings that were confusing and exhilarating in their complexity.

The yearning Bliss felt in Victoria's presence was instinctual and not tied to his voracious appetite for women's emotions. In fact, it rivaled anything in his experience. Her eyes, the turn of her nose, the curve of her cheek, each was so dear, so familiar to him. Just looking at Victoria brought him joy.

Although he wanted the feeling to go on forever, he was relieved when Rita joined them again. At least, she offered a form of protection. With her mother around, he had to control the temptation to take Victoria to bed. Bliss wanted her, yes—he wanted her, oh,
how he *wanted* her, but knew if he took her, she would be changed. And Bliss liked Victoria exactly as she was.

They continued on the tour, ending with his bedroom, another over-sized room dominated by an antique silk-curtained bed with color matched walls, papered in an airy print in varying shades of blue and green. A Persian rug that picked up the colors of the wallpaper accented the highly polished wide plank floor. Severes porcelains in stirring colors, created bright splashes on the bureau and tabletops.

Silk curtains framed the French doors leading to a balcony overlooking the pool area and the ocean beyond. But Bliss allowed them only a quick, cursory inspection; all the while imagining Victoria sprawled naked on his bed.

Before he ushered them out, Victoria checked out the master bathroom, straight out of a Cecil B. DeMille movie set with a yellow marble Roman bath complete with 14K gold fixtures and a seventeenth century statue of Bacchus, the God of wine, pouring water into the large Jacuzzi. A tent-like canopy of gold and blue draped the area.

At that moment, Bodkins interrupted the tour. "Dinner is served," he announced, looking straight at Victoria. It was the first time she had seen him smile. She smiled back.

Bliss thanked the powers that be for fortunate timing; he was relieved to be out of the bedroom, exceedingly uncomfortable with Victoria's nearness. She accidentally brushed his arm as they left the room, and his hunger flared. Bliss averted his eyes from her all the way down the winding staircase, trying to avoid the sight of the tantalizing sway of her hips.

In the formal dining room, the long oval table faced floor to ceiling windows that looked out on a dramatic ocean view. Another lavish chandelier shed an impressive glow over the antique cherry table covered with blue and white damask. Silver tureens and gossamer silk birds circled by small silver bowls filled with white orchids served as the centerpiece.

Bliss seated first Rita and then Victoria. As he pushed her chair forward, he leaned down and whispered in her ear, "I remembered how much you liked the orchids at Maggie's party."

His thoughtfulness made her feel special, and the meal was excellent, served expertly by Bodkins. Victoria would have felt better about him if he spilled the salt, dropped a serving fork or done anything that would indicate some human failing. *There is nothing more irritating than perfection in others*, she thought, dismissing her discomfort.

First, he placed a crisp, Caesar salad before them, followed by the main course of asparagus with bay scallops, shrimp and basil served with a side dish of porcini mushrooms.

These are some of my favorite foods; Bliss must be a mind reader, she thought as she washed down a delicate bite with a generous mouthful of Cristal Brut 1990 "Methuselah" champagne. Had she known that Bliss had purchased it at a Sotheby's auction for $17,625, Victoria might have fainted dead away.

She was sure the food was delicious, but her mind was on the man, not the meal. Her appetite had vanished. As they talked, she pushed her food from one side of her plate to the other, remembering to eat when the final course was served. Dessert was an elaborate concoction, a meringue swan filled with ice cream.

"What a lovely meal," Rita said, "thank you so much for including me."

"Yes, Bliss, thank you, it was wonderful," Victoria added.

Victoria and Rita left the table stuffed. Bliss grew hungrier by the minute.

Chapter 24

After dinner, they returned to the sitting room to relax and finish off a second bottle of champagne. Victoria sipped the fine wine and perused the bookcase shelves, delighted to find some of her favorite titles. She asked Bliss if he had read them.

"Yes, I have." Actually, he had consumed them.

Her hand caressed the bindings and came to rest on one book. It was a large tome, a compilation of research data on psychic phenomena. She removed it from the bookshelf.

"This one is interesting," she said, smiling like a cat with a bowl of cream.

"It's a fascinating subject, ESP," he remarked. Taking the book from her hand, he casually flipped through the pages. "I met another psychic when I was in New York. She helped me make some extremely successful investments."

"Really? I'm surprised. Do you know you are the only person," *aside from Bodkins*, she thought, "I've ever been unable to read. You say this other psychic perceived something with you?"

Bliss realized he had made a misstep. "Yes, she did, but her impression involved events that didn't concern me directly, you know, business trends," he shrugged. "There was nothing of a personal nature in the reading." He discussed his investment success

without revealing that the original idea had come from Victoria. How could he explain that?

Turning the conversation from himself, he asked about her work. The dam of nervousness inside her broke and a torrent of words gushed out. Victoria told him about Granny Mamie, her mentor and adviser, about the summers she had spent at Mamie's home place in the hills of Tennessee. Victoria spoke with passion about her work and the fulfillment in using her gifts. "I tap into sub-conscious and spiritual realms to reveal the truth, and I use the information to advise people, to counsel and sometimes, I locate missing objects and even missing people."

"Amazing, you can actually sense where something or someone is?"

"Yes. It's what brought me to Miami this time. I'm working on the third missing child case this year—it seems to be a serial killer. I assisted the police in finding the first two boys. Both of them were about the same age and had been brutalized in the same fashion." Victoria felt positive that the third child, only seven years old, was dead, too. Sometimes she hated the knowing.

Bliss sensed her reluctance to dwell on the subject. "How do you do these readings? Do you see things? Or do you hear things."

"As I said, my gift allows me to tap into the sub-conscious or universal mind," she explained. "When I touch a person or one of their possessions, in my mind, I see pictures, like a slide show or sometimes a movie. Sometimes I hear words or phrases. Timing is the most difficult aspect because in universal mind, there is no time or space, so it's all one continuous unbroken reality—the past, the present and the future all exist at once."

"How do you know which is which?"

"Sometimes, I don't," she admitted. "Timeframes are the most difficult things for a psychic to pinpoint. An event may already have taken place, be right around the corner or off somewhere in the distant future," she said, pausing, searching for the right words. "You see, each person carries within them the knowledge of the entire span of their individual life, plus the collective lives of all those around them. Sometimes my clients have to interpret the information for themselves as it relates to their own experience. Or I may call upon their guides or angels for assistance in answering a particular question or concern."

"Guides?"

"Yes, everyone has guides, spiritual beings who provide loving support throughout our lives."

"I see," he said. It was a concept he was familiar with, but could not, would not think about.

But he was not the only one who did not want to think about it. Rita, luxuriating in the mellow mist of the champagne, had daydreamed during most of their conversation. She had heard it all before. But she perked up, when Bliss brought up the subject of Victoria's work, thinking he might prove to be an ally. The man certainly seemed to have nothing against money and the finer things in life. Rita took one more sip of courage.

"Victoria, I don't understand why you don't charge more for your services," Rita said as she turned to Bliss, seeking confirmation. "She has some extremely wealthy clients who can well afford to pay much more. It's beyond me to understand why you settle for so little!"

Bliss rose to the bait. "If the client can afford it, why not charge more? Knowing the future seems an excellent way to become wealthy yourself." He wouldn't mind having such foresight. As it was, his telepathic abilities put him in touch solely with the present or with people's memories of the past.

"For one thing," Victoria said, glancing pointedly at her mother, "I don't need the money. My grandmother left me a trust that allows me to live comfortably, although not lavishly. But the real reason is; if I use my ability for personal gain, I feel it dilutes it. On the other hand, if I use my gifts to benefit others, it increases my effectiveness. The more I give, the more I get—in awareness."

Bliss understood, even if her mother did not. "I see," he said, in an effort to clarify the matter with Rita, "you're afraid that if you use the power solely for your own profit, it might eventually disappear altogether. You feel it's too important an asset, much too valuable to risk losing by abusing the ability."

"Exactly," Victoria agreed, "I couldn't have said it better myself." She glanced at her mother. "I find happiness in helping others with their problems; and for me, that's payment enough."

Rita rolled her eyes.

But Bliss was fascinated. "If the future is out there," he said, "already a reality you can tap into and see, then do you believe we have a pre-ordained, unavoidable destiny?"

"No, not really. There's always free will involved. Our Creator gave us that license, and it hasn't been revoked," she smiled. "I believe certain circumstances and situations are important opportunities, the catalysts in our lives. These events *are* unavoidable, but we do have free will and can make the choice of how we react or respond to any given situation. Everything is cause and effect. The course of the future can be changed at any time, change your mind— change your life. The challenges we face in life are our stepping stones to higher learning."

"I'm not sure I can accept that," Bliss said. "Not every issue in life can be overcome. Some problems have no solutions, they're not stepping stones, they're stumbling blocks." Suddenly, he was angry, repelled by the idea that he might somehow share the responsibility for what had befallen him. "Hatred. Revenge. Some situations can't be overcome or changed."

"I disagree," she said, softly, adding force to the words by her calmness. "I will admit that hatred is a powerful force, but there are stronger forces—those of forgiveness, creative thought and love. Healing ourselves of an undeserved hurt takes heroic surgery of the soul. By coming face-to-face with our true selves, we eliminate our weaknesses and find our strengths. When we come to know and to love self, then we truly have the ability to love others. And love is the great healer, relationships are what life is all about."

"For you, maybe," he said, looking at the fire to avoid her penetrating gaze. "For me, life is about freedom; doing exactly what I please, when I please, and with whom I please. Love means chains, pain and ultimately, heartache."

Victoria looked as if she had been slapped in the face. Tears swam in her eyes, and she blinked several times to clear them. She couldn't believe what he had just said about love, it was the antithesis of everything she knew to be true.

Someone must have given his heart an awful beating to bring on such a withdrawal.

"I'm sorry, if I've upset you, Victoria," he continued. "I do respect what you're saying, but most people don't believe in these virtues, let alone put them into practice. Some people are unforgivable and unchangeable. Trust me, I know." *I am one*, he thought. "But it's obvious that you believe in these things and enjoy helping others, and you're good at it."

"I've come to rely on the positive energies, it's a part of me," she said, glancing at her mother. "I enjoy being of service."

"There might be something you can help me with," he said.

"How? You know I can't pick up anything where you're concerned."

"True, but you did say you could locate missing objects?"

"Yes, it's simple, the person who lost the article brings me something directly connected with it. Then, I tune in on the vibrations, and through a process some psychics call 'distant viewing', I actually see the location. Have you lost something?"

My heart, he thought. "Yes, I've misplaced something, but I'm sure it will turn up," he said. "If it doesn't, I'll be sure to call on you." Victoria's distant viewing abilities could come in handy.

Having finished off the champagne, Rita was bored with the conversation. She had no interest in the psychic world or her daughter's profession. Rita stared at her daughter unable to fathom why such a beautiful young woman would devote her life to such a calling. If she didn't look out for her, Victoria would probably end up married to some penniless mystic. Rita loved her daughter, but could not relate to who and what she was. Why couldn't she have been a normal girl, interested in men, houses, clothes and jewelry, instead of running around spouting off about universal love and healing?

But as she watched Bliss and Victoria together, engrossed in their conversation, she was struck by a solid, singular fact;

they seemed to belong together. It was evident, there was a closeness developing, a thread of attachment, tenuous at best, but evident nonetheless. They meshed as closely in her mind as missing pieces of a puzzle. Somehow Rita knew her daughter's life was destined to intertwine with his, and for an unknown, unfathomable reason, it frightened her, although by every indication, she should have been pleased.

On the surface, she thought, eyeing Bliss closely, everything about him was perfect. He was obviously rich, intelligent, well mannered, handsome in a different sort of way, and he had a great sense of humor. But a discordant note struck her, something was off-key in his lack of any ties to the past, and the absence of any family photographs on the walls or mantles. There were no personal items in evidence in the house, anywhere, so far as she could see, no signs of school affiliations or past achievements, scholastic or otherwise. Bliss seemed to have no roots or beginnings, and with the exception of the one mention of some undefined past regret, all his conversation had related to impersonal matters.

Rita tried to draw him out, but each time he deftly changed the subject and successfully evaded her questions. Giving up for the moment, she excused herself on the pretext of the ladies' room. Actually, she wanted to have another look at that room full of goodies. His past might be packed away in a dusty box somewhere, and there might be important clues in the montage in the ballroom.

They hardly noticed her leave. As it was, Victoria was falling further under Bliss' spell. The man exuded mastery. His ease of manner and confidence was compelling. He made her feel more womanly and feminine. Warmed by his attention and the champagne, Victoria felt bright, alert and completely alive.

The conversation continued to flow easily. Somehow his interest in her was more significant than the actual words they spoke. He acted as if her statements were divine revelations and greeted each of her ideas as if she had just announced a medical breakthrough. When the topic moved to world affairs, Bliss startled her with an off-the-wall question.

"Why do governments put so much emphasis on enemies, weapons and arms build-up? Why don't they encourage the development of your type of talent as a means to improve the quality of life for everyone?"

"It would never work here. Most people in this country scoff at ESP, treat us like con artists and charlatans. Of course, the religious community is scared to death of us because we give people direct insight and guidance. But you don't need any intermediary, including me, you always have direct access to your Higher Power."

"Power to the people always creates fear in high places."

"Exactly. But the Russians have a different approach; they've supported parapsychology research since the '70s, to the tune of over 20 million rubles a year. I think our government is starting to play catch up, but of course the main thrust is toward technological applications, not humanitarian."

"What sort of technological applications?"

"I recently read an article that said the military has been funding a handful of mind-tapping technologies. Last year, the National Research Council and the Defense Intelligence Agency released a report suggesting that neuroscience might also be useful to 'make the enemy obey our commands.' The real goal of the government seems to be ESP-ionage. Pretty scary stuff."

"You're right. Military defense systems would become obsolete overnight if one country could control and confuse the minds of their enemies. Imagine waves of misleading information about weapon stocks or even incoming missiles." Bliss' concern was genuine. He'd hate to be trapped on Earth during one of their nasty global wars.

"Yes, but why would anybody bother with weapons at all," Victoria continued, "even atomic ones, if you can perform mass manipulation and stupefy whole cities through mind control. Our government is probably secretly delving into PSI research and hiding it from the public in an attempt to thwart the Russians."

"That could backfire," Bliss said. "Is there any proof?"

"There was an article about it in the late '50s. Granny Mamie had saved a clipping from a French tabloid, stating that the US atomic submarine Nautilus was engaged in testing sub-to-shore communications by telepathy."

"What happened?" Bliss was fascinated.

"Of course, U.S. officials hotly denied the story. Then, there were rumors that the Russians had planted the story in order to gain support at home for their own parapsychology program. Another rumor hinted that the CIA was involved and had released the story to cover their own leak."

"It's a dictator's fantasy, using mind power to control the masses."

"Can you imagine—the militaries of both sides, like some evil sorcerers, prying into our thoughts, manipulating us to do their will. It's terrifying and repulsive, yet at the same time fascinating." For an instant Bliss saw himself through Victoria's eyes, and it frightened him. "Are you all right?" Victoria asked.

"Yes, I'm fine, it's nothing," he lied, irritated with himself, with her and the entire population of Earth. "If there is such a thing as a psychic arms race, it's not a new phenomenon, merely a continuance of the arms race that has plagued the human race for decades. As I see it, unbridled greed, the lust for power, conspiracies, double dealing, and political intrigue, are all ancient practices."

On the verge of a tirade, he continued, "But why worry about it, Victoria. The potential possibilities of destruction are already endless; pollution, depleted natural resources, famine, runaway population, breaks in the ozone, not to mention the natural catastrophes, earthquakes, a new Ice Age, polar shifts and the resulting world-wide floods." He snorted in disgust. "It seems to me that Earth's researchers should be concentrating on eliminating the dangers that already exist, not in creating still more."

"But we are. Positive changes are taking place all over the world. The Berlin Wall came down. Plenty of people said that would never happen. Changes are being implemented by millions of people in a mass consciousness movement. Thoughts are things. When we dwell on something, we give it a strength and power. More and more people are getting a clear mental picture of what they want in the way of peace and prosperity . . . and believing they can have it."

"I'm no psychic," Bliss said with a doubtful look on his face, "but I'll make a prediction: In the next 20 years, mankind will decide whether or not to wipe most of its kind off the face of the Earth."

"Bliss, that's only one possibility. A raising of consciousness will bring about reforms on a global scale. There are uncharted realms of inner space, waiting to be mapped; the regions of the mind and of the spirit."

"Aquarius is possible, but so is Armageddon."

"I much prefer what the Age of Aquarius symbolizes."

"Victoria, every age has its own inherent drawbacks, advantages and disadvantages. I guess I've lived too long and seen too much. I am not at all sure of a positive outcome."

"Well," she said, "there's one thing that I'm sure of—the people who desire peace and a harmonious existence on this planet far out-number those who don't. Our unconscious relationship with the universe is very effective. We tend to get what we want."

With the fire of conviction burning in her eyes, Victoria looked irresistible to Bliss. He knew what he wanted.

"You're very beautiful, you know that?" he said, softly.

"Am I?" Somehow with him, she felt beautiful, radiantly alive.

"You seem surprised," he said with a puzzled look on his face. "Hasn't anyone ever told you how beautiful you are?"

"Well, yes—they have," she confessed. "But I never considered myself beautiful. I know I'm not ugly. But eventually, we all lose the beauty of youth, everyone ages."

He looked at her oddly. "Victoria, you are a very special woman. No one else can do the things you do. No one else even comes close, and you haven't even begun to tap the surface of what you are. You are filled with light and love, and the world is a better, kinder place for having you in it."

The tenderness in his voice touched her heart. Without having moved, he had drawn closer to her. Her hand reached out of its own volition to meet his and their fingers entwined.

At her touch, something inside him, cramped and stiff, broke ancient, dusty bonds and soared upward to infuse him with a rapturous, tumultuous enchantment. Without thinking, Bliss pulled her to him, he wanted to hold her, needed her as a man needs a woman; forgetting in the exhilaration of the moment who and what he was.

Victoria felt safe. It seemed right to be in his arms, like coming home. Looking up into his face, inches from her own, her feelings flowed out to him. The strong emotions bombarded Bliss, and the intensity of them awakened the hunger he had struggled all night to suppress. Her essence was intoxicating, tempting. Bliss was losing control.

Victoria's fingers gently traced a circular pattern over his back and the gentle stroking motions drove him crazy. Her scent filled his nostrils, enticing, beckoning. Bliss fought his urges, and the conflict raged within him. But in the end, curiosity outweighed his better judgment, and he gave into his urges. He wanted to know, needed to know what it would be like to kiss her.

At first, his lips touched hers cautiously as if she were a frightened doe under the hunter's gun. He moved slowly, carefully, and managed to keep himself under control as he kissed her tenderly. But Victoria's response was instantaneous and wholehearted, and she pressed her mouth to his.

Miraculously, he felt something flow out from him to her and back again, and there was magic in the moment as they melded and merged. Bliss had never experienced anything like it. The embrace transcended the physical, and moved into another higher realm. He was out of his body and out of his mind. They were two souls dancing in the light.

Then, the hunger he had fought to restrain, flared up and twisted his intentions, mangled his motives and demanded immediate gratification. His kisses changed, becoming more sensual as his tongue probed and invaded her mouth on a search and destroy mission, drawing her into the swirling cauldron of his emotions. Somewhere in the back of Victoria's mind, a warning flashed and in her mind's eye she saw the stone hounds at the gate.

But it was too late. In an explosion of passion, his hands moved over her body, caressed her breasts, roamed down her thigh, and up under her dress and slipped under the waistband of her panties.

Shocked by his sudden ardor, she knew she should pull away, but she was caught up in the intensity of her own involuntary response and sank helplessly against him. The blood drained from her veins, and her heart rate doubled as a rush of adrenaline surged through her, blotting out the rest of the world. It no longer mattered who she was or where she was; nothing could keep her from consummating her mad passion with Bliss.

Nothing that is, except the voice of her mother.

"Well, I can see you two are getting along just fine without me."

Victoria jerked free and pushed his hands away, leaving Bliss to clutch a handful of air. Breathing raggedly, she put a trembling hand to her chest, "Mother," she gasped, "you startled me!"

With a wicked smile, Rita said, "I'm sure I did." Her sharp eyes didn't miss a thing; she took in Victoria's wrinkled dress, and she enjoyed every minute of her daughter's discomfort and confusion. Victoria's goodness sometimes got on her nerves. Rita was pleased to find her daughter was human after all.

Bliss recovered first. "Your daughter and I were just getting to know each other better," he said, and then grinned at Victoria. Although his hands no longer touched her, his eyes did.

"A little knowledge can be a dangerous thing," Rita sniped.

Victoria blushed crimson, and she smoothed her dress in a useless attempt to diminish the damage. She knew every word her mother said held a double meaning, and she was mortified.

Bliss came to her rescue by putting Rita on the defensive. "You were gone for a long time, Rita. Did you get lost?"

It was Rita's turn to avoid their eyes. "Why, no . . .uh, actually," she stammered, "I've been in the ballroom all this time. Those lovely things just drew me back, so many beautiful pieces in one place at one time—it was irresistible. You were so involved in your . . . discussion, I didn't think you'd miss me. Obviously, you didn't." There was humor edged with envy in her eyes.

Bliss tactfully accepted her explanation, adroitly smoothing over the situation. They all relaxed, and Bliss the ever-genial host, offered them more champagne.

Rita remained standing and refused politely, glancing at her diamond studded watch. "Victoria and I really must be going. It's late and I, for one, have a busy day ahead of me tomorrow." The hours of primping she required to look her best, weighed heavily on her. Actually, it was barely past ten o'clock.

Victoria rose and joined her mother, reluctantly agreeing. "Mother's right, we should be going. It was a lovely evening, Bliss, thank you." Her eyes conveyed another message.

"It was my pleasure to entertain such lovely ladies. I wish you could stay longer, but I understand. I'll alert Bodkins, and he'll have your chauffeur bring the car around."

A few minutes later, their driver stood at the side of the car, holding the back door of the limo open. Rita walked briskly to the car, calling out her goodnights over her shoulder. Bliss held Victoria back with a light pressure on her arm, and then he bent down and kissed her on the lips. His face close to hers he said, "Victoria, I want to see you, again, to get to know you, even though I already feel as if I've known you forever."

The unexpected, unaccounted for closeness, growing all evening, had crystallized. She looked up at him. "I feel exactly the same way, isn't it strange?"

What am I going to do about her? Bliss wondered. *What can I do?*

He chose his next words carefully. "Ours will be, of necessity, a different . . . a special kind of relationship, for reasons I can't explain, right now." *Probably never.*

"You're married?"

"No, it's much more complicated than that," he said with a peculiar look on his face.

What's worse, she thought. *Is he gay? Not even a remote possibility, but what?* Her facial expression revealed all.

Bliss lightly touched her cheek. "Don't look so concerned, it will be all right." But his smile, meant to be reassuring, was tinged with doubt. "I'll never hurt you, Victoria, not intentionally. You're too important to me." Bliss was amazed at his own reaction, never having known a love that sublimated his own needs and desires for those of another.

His words were bittersweet in her ears and confusion reigned in her mind as her heart engaged in a tug-of-war with her head. She felt her mother's impatience to leave rising above the limo like a threatening storm cloud. Although Victoria wanted to stay, to talk it out and clear up the mystery, she knew she must leave.

"Good-night, Bliss," she said, thinking that all in all, in spite of the problem, whatever it was, it had been an excellent evening.

As he watched her climb into the limo, Bliss knew he had found something rare, and that he was in deep trouble.

In the car, during the drive home, Victoria's mother expressed her concern about Bliss' background, and his seeming lack of any personal history. She cautioned her daughter to proceed slowly. Then she blurted out, "Victoria I would feel much better about this situation if you never saw him again. Forget about him. He's trouble, with a capital T."

But Victoria was only half listening. Instead, she was going back over the events of the evening. It didn't matter what her mother said, what anyone said. Tonight, she had touched the stars, and her head was in the clouds.

Back at his mansion, Bliss was going crazy, mad with desire for Victoria. If his ship was available, he would have run, as far and as fast as possible, but he was grounded, stuck here on Earth with Victoria just a few minutes away. And he couldn't have her.

Two hours later, Bliss answered a soft knock at his door. It was Rita. He knew what she wanted and what he needed.

Chapter 25

Bodkins skillfully maneuvered the limo into a parking spot near Pier 11 at the Port of Miami. It was early Sunday afternoon, and Bliss intended to be one of the first passengers to board the cruise ship, the Viking Song. "Love Boats, they call them," he remarked to Bodkins. "I plan to do everything in my power to perpetuate that myth."

"Yes, but don't go overboard." Bodkins quipped.

"Perhaps it's time you had a routine service, old boy."

"Check my oil?"

"So to speak," Bliss said.

As usual, Bodkins had made all the arrangements for the trip, including the early boarding. Bliss bypassed the preliminary procedures and walked right past the cattle-call lines of passengers waiting to board. "Who is that?" a woman stage-whispered to her husband.

"A lucky bastard," he replied.

If he only knew how right he is, Bliss thought. *And about to get luckier.*

At the top of the boarding ramp, a preppy young woman in a cruise director's uniform greeted Bliss with a broad smile and asked to see his ticket. Visibly impressed, she personally directed him to his accommodations—a deluxe suite on the promenade deck, complete with a balcony.

Bliss viewed his spacious cabin from the open doorway. Champagne in the ice bucket, fresh flowers on the desk and Godiva chocolates on the nightstand. *It will do*, he thought. He returned to the main deck and secured a comfortable position where he could check out the other passengers as they arrived. Females of every age and description filed past him. The ship was a floating smorgasbord. He guessed that many of the single women on board, as well as a few of the married ones, were hoping to find a little romance during their cruise. Bliss' goal was to guarantee that this sailing went down in history as one of the most amorous ocean-going adventures ever.

Since his date with Victoria on Friday, Bliss had developed a thinking problem. Victoria was all he could think about and her intrusion into his mental montage made him crazy. It was getting crowded in there. Back to business, and to remembering that women were his business, his only business—his sole means of survival. After his close call with Victoria, Bliss realized he must put some distance between them until he could sort things out. *Who am I kidding? I just wanted to escape.*

He felt confident he'd soon forget about Victoria when the ship set sail, and he was lost in an ocean of blondes, brunettes and redheads. Not to mention the gorgeous prematurely gray vision coming toward him. As she walked past Bliss, the beautiful lady gave him a promising wink, and he always liked to collect on a promise.

Later, on his way back to his cabin to get his life preserver for the lifeboat drill, he saw the same woman coming down the hallway. Bikini clad with a tote bag on her arm, the lady in question approached. *Mint condition*, he thought.

"Has the luggage been delivered," he inquired, knowing full well it had not.

"No, I brought my bathing suit in my carry-on so I could take advantage of the pool and the sun. Our luggage should be delivered to our cabins sometime this evening unless the airlines sent it to Alaska or someplace else as a goodwill gesture."

He laughed and stuck out his hand. "I'm Jonathan Bliss."

She shook his hand. "Irene Tucker from Rapid City, South Dakota."

"The far north country," he said, still holding her hand as Irene unconsciously divulged her innermost romantic fantasy. "A place where the nights are cold."

Irene felt anything but cold.

Perhaps, I'll see you, later," Bliss said as he released her hand.

"Yes, that would be nice," Irene said as she walked away in a bemused state of mind.

Bliss entered his cabin and 15 minutes later Hugh Grant's exact duplicate emerged and sauntered down the hallway, following the faint scent of Chanel No. 5, lingering in Irene's wake.

A half-hour later during the lifeboat drill, two passengers remained unaccounted for. Everyone, according to maritime rules, was required to participate. Slightly miffed, cruise director Harry Landers phoned each cabin. *No answer.* Irritated, he stalked off to check each of the respective cabins to make sure no harm had come to the occupants. It would be just his luck to discover someone dead of a heart attack on his watch.

A few minutes later, Harry reported straight-faced to the Captain. "Ms. Tucker is indisposed and Mr. Bliss is attending to her." And there was some truth in that.

Later, back in his palatial cabin, Bliss carefully dressed for dinner, looking forward to fine cuisine, interesting conversations and stimulating companions. As he looked in the mirror, tying his tie, an angelic face intruded on his thoughts. What would Victoria think if she knew what he had just done, was about to do again—would be forced to repeat over and over? *What do I tell her—that I'm an emotional vampire? Victoria won't stick around to hear the rest of that story. She'll be out buying a crucifix and garlic.*

"The best thing you can do for Victoria is forget her," he affirmed as he downed another glass of champagne as a prelude to the feast to come.

Although the second dinner seating had already been announced, Bliss enjoyed a brief walking tour of the vessel on his way to the Rhapsody dining room. True to form, he checked her out, stem to stern. The Viking Song was a floating resort with two Las Vegas style entertainment rooms, a gambling casino, two swimming pools, a movie theater, health spa, game rooms, as well as several bars, lounges and discos—the perfect place for a man with his mission.

When Bliss entered the main dining room, his late arrival created a ripple effect. Women unconsciously adjusted their clothing, struck a pose or offered their best profile. As he passed near their table, two young women watched him with undisguised interest. One remarked to the other, "He's got it all."

Her friend retorted. "Yeah, and he's keeping it, too. That one is a heartbreak waiting to happen. Every woman in this room has her eye on him and vice versa. Been there, done that."

Her friend's eyes continued to follow Bliss as he crossed the room. "You're probably right, but he might be worth it."

The maitre d escorted Bliss to his table. Occupants of the most expensive cabins automatically received an invitation to be seated at the Captain's table. Bliss wasn't trying to impress anyone; the luxurious suite had been the only cabin available on such short notice. But as Bliss quickly learned, the arrangement proved to be to his advantage. Captain Swenson had an eye for the ladies and always asked the most desirable women on board to be his dinner companions. Swenson's ploy was a real time saver; Bliss wouldn't have to seek out these women, they'd been served up for him like featured entrees.

Bliss greeted the Captain. Introductions and hand shaking followed with the group of eight people gathered around the table. In addition to the Captain and Bliss, the other men at the table were Oliver Landis, a prominent plastic surgeon from Dallas and Andrew Comer, a retired mercantile magnate.

Andrew was by far the most interesting of the three; he was a charming man, on his fourth consecutive back-to-back cruise on the Viking Sun. When the ship returned to the Port of Miami next Saturday, Andrew would stay on board and sail out again on Sunday. Having outlived his family and his usefulness in the business world, Andrew did what he loved best—travel. An inveterate student of human nature, he never tired of the unfolding human drama on board ship, and considered it to be his own private soap opera. The

Viking Song and Captain Swenson were among his favorites. Andrew had followed the captain from ship to ship in the line until his current appointment. At 76 years of age, Andrew had been on 82 cruises, often staying on the same vessel for weeks, trip after trip.

The ladies at the table were either rich or beautiful, or both. Two were wealthy widows, one was a famous fashion model, and the fourth was a gorgeous, married travel agent from Orlando, Florida.

Everyone seemed to be in a good mood. It was French night in the dining room. The waiters attired in appropriate costumes had assumed the aliases of Pierre or Louie. Bliss ordered Escargot as his appetizer and two bottles of Dom Perignon for the table. The champagne loosened tongues and the conversation flowed.

The ladies vied for his attention, and the men engaged him in discussions on a wide variety of subjects. Whatever topic arose, Bliss shared an intriguing fact or insight. Andrew was particularly impressed with Bliss' wide range of knowledge. But he noted that Bliss seemed to be operating on two levels at once, although he actively took part in the discussion, a part of him seemed to be miles away.

Too many things reminded Bliss of Victoria. Sights and sounds, even smells triggered an emotional response tied to her. When he heard some interesting conversational tidbit, his first thought was to share the morsel with her. But Bliss bristled at the power she had over his thoughts. Irritated and angry with himself, he set out to drive her from his mind. *The best way to forget a woman is with another woman.* Bliss forced himself to think about choosing a companion for the evening, but not from among the ladies at his dinner table. These he would hold in reserve until nearer the end of the cruise when there would be less chance of complications. After dinner, he excused himself and started his auditions.

In the Casablanca Lounge, he paused for a moment to access the possibilities. After studying their faces and figures, Bliss asked Luanne Braxton, an auburn-haired secretary from Jackson, Mississippi, for a dance. She was happy to oblige. It was a slow song; a love song and she was a good dancer. Although Bliss was extremely attractive to women, he much preferred to assume another identity, using anonymity as a safety net. As Bliss held Luanne close, he tapped into her subconscious. *Ah, a familiar choice.* Her dream lover turned out to be a man he recognized, a transition made easier by practice.

The song finished. Bliss invited Luanne for a stroll in the moonlight. She accepted. The sea breeze whipped her clothing and pressed the fabric of her dress against her body, outlining her figure in moon glow and inviting shadows. His hunger stirred and Bliss was caught up in the familiar frenzy of the need to feed.

He escorted Luanne to an enclosed area near the pool, sheltered from the wind but with a good view of the stars and the ocean. "Would you care for a glass of champagne?"

"Yes, that would be lovely."

"I won't be long."

She stared out at the patterns of lights on the cresting ocean waves, searching for the moon that played hide and seek among the scattered clouds. A few minutes later, from behind her a strong masculine hand offered a tulip shaped glass. "You're back," she said as she turned. Luanne couldn't believe her eyes. "Do you know who you are? You're Brad Pitt!"

He smiled and handed her the glass. Luanne took it from him and drained the contents without stopping, never once taking her eyes from his face; afraid she might break the spell. Pitt was Luanne's idea of the ideal man. His photos were on the walls of her office and on the bureau in her bedroom. Never in a million years, had Luanne hoped to come face to face with the glamorous movie star. She was speechless. Maybe he was just one of those look-a-likes, but who cared, he looked enough like Pitt for her.

"I'm sorry if I startled you. I saw you earlier and wanted to meet you, so I sent my friend to bring you to me." With a hint of sadness, he looked down at his glass. "It's difficult for me to meet people, to really get to know them, without attracting a crowd." He paused, raised his head and gave a world-class imitation of Pitt's famous smile. "But I wanted to get to know you better."

Luanne's eyes dilated. It didn't matter that the entire situation was implausible. The arms reaching out for her were real enough. She dispensed with reason and reached for the brass ring. The empty champagne glass in her hand dropped unnoticed to the deck. Unbroken by the fall, the glass rolled crazily across the surface of the deck, underneath the ship's rail and over the side.

Late the next morning, Luanne sat on the edge of her bed in her pajamas and robe. She knocked back two Excedrin, held them on the back of her tongue and raised a glass of water to her parched lips. A throbbing headache and a pervasive chill added up to a heavy-duty case of anxiety. *It's just my luck*, she thought, *to come down with the flu the second day out.* She lay back on the pillow and waited for the pills to take effect.

God! Last night had been the most romantic, exciting, unbelievable night of her life. No one back home would believe it. The experience had been everything she'd ever dreamed of in even in her wildest moments. *My, my, my! The boys back in Mississippi sure had a lot to learn.*

The night had been so perfect, except for those last few moments. Right at the height of their passion, Luanne suddenly felt sick, on the verge of passing out. So embarrassing, but Brad hadn't seemed to mind. Luanne hoped she hadn't given him the flu. She decided to stay in her cabin and take care of herself. Brad might decide to call or come by.

Irene Tucker awoke at ten o'clock that Monday morning in her cabin two decks above Luanne. The ship had docked in Nassau three hours earlier. Irene sat up, rubbed her eyes and stared in disbelief at the clock radio. She had slept for 14 hours straight. A pleased smile touched her lips as the memory of her early evening adventure returned. She couldn't wait to tell her sister Renee when she got home.

Good grief, it's cold in here, she thought. Shivering, she pulled the bedspread around her like a cape and stood up. *Damn room steward—men always liked to keep a room the temperature of a meat locker.* When she was married, Irene always slept with her socks on for warmth and never realized until years later, that it was her husband's terminally high blood pressure that kept him so hot-blooded. It certainly wasn't his sex drive.

She tossed the covers back on the bed, rummaged through her as yet unpacked luggage until she found the rest of her pool paraphernalia. The image of a deck chair in the hot sun and a tall bourbon and coke beckoned. On her way to the main deck, Irene dropped by the purser's office to complain about the overactive air conditioning in her cabin.

Irene settled into a comfortable chaise lounge by the pool. Amply oiled, with her favorite drink by her side and a steamy romance novel in her hand, she waited for the sun to work its magic. The man in the chair next to her was already beet red and sweating profusely. Irene pulled one of the ship's towels around her shoulders for warmth. Nothing worked. She decided to go back to her cabin, get dressed and have an early lunch—maybe even a cup of hot tea. Later, she mused, perhaps there would be another rendezvous with her mystery man, the one who looked exactly like Hugh Grant.

Luanne and Irene each waited in vain for their dream lover to reappear. Bliss had already determined his best course of action—one-night stands—less risk for him, less harm for the women. His new motto was hit and run. Of course, his code of conduct had always been to avoid commitment at all cost. Bliss kept his options open, his bags packed. Whenever there ceased to be a payoff from a relationship, Bliss was out of there. Prior to Cassandra's curse, his lifestyle revolved around the joy of the chase, the excitement of a new sexual partner. Now, it meant fresh, exciting emotions and survival.

But if the truth were known, Bliss was damned tired of his life and of what he had become. Once upon a time, he had even tried fasting, but when his body began to break down and to age, he gave in to the craving. As far as Bliss knew, the only way to break the vicious cycle was death. For awhile, Bliss had lived life with a death wish, fighting for and aiding lost causes, hoping to be killed in action performing a good deed. But he seemed to lead a charmed life, absorbing the hatred and hostility of his enemies in a way even he did not understand. A steady diet of the heavy fare of fear and anger left him irritated and dissatisfied. Love and passion, even lust proved more palatable. Bliss emerged from such encounters refreshed and revitalized until he hungered again, and the cycle began anew, repeating itself in a maddening sameness. So, Bliss found his pleasure where he could, in beauty, in art, in ideas and in the affections of women.

As the voyage continued, the ship was rife with rumors of famous celebrities on board. The crew was besieged by inquires about the cabin number of George Clooney, Johnny Depp, Matthew McConaughey, Hugh Grant, Tom Cruise and Brad Pitt. When the ship's purser denied having any famous guests registered, the ladies grew insistent, protesting that they had seen them in the hallways or disappearing into a cabin. Captain Swenson wondered if his female passengers were suffering from a mass hallucination.

Bliss succeeded where others failed because he knew what women wanted—sharing, kindness, tenderness, consideration, and most important of all, appreciation freely given, not gratitude solicited or compliments paid on demand. Women wanted these things to spring naturally from a deep well of love and hated to ask or beg for these tender mercies. Wives, mistresses and girlfriends made investments of time, love and money in relationships with no compensating return. Until one night, they sat at the dinner table with a familiar stranger and asked—in a blinding moment of insight—is this all there is?

Bliss invoked and spoke all the words women longed to hear, words left unsaid in the sterile environment at home, words a woman like Dana Hayes needed to hear to soothe her soul.

On Tuesday morning while strolling on the main deck, Bliss retrieved the sunglasses Dana had dropped. As he returned them to her, he brushed the tips of his finger against hers, established contact and pulled from her mind every cherished desire, hope and unfulfilled wish.

The next day, the ship docked in St. Thomas. Dana's husband Jim refused to accompany her on a tour of the lush tropical island. Instead, he intended to crawl into a bottle of Jim Beam in one of the ship's bars.

So, Dana went alone to one of the most beautiful islands in the Caribbean. Near noon, she arrived at Bluebeard's Castle, located high on a mountaintop. Dana drank in the view from the terrace of the luxurious hotel. Lush green vegetation speckled with brilliant patches of tropical flowers cascaded over the mountains. White stucco homes with vivid red tile roofs perched precariously on the hillsides. In the harbor below, several ocean liners including the Viking Song loomed large, their great white bulk bobbing in the azure blue sea. It was a picture postcard view, a scene Dana wanted to capture. She raised her camera and moved back to include more of the panorama in her viewfinder and stepped on someone else's feet. She jumped away, stumbled, and dropped her camera.

"Excuse me," she muttered as strong arms helped her regain her footing.

She turned and found herself practically in the arms of a handsome gentleman.

"I'm sorry, I wasn't paying attention."

"No apologies, necessary. I'm glad we bumped into each other. You seemed to be enjoying the view as much as I am."

From the look in his eyes, she knew he meant more than the scenic countryside. With unusual grace for such a tall man, he bent over and retrieved her camera and checked it for damage, then handed the Nikon back to her.

"It looks fine. I was just about to have a drink in the Castle bar. Will you join me?'

There was more than a hint of danger about him and for a moment, Dana retreated in into the safe shell of her marriage. Then she thought, *What the hell, I'll never have a chance like this again.*

"I can't be gone long, I'm with a tour group." She motioned toward the waiting bus, dreading the ride back down the narrow, winding road.

"No problem, I have a rental car. I can take you back to the ship."

"How did you know I was on a ship?"

"Oh, I know a lot of things," he said and smiled.

And he did. Dana had the time of her life and returned to the Viking Song a changed woman. Now that she knew what she was missing, Jim was really in for it. Bliss had siphoned off her excess emotions, and Dana was prepared to deal with life on her own terms. She intended to demand more from people and fully expected to get what she asked for. Within her, thanks to Bliss, existed a rare harmony, a balance between her mental and emotional selves.

On the last evening of the cruise, Bliss stood alone on the windswept bow of the ship staring out at the ocean and the stars. Most of his fellow passengers were either asleep or stuffing themselves at the midnight buffet. Bliss relished the solitude and time to think.

He was ready to face facts. He might well be stranded on Earth, but Bliss was beginning to like this crazy little planet where people worked, with great energy, varying degrees of pain and absolutely no guarantees, to find their true destiny. Lost somewhere between immensity and eternity, humans struggled on, never giving up. Bliss felt a kinship with the people on the planet he sometimes thought was the insane asylum of the universe. *Have I been drawn here for a reason?* Bliss had come to claim Earth, but perhaps it had claimed him.

The night was crystal clear, perfect for stargazing. Strong winds earlier in the day had scoured the sky of the last remnants of cloud cover, leaving the air pure and pristine with an unobstructed view of the cosmos. Bliss threw back his head awed by the innumerable lights strewn like celestial sea foam on the waves of space. As his eyes followed the wispy trails and tendrils of light, Bliss experienced a deep sense of connection with all things. Small and insignificant, he was yet part of the vastness, at one with its infinite forces. He sensed a great power waiting to be tapped, needing only the proper conduit. Once upon a time, he had been a channel for that energy.

Bliss had never thought of himself as evil choosing to believe instead that he was merely a victim of circumstance. But on Earth, Bliss could not escape seeing the consequences of his actions. Firsthand, he was forced to witness the results of his reckless philandering and feeding.

Maggie, a warm, compassionate human being had become a cold, heartless bitch, an unrecognizable woman who preyed on the weakness of others while slowly killing herself. Kathy Elliott was as good as dead, plying her trade as a prostitute in L.A. And yes, the commodities broker, Nancy Burgess, had died as a direct result of his feedings. Taking another life was a serious matter and Bliss understood that from a spiritual point of view, the act forged yet another link in the heavy chain of karma he carried. For a moment, he considered the vast ocean as a possible solution, but he knew suicide would solve nothing. "Father, make me whole again," he whispered. Sorrow and regret consumed him, and he bowed his head in surrender.

If only I could go back in time, if only I could change things, make things right. His thirst for revenge had been slaked. Having been forced to drink from the bitter cup, Bliss even found himself thinking of Cassandra as something other than a degenerate lump of corruption, seeing for the first time, the person behind the deed and her motivation. *Starlight, star bright, I wish I may, I wish I might, have the wish I wish tonight.*

That night on the edge of sleep, Bliss astral traveled. In that realm, his spiritual guides at long last reached him, touched his mind and soul and nurtured the positive seeds he had sown in his heart.

When the Viking Song docked in Miami on Saturday, many of the female passengers left with considerably less emotional baggage. Bliss had lightened their load and allowed the women to view life in a more detached manner. For the most part, their one-night-stand with Bliss gave them a once-in-a-lifetime memory and moved them one step away from emotional dependency.

Bliss left the ship rejuvenated, revived, revitalized and changed in ways he did not yet understand. *What if, what if, what if,* resounded in his brain.

Chapter 26

After their dinner date, Victoria did not hear from Bliss for ten days, she knew exactly how long it had been because she counted every single minute. When he finally phoned, the reconnection was instantaneous and complete. They talked for hours and before Bliss hung up, he promised, "I'll call you tomorrow."

After that, he phoned every day, usually in the early evening. But Bliss did not ask her out; instead he seemed to be feeling her out, asking questions about metaphysical and spiritual issues. It was as if he was looking for the missing piece of a puzzle.

Bliss grilled her on a variety of subjects including reincarnation and karma. Victoria suggested he read about the life of the late American psychic, Edgar Cayce. "His work dealt with illnesses caused by the effects of experiences in other lifetimes."

"I'm more concerned with this lifetime," Bliss confessed. "I have a friend who has racked up a mountain of karma this time around."

"Sounds serious."

"It is."

"Well, my advice to your friend is to face up to the truth, deal with it. Take responsibility, forgive himself and anyone else involved, and do whatever's possible to make restitution."

"What if it's like . . . an addiction? What if he can't just stop?"

"The steps I gave you are part of the 12-step program for addicts and alcoholics. The most important step is surrendering to a Higher Power."

"Surrendering . . . you mean giving up?"

"Well, no, it's more like giving things over, letting them go."

"What if he can't surrender, what if he's evil through and through."

"Ever heard of duality—every sweet has it sour; every darkness has light; every evil its good. No one is evil through and through. Even Hitler had a choice. He made the wrong one. Human will is far stronger than random fate. People always have choices.

"You mean change your mind, change your life."

"Exactly, I suggest he read some books by John Randolph Price, Gary Zukav, Wayne Dyer and Deepak Chopra to start."

"Thanks, Victoria. I'll tell my friend what you said."

"You do that. Tell him to pray and to meditate. Prayer is talking to God, meditating is listening."

"What if they haven't spoken in a while?"

"Who left? God is always there."

A few days later Bliss rang and asked Victoria to meet him for a late lunch. It would be the first time she had seen him in person since their first date. Before she left for their meeting, Victoria consulted her guides. She knew Bliss was hiding something and felt sure there was no friend asking for advice. During her morning meditation she asked the question: *Is there a future for me with Bliss?* The answer came in a heartbeat.

Indeed. He will be an important part of your life. Each of you can achieve more together than you ever could apart. It is not only a relationship of great importance for each of you, but is also of benefit to the universe as a whole. Victoria found the revelation hard to believe, but the guides had never lied to her before.

As instructed, Victoria met Bliss at a popular but out-of-the-way beach restaurant, The Blue Dolphin. Although it was past the normal lunch hour, most of the tables were taken. The rendezvous had all the earmarks of a clandestine relationship. It was beyond her understanding, yet Victoria was unable to stay away.

From the moment Bliss greeted her in the foyer, she sensed the current of energy that flowed between them and a fluid sweet ecstasy that congealed around her heart chakra.

The hostess appeared and led them to a table by a bank of windows overlooking the ocean. The sun had already begun its nightly descent.

"Hello," she said.

"Hello, yourself. You are even more beautiful than I remembered," he said.

"You don't look so bad yourself."

"Oh, but I am bad. Bad to the bone."

"How's your friend?"

"My friend?"

"Yes, the one you asked me to give you advice for . . . you know, the addict."

"Oh, yes, him. Well, he's making progress." Bliss closed his eyes and let his guard down for an instant. *I'm trying, Victoria, I'm really trying to find a way out of this mess.*

"Ohhhh," Victoria said with a sharp intake of breath loud enough to catch the attention of two women at a nearby table.

They'll have what you're having, Bliss thought, realizing what had just happened.

Although Bliss had uttered no sounds, Victoria had heard him. His thoughts were easily identified, separate and apart from her inner voice and thinking self, different in both quality and feel, his unique timing and inflection were apparent.

"I heard you! First, you said, I mean . . . you thought . . . something about trying to find a way out of this mess."

He smiled, knowing sooner or later, it had to happen. *Never fool around with a psychic.*

"It's nothing like a psychic perception, and you know it," she said. "Some people think that's telepathy, but it's not. When I read for people, I see things in my mind, pictures that I try to translate into words. But I heard your thoughts as plainly as if you'd spoken them out loud. Amazing . . . do it again!"

Bliss reached out and placed his index finger on his lips. "Shhhh," he whispered. For the first time she noticed that his finger was deeply scarred and made a mental note to ask him about it later.

"You can do it, too, Victoria, just concentrate on the thought, focus on the words, see yourself releasing them to me."

Victoria gathered her mental powers and focused them with all the intensity she could muster. *LIKE THIS?* she sent.

Bliss winced. "Easy," he said. "Release your thought, gently."

"Sorry," she said out loud, "I guess I don't know my own strength." Her face reddened with embarrassment.

"Try again. Only this time, don't push quite so hard. Think of me as all ears."

Oh, I think there's much more to you than that, she thought. It was a whisper that danced in his mind. Bliss lost himself in the thrill of the moment, of having found someone to communicate with on a telepathic level.

Victoria sensed his joy. Tears stung her eyes as the enormity of the event overwhelmed her. She had reached out and touched his mind with her own.

Suddenly silent after her successful attempt, Bliss began to censor his thoughts.

Although on one hand, he wanted to be completely honest with Victoria, his fear of losing her was greater than his desire to be truthful.

One of her thoughts interrupted his. *Can everyone do this?*

To some extent, he projected. *But you're the only one I've ever shared this experience with.*

I'll bet you say that to all the girls, she shot back.

There are none like you.

"Good answer, Bliss."

"Victoria, I'm only saying it because it's true. I've never come across a woman like you, and I've known quite a few."

In her mind, she felt a massing of numbers and names. If what she sensed was true, as her ex-husband used to say, this guy's done more banging than a screen door in a hurricane. Victoria found it unsettling. Although she did not mind if a man was experienced, the sheer numbers distressed her. Bliss received the wave of emotional anguish and hastily closed off that portion of his past and spared Victoria the role of unwilling voyeur. There were some things she would be better off not knowing. Fortunately, it was possible to compartmentalize his thoughts and send those he chose. Normally, he had to touch someone to pick up mental chatter and stored memories. Victoria was unusual in many ways. *Finding you is like finding the missing half of myself,* he sent.

It sounded to Victoria like a declaration of love, yet he had not said the word. "I feel it, too, a sense of fulfillment, of completion."

The desire in Victoria's eyes clouded their brilliant blue with the smoke from an internal fire. Beneath the thin bodice of her sundress, the quickening rise and fall of her breasts tantalized him. An answering longing welled up in him. Never had any female affected him so deeply and on so many levels. A mere distance of two feet separated them. She could be in his arms in seconds and the qualities he loved most about her decimated in moments.

"Let's take a walk on the beach," he suggested. Although neither of them had finished their meal, he asked for the check. They strolled along the beach, hand in hand; Bliss could feel the hunger circling in his loins, gaining momentum. If it gained supremacy, Bliss knew he wouldn't care where they were. He had selected the popular restaurant and crowded beach, intending to use it as a bulwark between them, but his hunger pressed and prodded and threatened to break through the barriers he had erected. Bliss fought for control and willed himself to think of something else, anything else. He stared out at the ocean and struggled to make his mind a serene blank. Each time a sensuous picture of Victoria rose in his mind, Bliss pushed it back until such thoughts ceased to come. Then, and only then, did he trust himself to look at her again.

Victoria was totally confused, torn between a desire to fling herself into his arms and the compulsion to turn on her heels and run.

His mind touched hers again. *I want you. I need you, in a way that's incomprehensible and frightening to me. It's more than physical, it's mystical, it's magical.*

Victoria made a movement toward him, but Bliss held up his hands for her to stop. "No, please . . . don't come any closer. If you care about me, if you care about yourself, don't touch me right now. I'm not strong enough to resist the temptation. Believe me, trust me when I say, for your sake, we cannot have an intimate relationship."

"But why, do you have a disease?" *AIDS*, the thought popped out before she could censor it.

"No, I don't have AIDS."

"If you're not terminally ill, gay, married, or a priest— what is the problem?"

"Someday soon, I'll explain. I know it's asking a lot, but for now can you just go on blind faith. Trust me, what I'm asking is the best for you, something I'm doing because I care so deeply for you." *Explain someday? Who was he kidding? Tell her what, that he had an immune deficiency— absolutely no resistance to women?*

"Bliss, my guides have assured me that everything is going to be all right." Something within her told her to trust, if not in him, in herself.

Her ignorance of the enormity of Bliss' problem allowed her to smile sweetly and calmly, making a molehill out of a mountain. Her love for him was total and unconditional. She knew there was a mission and purpose in their lives to be fulfilled, and she silently resolved to help him, and if necessary, to heal him.

He heard the dialogue of her heart. "Thank you. You won't regret it. I promise." It was the first promise he had made in a long, long time.

"I will hold you to that."

"Good," Bliss projected. "I may have discovered a way we can be together more intimately, more often. Have you ever astral traveled?"

"Only once, during meditation. Suddenly, I found myself in the sky out over the airport. When I realized where I was,

I thought . . . it's the airport, and it brought me right back into my body. I've never been able to duplicate the experience. I have friends who claim to have astral traveled," Victoria said, her interest quickening.

"It's not all that difficult, especially if you're trained in the art of meditation as you are. Would you like to try it?" He rushed on before she could answer. "It's the only way we can spend a night together, but it will be a night you'll never forget."

Victoria hesitated. "Is there any danger of not being able to get back into my body?" She had no desire to be lost in space.

"No, that's a myth," he reassured her. "Any time you want to come back in, all you have to do is think, 'I want to be back in my physical body.' It's that simple. That's what happened to you out over the airport."

"What about other spirits?"

"There's no cause for concern. Don't worry, no matter what you might have read or heard, there's no danger of possession or attack by other entities."

"Could we use some form of protection," she asked, "you know, safe psyches?"

He laughed. "Use whatever normally works for you. Do what you always do before you go into meditation; invoke the circles of light as your protection."

"You're right, I do know how to protect myself."

"Now, may I take you out—way out?"

"Yes, but promise to kiss me first, before we go all the way."

He smiled, kissed her cheek and put his arm around her. As they stood at the edge of the ocean in silent communion, the Earth seemed to fall away, and for a blessed few moments, everything else around them seemed normal.

But time and tides wait for no one and soon, a foam-flecked wave broke over their feet and drenched their shoes. They laughed at the mishap and ran together toward higher, dryer ground. Bliss didn't stop until they reached the edge of the beach and the wooden stairway that led to the parking area above.

He checked the time as reality closed in. The sun was setting and people were gathering up their belongings and packing up their cars. Soon, they would be alone.

The crowd of people had been his insurance policy. There was safety in numbers and as those dwindled, so did his resolve. In the hazy colors of twilight, Victoria looked more beautiful than ever.

The hunger stirred. Soon, in spite of all his good intentions, his needs would make demands on his body. Bliss had already put a plan into effect to alter his life and although he had gone on a strict diet and done his best to limit his feedings, the hunger was always there. It complicated things whenever he was near her.

Feeling the pressure of his own time constraints, he wanted to confirm her answer. "We've got a date?"

"Yes, of course. You know I can't resist an opportunity to be with you, no matter how unconventional it is."

Bliss hadn't known any such thing, but was pleased by her reply, amazed that she trusted him or that there was the slightest chance he might be worthy of it. For the first time in a long time, something mattered, someone else mattered, and he was beginning to get a vague understanding—it all mattered. In his solar plexus something shifted, and he experienced an unusual lightness of being combined with an astonishing sense of freedom.

"My house, Friday at 11:00 p.m.?"

"Why so late?"

"It will be easier, if we begin around your normal bedtime. We'll use a form of self-hypnosis that allows you to program your sub-conscious mind ahead of time to leave your body in that millisecond before you fall asleep."

There's another reason, I don't want you in my house, in your gorgeous body for one minute longer than necessary."

Victoria sighed heavily. "I wish you would just tell me what's going on. Maybe I could help," she said.

"I I promise to tell you everything when we have more time." He looked at his watch. "I have to go," Bliss said, as he backed away, one of his feet resting on the first of the wooden steps in preparation for a hasty retreat. His internal time clock sounded another jarring alarm

. "Goodnight, love," he said before he blew her a kiss, whirled and bounded up the steps, taking them two at a time. *I'm coming back*, the demon whispered in his head. *No, you're not . . . not until I get outta here.*

Victoria called out her farewell to his retreating back. Then she remembered their telepathic contact and sent out a loving thought to him.

"I'll see you soon," he sent back just before the darkness of his hunger claimed him.

Chapter 27

When Victoria returned to her home after their beach encounter, her emotions ricocheted from joy at the promise of their next meeting to deep anxiety. She knew so little about Bliss and had so many unanswered questions, yet Victoria knew she loved him completely. She felt as though they belonged together.

But why, she wondered, are all these other women in his life, if he loves me? She sensed them intuitively, and last week there had been a confirmation of her suspicions. She had walked into one of her favorite restaurants and spied Bliss at a secluded corner table; engaged in a deep, intimate conversation with another woman. They were holding hands, and it sure didn't look like a business meeting— monkey business—maybe. Bliss had not seen her, and Victoria had fled the scene. Obviously, he wanted female companionship and physical contact, but not hers. Why?

Victoria could accurately predict the outcome of other people's romantic involvement. *Why can't I do the same for myself,* she wondered? Too much stuff in the way, she supposed. *I'm too attached to the outcome.* Was he strictly a womanizer, and she just another conquest? Or was she the last link in the chain, as she hoped? In her heart Victoria knew all the others before her must have thought the same thing. Doubts assailed her, tortured her, and made every other woman seem a more likely candidate for Bliss' lasting affection than herself.

Not knowing was the worst part. If he didn't love her, if there was no future for them, Victoria would accept it and get on with her life. What she couldn't tolerate was the feeling of being in limbo, tippy-toeing across the sinking sands of uncertainty, and waiting for the bottom to fall out. Now, she knew how some of her clients felt. Of course, she hadn't asked Bliss about any of these things, nor would she.

Victoria knew love on demand was impossible. Either someone loved you, or they didn't and no amount of talk could make someone fall in love with you.

As she prepared herself for bed, Victoria willed herself to stop thinking about him. She emptied her mind, let go of her problems and experienced the serenity of her own spiritual mountaintop. Victoria transcended her worries and fear and arrived at a secure, safe place where she found peace. In that relaxed state, her sub-conscious mind was in an open, receptive state.

Soon a vision began to take shape. She saw a familiar figure standing with her head thrown back and her mouth gaping open. A snowstorm swirled violently around the woman and the large, puffy flakes piled up rapidly until they reached her shoulders. The woman looked down in dismay at the deepening snow and whimpered. Then, her body slumped and disappeared into the suffocating accumulation.

Victoria jumped out of bed and ran into the living room to look for her client book. In her panic-stricken state, she was unable to find the number. Wait. Her cell phone Maggie had called her a few days ago. She scrolled down and found Danvers. *Thank God*, she thought as the phone began to ring.

Moments earlier, Maggie had opened her third vial of crack. Lately, it took more and more to feel less and less. The drug's adrenaline rush stimulated the pleasure zones, but now it brought her down much faster than she shot up.

Maggie heard the phone ring, but she ignored it. The bell continued to shrill. "Not now, dammit," she screamed and yanked the cord from the wall. She wanted to be alone. Several empty vials, their red and yellow caps scattered about like confetti on her bedside table, gave ample testimony to her dependence.

Maggie wanted up again, now. She took another hit—the rush was too much, too soon. When the crack entered Maggie's overloaded brain, her body rebelled and went into adrenaline shock. Instead of pleasure, there was sudden, incredible pain. She cried out and slumped to the floor, hyperventilating as her blood pressure skyrocketed and roman candles burst in her head.

Unable to reach Maggie, Victoria called the nearest ambulance service. "Hello, this is Maggie Danvers at 3509 Sunset Way. Please send an ambulance immediately. I'm alone. I'm having a heart attack. Hurry," she shouted as she hung up.

Fortunately, the dazed woman had forgotten to lock the patio doors. Maggie had forgotten to do quite a few things lately, eating and sleeping among them. The body the medics found on the bedroom floor was thin and gaunt, ravaged by her love for cocaine.

The medics immediately began giving her CPR. It was all they could do. There is no treatment for a crack overdose. Their best hope was to keep her alive until the drug wore off. On the way to the hospital, the medics struggled to keep her breathing.

Victoria waited an hour before she phoned St. James Hospital to check on Maggie's condition. "Critical," the crisp, calm voice informed her. Relief engulfed Victoria. At least, Maggie was still alive.

Was it what her vision in New York had foretold, the explanation for the repeated warnings, the sense of impending doom, the profound cold? *It must be*, she thought. *But why don't I feel a sense of relief?*

Victoria knew the worst was yet to come for Maggie. Surviving a drug overdose was just the beginning. When Maggie woke up in the morning, the real challenges would begin, the terrible ordeal of climbing up from the black pit of a mental and physical hell. But Maggie had already been to hell-and-back so many times she should have had frequent flyer miles.

Suddenly, the reason for the vision was clear to her. Seeing such events was the result of direct contact with the person, their possessions, or by contact with someone close to them. Much to her dismay, she knew. Bliss had been the catalyst. His involvement in Maggie's life had opened up the channel while Victoria was in her relaxed, meditative state.

But why couldn't she perceive anything about Bliss? Usually, she received some impression from even the most uncooperative subject. Sometimes people came to a reading prepared to mislead or test her; others were determined to prove her to be a fraud.

Those people did test her abilities, but not in the way they had intended, mostly they tested her patience. When she made contact, Victoria tuned in to their magnetic vibrations and viewed a series of impressions and pictures. The fabric of time flowed out, unmarked by any guideposts. Sometimes Victoria didn't know whether the event was past or present. Was it happening now? Or yet to be? The client always wanted to know how soon it would take place—next week, next month, next year? Victoria could only make an educated guess.

When a client cooperated and opened up, they helped interpret the impressions, gain an understanding of the significance of an event and establish a timeframe. If they resisted or lied to her, as many did, or worse yet, refused to answer any questions, Victoria wasted valuable time trying to piece the puzzle together.

But she always saw something. With Bliss—there was a blank wall. Could it be because of his telepathic ability? If he could send thoughts, then there was the possibility that he could block them as well. What deep, dark secret was he hiding?

Victoria had always expected that when she found her soul mate, the encounter would mean clear sailing. Instead, she had found as many obstacles, although different ones, as in any other relationship. *How disappointing*, she thought. *What ever happened to happily ever after?*

She realized her thoughts were caught up in yet another negative spiral. If she didn't change her state of mind, she would be awake all night. *Everything happens for a reason*, she thought, *even if it seems clear as mud at the time*. She invoked the Light of the Christ Consciousness and sent Maggie a healing, spiritual mind treatment, imbuing her with strength and courage. *The rest*, she sighed, *is up to you, Maggie.*

Victoria shuddered, remembering the vast emptiness she sensed within Maggie, unlike anything she had ever experienced. *Was that desolate emotional wasteland the result of the drug overdose*, she wondered, *or the cause?*

She yawned and looked at her watch. It was getting late, and tomorrow was a busy day. She needed her rest because early the next morning, she had an appointment with a member of the Miami Homicide Squad to assist in the investigation of a missing child.

Six-year old Christopher Rhodes had disappeared on his way to school. Widespread neighborhood searches had proved futile. No trace of Chris had been found. His was the fourth such case in as many months, and the people of Miami were clamoring for action. Last week, the frustrated Chief of Police had called Victoria in on the case.

She hated these cases because the things she saw in some of her visions were ghastly, and Victoria picked up on the fear, pain and suffering of the victims. But she felt it was worth her personal discomfort if she could end the ordeal of uncertainty for the victim's parents. She realized it was another avenue of thought best not pursued any further, so she stilled her mind and, in a few minutes, drifted off into a deep and dreamless sleep.

Chapter 28

When Victoria entered the Miami Police Station the next morning, she knew instinctively, it was not going to be an easy case. Outside in the bustling streets, the atmosphere was warm and sunny, but inside the building, the artificially chilled air was rife with tension. A palatable, unpleasant conglomeration of feelings permeated the rooms, seeped into the walls, and riddled the bodies of the men and women who struggled to survive in a southern tidal wave of crime and corruption.

The police poked and prodded and exposed the unsavory underbelly of Floridian society. Their daily dealings with the dregs of humanity made them watchful and wary, and they had learned through experience to question everyone's motives. The combined force of their suspicious natures hit Victoria like a slap in the face. *Wake-up call.* She had entered a different dimension.

As Victoria walked past a row of desks, several pairs of sharp eyes raked her in silent appraisal, then dropped, dismissing her as dull and uninteresting. Dressed in a light beige linen suit, she knew she appeared cool and aloof, confident and business-like. Victoria headed straight for the Chief-of-Police's office. At least, Tom Stanton was a friend, someone who respected her talents and believed in her abilities, having witnessed them firsthand.

As Victoria strode past his desk, Lt. Nick Feranti glanced up at her from a pile of paper work. He was the homicide officer assigned to the missing child case, consisting of three previous cases that had resulted in three dead children, all of them young boys. There were few clues and even fewer suspects. Now, the Chief had insisted on bringing in a psychic. Nick snorted in disgust. He had never worked with one and never wanted to. A veteran with 12 years on the force, Nick didn't believe in anything outside the realm of solid, bankable reality.

In his glass-enclosed office that overlooked the bullpen, the Chief greeted Victoria with warmth and did his best to make her feel welcome. But she could feel someone's eyes boring holes in her back. She turned and stared directly at Nick, who avoided her eyes, muttering to himself, "Stupid bitch, what a waste of time." Victoria read his lips and smiled.

The Chief picked up his phone, dialed Nick's extension and asked him to come into his office. After the introductions, Chief Stanton instructed Nick to give Mrs. Chambers his complete cooperation. Nick rolled his eyes and grunted a grudging, "Yes, Sir."

Nick led the way to his desk, where he snatched an envelope from his desk drawer, opened it and spilled the contents onto his cluttered work area. Among the items was a photo of a smiling 6-year old boy, a worn, grimy t-shirt and a small plastic car. From a paper sack, he pulled a tattered teddy bear with most of the fur loved off.

He turned toward her with a cynical grin bordering on a smirk that slashed across his ruggedly handsome Italian features. "O.K., lady, do your stuff."

"Lt. Feranti, why did you agree to work with me, if you have no faith in my abilities?"

"Lady, I didn't agree to anything. The Chief didn't give me a choice. So, let's get on with it." Don't waste any more of my time, he meant.

"I can't work this way, out here in the bullpen with all these people around. There are too many distractions and outside influences. I need someplace quiet where I can concentrate. Your skepticism and negative vibes aren't helping matters either."

"Look, lady—either you're psychic, or you're not. What's the big deal?" he asked, raising his voice.

"Nick, I'll put it into terms you can understand. It's like this; I know you think you're sexy," she said, lowering her voice, so no one else could hear, "but do you go around with an erection all the time—or only when you can focus, when other things don't intrude on your sensual thoughts." Sometimes, she had to break it down for them.

Nick's face reddened as he gripped the edge of his desk and leaned toward her. "What makes you think I think I'm sexy?"

"I'm psychic." Victoria paused for a moment. "Now that I have your attention, what I'm trying to say is, I have to be in the right *mood* to perform. Lt. Feranti, either you cooperate with me, or I walk out of here right now, and you can explain that to the Chief."

Nick had the good grace to look a bit sheepish as he gathered up the evidence and escorted her to a vacant, clerical office down the hall.

"Close the door, please," she said, as she extended her hand for the envelope.

She spread the items out on the bare desktop and stared intently at the child's photograph. Her hands stroked the t-shirt and the toys. Suddenly, Victoria began to receive vivid impressions.

She saw the boy, he lay face down, in a ravine, his face hidden in a puddle of water. Dressed in a blue, green and white striped shirt and jeans, he was wearing only one blue Nike tennis shoe. The child had been dead for several days. As the facts came to her, she relayed them to a stunned Lt. Feranti. He was amazed. Only three people knew about the tennis shoe, an unreported clue found early in the investigation.

"Can you determine where the body is?" he asked.

"I'm getting something—it's coming from the victim, his fear, his pain! Oh, God, I see him, it's the murderer," Victoria said, her voice shaking with excitement. "Take this down!" She waited for him to grab a pen. "He's about 5' 9", weighs around 180 pounds, has sandy, thinning hair combed across his head to cover a bald spot. He's maybe 35 years old with a round, boyish face. Oh, yes . . . he has a small mole on his left temple above his eyes—hazel eyes—God, those eyes!" Victoria didn't want to go on, she wanted a release from the child's stark fear and terror that still permeated that horrible place.

"This is a brutal, brutal man," she whispered, "one who really gets off on hurting people. He's sick, twisted, sadistic—with a perverted preference for young boys."

Lt. Feranti was furiously writing it all down. *Damn it, why didn't I bring the friggin' tape recorder!*

Victoria sighed heavily and forced herself to continue. "I'm getting more on the location. The highway forks near a road sign, the left fork takes you to the ravine, it's an excavation pit. I can see a sign." The words were beginning to come into focus. "Future home of Providence Baptist Church," she read. "It's a construction site."

Her eyes popped open, and the images continued to come. "Let me have your pen, and I'll draw you a map."

He handed it to her, and she began to sketch in a map of the terrain. "There's a big clump of bushes right here. The body is just beyond them," she said, making an X mark.

Without warning, her psychic perceptions shifted. She saw a tall, dark-haired man standing over a naked woman lying on a bed. It looked and felt like a hotel room. The woman's eyes were closed and she had a serene, blissful expression on her chalk-white face.

Victoria didn't understand what it had to do with the case. *What's going on?* But the impressions were so strong, she was pulled in. Victoria felt as if she were in the room with them. Without thinking, she automatically began to relay the information to Lt. Feranti as quickly as she perceived it.

"She's asleep . . . no, wait . . . she's dead. She's a slim woman, about 30 years old, girlish figure, around 120 pounds, curly blond cap of hair, and she has a birthmark." Victoria was elated. Any identifying mark was always important to the police. "It's just above the bathing suit line on her left hip."

Lt. Feranti flinched. It was a coincidence, the birthmark, but even so, the coarse black hair on his heavily muscled forearms stood up. *Jesus*, he thought, *this broad gives me the creeps.*

Having blocked out his negative vibrations, Victoria was ignoring Lt. Feranti and missed an important clue in his reaction. The images came fast and furious as her perception shifted to the man in the room. "Lieutenant, I recognize this man, but it can't be . . . he looks exactly like Alan Alda, the actor."

The man in her vision stared down at the lifeless body on the bed, his face sad and confused. Victoria vicariously experienced his pain and regret along with something else, the cause of death. She blurted out the bizarre notion as soon as it entered her mind. "The woman died during the feeding, it was a result of the feeding." Victoria was amazed at her choice of words.

Lt. Feranti snorted, and then broke down completely, dissolving in gales of laughter. When his amusement had passed, his face darkened. "What in the hell are you babbling about? You're trying to tell me some broad, shacked up in a motel with Alan Alda died from—what did you say, feeding? Now, I know for sure . . . lady, you *are* crazy. I knew this psychic bullshit was a waste of time!"

"Lieutenant, I know how crazy it sounds, but I saw it. I don't understand it, myself—it's what came through," she insisted.

He rose to leave, but Victoria stopped him with a torrent of words. "Wait, there's more, the man has an identifying mark, a mangled index fingertip." She hesitated, remembering an identical scar on Bliss' index finger, but there could be no connection, this man looked exactly like Alan Alda. Then another image hit her with startling clarity. "I know exactly how the woman died," she said, feeling a flood of passion. "It wasn't murder, more like involuntary manslaughter. She died while they were having sex!"

Lt. Feranti's mouth hung open. "This is the wildest bunch of crap I've ever heard. You've got some kind of imagination. How do you come up with this stuff?"

"I'm not imagining it," Victoria stated emphatically. "The woman had rheumatic fever as a child, it weakened her heart. When she climaxed, there was a sudden rush of adrenaline; her blood pressure shot up. The nearest thing to describe it is a cocaine high," she explained. "Her heart couldn't take the strain, the sex killed her."

Lt. Feranti grunted in disgust. "Oh, I get it. He fucked her to death. Mrs. Chambers, what exactly, does this have to do with the missing boy?"

"I don't know," she said, shaking her head, a pleading look in her eyes, "maybe nothing." Without warning, it came into her mind; Victoria was getting a name, the dead woman's name. It was Mary . . . *Oh, my God. No! Please, she thought, don't let it be true.* But it was, and she knew it without a doubt. The ballpoint pen Lt. Feranti had handed her had been the catalyst for the vision. *How could I have been so stupid?*

Victoria dropped the pen as if it were a hot coal. The name of the victim reverberated in her brain as the blood drained from her face. She felt faint. *This is horrible,* she thought, *I almost did an unforgivable thing.* Victoria's stomach churned in revolt at the idea as bile rose in the back of her throat, and she knew if she didn't get out of the office immediately, she was going to puke all over the desk.

Feranti watched her with an odd, perplexed look on his face, vacillating between total disbelief and a growing sense of apprehension. Victoria rose, a bit unsteady on her feet.

"I'm sorry, you'll have to excuse me," she said, avoiding his eyes. "I can't continue. Please, send these to me at my home address." She waved her hand to indicate the child's possessions. Her head throbbed with pain; it was the beginning of a sick headache, a form of psychic hangover. Without looking at Feranti again, Victoria bolted for the door.

She fled down the hall and ran into the ladies' room where she jerked paper towels from the dispenser, two at a time and wet the clump with cold water. In one of the stalls, she sat on the toilet with her head between her knees and mopped her face and throat with the towels in a futile attempt to keep from vomiting. But she was too late, everything came up anyway.

Lt. Feranti took his notes and went back to his desk and plunged into some overdue paperwork. Later that afternoon, he was called to the scene of a routine homicide investigation. A maid at a beachfront motel had discovered a body when she went in to clean one of the rooms.

But when Nick arrived, the coroner stopped him at the motel room door and blocked the entrance. "Nick, I wouldn't go in there if I were you," he said. "I don't know how to tell you this . . . we didn't know when they called you out here."

Nick's face blanched. In his heart, he knew what was coming. "Spit it out," he said.

"It's your wife, Mary. I'm sorry, Nick, real sorry."

Four hours later, Nick Feranti returned home to his empty apartment, having spent the entire time in abject misery, first at the motel, then at the funeral home making arrangements. When he entered his apartment, he automatically switched on the television out of force of habit. Then, he noticed a tape still in the VCR.

He pressed the eject button and the tape slid into his waiting hand. As he turned it over, the title jumped up and hit him right in the solar plexus. It was "Same Time Next Year," starring Alan Alda. As he clutched the tape, Nick sank to the floor, moaning, and the dam of tears he had been holding back finally burst.

The next morning, he placed several calls. The clerk at the motel informed him that the register at the front desk for his wife's room read James Green. A call to California confirmed the fact that Alan Alda was on location making a film in Europe at the time of Nick's wife's death in Florida—five thousand miles away, in front of cameras and a crew with dozens of witnesses. None of it made any sense. Mary with another man . . . dead . . . Nick felt his life was over, too. He loved her deeply, always had, always would, but he never knew how to show it. Now, it was too late.

The next afternoon, Victoria received a package from Lt. Feranti by special police messenger. It contained the child's photograph and toys, along with a recent snapshot of Mary

Feranti and a heart-shaped necklace pendant, her favorite
piece of jewelry. Attached to the pendant was a note.
"Please, see if you can pick up any more information from
these items. They found my wife in a motel room, yesterday
afternoon, just as you saw it." It was signed, "A believer,
Nick Feranti."

Victoria concentrated on the woman's face in the picture;
she stared into the warm, chocolate brown eyes, and saw the
pathos there. It was a familiar story. Mary had been lonely
and unhappy for a long time. Nick worked long, odd hours.
When he was home, he never talked with her about his work.
He closed himself off. The only time she felt close to him was
during sex because in the afterglow Nick was more open and
affectionate. During his off hours, Nick hung out with other
policemen, it was his social life; wives weren't included
because all too often some of the guys brought their
girlfriends.

The daughter of an alcoholic, she craved love and
attention, having been denied it in her youth. Without
realizing it, she had married a man much like her father.
Nick drank too much, too often. Mary felt frustrated,
disenchanted with her marriage, and guilt-ridden; somehow
feeling it was partly her fault. Everything had always been
Mary's fault; she shouldered the blame and the
responsibility. The man who took her to the motel room had
made her feel special, appreciated, alive and vital. Now, she
would never feel anything, again.

But Victoria was unable to pick up any more information
on the man in the room with Mary. She drew a blank; the
man seemed to have no past for her to tap into. All she saw
were scenes from an old Alan Alda film, a man with no life
outside the celluloid.

Giving up on him for the moment, she turned her
attention to the photograph of the child. Instant perceptions
followed with lightning speed as Victoria tuned her
awareness to that of the dead child's. The murderer . . . she
saw his feet walking back to his car . . . a blue Volkswagen
Beetle. Victoria followed him with her mind until she could

see the license plate clearly and read the numbers on the out-of-state Georgia plate.

Victoria scribbled them down and placed a call to Lt. Feranti before she realized he wouldn't be in the office. It was the day of his wife's funeral, but Chief Stanton was available to take the call.

Chapter 29

Friday dawned bright and clear, and a cooling breeze blew in from the ocean. The predicted high for the day was 85 degrees. Clutching a large tumbler of fresh squeezed orange juice in both hands, Victoria stood at the window and watched the sea gulls swoop and dive in the pristine sky.

Would astral travel be like the gull's free form of flight, she wondered, having always envied the birds' airborne antics and their unobstructed view of things from hundreds of feet in the air. Sometimes in her dreams she flew, and the episodes were so realistic, she woke up knowing how it felt to fly.

The dream sequence often began with her standing straight and tall, arms raised slightly away from her sides as she balanced on her toes in a ballerina style pose. All she needed to do was to think of flying, and the thought itself, floating in her head, lifted her body. She rose slowly at first, but soon she soared over the rooftops and trees. Coming back down was easy, she merely thought about it, and the thought moved to her feet, they grew heavy, weighed her down and brought her gently back to the ground.

Victoria smiled. Tonight, she was going flying with Bliss. *I've never gone this far with a man before.* Plenty of men had wanted to get into her body, but this was the first time anyone had wanted to get her out of it.

The gulls landed on the beach and brought Victoria's thoughts back to earth with them. She checked her watch. It was already seven and her first client was scheduled for eight. *Better get this show on the road*, she thought as she rinsed out her glass and put it in the dishwasher.

She was booked solid with back-to-back readings every thirty minutes until six that night. And there were always some drop-ins, people with emergencies, real or imagined, it was possible her readings would take her into early evening. At least her mind would be occupied.

As it was, the day passed swiftly, and at five minutes before eleven that evening, Victoria was escorted upstairs to a guest bedroom at the Haley mansion by Bodkins. *Ole Odd Bod* as she thought of him, with his physical perfection and total lack of personality, showed her to a guest room and promptly left her alone.

The bedroom was lovely, a restful and serene space, tastefully decorated in shades of peach, green and beige. On the nightstand beside the antique brass bed, she found a tape recorder and a note from Bliss containing detailed instructions for her to follow.

Victoria undressed and pulled on her favorite nightshirt, a white oversized shirt with "Good Happens" emblazoned on the front in bright blue letters. Then, she lay down on the bed and switched on the tape recorder to play the guided meditation. Low pitched and compelling, Bliss' voice lulled her into a highly receptive state. As she relaxed, the layers of the day's tensions peeled away, her mind cleared and then grew still. His voice hummed in her ear, and the words soon ceased to have meaning, the sounds were more like musical tones in tune with her spirit, soothing her soul with his song. She drifted nearer to the doorway of sleep.

Bliss' voice called to her, drawing her out. She felt lighter as something within her shifted, and she moved toward the sound. Victoria slipped effortlessly from her body. One second, she was inside, and the next second, she was outside—weightless, floating free, as she drifted up towards the ceiling high above her own sleeping form. The sight of her body drew her back. It felt so strange to see her body from a distance, eyes closed, completely relaxed.

Victoria gave in to the pull of the physical and began a slow descent back toward her body until a soft stirring of air nearby sent her into a spin. When she righted herself, the cause of the disruption, hovered to her left. It was Bliss. His transparent, smoky essence moved closer and stretched out long, tapered fingers of mist to meet her own. As they touched, their spirits met in a mystical union more intense, more pleasurable than anything she had ever imagined possible.

Bliss had intended to prolong the anticipation of the event by delaying the moment of unification until they traveled to some lovely, special location, but their pent-up longing was too great. Bliss melded and merged with Victoria as the two were united in mind and spirit and instantly achieved unity, oneness and completion as they bonded with a force larger and more infinite than their finite selves.

I like the way you say "hello" Victoria sent, her thoughts mingling with his.

And I loved your response.

Locked in a shadowy embrace, Bliss drew Victoria upward, through the ceiling into the calm, clear evening sky. Up, up into the black dome of night they climbed, higher and higher until Victoria felt as if she could reach out and grab the tip of the crescent moon that floated above her in a sea of glittering diamonds.

She exalted in the release from the burden of her physical body. *Freedom!* All the pressures of her Earthly existence lay back in that bedroom while her mind and spirit soared higher and higher, unfettered by the mundane miseries of her mortal self. No ears to pop or hurt as she soared to dizzying heights, no head to throb, no nose to itch, no aches or pains, no cold, no heat, no sensations of any kind, except for a deep sense of peace and well being.

Bliss directed their flight as Victoria gained confidence. He delighted in the opportunity to open up new avenues of experience to her and his consciousness expanded to accept the contentment he felt. Being with Victoria without the torture of his hunger, opened new areas of inner space previously unexplored.

No longer plagued by his physical needs and considerations, Bliss' mind functioned more clearly. The freedom allowed him to ask questions and actively seek the answers from a higher source. In the universe every action has a reaction; and by that very reasoning, Bliss suddenly realized that the curse Cassandra had placed on him must have an antidote, and he was determined to find it.

His love for Victoria had penetrated the fortress around his heart and shattered the walls he had built. Knowing how much she valued truth and honesty, Bliss was now prepared to risk losing Victoria's love by telling her who and what he was.

Below them, silvery shafts of moonlight glinted off the tops of the ocean swells interspersed with flecks of foam. The lights from the houses along the coastline reminded Victoria of tiny strands of white Christmas lights in a strangely silent night.

With no vocal chords to produce sounds and no ears to hear them, mental telepathy was their only means of communication.

Bliss directed a thought to Victoria. *What do you think of the experience so far?*

An indescribable sense of freedom combined with awe, wonder, exhilaration and joy filled her mind and flowed out to Bliss, reactions that mirrored his own.

I've never felt so close, in such complete harmony and accord. It's a magical night. Nothing will ever surpass this. Her love washed over him, warm and soothing as a summer rain. His happiness took the form of a wild, whirling dance in the heavens, and he pulled Victoria along in his wake as he swooped and soared, making the sea gulls look like novices. Gradually, they slowed to a more stable, serene form of flight.

Where would you like to go? Bliss asked.

Go?

"Yes, love—as in travel."

"I thought we were traveling?"

Yes, but we can go anywhere in time or space, just pick the place."

"Or the time?"

Actually, I'm much more accomplished at geographical or space travel than I am at time travel. Most of my astral excursions have been to gather data and information about the places I've visited. Not too much, too soon, he warned himself, no mention yet of other planets or lifetimes.

Can we really astral travel backwards or forwards in time?

Yes, it's possible; I'm just not proficient in that area. The idea of time travel stuck in his mind, and he filed it away for later. *I'm sorry, Victoria, you're disappointed. There's some point in time you'd like to visit, and I can't take you there.* He felt as if he'd taken a date to a greasy spoon after she's spent all day visualizing a French restaurant.

Are you kidding? I hadn't even thought of other places to visit, let alone another time. This experience is already beyond my wildest, most wonderful dreams.

Her fresh viewpoint of a phenomenon he took for granted blew through his mind, cleansing and dispersing the mental cobwebs that dimmed the memory of his first thrilling astral adventure. Somehow, Victoria possessed the unique ability to touch things in him buried deep in his subconscious, and turn those touchstones into bright, shining moments to be shared and savored. Together, they were as children again, discovering, learning, spontaneous, and open to new adventures.

We can go to wherever even if we can't go to whenever. What would you like to see? He sent. *Where shall we go?*

Many times before, on dates, Victoria had been asked that question, but never had she been faced with so many options. Given the choice of any place she wanted to go, Hawaii instantly popped into her mind.

Bliss pounced on it. *Perfect, great—it's daylight there, now. Are you ready?*

As I'll ever be. At least, I don't have to pack.

Then, we're off!

They moved as one horizontally, faster, faster, their speed accelerating as the night sky became a blur and gradually lightened. There was no sensation of heat or cold, no wind rushing past them, just an ever-increasing sense of rapid movement followed by total immersion in what looked to Victoria like liquid waves of color. Brilliant, intense neon rainbow hues more vivid than anything she had ever seen flowed around her in fluid hills and valleys. Mega white specks of light gleamed with a transcendent radiance, slipped through the streams of color and floated off from their view.

My heavens! Victoria thought, awestruck, as her mind expanded to take in the incredible beauty all around her. The riot of color permeated her being and filled her spirit. As each hue encompassed her, it elicited a different, positive emotional response, balancing and harmonizing with her own energies. Victoria became the colors, and the colors were her.

Bliss reveled in the passage, feeling but not fully understanding the healing process that was taking place within him. Having Victoria to share the experience with had heightened his awareness, and their consciousness seemed to be plugged into the same circuit as his joy was doubled and magnified by hers.

All too soon, they left the rippling waves and entered a gray in-between zone. Suddenly, they burst through a bank of clouds, then gradually their notion slowed and the sky surrounding them was a canopy of azure blue, giving way to a circle of misty vapors. Sunlight glistened on the tops of mountainous cloud peaks of pure, white smoke. Bliss released her as they passed through the top of a large, mushroom shaped cloud. Unable to distinguish his form from that of the fog, she panicked when she lost sight of him.

But he found her, even among the clouds packed as solidly as a snow bank, and during the descent toward the landmass below, he once more joined his energy field with hers. With their second union of mind and spirit, they created a link stronger than any that could be forged in the material world, and one Bliss prayed would endure the testing to come.

As the pair reunited, twin flames of spirit in the sky, they explored each other's minds. Victoria encountered much she did not understand, catching glimpses of strange places and even stranger people.

Bliss discovered in Victoria an inner grace and beauty, a wise and loving spirit. In him she detected compassion, a potential for great kindness, tenderness and other sympathetic vibrations that corresponded with her own.

When they dropped down through the clouds, their forms separated and sank closer to the land, a jade green chain of islands that wove indolently in and out of a sea of blue and green. Victoria soaked in the beautiful sight, while Bliss sorted out his private thoughts.

The moment of truth had arrived, but could he tell her the truth? How? Would she turn on him with revulsion and loathing? It was one possible reality and a painful prospect. Would she hate him? Although he knew Victoria possessed a broad understanding of human failing and a deep, abiding faith in the power of love and forgiveness, he couldn't help but wonder if it would extend to him and his bizarre circumstances.

Perhaps, I shouldn't tell her, he wavered. *But no*, he admitted, *cowardice would not serve them*. He knew he must face up to things and do his best to set them right. *Ignorance had been Bliss*, he thought, *but was no more*. Forgiveness for those who had hurt him in the past brought with it a sense of freedom and gave him the courage to tough out what he knew was going to be a difficult time in hope of better things to come.

With his thoughts on their future, he zeroed in on the island of Maui and spied a secluded beach protected by jagged peaks rising high into the low-lying clouds. He drew Victoria down to the top of a grassy knoll that overlooked the ocean.

As they settled down, he turned his mind to hers and eavesdropped. *Everything is so beautiful, just the way I imagined it would be, but I can't feel the sun on my face or the breeze in my hair*. And her hand passed right through the brilliant red flowers she reached for. *I can't touch them*, she thought, *or smell their fragrance. Astral travel does have its limitations*.

Yes, it does, Bliss sent. *Think about it*, he rushed on, having found the opening gambit he needed, *how it would feel to exist on this plane for a lifetime, missing out on all the sensory pleasures. Would you feel deprived?*

I suppose so, after a while, especially if I could never have another scoop of Rocky Road ice cream. I guess it would be like being a kid with his nose forever pressed against the window of a candy store.

Exactly, he thought. *Victoria, imagine you were a being on another planet in a distant galaxy, living in a spiritual dimension . . .*

And so, the tale began. At first, Victoria assumed Bliss was playing "what if," creating an intriguing story to illustrate his point for her enlightenment and amusement. She listened, delighted and amazed at his creativity. Then she suddenly realized, he wasn't making this up, Bliss was telling her about himself, in one stunning revelation after another.

Victoria's pale, shadowy form unconsciously shied away from him. Separating, she put distance between them. She wanted to leave, yet had to stay.

He was an alien and formerly, a Spirit Guide who had fallen in love with his pupil, Gabrielle.

Caught up in his story, she felt compassion for him, especially when she learned that the dangerous dark-haired woman she had sensed on their first meeting was Cassandra, the powerful sorceress who had placed a curse on him. It all went downhill from there.

When he began to bring her up to date with his activities since reaching Earth, her interest intensified. Now, she understood Maggie's sudden change of temperament, the aftermath of Bill's death and Kathy Elliott's departure. *Oh, my God, and that poor woman, Mary Feranti.*

She had come close to becoming a victim herself and now, she finally understood why he shied away from physical intimacy with her. She knew Bliss must care for her deeply, but his love for her paled in comparison to all the other things he had done. Victoria's mind reeled from the onslaught of his shocking confessions. Up until this moment, she had thought that whatever his problem might be, love would find a way to overcome it.

Bliss plunged on, afraid to stop, not realizing when his disclosures had accumulated to the point that they were too much for Victoria to accept. Her spirit shrank back to avoid any further contact with him. She wanted to be back in her body.

That was all it took.

Chapter 30

The force of her thought sent Victoria careening back. She traveled much faster on the return route than on her journey out, speeding past the clouds in a blinding blur. She moved like a phantom jet, zipping into the gray in-between corridor and whizzing through the vivid astral colors so fast that they were only a flash in her field of scan.

Then, she fell and plummeted down through the roof of the house, slamming into her body. The shock of reentry brought her bolt upright in the bed, in a state of stark terror. Her heart thudded in her chest and she hyperventilated, her breath coming in ragged gasps. Victoria sat up, swung her feet over the edge of the bed, and collapsed with her head in her hands.

"Oh, dear God, of all the preposterous, unbelievable, implausible situations," she wailed. "He's an alien!" And to think how freaked out her mother had been when Victoria dated a foreigner. Bliss' family background would send Rita into orbit. As if that weren't enough to adjust to, Bliss was a womanizing monster who fed on their emotions. But Victoria had to admit there were times when being cold and unfeeling might be desirable, like right now.

She was so confused. The fact that Bliss was an emotional vampire who turned women into cold, uncaring bitches was a terrifying prospect. *But,* she argued with herself, *doesn't everything have a flip side; aren't some women virtually incapacitated by an excess of emotions? If Bliss absorbed the excess, were they better off? Oh, hell, I don't know, I don't know anything, anymore.* Victoria's thoughts raced around in circles.

Suddenly, she thought she heard a noise down the hall. Was it Bliss? He might return at any time, and she certainly didn't want to be here when he came back. Victoria had no desire to see him or talk to him, all she wanted to do was get as far away from Bliss as possible.

Panic stricken, she sprang into action and snatched on her clothes, dressing in frenzy. Of course, nothing worked as it should. *Hurry, dammit, hurry*, she chided her body as her fingers fumbled, acting as if they had never encountered a button on a blouse before. *Stupid friggin' buttons*! She gave up and left the garment gaping while she looked for her missing shoes.

In a tizzy, she searched the area around the bed, and then got down on all fours to peer underneath. *No luck, no shoes, and no way I'm leaving barefoot.* Then, she remembered the closet and found her pumps inside neatly put away on a shelf along with her purse. *Bodkins the perfect strikes again.* She yanked one of them on and hopped on one foot toward the door as she stuffed on the other shoe before she jerked the door open and ran down the stairs, taking them two at a time.

At the foot of the staircase, Bliss blocked her path. Unable to stop, she ran headlong into his waiting arms. Victoria tried to twist out of his grasp and brush by him, but he caught her by the shoulders. "Victoria," he pleaded, "please wait, let me talk to you."

"No! I don't want to talk," she shouted, as she struggled to free herself.

"I need your help. Please listen to me. I have to explain."

"Not now, just let me go. You are either crazy or you are telling the truth. In either case, I'd be stupid to stick around." Victoria glared at him, and the clear blue of her eyes had turned to ice. Knowing anger and fear were walls too high for him to scale with mere words, Bliss relaxed his grip on her, and she wriggled free and fled. Tears blinded her as she bolted out the door, tears she fought to hide.

Bliss watched her hasty departure from the steps of the mansion. Victoria's car tore down the drive and fishtailed out the entrance. She drove as if pursued by the devil himself. *I have to be patient*, he thought, *and wait until she calms down.* Even in the midst of her anger, he sensed her love for him. It was a powerful force. *What would it be like to ingest such an intense emotion? Don't even go there*, he thought.

Strangely enough, the prospect of sharing such a feeling, and enjoying the effortless flow of it between them for years to come appealed to him much more than feeding on it briefly. Was their love strong enough to bridge the gap and unite them for a lifetime? *Am I strong enough to do what must be done?*

Meanwhile, Victoria was putting as much distance as possible between them. At the moment, her inclinations ran more along the line of installing moats than building bridges. She drove at a high rate of speed as she tried to outrun the pain, but it encompassed her. The disappointment, hurt, fear and anger hardened into a throbbing ball of anguish centered in her mid-section.

She halted for a stop sign and then sped away, shifting back up through the gears, her thoughts meshing with the movements. *If Bliss were just a womanizer*, she hit second, *a type she normally despised —* third *— perhaps she could deal with it —* fourth*— but this was way too much!* She slammed the gearshift into fifth and nailed the gas pedal to the floor.

Bliss rationalized as most womanizers did, saying that the women were willing partners, getting what they wanted. But she knew most women expected the relationship to continue and expected more than just a few nights of Bliss. The trade-off was a killer, the high peak the women reached might be pure ecstasy, but the compensating low must be sheer hell.

A warning blast from another car horn when she drifted into oncoming traffic brought her back to reality. As she swerved back into her lane, Victoria realized she had been inches away from a head-on collision. Slowing down, she steered her car to the side of the road and stopped to collect herself, accepting the fact that it was much too dangerous to drive in her mentally distraught condition.

As the engine idled, Victoria's thoughts eased their rapid race. She decided to examine the other side of the coin. For one thing, whatever else Bliss might be, at least he had been honest with her and had placed himself at risk by telling her the truth. And she had to admit that Bliss hadn't tried to harm her; instead he seemed to be making an impressive effort to protect her, albeit from himself.

In spite of what he was and the unspeakable way he used women, she loved him. His condition, his addiction was something she couldn't change or wish away. Her dilemma reminded her of a favorite childhood fable, "Beauty and the Beast." Was she predestined to love the unlovable?

She knew Bliss had come into her life for a reason. Why else would there be such an uncontrollable attraction? Such meetings and experiences in life were unavoidable, but there was always free will, the choice was hers—to forget him, to turn him over to the authorities, or to forgive him and try to help him. It was her decision and hers alone. She needed time to think.

Victoria steered her sports car back onto the highway, determined to keep her spooky mind on the road. After all, dead women were little help to the living, except for Granny Mamie, that is.

Back in his mansion, Bliss sat alone in the darkness, deep in thought—a prisoner of hope.

Chapter 31

Saturday was Victoria's day off, a catch-up day she intended to devote to a good overall cleaning of her condo. She could easily afford maid service, but Victoria preferred to do it herself—a form of therapy—the one thing in her life she had some control over. At the moment, Victoria found a measure of comfort in the mundane chores of everyday living. When she finished, she planned a trip to the market for groceries and her reward, a half-gallon of rocky road ice cream.

Although she loved to sleep late and seldom got the opportunity, Victoria had risen early. Drowsy and fuzzyheaded from lack of sleep; she smiled as she recalled a friend's answer when asked if she believed in life after death. "It doesn't really matter to me," the old lady had replied, "there may be another higher, better dimension or death may be nothing more than the BIG sleep. Either way, I shall be very happy because I so dearly love to sleep. *So do I*, Victoria thought, *except I couldn't get any sleep.*

Victoria didn't doubt that there was life after death, but at the moment, it was life after birth that concerned her. Victoria intended to keep busy, much too busy to think, "as if that's possible," she mumbled to herself as she tackled her tasks with unusual gusto.

The phone rang incessantly, an unwelcome distraction. She ignored the ringing and turned on her answering machine. As her hands dusted, washed, sorted and put things away, her mind tried to unravel the tangled threads of destiny.

Victoria knew that sometimes the best thing to do about a situation is to do nothing, and if she could just let go of the problem, her subconscious mind would deliver the answers to her questions.

But she could not let it go, the tape of last night's events played and replayed in her head over and over again. For a while, she bought into it and played the "what if" game. But, in her heart she knew it was useless. *I'm smack in the middle of a what is*, she admitted to herself.

I need to deal with the facts she reminded herself as she kicked the vacuum cleaner into high gear. *For one thing, although he is an alien, Bliss doesn't appear to be planning any kind of attack or take-over so he doesn't represent any apparent threat to national security. Even his acquisition of wealth had been accomplished without upsetting the economic balance. Bliss could just as easily have counterfeited the money and caused economic chaos.*

"On the other hand, she muttered, kicking a throw rug out of her way, "he lied to me." Or did he? Yes, Bliss had hidden things from her, and Victoria had known he was hiding something from the beginning, so it wasn't as if her instincts hadn't sounded an alarm. But Bliss was so compelling, so charismatic that Victoria had been drawn to him in spite of her better judgment and innate common sense. "Girl," she chided herself, "you don't fool around with emotional vampires." What had she gotten herself into?

But she also knew that if Bliss had wanted to, he could easily have taken her, used her and moved on as he had done with so many others. Her passion for him was so strong; he could have easily overcome her resistance. "Who am I kidding? What resistance? If he had called me in the middle of the night, I would have gone to him." Bliss knew exactly what to say and do, where to touch her, to what intensity and for how long. Just thinking about it made her pulse quicken and her skin flush. *He has power over me*, she realized, *a power I gave him*. The thought terrified her.

Yet she knew her feelings for him involved more than mere chemistry and passion. She sank down on the sofa. "I love him," she confessed, "and if I never see him again, I will always love him." Her love for Bliss defied logic. Was it a gift or a trick of the fates?

She had seen the roses around his head, the absolute sign of her spiritual soul mate? *Is this some great cosmic lesson? Is this my stuff or his stuff or both?* If there was something to be learned, she wanted to "get it" and soon. She knew she was at a crossroads, the one her friend and psychic counselor, Alice Tubbs, had spoken about in Victoria's latest reading.

"God, how can this happen, just when I thought I knew where I was going," Victoria wailed as her thoughts careened out of control and hit a wall of despair.

"Granny! Alice! Help me!" As soon as she spoke the words, she felt a light touch on her shoulder and inhaled the faint scent of roses. The words, *all is well* floated into her mind. "All is well, all is well," Victoria repeated until the darkness abated.

At 11:00 a.m., she switched off the answering machine and played back her messages, three calls were from clients wanting to make appointments, one was from Lt. Feranti and twelve messages were from Bliss.

She returned Feranti's call.

"Thanks to you," Feranti said, "the suspect in the blue Volkswagen has been apprehended. We nailed him before he could grab another kid. There was enough evidence in the car and his rooming house to indict him. But that's not the worst of it. When we traced him back to Atlanta, we found connections with another series of missing children in Georgia—looks like you've helped us capture a mass murderer."

Victoria shuddered. "Thanks for letting me know, Nick. I'm glad you got him."

"What about Mary's case," he asked, with a catch in his gruff voice, "anything new there?"

Her face paled. "No, Nick, nothing. I'm sorry," she said, withholding information from the police for the first time in her career.

"Well, if you get any of your psychic flashes, let me know. And thanks again, lady."

"You're welcome, Nick. Take care of yourself, O.K.?" And don't drink so much, she wanted to add, but she didn't, knowing it would be a waste of breath. Nothing could change Nick but Nick.

"Will do," he said.

"Good-bye, Nick."

As soon as she placed the receiver in its cradle the phone rang. Automatically, she answered it.

"Victoria, it's you," Bliss said.

"Yes, it's me. I live here, remember?"

"You sound so far away." *Light years.*

"I have a lot on my mind."

"I know. Victoria, we need to talk. Please, give me a chance to explain," he pleaded.

His voice seemed to come from somewhere inside her, it was as if her heart and his heart were one and the same. She felt his pain and confusion. It touched her soul and the ice pack around her heart began to crack as a sudden thaw set in. Victoria steeled herself against him, thinking, *is that all it takes, his voice on the phone.*

"I'm listening," she said, and melting, and dying.

"You left so abruptly, Victoria, I didn't get a chance to tell you the most important thing. I think I've found a way out of this mess."

"Which mess you're referring to?" she asked, deliberately misunderstanding, playing for time.

"You know what I mean. The situation I've gotten myself into—us into—the mess I've made of my life. But before I can do anything to clean it up, I have to find my ship."

"Your what?"

"My ship . . . my spacecraft."

"What's the matter, Spock, forget where you're parked?" she snapped. When she was hurt or angry, Victoria had a tendency to become sarcastic as a cover. And she was both, just now.

"Yes, and I need your help to find it. Will you do that for me?"

"How could you misplace an entire spacecraft? It's not like losing a pair of sunglasses or a briefcase."

"I hid it in the Everglades—before the hurricane hit."

"Good God! What makes you think it hasn't been destroyed or damaged?"

"The ship's shields are virtually indestructible; my vessel is ultra light and extremely durable. If I can locate it, I'm sure it's still space worthy. The problem is that the landmarks I used to locate it no longer exist. It's too dangerous for me to mount a search party; too many people are still roaming about in the area. But I think you can find the ship, using your psychometry talents."

"I've never tried to find anything like this before." What was she saying? There had never been anything like this before. "Anyway, I seem to have some sort of psychic block where you're concerned."

"I created the block, I'll remove it."

"Interesting. So, tell me, what happens when you find your ship? Is leaving Earth just another way to avoid confronting your problems?"

"No, not this time. I believe I've found a way to solve my problems. Remember when we were astral traveling and you asked about time travel? It gave me an idea. I've been up all-night thinking and traveling."

"I thought you didn't know how to do that very well."

"I don't. I didn't. But last night I experimented, I astral traveled in time as well as space. Actually, it's not much different. When you enter light sleep, you focus on the exact time and place you want to visit, zero in on it and-zip zap-you're there."

"O.K., so you zip-zapped yourself back in time. What does that have to do with anything?"

"It has everything to do with it. If I can retrieve my ship and return to Scorpious, there is a strong possibility that I can go back in time and alter my future, along with the future of everyone I've encountered since then."

"But why do you need the ship, can't you time travel from here?" Suspicion clouded her mind.

"Yes," Bliss explained, "but not for a distance of light years, and there's another problem, my astral body is incapable of any physical action in another time and dimension. I need someone to help me, someone alive during that timeframe, someone who can take action in the physical realm."

"Bliss, this all sounds terribly complicated and dangerous. Isn't altering time a drastic measure? Can you really expect to do that?" she said. *And survive*, she thought.

"I won't know until I try, and I must try. When the curse was first placed on me lifetimes ago, and I realized what I had become, I wanted to die. But three females who were losing their lives, offered to save mine and ultimately, my will to survive proved much stronger than my self-loathing. I adapted as best I could and accepted my fate."

"It seems to me that you have adapted a little too well," she said, thinking of his many conquests.

He sensed the direction of her thoughts. "Victoria, seducing women and feeding on their emotions has become the punishment Cassandra intended for it to be, one without end. Mine is a lonely existence. I have formed no friendships, no lasting relationships in several hundred of your Earth years. It is a long time to exist without companionship, there are no other of my kind."

"What about Bodkins?"

"Bodkins is a facsimile, a computerized android. His features may be changed to suit his environment, but his personality is a standard program. He has no feelings or spirit. He is a machine, devoid of the ability to be a true friend, yet after all this time," he admitted, "I do feel a kinship with Bodkins."

Bodkins weird behavior suddenly made sense. "How long has he been with you?"

"Since before I made my ill-advised stop on Scorpious, a long, long time ago," Bliss said, his voice heavy with fatigue.

"If I'm going to help," she said, "and I'm not promising anything, I have to know why, after all this time, you want to be free of this affliction."

"You of all people should understand. I'd much prefer to talk to you in person, face-to-face, but I'm afraid of losing control when I'm near you."

She did not want to go there. "Don't try to change the subject, just tell me the truth," she snapped.

"My decision is not easily explained, but I'll try. When I came to Earth, the only thing I was looking for was a way to ease my hunger. The intense emotional vibrations of your planet drew me like a beacon. What I found here was place where humans constantly seek instant gratification through material possessions, food, sex and drugs, and I was forced to face the similarities of my own existence. In your world, for the first time, I clearly saw myself, trying to have it all, yet having nothing. Then, I met you and everything changed, including me. I suddenly realized that all the knowledge I had acquired prior to coming here had not moved me one step higher or added one whit to the sum total of my immortal soul. I had been looking in the wrong place, outside myself, for a solution to a problem that comes from within. That was my first step in the right direction."

For a moment she was silent. "So, in us, you see yourself, we've enlightened you—now what?"

"When I time-traveled back to the beginnings of human life on your planet, I discovered something unusual—Earth is actually a star seed colony. Humans were placed here hundreds of thousands of years ago on the edge of the known universe to make a new beginning. Your ancestors were more advanced and highly spiritual, and wished to express themselves fully and to create.

When they entered into a material, physical life and immersed themselves in it in order to survive, they soon lost the knowledge of who and what they truly were. I suffered the same fate. But each of us have free will, given by our Divine Source, the opportunity to change our minds and choose the path of light."

"Bliss, that's true, but it's not that easy. I don't think you understand how badly others have been hurt by your selfish actions. We're here to do more than learn. How we treat others is vitally important. The basic tenet is; harm no one, because by hurting another, you harm yourself."

"For a long, long time you've been making others pay debts they didn't owe, extracting their feelings with a false promise, one you didn't even know you were making. None of these women understood the exchange they were making. Any female would jump at the chance to have her fantasies fulfilled, if they didn't know about the trade-off."

"Victoria, I understand that now, but before I came here, it was a game I played with myself, a delusion I fostered, pretending there was no real harm in my actions. It was sport, conquest, and I focused on the pleasure. Until I was forced to stay on Earth and see the ultimate outcome of my actions, I could avoid facing the pain of the consequences. What can I say, except that I do know what I've done, and I'm sorry. The only thing I can do is ask for forgiveness and try to go back and attempt to change the past and make amends."

"But you can't be sure of the outcome, Bliss. You've done terrible things to a lot of innocent people. How can you expect me to help you ride off into the sunset? Why should I?" she said, her anger rising.

"Victoria, everyone sows a few wild oats," he said, attempting to lighten the moment with some humor.

It fell flat. "A few wild oats. You could qualify for a farm loan!"

"You're not going to make this easy, are you, Victoria?" he asked, a hint of desperation creeping into his voice.

"No, I'm not! It's obviously been too damn easy for too damn long. All your conquests before this curse were to keep anyone from getting really close to you. What does love represent to you, Bliss? A cage? Some sort of prison a woman puts you in? Gabrielle or Cassandra or any of the other thousands of females you've known didn't forge those bars, my philandering friend. You created them yourself, and you carry your cell around with you."

There was total silence on his end of the line as Bliss experienced a whiplash of the soul.

"Don't you get it, Bliss? Those high, cold walls you've built, didn't keep others out—they've kept you in."

"I did it to protect myself," he said.

"Never loving anyone, never allowing them to get close doesn't protect you—it isolates you, it keeps you from growing, it keeps you emotionally immature."

"After everything I have just said to you, the only thing you have to say to me is that I'm a child!"

"Exactly," she spat. "Grow up!" Victoria slammed down the phone.

Bliss held the receiver in his hand and listened to the dial tone for a long time before he hung up.

Chapter 32

After the phone conversation with Bliss, Victoria tried to meditate, but found it impossible to get centered and into the right space. Hurt and confusion enveloped her, making it difficult for Victoria to think clearly. She needed guidance and counsel, so she turned to her friend and mentor, Lynette Sawyer, a psychic and hypnotist by profession. Luckily, her office was open on Saturday.

The urgency in her protÉgÉ's voice convinced Lynette of the seriousness of the matter. She cancelled the rest of her afternoon appointments to make time for Victoria.

Victoria arrived breathless and out of sorts in the lobby of Lynette's high-rise at exactly one o'clock. A few minutes later, she fell into Lynette's open arms, and rested her head on her ample bosom. Years ago, after Granny Mamie's death, the older woman had taken Victoria under her wing. They had spent a considerable amount of time together in the psychic community of Cassadaga, Florida; further developing Victoria's talents. It was there that Victoria gained a following, a number of clients who drew her back again and again to the region, until Florida became her second home.

Lynette was in her early sixties with graying hair and an expanding figure. An imposing woman, she stood 5'11" in her stocking feet. Her face shone with wisdom, kindness and a deep concern for the problems that plagued humanity. She used hypnosis to heal and help her clients learn about their past lives in order to resolve problems in the present.

After advising her secretary that she did not wish to be disturbed, Lynette ushered her into her office. Victoria related the events of the past few months, telling her friend and confidant everything. Lynette's eyes widened in surprise, but she was neither shocked nor disbelieving, having heard a multitude of strange things during her many years of practice.

Beings from other planets were something she already knew existed. She related curses to karma. To Lynette, wizards and sorcerers were merely altered states of being. What intrigued her most was Victoria's role in this cosmic soap opera.

It was apparent that Victoria loved this being, but couldn't consummate the relationship in the normal physical way without being destroyed in the process. And yet, with his enormous powers of persuasion, Bliss had not acted to bring it about, a positive indication to Lynette of his devotion to Victoria.

Lynette knew it was entirely possible to love someone and hate his or her ways at the same time. It was obvious— Victoria was torn between her love for Bliss and her natural revulsion at what he was and what he had done.

"He wants me to help him escape," Victoria said, "to leave Earth. He says he has found a way to make it right, to undo the evil. But what if he's lying? What if he's just going to run away, as he has so many times in the past? He might go on to wreak further havoc in the universe. Even worse," she added, "what if he stays on Earth?"

"The police are skeptical of me as it is," Victoria moaned, "if I go to the authorities with this wild story about an alien who feeds on emotions, they'll probably lock *me* up. Lynette, it could ruin any credibility I have," she said nervously, running her fingers through her hair.

Lynette sat back in her chair and assessed the situation. "Yes, you're right, the powers that be would either pat you on the head and send you on your way or put you away, and Bliss would be free to go on doing exactly as he pleases. Lt. Feranti, might believe you since he has a vested interest, but

Bliss' ability to transform himself and change identities would make him damn near impossible to apprehend. Obviously, turning Bliss in is not the solution to the problem."

"But what is?"

"You, Victoria, are the only one with the answer to that question. Remember your teachings, there are no accidents in life. We bring events upon ourselves. No matter how unpleasant a situation may appear to be, at some level we helped to create it. And sometimes, the steps we take are necessary to reach the places we have chosen to go. You are looking at this challenge with tunnel vision, focusing on a small part of a much larger picture. Stop looking at the problem, find out why Bliss has come into your life, find out what the lesson is—for you—for him. Then, you'll know what to do."

"You're right," Victoria sighed. "I've been so busy judging Bliss, I lost sight of my own spiritual path. Whenever I used to moan and groan about some unfairness or injustice to Granny Mamie, she always chided me to 'rise above it, child.' I suppose forgiveness is the place to start, but each time I try, my emotions get the best of me. I'm so angry at him for being what he is."

"Victoria, don't lose sight of your purpose. You are not here on Earth to judge others, or to punish them, but to love, to teach and to heal. Let those be your only considerations, and you will make the right choices, always." She reached for Victoria's hands and clasped them in her own. "Don't lose faith. I know you, well, Victoria, you have courage and strength. Remember, creative thoughts and love are the strongest forces in the universe, the forces which created it. There is no spot where God is not, including this Bliss fellow. Nothing is hopeless or impossible, unless we think it's so."

"I know, you're right," Victoria agreed, "I guess I just got caught up in the coulda, shoulda, wouldas."

"Change your mind, change your life," Lynette affirmed. "Isn't that what this Bliss character is trying to do?" Victoria nodded and Lynette let go of her hands and sat back in her chair. "Now that we've released some of these negative feelings, we can approach the solution to this problem in a positive way. Are you willing to try hypnosis?"

"Whatever you suggest, Lynette. I'm open to anything."

"I have a strong feeling that a past life regression might shed some light on the subject. An intense attraction like this is often an indication of a past life link." She patted Victoria's hand reassuringly. "Let's see if we can find that connection."

Victoria stretched out in the recliner and took several deep breaths as Lynette switched on her recorder and began to talk her down. Lynette took her eager and willing subject deeper and deeper into a relaxed state until Victoria's breathing became steady and even, indicating a light trance.

Then, Lynette began the regression, slowly taking Victoria back to her childhood and beyond. They delved deeper, past her birth, into other identities, and other lifetimes.

At one point, Victoria spoke with a soft southern drawl with a hint of a French accent as she described her surroundings. "It's early mawnin', just before dawn. So misty, it's difficult to see. I can barely make out the outline of two men. They are standin' back to back in a grove of Live Oaks."

"What are you doing there?"

"I'm hidin'. I shouldn't be here, but they are about to fight a duel over me, and I must stop them."

Lynette took her out of that moment and moved on to briefly explore another lifetime. This time Victoria was a fair maiden in Avalon during the days of Camelot, an interesting time but it had no connection to the current events.

Back, back through the mists of time, they retraced the steps of her soul's journey. "Where are you?" Lynette probed.

"I don't know," Victoria said in a confused state. "Nothing looks familiar. I see things, but I don't feel a part of them. I'm in a wilderness above a grave with stones piled on it." She paused. "I think it's my own grave."

Lynette gently prodded her on, urging her past the in-between state. Suddenly, Victoria began to speak in a unique, lilting voice in an unknown tongue.

"I can't understand you, translate into English, please."

"I am in my favorite spot at the foot of the Kaperth Mountains where the waterfalls empty into the sea. It is near the time of the setting of the dual suns. The white sands grow pink with their fire."

Lynette's pulse quickened. "Dual suns—where are you?"

"I told you," the girl said impatiently, "I'm on the beach."

"But where is the beach? You mentioned dual suns, are you on another world, another galaxy?"

"Oh, I'm sorry, now I understand what you mean. My planet is Arias, fifth planet from the binary suns in the constellation of Orion." In a conspiratorial voice she whispered, "But you must promise not to tell anyone of our planet's location, it's a secret."

"I promise. Please tell me, what are you called?"

"Gabrielle."

Lynette gasped, "Gabrielle, are you alone?"

"Yes, I'm waiting for someone, but he has not come," she said, disappointment weighing her voice down. "I don't know why he's not here, it's our special meeting place. I don't understand."

"What is he called," Lynette asked and held her breath.

"Most refer to him simply as the Guide although his name is Andreas, but I have named him Bliss because that is what he brings me."

"You mean he is your Spirit Guide?" *Oh, my God!*

"Yes, but he is much more than that, Bliss is my soul mate." Her voice changed and grew sad. "But my parents say he is not for me, they want me to think of my future and forget him."

"But you haven't done that, have you." Lynette stated.

"No, even though they are trying to keep us apart by forcing a union between me and one of my own kind. Aryon has already claimed me in the mating ritual, but it was done against my will." A tear slid from beneath Victoria's lashes. "I love Bliss, and I will wait for him—my mind, heart and soul belong to him and always will—always."

"So, you've been waiting for him a long time?"

"Yes—you see—he doesn't know how much I love him. He will return, he will come for me, I know it."

"Yes, Gabrielle, I'm sure he will."

Lynette slowly brought Victoria up out of the trance, back into the present. "You are coming into a full awareness of the now. At the count of five, Victoria, you will awaken, feeling relaxed and refreshed, as if you have had several hours of sleep. One—you are awakening—two, three— wider and wider awake—four—five—wide awake." Lynette snapped her fingers and the trance ended.

The women stared at each other without speaking. Lynette played back the recording, watching Victoria's face as all of the pieces of the puzzle fell into place.

The two of them together, lifetimes ago—Victoria reeled from the implication— *she had been the catalyst for this vicious cycle of hurt and revenge.*

"Lynette, I'm partially responsible for what happened, I helped to set it in motion." Suddenly, it all made sense, and the women exchanged shocked looks of total comprehension.

"You'll know what to do, sweetheart," Lynette said as she hugged Victoria. "If you need anything else, I'm here."

"Some prayers would be nice."

"You got it."

Victoria thanked Lynette and retrieved the recording, knowing she was being given the chance to end the cycle and redeem not only Bliss, but also herself. It was a sobering experience to find that she was directly involved. *It's funny how blame tends to ricochet once you cast it,* she thought.

By the time she arrived back at her condo, she knew what she had to do and why. *Love had chained Bliss, could it also set him free?* She was saddened by the thought that all this misery had come about as the result of jealousy, misunderstandings and a total lack of communication—the reasons for much of the unhappiness in the world.

When she called Bliss on the phone to inform him of her decision to assist him, he let out a whoop that nearly deafened her.

After he settled down, he asked, "I'm curious, what brought about this sudden change of heart?"

"Bliss I don't want to talk about it on the phone. Come over, right away and bring me an object directly connected with your ship. I'll need something to tune it to. I'll tell you everything when you get here."

"You're not afraid to be with me?" he asked, surprised.

"No, not any more."

"You don't have to be. I wouldn't hurt you. I love you, Victoria."

There they were at last, the words she had waited lifetimes to hear.

"I know," she said, getting misty. "And I love you, Bliss. Now, get your spacey butt over here on the double!"

Within the hour, his car pulled into her driveway. Bliss instructed Bodkins to wait in the limo, patience robotified. It was the first time Bliss had visited her condo, and he found it to be exactly what he expected; a home furnished in classic, simple, understated elegance, filled with beauty and light, just like the woman he loved.

When Bliss was seated comfortably on the sofa, Victoria related the events of the day, giving him a blow by blow of her session with Lynette and the outcome. At first, Bliss was amazed, then skeptical.

"You—Gabrielle reincarnated. Impossible lady, no way," he snorted. His face was a mask of disbelief. During their astral date, he had briefly explained about his first love, the pain and rejection and the fact that he had run away to seek revenge. Victoria's subconscious must have been playing tricks on her, he thought, using information he had given her.

"There must be some way I can prove it to you. Did you, at any time, tell me the name of the mountain on Arias, the one near the beach where you and Gabrielle secretly met?"

"No, I most surely did not," he said as his eyes turned to jade stone. He had not gone into any great detail regarding that period of his life.

"Have you at any time opened yourself up to me so that I could have obtained the information using my psychic abilities?"

"No," he admitted.

"The block is in place even now, isn't it Bliss? I can feel— the wall."

He had been caught in the act.

"It's all right, Bliss don't remove it, yet. The name of that mountain range on Arias, its Kaperth, isn't it?"

"Spirits of my fathers!" Bliss exploded, his face a storm cloud, threatening. "How do you know that? Who told you? Damn it, Victoria, tell me the truth." His mind searched for some explanation. *Could Bodkins have given her the information? Not likely.*

"Bliss, I'm telling you the truth, and you don't believe me. Astonishing—you've confided all manner of implausible, mind-blowing things to me and expected me to accept them, yet when I tell you something so revealing about our relationship, the reason for our instantaneous connection— you reject it!"

Victoria wasn't prepared for his denial and struggled to find a way to convey to him the importance of what she had learned. "Bliss, you asked me why I've had a change of heart, why I'm willing to help you. I'm trying to tell you—it's because we shared a love in a past life, and we weren't able to complete it. Both of us were at fault."

He shook his head.

"Why would I lie? Don't you understand what this means, for both of us?

Bliss sprang to his feet and paced the floor. As he turned to face Victoria, the anger flared in his eyes. "You're the one who doesn't understand. I thought you did, but I can see I was wrong. Gabrielle and I didn't share a love," he argued. "She gave that away to someone else because I couldn't satisfy her. I couldn't give her what she wanted!"

He towered over her, his arms crossed. "Do you want some more truth, Victoria?" His tone practically frosted up the windows. "When I ran away from Arias, I didn't have sex with all those women for revenge alone. Oh, I'll admit it was a big part of it, but mostly I did it because I was trying to prove something to myself, to convince myself that I could actually satisfy a female."

Victoria looked up at him in amazement. *It's worse than I thought.*

He eyed her coldly and continued. "Yes, Victoria, I did it over and over, only it was never enough. My mind always returned to Gabrielle and my failure, my inability to fulfill her." His anger abated with his confession, and the warmth returned to his gaze. "So, please, dear lady—don't speak to me again of Gabrielle and our love. It never existed, except in my dreams."

"Bliss, you must listen to me. Gabrielle didn't give herself to another; she was manipulated into it by her parents. There was some sort of mating ritual, a forced marriage."

Bliss walked away from her, his face averted, but he listened. *A Zaroulis arrangement demanded by Gabrielle's parents.* He knew that such a thing was possible, but he didn't want to believe it, didn't want Victoria to be connected with Gabrielle, let alone be her—reincarnated. Years of hatred couldn't be washed away in an instant.

Forgive her, yes. Forget—hell, no!

His love for Victoria was fresh—new, and Bliss rebelled against seeing it transformed into some dusty relic from the past.

"Shall I play the recording for you?" she asked, unable to read his mood.

"Do what you like." he replied.

She rose, took the thumb drive from her purse and inserted it in her laptop and selected the file. As she turned to face him, she said, "Gabrielle loved you. She waited to tell you, and she prayed for your return, but you never came back. She didn't know why, and Gabrielle lived with that unanswered question for the rest of her life. I know you suffered, but don't you think Gabrielle suffered, too?" There was pain in Victoria's eyes and a deep sadness in her voice. "Does the hurting have to go on forever? Can't this be the end of it?

Feeling remorse, Bliss crossed the space between them, pulled Victoria in his arms and held her close as they listened to the recording. Without a doubt, the voice was Gabrielle's. Instantly he knew he had misjudged both women. "Victoria, I'm so sorry, forgive me for not believing you, forgive me for everything."

There was a catch in his voice as he continued, "It's so difficult for me to accept, to acknowledge that it's all been such a stupid waste." He held her and luxuriated in the feel of her body against his.

"If I hadn't run away, if I had stayed and faced up to the situation, none of it would have happened," he said, "none of it." Bliss removed the barrier blocking Victoria's powers and opened himself fully to her without reservation.

Victoria smiled up at him. "There are no accidents, Bliss. Some say coincidences are really God's fingerprints. I think He had a hand in here somewhere. Let's not spend any more valuable time on regrets. There is a reason for everything, including your being here, right now. Did you remember to bring an item associated with your ship?"

"Yes, I did," he said. "It's in my pocket."

"What are we waiting for? Let's find out where you're parked."

They sat down on the sofa, and Bliss placed a small instrument that looked like a key in her hand. She closed her fingers around the metal object and emptied her mind. Immediately, images formed, vivid and clear. Victoria used her newfound telepathic skills to relay the information to Bliss, showing him the way back to his vessel.

In less than five minutes, he had the exact location. In his mind's eye, he could see his vehicle, covered with a thick layer of prairie mud, camouflaged even further by piles of debris from the storm.

"When will you leave?" she asked.

"Tonight," Bliss said as he looked away, not wanting to meet her eyes and see his sorrow reflected there.

"So soon," she sighed, biting her lower lip.

Bliss contemplated the carpet. "The sooner, the better. The feeding won't allow me to wait, and I can't stay here under these conditions. I don't want to hurt anyone else. If I'm to succeed, I'll have to coordinate things precisely, timing is everything."

Bliss reached for her hand. "You realize that if my plan doesn't work, I won't return to Earth."

"I understand," Victoria said, knowing full well she night never see him again. She yearned to give herself to him, to give him something to take with him, a moment that would live in his memory.

He held her face between his hands. "Victoria, no matter what happens to me—you'll survive, and I need to know that—that you'll make it without me, just as you did all those years so long ago. You were a great healer then, and you have a similar mission and purpose in this life."

What he said was true. If Bliss never returned, she would grieve because something beautiful had died, but it wouldn't end her life. *She would go on because that's what life is all about*, she thought, *getting up and going on, rising above it*. "I'll be fine," she whispered, laying her head on his shoulder. "I promise."

They embraced, and he clutched her to him as she cried softly into his shirtfront. When she lifted her tear-stained face and brought her eyes up to meet his, Bliss took a moment to memorize every line, each soft rounding of her features.

"If everything goes as planned, none of this will have happened. When I come back to Earth, you won't know me. I'll remember what took place, but you won't. Except for our past karmic connection, I'll be a stranger. My intervention in time, and my return to Earth will be at a point before we met. Cassandra's curse, my arrival here, none of it will exist, all will be wiped out, including all the harm I have done to others." He stared at her as a feeling of certainty setting in.

"Yet, somehow, I can't help but feel there will be something—the way I walk, the shape of my head, or my smile—something that will tell you that we are meant for each other, that we are soul mates."

They kissed, pouring out their hearts and souls to each other, wanting nothing more than to spend eternity in each other's arms.

Afraid of getting caught up in the mounting passion, Bliss pulled away first.

Their time together had come to an end, and they both knew it. Victoria walked him to the door and they kissed farewell. "Oh, Bliss, I wish you didn't have to leave, if only I could go with you." Knowing it was impossible, she dreaded the moment when he walked out of the door and very possibly—out of her life.

"I'm not leaving you, Victoria. Wherever I go, I take you with me. You live in my heart, you are a part of me."

Chapter 33

Bliss left Earth later that same night, shooting up into the velvet blackness until it engulfed his ship. On Earth's surface, near the time of his take-off, Victoria stood and stared up into the star-strewn night sky. She knew he was out there somewhere. She closed her eyes, concentrated on her breathing, and stilled her thoughts. A deep sense of knowing and peace enveloped her. It was a feeling of interconnectedness with all things, a feeling of oneness with the Creator.

She raised her head, flung her arms open to the heavens and projected her thoughts out into space, and spoke the words of power.

"I surround Bliss in the pure light of Love and ask that we both be channels for Divine Communication and healing. I invoke the Christ consciousness within Bliss and within myself."

Then she began to pray the Lord's Prayer, quoting the words of one of the less familiar, but equally beautiful, direct translation from Aramaic into English.

"O Cosmic Birther of all radiance and vibration! Soften the ground of our being and carve out a space within us where your presence may abide. Fill us with your creativity so that we may be empowered to bear the fruit of your mission. Let each of our actions bear fruit in accordance with our desire."

"Endow us with the wisdom to produce and share what each being needs to grow and flourish. Untie the tangled threads of destiny that bind us, as we release others from the entanglement of past mistakes." She paused, tears running down her face as the words took on a new deeper, more personal meaning.

"'Do not let us be seduced by that which would divert us from our true purpose, but illuminate the opportunities of the present moment. For you are the ground and the fruitful vision, the birth, power and fulfillment, as all is gathered and made whole again."

Rose, mauve, sunlit yellow, neon green, ethereal blue, brilliant orange and crimson red hues danced and flowed in rainbow waves that surrounded Victoria until she appeared to be floating in the shifting halos of color and light.

She sent more thoughts to Bliss, praying the affirmations might lodge in his being to shield and inspire him with their healing powers. *My soul traverses the mystical pathway of the Light, and we are enfolded by infinite beauty, surrounded by infinite good, blessed by infinite intelligence and inspired by infinite joy and love. We are surrounded in the magic circles of love, peace and harmony, and Bliss is free, free, free!*

Tears flowed freely as she said aloud, "Thank you, Mother/Father God for hearing me . . . thank you for always hearing me."

In deep space, Bliss' mind was attuned to Victoria's. He thought about how grand and wonderful it felt to find love and at long last, know the unrestrained joy of loving another more than life itself and to place her well-being above his own. Responsibility, commitment and self-sacrifice were all aspects of his unconditional love for Victoria. The loophole of love had set him free—the one out provided by the sorcerer Colin now liberated him from the curse.

But Bliss remained unaware of the change. He mistook the eerie feelings churning within him for the normal pangs of his hunger, when in reality, the chemical process was being reversed in his body in a slow, gradual way much like the initial advent of the curse. But he was much too preoccupied with his plans to take any notice. Totally absorbed in the details of his undertaking, Bliss sublimated his bodily distress as he had done so many times before.

He did, however, sit up and take notice when the powerful thoughts of Victoria's meditation reached him. Her loving thoughts and the words of power she spoke for him brought a sense of peaceful serenity that placed him in a zone that allowed him to relax. In that state, his healing process sped up. As the vivid astral colors pooled in puddles of light in the ship's interior, the high-frequency vibrations infused Bliss with the strength and courage he so sorely needed.

Victoria's communications came in the nick of time, seconds before his space cruiser went to full power and neared warp speed. Time at first, slowed down then sped up as Bliss exceeded light speed, creating the side effect that induced rapid aging in spacers. Fortunately for Bliss, the leap into the Tabot galaxy to a point near Scorpious required only a short span at hyper-speed.

Unfortunately, Bliss had to stop for rejuvenation somewhere in the area, an event he no longer looked forward to. But he consoled himself with the thought that if his calculations were correct, and things went according to plan, it would, thank God, be his last feeding and the final scourge of his soul.

In due time, they landed on Petoria, a planet not far from Scorpious. Bliss left Bodkins in the ship scanning the sector, searching for the asteroid home of Cassandra's father, the infamous sorcerer, Colin. In a rare moment of sharing during the last darkness Bliss had spent with Cassandra, she had spoken of the old one and their relationship, or more on target, the lack of one. Always on the lookout for valuable information, Bliss had extracted Colin's whereabouts from her mind, thinking the sorcerer's location might be useful in the future. It was the future, and Bliss had total recall.

When the dastardly deed of feeding was done, Bliss returned to the ship—his countenance aglow with the flush of renewal. In his absence, Bodkins had pinpointed Colin's asteroid hideout. In a confident mood, Bliss set the course for the asteroid, and in a short span the ship slipped into orbit around the solitary sphere. Prior to initiating landing procedures, Bodkins scanned the rocky terrain for life forms.

Bliss didn't expect to find Colin in residence since the old one must have made his transition long ago. But he feared some other creature might have taken up residence in one of the asteroid's many caverns. The scans eliminated any doubt; the place was deserted. Without further delay, Bliss embarked on his plan to turn Colin's secret chambers into his own base of operation.

The ship slipped into the landing mode and descended rapidly. When they touched down on the surface, Bliss programmed Bodkins and instructed him on his duties before he entered the maze of caves to search for Colin's inner chamber. *Thank heaven for Bodkins, without him, this plan would never work.*

He utilized a computerized bio-map to track through the corridors and followed the diamap straight to its blinking target. Bliss counted on using the advanced technology on board his ship to create a livable atmosphere for a short period. *Will it be long enough,* he wondered? Time was something he had always had plenty of until now. Bliss was no adept or wizard with awesome powers like Colin, so more mundane measures would have to suffice. He took solace from the words of Victoria's meditation and added a plea of his own for guidance.

His goal was to initiate a major change in the past, a virtual rending of the fabric of time itself, affecting not only the Earth, but countless other planets. Changes in the past were frowned upon by those with any knowledge of time travel—an action often warned against. On his trial forays into the past on Earth, Bliss had been aware of the need for nonintervention and had avoided interaction in any way with the remnants of the past for fear of somehow altering the future. In his out of body state, Bliss was unable to act in the physical world, but he realized that he could influence others to do so, and even the slightest change might have major repercussions.

Of course, he had thought it through, pondered over and over every possible contingency, and followed to its conclusion every conceivable result from the course of action that he was about to take. His plan seemed plausible enough with nothing but positive consequences. *But what if I have overlooked some important tiny detail?* What if Colin declined to participate or flat-out killed him? Bliss knew he could go on playing 'what if' until the end of time. *And time,* he thought, *is something I have wasted far too much of already.*

Chapter 34

When he arrived at his destination, he found Colin's cavern much to his liking. It was big but not too large and seemed to have its own unique lighting system in the form of lustrous, glowing mineral deposits in the walls. To his surprise, when Bliss tested the atmosphere, he found it still spellbound and able to support life. He wouldn't need the ship to create a breathable atmosphere. Immediately, he contacted Bodkins and asked him to join him in the cavern.

Colin was apparently a powerful wizard, indeed. *Good*, he thought, *I came to seek his assistance and guidance, so the more powerful he is, the better.* He also hoped great wisdom went hand-in-hand with great power, but knew it was not always so. Bliss needed another person's cooperation in order to carry out his plans in the past—someone to do the things he could not.

His first thoughts had been of Elena, and Bliss knew she would eagerly assist him, but he soon realized her youth and inexperience might be more of a liability than an asset. In the end, Elena proved to be the primary reason for his return to that particular point in time. If he returned earlier, it would be possible to completely bypass his visit to Scorpious and avoid Cassandra's curse. But if he made that choice, as far as he knew, Elena would remain enslaved on Scorpious. Her safe return to her home planet Althea and her union with the leader from Kryon had created a major impact on life in that corner of the universe. A decision to bypass her rescue was out of the question.

Resigned to his fate, whatever it might be, Bliss knew the moment was upon him—there was nothing else that remained to be done in this dimension. He reached out to caress one of the walls of the chamber, wondering if he would ever touch anything so solid again. "Victoria," he groaned and bowed his head against the stone. "Help me," he pleaded.

He missed her, he loved her, but Bliss knew it wasn't Victoria's help he needed now, but the aid of a Higher Power. He must prepare himself to reach into the past and attempt to enlist the aid of Colin, the man who held his future in what Bliss hoped were compassionate hands. He turned his back to the wall, "No time like the present," he said to Bodkins with a rueful grin.

As he walked to the center of the cavern, he wondered what kind of reception awaited him in the past. He would soon find out. Bliss placed a body length silken pillow in the central area of the cave and stretched out on it. Then, he instructed Bodkins to stand at the entrance to the chamber and guard his body while he was in the trance state. Next, Bliss closed his eyes and entered his world of inner stillness and meditation. A few moments passed before his shadowy spirit form rose from his body, trailing its connecting silver cord. Directing his thoughts to the point in time he wished to reach, and in one whizzing buzzing blur, Bliss was there.

An old man in a long black cape stood with his back to Bliss, he was busy muttering an incantation over a concoction brewing on a long, low worktable in front of him. Sensing a presence, he turned. His eyes widened at the sight of the disembodied spirit that appeared in front of him. "What manner of visitor are you?" he asked, the epitome of calm courtesy.

Bliss' thoughts reached out to touch Colin's mind. *I have come to you from the future. I am Bliss, a being from the planet Arias in the constellation of Orion.*

"I know of it," the old one answered, "but what is your business here, Spirit?"

I come on a mission of mercy, involving your daughter, Cassandra.

"Cassandra?" Colin was confused, Cassandra had just moments ago left for Scorpious after one of her infrequent visits and had appeared to be in an excellent mood. Colin sighed heavily. "It has been a long lightness and gives every appearance of continuing as such. My mind is strong and willing, but the vessel housing it grows frail. Allow me to sit and make myself more comfortable," he said, easing onto a seat. Then he waved his hands in the air. "You may sit or hover or whatever it is that spirits do under such circumstances."

After arranging his robes around him, Colin continued. "To what do I owe the honor of a visitation from the spirit realms?" He drew himself up in consternation as a new thought crossed his mind. "You have not come for me, I trust?" He was not, as yet, prepared to go.

No, I assure you, that is not my mission. I am not the messenger of death, and I don't wish to meet that fellow myself. What I came to do, rather what I hope to do, with your help, is prevent the demise, the destruction of many females in the future.

"I am open to hearing your request, spirit, pray continue," Colin said.

May I have your permission to show you the future as it now exists? I will need to merge with you.

"Merge if you must."

Bliss entered Colin's mind and filled it with scenes of things yet to be. Colin sat enthralled in fascinated silence as Bliss' future unfolded, and Colin saw for himself the devastating results of the curse he and Cassandra would soon place on Bliss. Colin accepted the information without any indication of judgment or scorn.

As Bliss vividly recreated his sojourn on Earth and conveyed his love for Victoria along with his compelling desire to change what he was, Colin nodded his head as if in agreement, or was it merely a sign of fatigue?

I have come to you to seek your aid in revoking the curse Cassandra placed upon me. If not for me, do this deed for your daughter. Such hatred and revenge can only destroy her and kill any chance for her happiness. I speak from experience, for I myself have been held captive by those negative emotions for far too long. Your daughter is a complex being, there is much more to her than the cruelty displayed by her vendetta. Bliss wondered if he had gone too far.

"Spirit Bliss, there is much truth in what you say. You ask for my help, but what is it exactly that you expect from me?" Before Bliss could answer, he said, "I tell you one thing, I will do nothing to harm my daughter. I have done enough of that already. Do not ask it, do not even suggest such a thing!" His eyes flashed with fire.

Colin, I truly wish her no harm. I promise you that. There is much to be gained by what I propose. The only one who can possibly be hurt is me.

"Tell me then what you require of me and be done with it!"

I intend to change the events of the past and bypass the circumstances that brought about the curse. To do this, I need your help.

"Well, here you are, already in the past. Surely, you can do this alone," Colin scoffed.

I'm afraid not. In order to return to Earth and Victoria at the age of thirty-three, I must put the body of the me that exists in your time into suspended animation for the passage of time between leaving Scorpious and my arrival on Earth in the distant future.

"You mean freezing!" Colin said, amazed. "No being has used that antiquated, out-dated practice in over 20 life spans."

I realize that, it's the only thing I could think of. Doesn't it make sense to use something out of the past to change the past? That's why I need you. As an astral traveler, I'm physically ineffective. Someone else must do the freezing. In your timeframe, my robotic facsimile, Bodkins will assist if approached with the right password, but there must be someone to program him, someone who exists in the same timeframe. As a spirit, I can't do it. And there are other things to be done that require someone who can operate on the material plane, someone I can trust.

"Yes, I understand that you must be aided and abetted by someone in my time, but why have you chosen me?"

Who else is there? Who else would be as concerned about the outcome? Does anyone else care about Cassandra and what ultimately happens to her?

Colin shook his head, knit his brows and stared at a point in the rocky walls somewhere out past Bliss' transparent form. "But how will the Bliss that's here now, in my timeframe—and in your past—know what happened to you in the future and believe it? That is, in the event we can get him to leave Scorpious on good terms with Cassandra before this curse takes place?"

Before Bliss could answer, Colin held up a hand to silence him. "In my timeframe, Bliss has never met your beloved, Victoria, or seen planet Earth, the place you now say you wish to make your home. Why would he go there? What will stop him from going home to Arias or somewhere else, anywhere else in the universe but Earth?"

"You."

"Me!" Colin exploded. "What do you expect me to do about it? Cast more spells? Hypnotize him? Force him to obey my will?"

Exactly, Bliss sent, *use whatever means you have to. If we can get him on the ship and into suspended animation, the rest is simple. When he thaws out several hundred Earth years from now, Bodkins will restore my current memories, personality and feelings into my body, reuniting me with all that I have been and all that I wish to be. Bodkins will travel with me: He will be my keeper, the guardian of my physical body. Since Bodkins is not a human being, he has a long lifespan, and he never gets tired or bored.*

"I must say I'm relieved to find you don't expect me to travel endlessly in space with you," Colin commented, but he still looked puzzled. "Bliss, what is so fascinating about this obscure planet Earth? Why not take the woman and go home to Arias. Surely, civilization is more highly developed and advanced on your home planet?"

I've considered that possibility, but Earth is my home. To me, it is a microcosm of the universe. Everything is represented there, light and darkness, good and evil, materialism and spirituality. It is the place where I have the most to learn and the most to contribute. The planet is at a crossroads, balanced on the hair's edge of annihilation—or elevation.

"And you think you can tip the balance," Colin mused aloud. He had once thought the same things himself in other times on other worlds.

Not by myself, but with the help of Victoria and others of like-mind. Anything is possible. If I can change, anything is possible. Bliss was speaking more to himself than to Colin.

"You have given me much to think about, Bliss," Colin said, shaking his head. "Allow me some time to dwell on these matters, and I will give you your answer."

Colin, time is in short supply.

"You have waited hundreds of years, a few more time spans won't matter," he said as a gentle chastisement. "Patience. Come to me again in the early time of next lightness, and I will give you my decision." With those words, Colin closed his eyes and relaxed into a deep sleep, leaving Bliss no choice except to return to his body.

Chapter 35

Bliss snapped back into his form with the force of a guided missile. The rapid entrance jarred him wide-awake. He was grateful, he needed time to think, to work out the details of his plan. By the Gods, he would proceed as if he already had Colin's support.

Bliss turned his mind to the matters at hand, studying the information he had gleaned from the archives of the ancients concerning the outmoded practice of suspended animation. It seemed that freezing had been perfected in the early era of space travel prior to the discovery of the heavy duty, space warping powers of the Carduvian crystals.

At first, he learned, freezing had been used to make space travel possible over great distances of time and space. But then someone had latched onto the idea of freezing as the means to obtain immortality. After the discovery of the restorative chemical ZERO 3, reanimation became an easy, practical procedure. About the same time, the technology had been developed to store key elements of memory and personality. These aspects were fed into a computer and retained until the body was reanimated, then the respective memory and personality factors were restored to the body with few, if any, side effects.

He discovered that cryogenic internment had gained widespread popularity throughout the galaxy. Millions of beings had opted for the temporary postponement of their death. Eventually whole moons of planets were given over to the storage of an increasing stockpile of bodies entombed in the naturally cold mortuaries of the moons. As a result, thousands reaped a harvest of riches from the crops of corpses by charging exorbitant fees for their storage.

Later, when the bodies began to be reanimated as cures were found for their maladies, many worlds became overpopulated. Entire civilizations sank beneath the teeming load of the reanimated. Many in that period, chose to emigrate into deep space to escape the crowding and created new colonies in a bludgeoning rash of space exploration.

As he researched deeper, Bliss learned that there were many problems for the beings that were reanimated. During the many years of storage, programs for their restoration had been inadvertently deleted or simply lost, along with their bodies' identity. The fate of those who had been fully restored from the distant past was not much better. Many of them awoke to a world they could not understand. Someone who had been brilliant when last he lived might lag hopelessly behind in a later, more advanced era.

Bliss learned of other hazards. He found that the promise of awakening young in body and mature in experience had proved to be utterly false. After the passage of five, six or even ten normal lifespans, the knowledge and experience gained in one lifetime might be less than that a child in the future.

But the worst of it, according to the documentaries he viewed, was the loneliness. Many times, the reanimees awakened as the sole survivor with no friends, family or loved ones. Mates frozen at the same time might be reanimated many time spans apart when a cure was found for their respective illnesses. If Mary woke up before her mate John, should she find a new mate or wait for the old one to thaw out?

Fascinated, Bliss plunged on with his research, feeling that it might somehow benefit the people on Earth. Already some of them were experimenting with the process, and he found himself deeply interested in the outcome. As he delved deeper, he found that many of the reanimated ended up as displaced entities—the street people of the universe— long before Earthlings had coined the phrase. Elaborate social programs were established, and World economies sagged under the strain of the high cost of financial assistance.

To his surprise, Bliss discovered that Scorpious had once been a gateway in the FSR (Freeze-Store-Reanimate) program. Its three moons served as warehouses for a multitude of containers of frozen bodies. The planet had originally been called Vadanix, but the name had been changed to Scorpious, a term long associated with power and death.

Freezing had created more problems than it solved and the practice had gone into a sharp decline. Funds ran out, and the facilities around Scorpious were abandoned. But the name stuck, along with the morbid memories of the planet's moons as an intergalactic mortuary. Those who remained on the world formed a closed society. Few newcomers were attracted to such a place. As time passed, Scorpious became a dropping off place for the terminally troubled, like Cassandra. Using the cryogenic freezing process as part of his means of escape from her curse seemed to him to be a form of poetic justice.

Meanwhile in the distant past, Colin had awakened from his slumber and was deliberating. He decided to do some reconnoitering of his own to ascertain the facts. In the middle of his chamber, he stood with arms folded across his chest. Suddenly, his body appeared to be a multiple series of mirror images that stretched to infinity, telescoping to nothingness at some unseen distant point.

Much later, when he returned, Colin had acquired all the information he needed and much more than he expected. He paced the floor of his chamber, his long limbs eating up the distance as he pondered what to do. *Should I tell Bliss the truth?* Or perhaps tell him a partial truth—that the curse was already in the process of being revoked by a stipulation Colin himself had insisted on? Will he run immediately back to Earth and Victoria?

Or should he simply go along with Bliss' plan and allow him to make his sacrifice? Cassandra would benefit. It might even change the course of her life. There were many variables and his decision might make a vast difference in the course of another life of equal importance to him.

Countless others throughout the galaxy, and many on Bliss' precious Earth would benefit—all of the females Bliss had victimized plus the lives each of them had touched and altered. The ramifications were staggering in their immensity.

And what if Bliss' plan should fail?

Something could go wrong during those years of waiting in deep space. What if there was a system malfunction, or he was only partially reanimated? Colin weighed the possible loss of one life against the lives of so many. "By all the sons of sorcery," he swore, "Bliss has handed me a problem the size of a super nova."

But it was not the first huge problem he had been asked to handle. Colin was a sorcerer of great fame and renown. In the past, he had aided and abetted those in power on the ruling worlds until the time came when he had been through it all before. Exhausted by the duplicity of interplanetary politics, he became ever more suspicious, critical and moody. The sobering thought of his advancing age, the arduous task of tying up the loose ends of life on the material plane overwhelmed him and forced him to seek solitude in search of his own destiny.

Unwittingly Colin, by casting himself adrift and assuming a distinct detachment in his attitude toward life, lost control of the very destiny he sought. For far too long, he had wandering aimlessly, usurping his own goals by living without any real purpose.

Now, the situation with Bliss and his daughter Cassandra had been thrust upon him, and for the first time in a long time, Colin felt fully alive with an invigorating sense of purpose. His feelings of detachment had been transmuted into optimism, hope and strangely enough, faith in the future—the one that Bliss foresaw.

What an incredible being, Colin marveled.

Never had he known anyone who went from the spiritual plane to the material plane and aspired again to the spiritual, all in one lifespan. But of course, the curse added to that lifespan and gave him additional time and opportunities, plus untold realms of experience.

The last bundle of thoughts had tipped the balance of the scales. The old one had made his decision. Helping Cassandra move in the direction of a better life infused his own existence with new meaning. Now his movements were purpose filled and an expectant light shone in his tired eyes as he gathered together the tools of his trade and prepared to join Bliss on board his ship.

Chapter 36

Bliss was hunched over the computer coordinating his calculations for the freezing process, when Colin suddenly appeared on his ship's bridge. The old one stood beside him, tall and erect, his arms filled with books and bottles. A smile curved his lips at the obvious chagrin on Bliss' face.

"Why, you old spacer, you can transport, physically and I'll wager you can time travel, too!"

"Of course," Colin said with smug satisfaction.

"How did you do it?"

Before he answered, Colin carefully placed his armload of supplies on the console. "What good is a sorcerer without some secrets? The knowledge of time travel was a long while in coming and is not so easily imparted to another. We will save that for another time and place," he said with a wink. "So, let us get to the reason I am here. What would you have me do to assist you in this madness?" Colin's words were harsh, but his eyes were kind.

Bliss reached out and placed a hand on Colin's shoulder. Equal in height, the two looked each other squarely in the eye. "Colin, you will not regret this," he said, as he struggled to suppress tears of gratitude, thinking his inadvertent display of emotion might be perceived as a weakness. But Colin saw no weakness in the tears; he saw only Bliss' courage.

"What I plan to accomplish, with your help," Bliss explained as he pointed to the large viewing screen filling with data, "seems plausible and possible. What do you think?" The two heads bent in silent contemplation as they watched row after row of equations appear on the screen, the documentation of all the facts Bliss had gathered.

Colin nodded his head, repeatedly and stroked his chin. "By the Gods, I believe it can actually be done!"

Prior to this moment, doubt had been Bliss' constant companion, but Colin's positive reinforcement put him back in control, and his anxiety dropped to a bearable level. With renewed confidence, he laid out the entire plan for Colin, who stopped Bliss frequently to interject his own ideas amid a series of penetrating questions.

A feeling of unity and mutual respect developed between them as they worked out the intricate details and conspired to pull off Bliss' trick with time.

When at last Colin's instructions were complete, he bid farewell to Bliss and went forth to intercept and change the life pattern of the Bliss that had been. With him, he took the essence of Bliss; his entire inner being, his memory, his feelings all recorded in minitron to be inserted in the storage banks of the ship's computer in the ship now docked in the past on Scorpious. Those vital elements were the key to his survival, ready to be retrieved when Bodkins reanimated Bliss and restored his present knowledge to his regenerated body.

Colin felt great admiration for the woman who had inspired such a great love and who had been the catalyst for such a monumental change in Bliss.

I would like to meet this Victoria, he thought as he headed for Scorpious.

He carefully selected his arrival time on the planet to coincide with the mid-point of the evening. When he checked on Bliss and Cassandra, he found the two lovers fast asleep in her dim chamber. He placed a light sleeping spell on them for added insurance before he materialized in his daughter's computer control room where he played back the information chronicled during the previous two lightnesses.

Editing carefully, he removed any evidence of the time Bliss and Elena had spent together and then created a malfunction to explain the gap. For the time being, his daughter's surveillance system was inoperable, and there would be no record of Bliss' alliance with Elena, nothing for

Cassandra to obsess over. As a result, she might well be angry and upset when her lover left, but not vindictive.

Satisfied, he placed his thoughts inside Bliss' ship in the spaceport and appeared there, instantly, knowing from the information the Bliss of the future had given him, the Bliss of the present would arrive later to check on his cruiser. Colin found a deactivated Bodkins in a storage pod. Following his owner's instructions, Colin reprogrammed the facsimile to, in turn, reprogram the ship's computer for the long journey ahead.

Time grew short. He left Bodkins to his own devices and took on the task of replacing the worn Carduvian crystals in the ship. Bliss would need their power boost to warp into the Tropssap galaxy, a destination chosen because of the vast distances between its virtually uninhabited young planets with no intelligent life forms or space transport. On one of those planets, Bliss planned to wait out the intervening years until his time of restoration. Colin added twenty new crystals to the stores in the engine compartment, his gift of gratitude to Bliss.

Who knows, he thought, *he may need them sometime in the future.* "Forgive me, Bliss," he murmured, "for not telling you everything."

Outside, right on time, he heard the sound of booted feet on the approach ramp. Seconds later, Bliss entered as Colin raised his stun gun and fired a disabling spurt that rendered him most cooperative. Then, he and Bodkins dragged the body inside and closed the doors. When Bliss began to revive, but before he could completely regain his senses, Colin placed him under hypnotic control. Bliss was an apt pupil.

With Bodkins' able assistance, Colin followed the Bliss of the future's explicit instructions as he prepared the body for freezing. When Bliss' body had been drained of its life force, the bodily fluids were replaced with ZERO 3 to insure a rapid and complete restoration. Swiftly, they lowered his body temperature until Bliss was frozen solid.

Colin performed one last series of checks, and when he was convinced all was as it should be, they carried Bliss into a chamber for cold storage.

"Be careful, ease him down, Bodkins," Colin warned. "If we drop him, he'll shatter into a million pieces." Bliss' frosty form glistened prettily in the light as they slowly lowered him into the heavily padded storage pod.

Back on the asteroid, the Bliss in the future waited, feeling completely drained. Hunger pangs demanded attention, but there were no females around, and he wouldn't have made use of them if they were. Whatever the outcome of this venture, the feeding was over. To fill his time, Bliss decided to use the ship's computer to create an actual edible meal.

When it was ready, he wolfed down the food, thinking of Colin, wishing he knew what was going on back in the past on Scorpious. Suddenly, he realized something strange had occurred. The food he had eaten had appeased his hunger— it had satisfied him. For the first time in several hundred years, he had eaten and been nourished.

Bliss jumped up, he was ecstatic as the meaning of the accomplishment dawned crystal clear. The curse had been lifted. He brushed his fingers through his hair and was pleased when a few stands came away in his hand. Bliss rushed to the nearest mirrored surface and peered into it, searching for telltale lines on his face, jubilant at finding them.

The curse is gone—it's over.

His first thought as he stared at his reflection was, *I must stop Colin! There is no need to alter the past. I can go directly back to Earth.* He wouldn't have to wait hundreds of years to see Victoria again.

With his index finger, he caressed a tiny crease near his eye. The maimed tip of that finger was a painful reminder; a signpost pointing to the scarred lives in his past. The thought brought Bliss back to the reality of the situation. If he didn't go through with his plan, countless people would suffer. Would Victoria want him back on those terms? But of greater importance, would he want to live on those terms? His mind flashed on the many females from his past including Maggie Danvers and Mary Feranti, and Bliss knew without a doubt what he must do.

He stared out the view port in what he thought was the direction of Earth. A startling, slicing shaft of insight lit his face, and in that micro insta-span, Bliss, Bodkins and the ship vanished, canceled out by a cosmic time rend.

On Scorpious, the ship carrying Bliss in cold storage had taken off, altering the past and rippling through the fabric of the future. Colin applauded the departure, pleased with the way things had gone. Immediately, his mind turned to Elena, and his next task.

In Cassandra's empty chamber, Colin placed a miniaturized computer message capsule on his daughter's pillow, containing a previously recorded farewell message from Bliss. The encapsulated good-bye intended as a peace offering might help to soften the blow of his unexpected departure. The message would make life easier for all of them. Cassandra could not do battle with a memory.

A few minutes later, Colin slipped from her chamber and re-entered the palace by his normal route, asking to see his daughter. Cassandra soon joined him, greeting him formally, perplexed by her father's unannounced visit. To her knowledge, he never left the asteroid.

Colin came right to the point. "Daughter the reason I'm here is . . . I am lonely. I came seeking companionship."

"Father, I visit you as often as possible," she protested.

"I know, daughter. I'm not complaining about the frequency or infrequency of your visits. What I'm trying to say is, I need someone to attend me on the asteroid."

"Why, you old rascal! Cassandra chortled; delighted to at last have something he wanted.

Colin bridled at her tone, finding it offensive. "I'm not seeking a bedmate, Cassandra, merely a companion, someone to talk to, a helper. I wish to purchase a slave from you, preferably a female."

In Cassandra's manipulating mind, their mutual needs converged. She seized the opportunity to rid herself of the fair Elena. A cunning smile appeared on her face. "I have just the one for you, father. Her name is Elena. She is young, intelligent and strong. But you must promise me two things, you will take her immediately, and you will not school her in the arts of sorcery." Cassandra jealously guarded her power and wished to share it with no one.

"Certainly! There is no need for you to speak to me of that. I'm well aware that sorcery in the wrong hands can be disastrous," he said, staring at her pointedly.

But the look was lost on Cassandra. "Then consider it done, you may take her with you now." She smiled at her father benevolently, secretly amused at his needs, desires she felt sure he was taking great pains to disguise.

Companionship, indeed!

Shortly after, Colin departed from Scorpious with Elena. Instead of taking her back to his asteroid home, he escorted her safely back to her home planet Althea. During their journey he told Elena the rest of the story of Bliss, what had become of him, what the ultimate outcome had been and the part she had played in it. Elena accepted Colin's wild tale as the truth and expressed her gratitude to him and to Bliss for their intervention.

Light years away on a desolate planet, Bodkins faithfully stood watch over his frozen master.

Chapter 37

Meanwhile on Earth there had been an imperceptible gap as the stream of time was disconnected and then spliced back together again in a seamless joining that left no evidence of disruption. Neither Victoria, Maggie, Mary nor any of the others whose lives had been touched by Bliss even noticed the wobble in their reality as all memory of one particular series of events was wiped clean.

Far away in the Tropssap galaxy, at the appropriate moment, Bliss had been successfully, totally reanimated by Bodkins. All of his memories, including the now missing stitches in time, were fully restored. Within him lay the sum total of his experiences, all the knowledge he had gained, the lessons he had learned, and the wealth of emotions that were connected with them. Bliss at long last was whole and complete.

His first coherent thoughts were of Victoria, and when he had fully recovered from the effects of the freezing, Bliss immediately plotted a course for planet Earth. Bliss timed his second landing on Earth to arrive 24 hours in advance of his former touchdown, and he planned to use the additional time to his advantage. No longer a starving being headed for a banquet, Bliss stocked his ship with an abundant supply of nutritious food, and he felt strong and in control.

Although Bliss was still as handsome as ever, a faint feathering of lines has appeared around his eyes. In his quarters, Bliss looked at them often. In fact, he took great pride in these signs of aging, even going so far as to thank the Infinite Power of the universe for having allowed him the opportunity to display life's battle stripes.

Upon his landing in the Everglades, Bliss calmly secured his spacecraft and recorded clear, concise notations of the coordinates. Then, he checked them again with the computer to insure complete accuracy. Using both mechanical and natural camouflage, Bliss created a shield to conceal his ship.

Finding Maggie Danver's beach house again was child's play, and while Maggie was in Miami on her boring first date with David Trenton, Bliss and Bodkins staked out the house. When the dog, Daniel, bounded out of the darkness, Bliss fired one stunning spurt to disable him, and the two of them entered the house by the back door. Inside the house, Bliss used Maggie's computer as he had before to establish an identity and secure funds, but this time he intended to replace the money before it is even missed.

The next morning, he signed the contract on the Haley mansion and headed for Las Vegas. Later, when Bliss arrived in New York with his pile of gambling winnings, he carefully selected a male commodities buyer on Wall Street to handle his investments. The transactions are handled in a prompt, efficient and profitable manner, and once more, Bliss is fabulously wealthy.

With no romantic distractions, Nancy Burgess dutifully continues to take her blood pressure medication, bored but alive.

Bliss quickly makes the purchases necessary to refurbish his mansion and returns to Miami the night before Hurricane Sidney devastates the Everglades. Knowing that the storm is approaching, he had programmed Bodkins to ferry the ship out into space and then return when the storm has passed. As an additional safety measure, Bliss selected another isolated site in a western range of mountains as an alternate hiding place.

All the while, he thinks of Victoria, and wonders what she is doing. He wants to go to her, and finds it difficult to hold himself back. The urge to run to her condo is strong, and he is tempted to go to her and announce, *I'm back, I did it, and I'm alive*—to a complete stranger.

Instead, he musters control of his emotions and lurks outside Maggie's back door the next morning and waits for her to leave. When she finally backs the car down the drive, he slips into the study, turns on her computer and restores the purloined funds to Danvers Pharmaceuticals and then erases every record of his earlier transactions.

That Saturday morning, he trails Maggie to the parking lot of a grocery store. He strolls in behind her and selects a grocery cart and rolls it along in her wake. When he sees which aisle she is taking, Bliss turns his cart and speeds down the adjoining aisle until he comes to the end and makes a U-turn.

Between the canned nuts and frozen food, he rams his cart into Maggie's buggy and apologizes profusely.

"I am so sorry," he said, "are you O.K.?"

"Yes, I think so. It was an accident, no problem," Maggie said, blushing, finding herself a bit flustered by the run-in with the handsome stranger.

"There are no accidents," Bliss says as he holds out his hand. "I'm Jonathan Bliss, but my friends call me Bliss. Glad I ran into you," he says and laughs. "No, seriously. You see, I've just moved here, and I don't know anyone. "

Maggie takes his hand in hers and gives it a gentle squeeze. "I'm Maggie Danvers, we're pleased to have you here," she said politely.

But Bliss did not answer, he had done what he set out to do, he had made telepathic contact. Maggie froze, her hand still in his. *Forgive me for the intrusion, Maggie, it won't happen again*, he whispers in her mind before he places several suggestions in her subconscious mind.

"When I say three, you will awaken as if from a deep, relaxing sleep, fully awake, feeling good, feeling rested, as if you have had several hours of sleep . . . one, two, three!" Bliss released her hand.

Maggie blinked. "You know, I've just had the most marvelous idea. Why don't I give a party for you, introduce you to some people? It's been ages since I've thrown a good bash!"

"That would be wonderful," Bliss said. "You're too kind."

"Kindness has nothing to do with it. The party is as much for me as it is for you. I've been rather depressed lately. This is the first time I've felt excited about anything." Already she was thinking about the menu and the entertainment.

"What would be a good date for you?" she asked as she fumbled in her tote bag for her appointment book and a pen.

"How about Friday, the 24th?"

"Let's see . . . maybe," she said tentatively. "Well, yes, I mean, that works for me."

"Perfect. Thank you so much Maggie, I can't tell you how much this means to me."

Maggie had a bemused look on her face as they exchanged addresses and telephone numbers. She waved a jaunty good-bye to Bliss. Now in high spirits, she wheeled her cart from aisle to aisle, thinking about caterers and florists and mentally making up the guest list.

A party, she thought, was exactly what she needed, a humdinger of a blowout, a way to show everybody, including her about-to-be ex-husband Bill, that she was doing just fine, thank you very much. *I'll invite the neighbors, the people from my interior decorating class, show off the house a little, my friends from the club and all the folks I know at Danvers, except for that bitch, Kathy Elliott. But what about Bill, should she invite him?* His name stuck in her mind with a melancholy hook.

Well, why not ask him, see what he says?

He was still legally her husband and friend in spite of the fact that he had succumbed to the middle-age crazies. Anyway, she missed him and she was going to invite him. After all, the worst thing he could do was say no.

David Trenton's name flashed in her mind. *No, not now, not ever, his idea of the perfect woman is probably a nymphomaniac with a cocaine connection who owns a Ferrari dealership.*

Trenton might be useful to make Bill jealous, but it wasn't worth it. Maggie crossed him off her list for good.

At home later as she made out her invitation list, she came across Victoria Chambers name, but Maggie dismissed the idea. *Victoria is probably in New York*, she thought, *she wouldn't come down just for a party.*

She addressed several more envelopes but Victoria's name seemed to jump out at her, crying for attention. Finally, Maggie gave in to the intuitive nudge and called her, surprised when the famous psychic herself answered the phone. *ESP, no doubt,* she mused. Victoria already had plans to be in town, and she accepted the invitation. Now, everything was set for the party Friday night.

Meanwhile, Bliss kept himself busy supervising the restoration of his mansion and tying up loose ends before the big event. One of the tangled threads of destiny he was following involved finding a high-paying advertising position for a certain young woman. The owner and CEO were a young, single multi-millionaire. He arranged for the call from an executive recruiter in Los Angeles, the rest was easy. Bliss' telepathic powers worked wonders and with a few well-placed thoughts Kathy Elliott handed in her resignation at Danvers Pharmaceuticals and headed out West, going for the gold, leaving a heartbroken, lonely Bill Danvers behind.

Perfect.

Earlier, Bill had declined Maggie's unexpected invitation to the party, knowing it did not extend to Kathy. But after Kathy left him flat, Bill dreaded spending another night alone and changed his mind, accepting Maggie's invitation. Secretly, he had been pleased that Maggie included him.

Maybe, just maybe, we can talk.

On Friday, the elements conspired to deliver a delightful tropical evening with clear skies, low humidity and a light, cooling breeze, a pleasant atmosphere for grazing and mingling.

Bliss arrived early to stand by his hostess and be introduced as the guests arrived. He shook hands, made small talk, and waited. Soon, the place filled up. Bliss craned his neck to see if Victoria had slipped by them.

"Are you all right?" Maggie asked. "You seem nervous."

"Yes, I'm fine," he reassured her. *Like hell, I am,* he thought.

Then, it was Maggie's turn to feel nervous as Bill Danvers entered the room. They greeted each other stiffly, and she introduced Bliss. Bill took one look at the tall stranger and put his arm possessively around Maggie. "May I speak with you privately?" he asked.

"Excuse us," Maggie said, with a pleased smile.

Bliss moved among the milling crowd, watchful and waiting, expecting Victoria to appear at any moment. Several times he glanced at his timepiece, thinking it had stopped. *Where is she? What if she doesn't show up, and if she does show up, what if she isn't attracted to me?* Bliss continued to beat himself up with "what ifs". Then he piled on one more, *what if, after all he had done, this was all in vain?*

Suddenly, Victoria emerged from the darkness at the edge of the pool area. Time stood still, at least in his mind, as the moment from his past recreated itself right in front of his eyes. *She is even more beautiful than I remembered.* His heart hammered in his chest and his throat went dry. Bliss experienced a familiar joy at seeing the sparkle in her eyes and he sighed in relief, feeling the comfort of her presence.

I'm here, Victoria, I'm home.

His eyes caressed the curves of her face, followed the fullness of her lips, and devoured the rest of her. Smiling a welcome, he started toward her.

Victoria glanced at him, made eye contact, then immediately looked away and walked off toward a knot of people engrossed in conversation. There was no light of recognition in her eyes. He had to remind himself that although he knew her, she didn't as yet, know him. The realization brought him up short and reminded him to move more slowly.

For now, it might be better to stand and watch her from afar. But seeing her chatting amicably with a handsome man was pure agony for Bliss and his eagerness to have her in his arms tempted him to throw caution to the winds. *Patience, old man, patience*, he thought as he held himself back— poised and ready—waiting for the right moment.

But she will recognize me on some level, won't she? He hoped his image was stamped in her sub-conscious or imprinted in her chromosomes as a genetic memory, something she carried from lifetime to lifetime, a trigger designed by fate to give them a second chance at love.

Isn't that how it works with soul mates?

But in spite of her actions, Victoria had already noticed Bliss. She couldn't help it. She averted her eyes and struggled to remain cool and aloof, unaffected by his presence, it was useless. Each time she stole a glance at him, his arresting emerald eyes stared right back at her. His gaze caught hers again and held, and the warmth in his eyes penetrated her wall of cool reserve. Victoria knew she was defrosting way too fast, her knees felt like they were melting, turning into jelly.

But she grew uncomfortable under his knowing look of appraisal, feeling as if Bliss had just mentally undressed her. She broke the eye contact first as color suffused her face. Turning her back on him, Victoria feigned interest in the conversation that flowed around her. But she still sensed his magnetic presence as once again her eyes were drawn back to Bliss. She positioned herself so she could talk to others and still see him. Something about him—something in his unusual emerald eyes—compelled her.

She forced herself to look away, feigning indifference. Unable to bear the suspense any longer, Bliss started toward her. Turning to sneak one more covert glance, Victoria found herself face-to-face with Bliss, mere inches apart. She stepped back.

"Good evening, Victoria," he said, his voice husky with suppressed emotion. "I've been waiting a long time to say 'hello' to you."

Much longer than she could possibly imagine.

"Well," Victoria said with a nervous, confused smile. "I'm afraid you have me at a disadvantage. You know my name, but I don't remember yours." She searched her mind for the elusive memory. She didn't think she had ever seen him before, yet he seemed so familiar.

"I'm Jonathan Bliss," he offered. Bliss took her hand in his and kissed it.

Victoria's mind was flooded with images, overwhelming in their magnitude. None of the visions she saw made any sense to her at all, except one. When Bliss raised his head from her hand, he was surrounded by a glowing white aura, and mixed in it, circling his brow was a crown of red roses, the symbol of spiritual love and the sign denoting the arrival of Victoria's soul mate.

Awe and wonder filled her heart as she asked, "Have I met you somewhere before?"

Epilogue

At long last, Colin received word from Scorpious; the time had come. Before he left his cavern home, he placed a thick, heavy book in a golden box and sealed it with a mystic's spell, sure in the knowledge that only an incantation intoned by a direct male descendent could remove the protective spell he had invoked. Such powerful protection was necessary for contained within the book's pages were instructions meant for the eyes of a master practitioner in the arts of sorcery. Included in the tome was all Colin had learned about time and astral travel.

But most important of all, the leather-encased volume chronicled the history of the being, Bliss. The Chronicle of Bliss included a complete record of his origins and exploits, along with a map of the solar system showing the exact location of a remote planet in a distant galaxy. Colin took the box with him. It was to be his gift, his legacy.

When he arrived on Scorpious, he walked into his daughter's chamber and found her in the last stages of childbirth. She was attended by several slaves, but dismissed all of them except one upon the news of Colin's arrival.

As she watched her father cross the room, Cassandra brushed back spiraling strands of sweat-drenched raven hair from her forehead, hating to have him see her like this. He came to her side and took her hot hand in his, offering comfort.

"Oh, Father, thank the stars, you are here. I never knew what exhausting, hard work having a child would be," she wailed. "Somehow, I imagined it would be easier, a beautiful experience. But look at me ... I want this over with, now!"

"Daughter, don't be ridiculous! All new life is brought forth in the pain of creation. Nothing worth having ever comes easily. Did you really think this would be any different? Your child may be unique, but the process is the same throughout the universe."

He placed his cool, soothing hand on her damp forehead. "There, there, it will be over soon, don't hold back, go with it. If it hurts, scream, let it out."

When the next pain came, Cassandra tried to suppress the urge to scream, but soon her low-pitched moans escalated to piercing screams as she twisted and turned on the pillows, unable to lie still in her torment. Gradually, her shrieks abated and became an indistinguishable murmur. Cassandra turned her head to avoid her father's eyes and whispered in agony into her pillow. "Bliss, Bliss . . . why aren't you here with me? I need you." Tears streamed down her cheeks and mingled with her perspiration.

As another brutal pain twisted Cassandra's face, she bit her lip and struggled to stifle yet another rising scream. Blood oozed from her, now raw, lower lip. The cry escaped, and the attending slave flinched, her nerves as frayed as the lips of her mistress.

Cassandra fought the pain with a savage desperation as if it were a force she could conquer. Another overpowering urge to bear down and to push seized her and although it was not a thing she decided to do with any rational part of her mind, she gave in to the irresistible force that swept through her body.

Then abruptly, she was lifted up and out of the pain by the age-old urges—passionate, intense, and thrilling—the nearest thing to overwhelming sexual excitement that Cassandra had ever experienced.

Colin was the first to see the top of the baby's head emerge. "Cassandra, the child is coming!" Colin announced. He looked upon the miracle of birth in a state of awe and wonder as his grandchild entered the world. There was no greater magic.

He watched as the tiny form slipped into the waiting hands of the attending slave. Wailing, the child thrashed its diminutive limbs about wildly as the woman muttered soothing words and held the babe close to her breast.

"May I?" Colin asked. With great care, the slave placed the babe in his arms. He examined the child closely. A smile of satisfaction creased his wise old face. Of course, he had known it would be a boy. If he did say so himself, his grandson was the finest looking newborn he had ever seen. The child's skin was alabaster, his features perfectly sculpted.

Pride evident in his tone, Colin proclaimed to Cassandra, "It's a boy!"

The attending woman stared at him in astonishment, an emotion that quickly turned into exasperation. She took the child from him and began to gently wipe it dry. "Master Colin, your eyes must be growing dim, this is a female child. Don't be teasing my lady, after all she's been through." A girl baby was what the slave wanted, someone to dress pretty and play games with, not some troublesome little boy.

Cassandra snorted in disbelief. "Will someone please tell me which one the child is, male or female?"

"It's a male!" Colin quickly shot back.

"A female!" the waiting woman insisted.

"Give the child to me," Cassandra demanded, disgusted.

The slave laid the baby gently on its mother's stomach and watched in dumbstruck amazement as the gender of the infant changed from female to male.

Cassandra caressed the tiny head and fingered the damp hair, knowing that when it dried, his hair would be snow white and shiny as moon glow. Then, the babe opened its eyes, and she saw that they were already a brilliant shade of emerald green, brushed with the luster of an ancient wisdom.

With a sad, bittersweet smile on her face, Cassandra watched in amusement as the gender of the child changed again, back to female and once more to male, following the whims of her wishes. *Already, he's so much like his father*, she thought, *so eager to please.*

At long last, Cassandra had someone to love, if only she could.

Bliss

* * *

It was the end of the beginning.

Bliss

Bliss

Made in the USA
Lexington, KY
14 January 2019